IT WAS ALWAYS GOING
TO END THIS WAY

IT WAS ALWAYS GOING TO END THIS WAY

ASHLYNN HEATHER POULSEN

ROGUE

For my grandfather, Robert,
a person whose love for literature surpassed even my own.
Miss you forever.

CHAPTER ONE
SEEING HER

Emptiness is all that my body has housed for as far back as my memories stretch. Sadness, embarrassment, sympathy, happiness—their chemical formations have never taken root in my brain. But it is a gift to not be burdened. I could never be the person that I am if clouds of emotions loomed over my every action. My life is a simplistic machine; actions result in consequences.

Still, I have sometimes wondered what it is to feel.

Today is Sunday, my favorite day of the week. No work. No requirement for tiresome social interactions. The day of the week where my life is my own. Where I have total control.

Clouds crowd the sky with their stainless tufts. Moisture clings to the air with the threat of a late-night storm, but that is the most electrifying thing out tonight. This evening's run is just as mundane as any other.

Running through neighborhoods provides dull insights into ordinary people's lives. A brief glimpse into a yard shows a mother watching over her children. A lawn sprinkler shoots water at them as it rotates predictably back and forth, resulting in incessant squeals of laughter. The lazy mother stays seated on the porch, her swollen belly keeping her in place.

In the seconds that I steal from them, all I think is how strange it must be to be enthralled by something like an attachment to a hose—to find enjoyment in anything as simplistic as water.

While I myself have never felt joy, certainly it is not that easy to find?

Water mists me as I pass by. If it were a warmer night, I might welcome the assault instead of shooting the mother a frosty glare.

A few houses down, an oversized man unloads groceries in the driveway of his quaint one-story home. No wife appears to help him as he grabs the plastic bags burdened with too many items. Each one taunts the man, threatening to overflow. One particularly cramped bag, brimming with cans of chili, begins to tear. Its contents yack onto the sidewalk, attacking the cement in a cacophony of harsh metal colliding in the spillage. The plump man takes one look at the massacre before abandoning it, deciding to bring in the bags that are still intact.

I run through the carnage, adjusting my stride to evade the neglected cans.

Witnessing these shreds of strangers' lives calms me. Strangely, it is like my therapy. It helps me disembowel and rearrange my tangled thoughts while my feet pound the concrete over and over again, propelling me toward a familiar landmark: a mansion precisely 4.7 miles from my home.

Before my grandfather's passing, he told me about his time spent working for the city as an electrician. He pointed to this exact home—not as hidden then by overgrown trees and hedges, not yet dusted with age and worn by weather—and explained how difficult it was to work on it, as it was one of the Historical Society's homes of historical importance. Its historical accuracy was of the utmost significance and had to be maintained, no matter what. Even if that meant spending thousands of dollars on vintage piping to conceal modern wiring. It did not matter that inside the cast iron lay twenty-first-century wires that passed inspections, only that it mirrored the rest of the fossilized home.

It is one of the only things he ever told me that I understood.

Tonight, I give nothing more than a cursory glance as I pass the seemingly empty home. I have memorized every visible inch of the auburn brick and faded stained glass, and I have never seen people in or around the property. I do not believe in ghosts, as there is no evidence to support their existence, but this home on Sycamore Street is the only place I fathom capable of housing such haunts. The only place I imagine spirits might linger.

Taking into account the forty-nine seconds spent waiting for the crosswalk sign to change, it is now exactly 9:01 p.m. Wanting to complete an even hour of running, I loop around the street and head toward the park less than a quarter of a mile east of my location. I should arrive back home at exactly 9:30 p.m. The perfect amount of time to execute my nightly routine and sleep a solid seven hours before starting the week over again.

A few couples pass by on evening strolls, walking hand in hand, content with the familiarity of their company. Unattended children run rampant in the streets participating in games I have never indulged in; they kick cans and hide behind bushes, their uncontrollable giggles giving away their hiding places. A bird occasionally coos, settling down after a long day of collecting twigs, worms, and leaves in efforts to survive and provide. Porch lights flip on, screen doors crack, and the sounds of bugs slowly charges the air. Each action is predictable. Expected. Normal.

Subconsciously, I count the things around me, both occupying my mind and honing its focus. Forty-two inhales and forty-three exhales drain and fill my lungs with air. My running shoes smack twenty-eight sidewalk cracks and narrowly miss thirty-nine. Four children, crazed with youth and dirtied from play, dart across the street without looking. Fourteen pieces of littered trash, fifty-two parked cars, and six bikes toppled over in a yard. I count the falling leaves, the doors that are brown, and the shutters that are white. I add up the sounds around me until they equate to something dull.

I count and I count until I catch myself staring at *one* thing —one that has ensnared my attention and interrupted my impeccably timed run.

A young woman, sitting on a hanging bench on the other side of a steel fence. She appears to be right around my age, maybe a year or so younger. And although she is pretty, it is not her beauty that has stopped me. No. No, the reason I have stopped is because she is completely captivated by the novel that sits astride her palms, ignorant of everything else that surrounds her. When she turns the page, her eyes shift to the top of the next, her gaze drifting just high enough that she could spot me in her peripheral.

My knees creak from bending slowly, trying not to draw her attention as I pretend to tie a lace that is already perfectly knotted. One of the many practiced performances I have perfected to distract people from noticing my less accepted practice of watching others.

She looks up then, and the breath in my lungs freezes. I feel certain I am about to be caught, forced to stop this harmless practice—but her eyes do not meet mine in the fading light. They don't see me at all. Instead, she looks up a few degrees above my cowering head at what I imagine is the horizon.

It is then that I realize she is watching the sunset.

It is also then that I get a much better look at her face.

She is much more beautiful than I first noticed. I do not care about beauty, but I do notice it. Appreciate it. I can admire the symmetry of facial features, the cohesiveness of a palette.

Brown hair, meticulously pulled up in a clip that conceals its length, with a few strategically pulled strands that frame her sharp face. A straight nose, narrowed eyes, and thin lips sit evenly around one another, trapped between her defined jaw and prominent cheek bones. From this distance and in the fading light, her eye color is impossible to distinguish, but melds with the shadows to match the hue of her dark hair. It all seamlessly blends to produce a woman not so different from the rest, but one who is enamored by things like ink on a page and colors in the sky.

What has always been light reacting to the particles in the atmosphere to me is a sunset to her. To her, this chilly air and bench make up the perfect setting in which to comfortably read.

She tilts her head ever so slightly. The motion allows one of her calculated strands to drift from its place, but she cannot be bothered to replace it.

She is so wholly herself.

And it is exactly what I have been hunting for.

Her foot finds the ground and begins to swing her back and forth, back and forth, as she returns to her book. The movement is methodical, impeccably timed, and the sound of the squeaking mixed with the sight of her makes me tipsy with anticipation—with the thrill of what's to come.

She smiles then at something she reads, and the Earth actually tips off its axis. It is so perfect, so natural, so *human*.

I lean forward by impulse, having no choice in the matter. This smile is like nothing I have ever seen before. I watch people smile all the time—they give you one while passing on the street—yet this smile is something entirely different. This smile was not meant to be seen.

It was not placed on her face for anyone else. The corners of her lips were not lifted by obligation or courtesy; it was not a twitch, nor something to stifle. This smile is something I have never experienced before. It is completely mesmerizing, this selfishly formed smile, and too quickly it is gone.

By now I have made it an effortless task for any onlooker to take notice of my gawking, but my impatience makes it difficult to tear myself away.

I want to demand that her eyes lock with mine. That her gaze should crash through the fence and into me. I want to look at her and know exactly what is going on in her head. I want her to look at me and allow me to learn what that look means. I want her to blink and let me interpret it to death. It is maddening, this guttural need for human contact.

It is not the connection that I demand; I am not capable of such things. It is *her*. I need her—next to me, with me, around me—where no one else can see. She needs to be mine and mine alone. I need to take her mind apart and put it back together, to model the clay into something digestible, place it back where I found it, and do it all again.

She is what it means to be human, I think. To be utterly, completely human.

And by watching her, I might finally understand what it is to feel something.

The night covers me when I leave. She never notices my presence.

I will find a way to insert myself into her life—falsify a fender bender to exchange numbers or find where she works and integrate myself there. Making her mine will not be difficult.

The challenge will be making her think it was her idea.

But I am patient. I will manage.

I always do.

I will change the way she measures time; its parameters will morph into befores and afters. A clear line will be drawn that dictates the rest of her life.

There will be a before me, and there will be an after me.

She does not yet know that there is not much "before" left.

CHAPTER TWO

I look up restlessly from the book lying in my palms, unable to ignore how uncomfortable I still am with reading out here. The iron fence posts do little to conceal what they surround; each three-inch gap allows the prying eyes of passersby to catch small glimpses inside. There's nothing to hide in this backyard—nothing to be ashamed of, nothing that requires shielding from these onlookers. It's only me, sitting innocently, while the people on the jogging trail instinctively glance my way.

It's an innocent act, I suppose, the looking, but it renders any sense of privacy void all the same. Their looks strip me, leaving me vulnerable every time, and it's always an awkward exchange. Do you smile and wave to the people interrupting your evening in your own backyard? Or do the two parties just pretend not to notice, ignoring the other's existence?

This is just something I need to get used to, sharing my life with strangers. It's only natural for their eyes to wander toward the exposed fence line. I can't blame them for being human. It isn't their fault that their innocent prying eyes make me feel like a caged animal.

Looking back down at my book, I try hopelessly to refocus.

I've been on the same page for a few minutes too long now. I can't prevent my thoughts and my focus from strolling away from me, hand in hand. I can't think of much else other than how I miss the feeling of home. That's why I'm out here, reading. Trying to feel some semblance of comfort, some reminder that not everything has changed. That some things remain constant despite the distance.

But it's only been a few days. Soon, I will get used to this feeling. Soon, this will be home, too.

I place one foot on the concrete and begin to rock the bench beneath me in an attempt to ground myself, praying that the droning motion will drag my attention back to my book, and after a while, it does. The methodical sway welcomes me into the comfort of another world, one of fiction and absurdities, but real all the same. The lovingly crafted letters, strung together in poetic madness, hug me close. They whisper emotions to my heart and leave visions dancing around inside my skull. I can see everything the author wants me to, hear each shaky breath, and feel each tear as it rests on my cheek.

Each time I dive into a book, I get to live another life. At times I sit still, struck with awe that something as incredible as this can exist in life, and other times I'm struck with disbelief that some people choose to go through their lives without such pleasures.

I smile down at the book, my favorite character making a fool of himself once again. It's adorable how clumsy this fictional man is. I can't help but find him amusing, even if he only exists in the ink between these pages and in my thoughts.

It's only a moment more before I find myself looking back up at the darkening sky. Clouds that were just moments ago steeped in the hues of autumn are now leeched of life. The only remaining color is the bit of mustard perched on the tops of the distant mountains—if you can even call them that. The mountains back home put these ones to shame.

I bite my lip. *This* is home now. I chose to come here, to stay with my family. But still my eyes search for something familiar, something that this place has in common with the last. Something comfortable. And so I have sat out here for an hour, watching the sunset and now waiting for the stars to come out. I have yet to see them, the stars, but I'm holding out hope that they are more visible here. That their light reaches me here in a way that would be impossible with the smog and city lights in Utah. At least in the city, only a few of them ever managed to shine their way through. It was criminal.

It isn't long before the moment comes between the brilliant colors of sunset and the first gleams of starlight. When the sun has gone, but nothing else has yet found the courage to peek through the atmosphere. Only grey remains, stitching the two pieces of woven fabric together, but it is beautiful all the same.

The lifeless clouds are bruised with fuzzy shades of violet. The twilight sky still dances with color like it did before, but instead of a waltz, it sways slowly back and forth as two lovers do when they wish to linger. The steps are less defined, no longer important, nor even the focus—what matters instead is the closeness, the touch, and that is what this in-between moment does for its viewers. This portion of the day, where the light gravitates to the dark, is when the world hugs you a little closer. When children settle, and when thoughts become a little less chaotic. The soul stills as the world covers itself in a dark blanket.

I decide to read for a minute longer before going back inside. Although it's rather warm here compared to Utah in January, a chill sneaks up on me from the lack of warmth the late sunlight provided. In its absence, I snake an arm around my torso and tuck both my legs in. I didn't think to bring a blanket outside with me; I imagined Arizona to be warmer than it has proven to be so far. But I don't let the cool breeze push me back into the warmth of the house just yet.

The remaining minutes that I invite to join me do so eagerly, pulling me by the hand to enjoy each second of theirs.

They watch as I read the pages splayed across my hands, chuckling when I become so engrossed in my thoughts that I let more of them slip by than I intended. We breathe in the cool dry air, and together we sit in this moment.

I stay as long as I can manage before the night chill bullies me back inside. Back into the house. Back inside my new home.

"How was reading, hun?" my mother asks, her hands furiously typing away on her laptop. The sound of fingers colliding with the keys is a white noise I wish I could capture. I could sit and listen to it forever, letting the sound wash over my brain and clear it out.

"It was nice." I shamble over to the kitchen table and take a seat beside her. "I was a little distracted, but I'm almost finished with this book."

"And why is that?" she asks, her eyes never leaving the screen as she continues typing.

"It just feels creepy that people can see me. Every other minute, a person is jogging by, or a couple is taking a walk, and they always look in. It's fine, just weird—different, I guess."

My mom finally meets my eyes. The deep honey-brown hue in hers is a perfect reflection of my own. "Yeah, Dad and I were talking about that before we bought the house. We ordered some hedges that were supposed to get here this morning, but there was an issue with the trucks. Should be here tomorrow, though, so no more interruptions." She smiles and taps my nose with her finger, despite knowing I dislike being touched, then returns her gaze and traitorous finger to her computer.

I smile to myself at the news. People will still walk by, but at least they won't be able to look in on me anymore. The partition will keep me safe from onlookers' gazes and allow me to read in the privacy I've become accustomed to.

I stare at my mother for a moment. She's a tall, lengthy

woman, reaching about five feet ten. Her brown hair is a couple of shades darker than mine, as close to black as brown can get, and reaches the middle of her back, but she usually wears it up in a clip. She's loud and talkative, always has an opinion, and will share it even if you don't ask her to, but her insight is rarely unwelcome. I don't get much from her other than that we share the same face: the same almond eyes, thin heart-shaped lips, high cheekbones, and straight noses. I'm shorter than her, and not the same stick-skinny that she was at my age. Fortunately, our rather opposite personalities draw us closer together than most mothers and daughters. We get along more as best friends than as family.

"What are you working on?" I can't help but ask. She is so immersed in her screen that it compels me to know for myself.

She smiles at the screen, the bright white light illuminating her high cheekbones and arched brows, but still does not look up. "I am putting together a website," she sings, "for my new business."

"What?!" I exclaim. "What new business?"

My mother has not had a job in over twenty years, as she's been a stay-at-home mom for my entire life and then some. It's hard to imagine her working, even with us kids all grown.

"It's a cleaning business." She hits a few more keys, finalizing whatever she is working on, and then shuts her laptop. "I figured I might as well do something with all this extra time. Kayden says he wants to be in on it, too. He wants to detail cars, and I think a range of services would make us stand out."

My jaw drops, mouth agape. "Kayden? *Kayden* wants a job? Like a real job?"

"It would seem that way." Her face is neutral as she gets up, not nearly as shocked by this information as I am, to get dinner out of the oven. It looks like lasagna and cheesy garlic bread are on tonight's menu.

"We can't possibly be talking about the same brother," I

insist. "There is no way Kayden would ever willingly offer himself up for manual labor."

"Think again, Gray!" My head is suddenly prisoner to the noogie my younger—but much larger—brother has decided to give me. Coming from any other mouth, my middle name would make me cringe, but my baby brother gets a pass for this, like he does most things.

"Hey!" I swat at him, no doubt adding fuel to the fire and making his devious grin spread wider. "Knock that off." I let out a groan. My hair, although always a tad chaotic, is now a complete disaster.

Kayden saunters over to the kitchen counter to dish himself out some food, scooping enough out for three people.

"Can't help it," he says. "Sometimes you just need to be put in your place, and who am I to say no when such opportunities arise?" He flashes a grin and brings his heaping plate over to take a seat next to me. I punch his shoulder, a little harder than necessary to relay the joke, but of course he ignores the assault, as if the force of my hit is unnoticeable.

"So why are you interested in a job all of a sudden? I thought that kind of thing was beneath someone like you." I poke his skinny arm as I get up to get some dinner for myself. We still have yet to fully unpack, so mismatched cutlery sits out on the counter. I use a Strawberry Shortcake dish I was unaware we still owned to plate my meal, covering her face is red sauce and cheesy garlic bread before taking my seat again.

Kayden has always danced to his own tune. He is intrigued by all things technology, and none of us know where he gets it from. His obsession started when he was young. He found an old laptop in the garage that wasn't working, tore it apart, and set to work putting it back together until one day, we found him sitting in his room playing a game on it. He had gotten the thing to work all on his own! Since then, he's spent most of his time on computers, doing whatever it is that he does.

My brother has never wanted a traditional job because,

according to him, it's a trap. He thinks that once you start making money like the rest of the world, you will never truly succeed on your own, and so he's taken a more outside-of-the-box approach to making income: he starts his endeavors and sees them through to the end, or he pawns them off on someone else when he grows bored. I'm shocked he would consider working for someone else now, even if that person is our mother.

He shrugs. "Well, this new business venture is taking longer than expected to jump-start. I figured I might as well make some money in the meantime. That way, I'll have some extra cash for when the next opportunity presents itself. Then I can just hire out my position as the car detailer in mom's business." He starts to shovel food into his mouth, and I don't question him further.

Kayden isn't one to overshare. Most of his "business ventures" are a mystery to us. All I know is that all of them are most likely legal and my youngest brother always seems to have cash on hand.

The three of us are talking and enjoying our dinner when my father makes his way into the kitchen. He says his quiet hellos, dishes out his food, and joins us at the table.

Where my mother is all things loud and exciting, my father is the complete opposite. Time has been slowly tracing his face for decades now, evident in the few greys dappling his mostly dark beard. He is always calm and collected, though you wouldn't guess it by looking at him. All five feet and eleven inches of his physique are constructed of solid muscle that he does nothing to maintain. Most people are intimidated by his build alone, but his face, constantly smooshed into an emotion-less stare, intimidates the rest of them. Crowds part for him like his build and expression alone are enough to tell them that he is *not* someone to mess with.

These assumptions, however, are blatant lies in the face of who my dad is. He's the biggest teddy bear I've ever known.

He's the kind of dad who spends the weekend building Valentine's Day boxes for his little children and stays up late watching cartoons with us after a scary movie. He thoughtfully listens while we yap about the trivial problems we create for ourselves and gently gives advice.

Truthfully, the most aggressive thing about him is probably his love for watching sappy romance movies. I have no doubt he would stand up for us or protect us if we needed it, but I don't see him as the mean guy that everyone else does. Maybe it's just because I'm one of his kids, but when I look at him, it's warmth and safety I feel, not nervousness.

When my dad sits next to Kayden, it's like looking at a younger version of him. They share the same dark hair and build, but Kayden has the same dark honey eyes as my mother and me. My father's are a kinder hue.

He kisses my mother on her cheek. "Where's Collin?"

"He's out on a date with some girl. I think her name is Mandy? Or maybe this one was Claire. Honestly, I've stopped trying to keep up. He should be home sometime soon, though."

Fresh out of high school, my eighteen-year-old brother, Collin Blu Collymore, decided to get into music and threw himself into it headfirst. He taught himself how to play guitar, drums, and piano within a year, and now, here in Arizona, he's roped himself into playing drums for a local band. If it were anyone else, I'd be shocked that they could accomplish something like this within a matter of days, but that's just Collin. If anyone could move to a new state, join a band, and go out with multiple girls in three days, it would be him.

He takes after my mother in most things, personality and looks especially, and they're rather close. Collin and Kayden both exhibit a rather boastful confidence, but when combined with their playful grins, you can't help but be charmed. The only thing Collin shares with my father, though, is his affinity for sentimental films, and the two of us don't share any similarities. We both resemble my mother, but somehow in opposite ways. But despite having nothing in common, we get along just fine.

Collin is the most dedicated of the family, a middle child with the intrinsic need to prove himself as the best in every aspect of life. He forces himself to excel at everything he tries—sports, dating, music, work—and once he's determined to do something, he can't be stopped. He is highly predictable in the way that he is always unpredictable. His dating life is a constant revolving door of girls; he hardly ever goes out with the same girl twice and never brings them home to meet the family. We hear their names and occasionally brief descriptions, but no one tries to keep up with them anymore. We let him live his defiant life and say nothing of it.

The rest of dinner is mostly quiet. Mom animatedly discusses the new business with Kayden, who nods along to her ramblings. Dad listens and gives advice now and then, telling them the best ways to market, how to set up an LLC, and the importance of sticking to a budget.

And all the while, I sit here. Not as an outsider, but as an observer. I take in each word and swish them around in my mind, considering but never offering up any of my own. Not because I don't want to, but because I don't want to mess up the easy conversation taking place. I don't want to intrude on the flow of their thoughts with the sound of my own, though I know full well I could; I just choose not to. I find I'm like my dad in that way—quiet, but not ignorant.

Once I'm finished eating, I say goodnight and head up to my bedroom. Most of my boxes are still lying taped up on the floor. The only things I've put away are my books and clothes. I'll unpack the rest tonight, I decide, but not quite yet. First, I take out my phone and dial the ten numbers I have known by heart for years now.

"D! Oh my goodness, how are you? I miss you *so much!* Tell me everything! How was your day? I have *so* much I need to tell you!"

Boston's chirpy voice and onslaught of questions come barreling through my phone speaker and into my ear. Her every word is punctuated with enthusiasm.

"Holy crap, slow down, Boss, or you'll give me a migraine," I say, smiling to myself. It's only been three days since I last saw her, but I already missed hearing her voice.

"Oh, shut up! You know you love it when I pester you with questions until you inevitably get whiplash. Now tell me, how is it down there?"

"It's good," I answer lamely, trying to hide the lie in my voice.

"Good, huh . . ." She trails off. "Sounds like some BS to me."

I've known Boston for almost eight years. She knows what it sounds like when I'm hiding something, or when I'm trying not to dull a moment. I'm not even sure why I tried to play off how I'm feeling; she knows me better than anyone. She can always tell when something isn't right.

Plus, I can't lie to save my life. Not even over the phone.

"Okay, maybe not so good . . . but it's only been a few days. I just need to get used to it." I stop there, not wanting to bring the mood down, but then I sigh, knowing she'll just keep pushing me until I tell her. "I just miss you, that's all."

"Oh, D," she sighs. I can hear the weight of my worries carried into her words, and I feel a quick sting of guilt for having said anything at all. "It sucks right now, but change is good. You'll see. One day you'll look back, and you'll miss having all these endless opportunities in front of you!" She laughs. "I know you'll at least miss unpacking all those books of yours and getting to stack them up all nice and neat, you nerd!"

I laugh, too, because it's true. I do love organizing all of my books.

"You're right," I agree, letting her perfectly pivot the conversation in the way only she can. "Promise I'll stop moping." I kick an empty box to the side and settle onto the floor.

"Well, good." I can hear her mischievous smile through the

phone. "Because you're going to need a date for my wedding, and I don't think you'll be meeting anyone holed up in that book-infested room of yours."

I roll my eyes and shake my head even though she can't see. *Not likely.*

Boss has been dating Max for a little over a year and a half. They met on campus and, like most guys do, he fell for her instantly. Who could resist the tall, beautiful, and kind blonde girl whose every movement is laced with confidence and swagger? How could he not plead for a moment of her time when he first heard that infectious laugh of hers? And in just five short months, he'll never have to again, because they'll be married.

We keep talking and laughing for as long as we can. I don't have to look at a clock to know we've babbled our way through most of the evening hours, but I don't care. It's not often we both have time to talk like this.

It doesn't matter how long we go without talking; it's always the same with Boss. Somehow, we just pick up right where we left off like we never stopped. It's easy to fall back into the groove our years of friendship have formed, and I can't imagine anything changing that. Fights, distance, time—none of it could form a big enough rift between the two of us.

"Oh, hey, I've got to go—Max just stopped by with dinner, but I love you, D! We'll talk soon. There's still so much I need to tell you—you're going to *die* when you hear about Max's mother," she says, laughing that contagious laugh of hers. "Oh, and good luck at the new job!"

I let out a breathy laugh of my own, not nearly as full of life as hers. "Tell Maxwell I say hello! I'll let you know how it goes."

Once we hang up, I drop the phone to my chest. I close my eyes and take a deep breath, and after who knows how long, I find it in me to get up and start organizing my books.

This is going to be good. This change will be exactly what I need.

At least that's what I'm telling myself.

CHAPTER THREE

"Order for Stacy!"

A tall and severe-looking woman approaches the counter, her clothing and eyes even darker than the black coffee she retrieves. Her smile is polite, her fingers quick to pluck a few napkins from the dispenser, and her feet determined to head out the door.

Customers like Stacy have become a staple in my life since I started working at Lava Java—a Hawaiian-themed coffee shop —a month ago, and I love the job more than I thought I would. The morning and afternoon rushes have been so full of brewing, stirring, mixing, and serving that before I know it, half of my shift is over. During the lulls, we take extra breaks, which means throughout my workday, I get the chance to dive back into my books.

I truly am living the life.

My coworkers aren't that bad, either. Molly—a crazy, perky twenty-four-year-old caffeine addict working her way through college—is the only one I'm close with. At any given moment, she is hyped up on a minimum of four shots of espresso. Her caffeine addiction, although not her only personality trait, certainly makes up the majority of it. Otherwise, she just groans incessantly about her anthropology classes, rarely completes her homework, and, to my knowledge, hasn't considered any career possibilities within her future degree.

The other employees are nice, but we don't talk, really. Most work the drive-thru and are so busy that there isn't time to chitchat. Anyone else who works the front with us usually pops in their headphones and clocks in and out without a word, somehow going whole shifts with only nods, grunts, and pointing fingers as forms of communication, but I don't mind. Molly likes to bus tables because she's always jacked up with energy, I usually work the register, and whoever else is scheduled typically makes the drinks and pastries. I love the consistency of it all.

Our tables usually fill up with college students and professors working on their laptops, but there always seems to be at least one or two people here solely to read with a cup of coffee that they leave untouched on the table within minutes of sitting down. Last week, a petite girl came in with an autobiography on Gandhi, and when I asked her what she was reading it for, she just shrugged and said, "I thought it looked interesting."

I scan the patrons at each table in search of some interesting titles only to find the room void of literature today. Frowning, I catch a glimpse of the clock.

Off in ten minutes? How?

"You're sure you don't need anything else?" I ask Molly as she rounds the counter to take my place at the register. Cool condensation from my freshly made drink collects beneath my hand.

"Girl." She pins me with one shockingly high brow. "I'm pretty sure we can manage the mid-afternoon lull without you. Get out of here! Go home. Relax. Do something stupid. I don't care, just get!" she exclaims with feigned exasperation before shooting me a sneaky little wink. Molly is only two years older, but she enjoys acting like she's much more than that.

"Okay, okay." I hold up my hands in defeat.

Once I finish my goodbyes, including an awkward exchange of nods with a coworker I don't know, I start the search for my keys in the never-ending pit that is my purse. The frappe nestled in the crook of my arm threatens to spill with every step I take toward the exit. Back and forth, my fingers swipe inside my bag, searching for the clinking metal that taunts them.

I push my hip into the door, opening it just as my fingers touch the cool material. But before the smidge of pride can warm my chest, the door is jerked away from my body, yanking me toward the opening and causing me to lose my footing.

Someone rushes in so quickly, head turned behind him as he locks his car, that he doesn't see me right in his path. Before I can regain my footing, the man slams right into me, spilling my untouched drink and completely *drenching* me from the chest down. The sweet liquid plasters my shirt to my torso and infects the air with its vanilla aroma.

"Oh, my! I-I am so, *so* sorry! I swear I didn't see you there, I—gosh, I am so daft," the man stresses, the deep timbre of his voice tinged with the panic of someone running late. He frantically begins to collect napkins from a dispenser. "I am so sorry! I should *not* have come running in like that."

"It's fine. Are you alright?" I ask. Drops of pale sugar water fall from my clothing and collect around my shoes in obnoxious pools. How can so much drink fit inside such a tiny cup?

"Am *I* alright?" he sputters. "Never mind me—are you okay?"

"I'm fine," I insist. "It's fine, really, it's—"

I finally meet the eyes of my accidental assailant and falter. The green in them so vivid against his scarlet-tinged face, so jarring against his dark lashes, so piercing with the rest of his sharp features. His thick dark brows pull together with concern, and his eyes pinch with worry.

"It's okay. It was an accident," I manage.

"No, it wasn't. That was pure negligence—I should have

been paying attention." The attractive stranger hands me the napkins bunched in his hand.

He's rather tall, at least six foot, and through his tight-fitted shirt, it's apparent that he's also quite muscular. His hand stretches out toward the napkin holder, revealing tanned muscles that flex beneath his sleeve. Freshly cut dark-brown hair works its way up to thick waves.

I've never met someone that I thought was a walking definition of "tall, dark, and handsome," but as his perfectly symmetrical face turns back toward me and his brilliant green eyes find mine, the thought occurs. I don't *mean* to notice him, but it's hard not to when I've quite literally collided with the man.

"Let me buy you another drink." He heads toward the counter but stops when I arch my brow.

"That's nice of you, but I'm not wearing this Hawaiian shirt just for kicks." I gesture to the sopping-wet button-up. "I work here. I get these for free."

He takes a glance at my clothing, as if seeing past the mess for the first time, and lets embarrassment seep into his light laugh. "That appears to be quite obvious."

We both crouch down to clean the mess on the floor and all the while he apologizes, his cheeks never fading from that scarlet shade.

"Seriously, I am so sorry—"

"Stop," I cut him off, giving him what I hope is a reassuring look. "I promise you, it's alright. Thank you for helping me clean up, but *please* stop apologizing. It was an accident." I throw away the last of the napkins, somehow feeling messier now that the sugar has dried to my skin.

He debates something for a moment, confusion flickering across his face, before he breaks out with a perfect smile.

Of course he would have perfect teeth.

"Okay, I'll stop apologizing," he says, leaning onto a tall table. "But only if you let me make it up to you."

My eyebrows shoot up again as I begin to seriously consider the possibility that this man suffers from short-term memory loss. It might be better to walk away now and let the forgetting-me part happen quicker. "I told you, I work here. I get these things for free. Perk of being a barista."

He throws away his remaining napkins and turns to me. "Yes, I do recall."

So not brain damaged, just ignorant.

"Let me make it up to you anyway. I'm sure you're hungry, and I've just ruined the only sustenance you had." He gestures to the trash containing the empty cup and frappé-soaked napkins. "This new café just opened up down the street and I've been wanting to try it out . . ."

He looks me up and down like he's just now remembering why we started this conversation in the first place. "I'm sure you'd like to change before, though, so here." He steps closer, leaving only a foot or so between us. I get a whiff of his cologne, something woodsy with a sweet undertone. "Let me get your number. You can go home and get changed into something less . . . drenched, and I'll meet you there."

He places the phone in my hands, but it takes me a moment to realize what exactly is happening.

"Are you *hitting* on me?"

His mossy eyes light up with mischief. "What if I am?"

I glance at the phone in my hands. "I don't even know you."

"Come on, now, we've been through an entire tragedy together," he laughs. His eyes never leave mine as his lips turn up in a lopsided grin, the red of his cheeks now giving way to his tan complexion. He extends a hand between us. "I'm Bodhi."

The outstretched hand waits for me to accept the invitation, and I consider leaving it there. How long would he let his hand hover in the air, I wonder, before dropping it back down to his side? Before he leaves us as the same strangers we were before right now? I'm tempted to test it out, but then a different bout of curiosity fills me instead. Hesitantly, I lift my hand.

"I'm Delilah," I say, taking his hand. I shake it slowly, still cautious. His skin is soft, not affected by the lifeless air that fills this place.

I find that I like the way my delicate hand fits in his strong one.

Bodhi's smile widens, revealing a singular divot in his cheek. The sight of it scrambles up my nerves. "It's a pleasure to meet you, Delilah."

CHAPTER FOUR

"It's not a date."

"Well, if it walks like a duck, and it talks like a duck..." Boston trails off.

"It's *not* a date," I reiterate, grabbing two shirts from my closet. I called her as soon as I got home and caught her up on what had happened, leaving out the part about how looking at Bodhi's perfect smile made my stomach flip. "I'm pretty sure I'd know if I had been asked on a date."

Boston's sharp laugh echoes in my ear.

Strewn across my bed, a white T-shirt and an olive button-up wait to be chosen. The uneven padding of the dove comforter ripples the cotton and polyester and does the same to the periwinkle blouse I add to the mix. "This is just an apology. Nothing more."

"Uh-huh," she says, unconvinced. "What are you going to wear?"

"I don't know." I throw the green and blue shirts back on their hangers and start sifting through other options.

"Wear a white shirt," she says with a smile in her voice. "You look good in white."

My head whips to the white shirt still on my bed. I'm almost convinced she's spying on me with hidden cameras.

"Maybe." The clock on my desk ticks one number higher, and I know I'm taking too long to get ready. "Hey, Boss, I gotta go. I'll call you later."

"Don't have too much fun without me!" she exclaims before ending the call.

I hold the white shirt up to myself in the mirror. The fact that I'm giving any thought at all to how I look tells me that I probably shouldn't go; I know better than to let myself get carried away in something like this. I know better than to put any stock in it. I won't let this become anything of substance, I tell myself, so there's nothing to get worked up about.

But when my eyes meet my reflection in the mirror, it's obvious from the stress I find there that I'm not fooling anyone. Not even myself.

My phone dings. On the screen is a text from Bodhi.

> I'll be there in ten minutes to get us some seats.
> See you soon.

I throw my phone onto my pillow without responding and fall face-first onto the bed.

The conversation with Bodhi is a total blur. Somewhere between the messy introduction and me getting home, we exchanged numbers. And now, here I am, getting ready to meet up with a man whom I can't even text back. *Pathetic.*

This is definitely a date.

It's not like I haven't been on dates before. I've been on plenty—I just don't care to go on any *right now*. I like my life exactly how it is, and I don't want anything about it to change. I've got a good routine: I wake up, exercise, work, come home, read, spend time with my family, and go to bed. Then I repeat it over and over and over again. It's consistent. Predictable. Why mess with something that's already so good?

Sitting up, I point a stern finger at my own reflection. "It's just a date! Once it's over, you can get back to your life. Maybe it will go horribly, but then you won't have to talk to each other ever again." The girl in the mirror is not convinced, but for whatever reason, it's this possible negative outcome that motivates her to get up and get dressed.

I grab the green shirt back out of the closet and leave my wet hair down to air-dry, not bothering to listen to Boss's suggestion or throw in some leave-in conditioner to tame the frizz. The reflection in the mirror receives one final nod of approval.

Boston was right. I would have looked good in the white shirt, but the deep-olive top, distressed jeans, and worn sneakers make me look exactly how I need to: like nothing special. Nothing worth remembering.

I text Bodhi back.

On my way!

———————

I show up completely underdressed. Not compared to the other patrons—I fit in great with them—just compared to Bodhi. And yet somehow, I feel like *I'm* the one out of place.

How I didn't take notice of his clothing during our encounter is beyond me. His dark-green dress shirt, with sleeves rolled up to his elbows, is an unfortunate near-match for my shirt. Tan pleated slacks hug his waist with a hickory belt that matches his shoes and watch annoyingly well. Meanwhile, I had enough time to throw something decent together and still chose to show up looking like I picked up the first things I found on my floor.

Bodhi waves from a table near the back. I bump into two chairs on my way there, nearly tripping before making it to him and the two glasses of water accompanying him.

"Hey, sorry it took me so long," I greet him. "I had to wash up real quick." I stutter a surprised "Thanks" when he gets up and pulls my chair out for me. "This is . . . quite the café," I comment, laughing softly.

The restaurant, Oui Oui, is entirely European-themed. Every wall, every tablecloth, and every napkin and utensil is either painted, engraved, or embroidered with something representative of one of its countries. Each and every inch of the place is a delightful sort of chaos. Our table, with its Eiffel Tower and Chanel No. 5 salt and pepper shakers and ceramic baguette holding the sugar packets, represents Paris. Tables for Rome, Florence, and Berlin surround ours, but without the city's name embroidered along the edge of the cloth, I embarrassingly wouldn't have recognized them.

Bodhi hands me a menu. "Get anything you'd like."

I scan the menu, finding that it follows the same rigid theme as the decorations: every dish is European. But then I feel Bodhi's eyes watching me, making me feel like I'm under a microscope.

"What?" I ask, unable to ignore his stare.

"I'm just admiring how intently you're investigating that menu," he admits. He takes a sip of water and maintains that same scrupulous gaze, unbothered by being caught.

Embarrassment colors my cheeks. I had expected a simple "Nothing" or a sheepish tint to his own cheeks. "How else should I look at it?" I ask, my voice too timid to house any real hostility.

Bodhi lets out an easy laugh that relaxes into a sly smile, as if this is something that comes all too easily for him. "I think your way is just fine," he says, finally dropping his gaze to his own menu.

I rub my thumbs over the shiny laminated paper and bite my tongue. If it's just fine, then why is he staring at me for it?

"What are you getting?" he asks after a minute of silence.

I glance quickly at my menu, trying not to *investigate* it. "I think the Caprese pizza."

Then Bodhi does the funniest thing: he frowns.

"What?" I ask, confused. I can't figure him out.

"Where's the fun in that?"

"Excuse me?"

"I said"—he leans forward, his vivid eyes locked on mine —"*where's* the *fun* in that?"

I place my menu on the table and cross my arms over my chest. "I heard what you said," I respond coolly. "I'm not deaf. I'm just curious why you're so judgmental over how and what I order." I lean forward, mimicking his posture. "You said to get anything I like, and what I would like is a Caprese pizza."

He smirks then, and I wonder if his agenda for this meal was to rile me up within the first fifteen minutes.

"There's no need to get defensive, Delilah." The peeved puff of air that jumps out of my lungs goes ignored as he leans back into the seat. "I just mean it would be such a waste to only order *one* thing at a new restaurant." He looks back up at me intently. His stare is missing some of that smug humor it had before. "I told you to get whatever you like—and I mean it. Get anything you want to try."

"You mean to *literally* get anything I would like to try?"

He nods.

My brows shoot up. "Anything?"

"Yes."

I stare at him for an elongated moment, lost for words. But he seems to genuinely mean it. "Okay," I say hesitantly. "Well, um, thank you."

"Don't thank me. I owe you one, remember?" He smiles broadly, and my eyes dart to that singular dimple. "So, Delilah, tell me something about yourself."

"Like what?"

"Anything. Tell me anything you'd like." There is a kind of tenderness to his words, like it's a request or a plea instead of a demand. Like he might really be interested in what I have to say.

It would be easier if we could go back to the silence from earlier. If it could stretch and linger, we might be able to leave this café the same way we came: as strangers. But life rarely lets things be easy, and it's hard not to give in with him looking at me like that.

"Well . . ." I try to think of things that have no real consequences once they leave my lips. "I have two younger brothers. I grew up in Utah and just moved here last month with my family. I don't like television, but I do like movies. And . . . umm . . ." I trail off, racking my brain for something else to say. "I don't like coffee."

Bodhi's brows furrow in perfect confusion. "But you work in a coffee shop."

I shrug and sip on my water. It's not uncommon for someone to dislike the taste of coffee, but apparently, when you get paid to make it all day, everyone expects it to be a given that you do.

"Then what was the drink I spilled all over you?" he laughs, the question funnier to him than it should be.

"A frappé," I answer. "I can't stand how jittery I get on caffeine. I'd honestly probably get into a car wreck if I had to drive home on it."

Bodhi's eyes narrow with mischief. With him looking at me like this, with that devilish grin and those wicked eyes, it's hard to remember my reason for not wanting to let him get to know me, and me him.

"Are you a bad driver?" he asks.

"I wouldn't say that. I mean, I've had a lot of close calls, but I've never been in a wreck—at least not one that was my fault." The explanation tumbles from my mouth, picking up speed as the urge to defend my driving increases. For what reason? I don't know. I don't care what he thinks of me, but still, the words come spewing out. "I've had a couple of people rear-end me, some high school kids sideswipe me at a light, and one old lady reverse into the side of my car, but that's it."

"Oh?" Bodhi chokes back a laugh, not believing a word of my protest. He tries and fails to hide his amusement behind his glass of water. "That's it?"

My face flushes again, but I'm not sure what about this I find embarrassing. "Yes. That's it."

A waitress—Betty, her name tag states—interrupts our conversation, and I feel like I could kiss her. It's so much easier talking to someone whose job it is to do so. She asks to take our orders, and when Bodhi begins to list off dishes, she looks baffled for only a moment before her pen begins scrambling across the page, jotting it all down.

He wasn't kidding when he said to order as much as we'd like. Just for himself, he orders a Hungarian beef soup, pumpkin-stuffed Italian pasta, and a French steak dish. I order my Caprese pizza, mostly just to be petty, but per Bodhi's request, I also order Polish dumplings, a cheese and pepper Italian pasta, and a chocolate Austrian cake to share. I shrug at him as I hand my menu to Betty, though he seems pleased that I ordered so much. I just feel wasteful.

"Tell me something about you, Bodhi," I prod before he can ask me something else. I'd rather make him talk and eat away at the time than do it myself.

"Like what?" he says. His lopsided grin makes my stomach somersault, and I pretend not to notice how heady it makes me feel to have it directed at me.

"Whatever you want." I start to tear a napkin into tiny pieces just to give my hands something to do. It's distracting, and probably impolite, but the miniature squares torn from the paper pile up below my hands anyway.

Bodhi shifts in his seat and glances down at the shredded napkin before he answers. He lists his facts like he's rehearsed them: quick, informative, and straight to the point. "I'm an only child. I grew up here in Arizona. I make some killer pancakes. I work at an investment bank."

I pick up my glass . . .

"I only listen to classical music."

Take a sip of water . . .

"And I think you are the most beautiful person I have ever seen."

And choke on it.

Coughing furiously, I move to wipe up the mess, which seems to be a common reoccurrence when I'm with this man. I wait for him to tack on that laugh that people add to sentences that go an inch or two past the point of no return. I wait for him to brush it off and shoo away the awkwardness like anyone else would.

But Bodhi doesn't so much as blink. He doesn't laugh or try to take it back. He said it as if he were casually mentioning a truth. Like saying his vehicle runs on diesel fuel.

He expects it to faze me, though—I can see it in the glint of his eyes. And it does, as is apparent from the spillage and the redness creeping into my neck. But letting him know that feels like I'm losing whatever odd game he's playing. Because he doesn't mean it; he's just a tease.

I look him dead in the eyes, refusing to give him what he wants. "Why do you only listen to classical music?"

If it weren't for the ever-so-slight widening of his eyes, I would have thought he didn't hear me. Not even a twitch of his lips betrays him the way my reddened cheeks do. But I've surprised him. He wasn't expecting me to ignore him like this.

"Well . . ." He pauses, rearranging his thoughts to something that fits on this track, I imagine. "I don't like to be influenced by anything. That includes substances—I, too, am not fond of caffeine—but that also includes things like music. I like to think that I am an individual and not someone made of societal norms. Most music puts other people's thoughts in our heads and emotions in our chests.

"Classical music, however, brings out our ideas. It influences us to think instead of just hear. It inspires us to feel, not just relate. It moves you." He shrugs, and I don't know if he's just copying me or if he truly feels indifferent about this. "But I can appreciate other music. In fact"—he sits up a little straighter—"I happen to have a soft spot for Led Zeppelin."

I can't help but let a small smile briefly flicker on my face at his childlike pride.

"I've never thought about music like that before," I say. "I think that's refreshing, actually—to care that much about how you're influenced." I pause, my smile returning. "But do you really like Led Zeppelin?"

He nods. "I most certainly do. No matter how much I try to ban lyrical music from my life, I always end up making an exception for them." He raises an inquisitive brow. "Have you listened to them before?"

"Not really. I mean, I'm sure I've listened to some of their popular songs, but I don't think I could confidently name any."

I expect a twinge of sadness, or to detect some level of disappointment in him. To feel like I've failed some sort of test and let him down. But I'm once again taken aback by how he reacts. Instead of seeming displeased, he smiles.

"How exciting for you. You have a lot of good music to look forward to listening to." He places both of his hands around his glass and holds it casually in front of him, staying still for a moment before he takes a drink. "What music do you like, then, if not the good kind?"

I give him a lackluster glare, and he smirks in return. "Well, I like a little bit of everything. I listen to classical music, too, but only when I need to focus or relax. I like some pop, some rap, a little bit of country." I grab my water and mimic him, raising it to my lips only to wait to drink until I finish answering. "I just like it all, for the most part."

He chews on my words for a moment before responding, "So, you are either indecisive or open-minded."

"I like what I like," I say simply, and I mean it. There is no rhyme or reason to the music I chose to listen to; I don't even organize the diverse music in my playlists by genre. I separate them only by the month I listened to the song. Hitting Play on any one of them is to gamble with your emotions. "I'm more drawn to lyrics than to specific artists or categories."

He examines me thoughtfully, seeming to pick the words that have flittered from my mouth off the table and read every curve and arch of each syllable and consonant. Underneath his gaze, I'm left feeling exposed, like I've said something more vulnerable than I intended. I don't know that I like him dissecting these delicate portions of my personality and inter-preting them beyond my comprehension.

I start to shred another napkin.

"What is something you love?" he asks, leaving whatever assumptions he's made about me to my imagination. "What is something that makes you happy?"

Bodhi places his elbows on the table and crosses his arms as he waits for my answer. He leans forward intently, his soft eyes asking me to give them what they plead for—like the answer I give might be the key to unlocking the deepest parts of me.

I don't care to confess anything meaningful about myself, but something in those emerald eyes short-circuits my brain into trusting him with one small part of me. Or maybe I just suffer from the human addiction of desiring to be known.

A soft unavoidable smile burrows into the creases of my lips. "I love to watch sunsets and sunrises. I try to watch them whenever I can. I also love to read. Like love, *love* to read. I read at least two or three books a week, but I used to read more. Once I started working, I just didn't have the time." I shrug one shoulder like this sentence holds no weight, but as he nods, the ghost of upturned lips lingering on his face, I can tell he feels how I'm saddened by this compromise.

"Why do you enjoy reading?"

"I just do. It's hard to explain."

Bodhi tips his chin toward me. "Try anyway."

Although I know I love books, I've never wondered what

about them intrigues me. I've never thought about what continues to draw me to them after all these years.

How exactly do you explain the complexities of an old friend to a total stranger?

"I don't know . . ." I begin. "I think when I read, it isn't about forgetting who I am, or pretending to be someone else, or living another life. I think when I read, it's about finding myself. I read someone else's thoughts and find a piece of me that somehow also exists in them. It's just nice to sometimes realize that we are not all that different from one another. That there's always someone in the room who understands even a small part of you."

I grow quiet, the silence between us humming, whispering in our ears sweet nothings and lies. In its hushed tone, I find embarrassment and let it pinch my cheeks, wondering why I can't seem to stop them from burning with its touch over and over again. Talking about something you hold dear is always a dangerous thing when you're not comfortable being vulnerable. When the person you're with lets the seconds drag and elongate in the absence of their catalytic words.

"That is . . ." he murmurs. "Well, that's kind of beautiful, actually."

Damp curls fall off my shoulder with a shy dip of my head, leaving streaks of a deeper shade of olive where they touch my sleeve. Any words that would have followed die on our lips as Betty interrupts us with a pitcher of water.

She refills our glasses.

We clear our throats.

And the conversation lightens.

We continue to talk, but now only about trivial things—like the movies that are playing and the weather here compared to Utah—until Betty returns with our food in tow. It takes her three trips to get it all out to us, and we end up pulling Berlin's empty table next to ours, invading its surface with our plates.

Each dish greets my taste buds with a different slice of

heaven. Even the pierogi, which I was skeptical of, is incredible. Bodhi tells me to try his dishes as well, and I don't hesitate. He takes bites out of the food on my plates as well, and together we share the meal. I'm a little shocked to find that I like every single one of them.

Between us, it's decided that the tortelli and steak au poivre are staples on the menu and should be ordered on every visit. We split my dessert and end up leaving the table with six to-go boxes, because eating that much food is simply impossible, no matter how determined two people might be.

I thank him as we make our way out of the restaurant and find myself feeling like the outing went alright—maybe even better than alright. We made it through the entire meal without another flirtatious comment from Bodhi.

"Thank you for letting me take you to lunch," he says as he holds the door open for me.

I step outside. "You didn't leave me much of a choice," I joke. He lets out an exhale that straddles the dangerously fine line between a sigh and a laugh.

"If you want," he starts as he walks with me toward my car, "I know of this cool bookstore in downtown Phoenix. It's about a twenty-minute drive or so from here. Kind of a hole-in-the-wall place, but I've never seen anything like it before. I can take you there—if you would like."

"Um . . ." I say, looking down at my car keys and stalling for time. An apologetic meal is one thing; going to a bookstore downtown is something entirely different. Was this a good time? Sure, I can admit that. But do I want to encourage him into thinking this could go anywhere else? No. It wouldn't be right to.

His green eyes invite me to betray myself—they *beg* me to do so—but I shouldn't. I need to stop this now before it gets more difficult to untangle the knots in the line.

"Listen, Bodhi, I—"

"My treat!" he nearly shouts, catching me off guard. "I still feel bad for spilling your drink and probably ruining your day. This would most certainly make things right between us."

I nearly laugh at the absurdity of it all. How could anyone look at the events of this afternoon and come to the conclusion it's been spoiled? But he continues talking before I can muster up the breath.

"We could go right now and be back before dinner," he insists.

Once we make it to my car, he leans effortlessly onto its side.

"Well . . ." I trail off, trying to think of a reasonable excuse not to go. Bodhi isn't horrible company, and it *would* be someplace I'd like to visit . . .

I look at him sideways, surprised he's found a way to get me to even entertain the thought.

My teeth dig into my bottom lip. "You promise we'll be back before dinner?"

Bodhi's face beams with the biggest grin I've ever seen, that one dimple shamelessly piercing his left cheek. "Promise."

CHAPTER FIVE
AFTER

It is a delicate thing to be known. One must be meticulous in the way they unfold and lay out the pieces of themselves. It takes skill to select the proper piece, to show someone at the right time, in the right light. Choose the wrong piece, or show it too quickly, and being known can be a mortifying experience. A horrific one. Do it right, though—lay out those shards and spikes in precisely the correct manner—and their edges seem to dull. Their points grant more forgiveness. Suddenly, there is beauty and understanding, even for the most twisted parts of us.

The scary pieces become the ellipses of our stories. They weave moments together in beautiful, smooth lies, leaving imagination to fill in the spaces between with something more soft, something more kind, something easier to swallow. Something that isn't true.

Because no matter the justification—no matter the lighting, the timing, or the angle—some pieces will be just that: lies. Ugly, filthy lies. No excuse, reason, or motive changes that. No matter the why, when you infect a girl's life with your poisoned fragments, those beautiful ellipses will eventually be filled with your ugly lies instead of those pretty wishes.

For all I know, there's a specific time and place for each of these complicated puzzle pieces to become known, for them to fit seamlessly together. For all I know, there's something to excuse each barb, each nick from accidentally grazing against another's splintered piece. There might be some way to forgive yourself for not feeling the razor's edge as they gradually dig into your palms, so slowly that what you thought was a gentle whisper was really them beginning to burrow. For all I know, those pieces may remain drilled into us for as long as our breath gives them life.

This, I know, because I have seen firsthand what happens when these fragments fuse together in a parasitic attachment.

I can feel the sharp claws digging in even now. The pieces are here in front of me—they always have been. They crept up on me unexpectedly, like the end of a dream. It was so sudden, seeing his pieces laid out. It wasn't vulnerability or honesty that brought us to this point. It wasn't a conversation. Yet it wasn't accidental, either.

It was a mask being removed. It was the bow after the play. A smile dropping from a face after a photo. I had just witnessed a confession—that is all. I was conned into believing the pieces laid out before me were the shapes they claimed to be though they were obscured, covered in bubble wrap. I had seen only their shadows and was not privy to the fact that they were puppets crafted for me and me alone. The strings were pulled just enough to give them life, mimicking pieces I have seen and held and known my entire existence. But when the strings were no longer taut with the puppeteer's deceit, I saw the lifeless shards for what they were: a ruse.

It seems impossible to imagine misjudging another person's pieces so, so horribly. It is an impossible thing, indeed. But still, I stare at the figure in the doorframe, and I no longer feel . . . well, anything. I no longer feel at all.

I used to know what it meant to cry. The feel of a tear on my cheek, the taste of the salt in my body's moisture. I knew what it was to be able to feel things. Humiliation. Regret. Longing. Embarrassment. Anger.

Fear.

I used to feel fear.

But I have grown so numb that I no longer feel even this hardwired emotion. Deep in my DNA, written across generations, this feeling was embedded, and somehow the person in the doorframe found a way to rewrite all the human evolution it once contained.

The figure stares back for what feels like a small eternity, but logic tells me it's only a moment, before stepping inside my perfect prison.

The puppeteer sits before me. I know better than to examine him the way he does me. He does not feel; his pieces now hang lifeless from the strings that once made people believe they *danced*. Those strings now only act as the noose, while anything human, anything normal, sways ominously in their grasp. That is all there is to see, and all there ever will be.

I wonder if that is all that can be seen in me now. I wonder if all that is left of me is the noose wrapped around my pieces.

I used to cry. I used to *feel*.

I used to be *alive*.

But I've misjudged the pieces that this monster showed me. I saw their shadows as they danced in the light but didn't turn around until it was too late. I didn't look until it was all too late.

"How did you do it?" There is no emotion in the question, no indication that the answer I receive will sway my mood one way or another. There is only indifference. The slight curiosity that should be present is instead caked in a dull boredom.

I don't know why I ask; if anyone does, it is the monster before me, because he knows me better than anyone. Knows me better than anyone should ever know another person.

My captor seeks no clarity. Not verbally, anyway. It is not needed here, not within these four walls. The only thing this painter of pieces needs is his canvas: me.

He answers the vague question with absolute precision.

"I took control of your life."

His words make it sound so simple. Like the task was not a difficult one to complete, and yet I believe it wasn't. Not for him.

The nod comes on its own. Slowly, my head bobs with a bit of life. The corner of the table blurs with the distance in my eyes. I'm here, but for how long? I'm drifting. Away and away I'll soon go, and I'll remember. I'll remember, again, but the memories are so worn, they don't possess the same grip on my heart they once did. They'll play endlessly in my mind to pass the time. As a way to fill the silence, though there will be no noise. Only the memories.

"You influenced what I read, who I talked to, how I carried myself—hell, even what I ate." I scoff, but there is no humor, anger, or annoyance in the sound. Just noise. "But *how* did you do it?"

I force myself to focus hard enough that when I meet the gaze of those two beautiful eyes, I can see every pixel of them. I let my eyes meet his, even though it means he'll see me more than I see him. "How did you get me to believe you? How did you get me to *love* you?"

The hollow notes leave my lips so casually, meeting the ears of someone I once called a friend. Someone I once loved—*thought* I loved. They kiss the ears of the liar before me, and for the first time in my life—my "after" life—the liar conjures what might be a smile. But it's too forced, too unnatural, on his face.

Deep within my stomach I feel a dull twist, like a weak flinch in a limb riddled with rigor mortis, and realize that this could be construed as feeling something. The sensation is odd. Unfamiliar.

"How did I do it?" The squeak of the chair. A blur as his arms cross. "How did I make you fall in love with me when I have never felt anything at all?" A pause.

"The simplest explanation is that I took my time." His gaze

rakes me up and down, drawing conclusions from my breaths and posture and my dead expression alone. "But that is not what you want, is it—the simple explanation?"

I let my silence speak for me, saying all the liar needs to hear.

"It was easy. I was always there. Even when you didn't know it, I was there. Watching. Waiting. Observing. There was not a book you read or a person you met that I didn't know about. That I didn't study the way I studied you."

And like that, the monster becomes a storyteller. The words paint the air around me with pictures of things I know I once lived. I see turning pages, spilled coffee, fleeting glances, crinkled eyes, and first kisses. I see the moment I fell in love and the moment I allowed myself to do just that, despite being so scared of what that would mean. I see the moment I let the monsters in, and how naïve I was to do so.

I see all of the happy moments dance around me, taunting me with things I'll never have again and things I never had at all. I relive all the memories like I have so many times before, only this time, I start to see them for what they are.

Lies.

CHAPTER SIX

I t doesn't occur to me that willingly hopping into the car with a practical stranger may not be the best idea I've ever had until we're merging onto the freeway—too late to insist on meeting there now. Not that I think anything is *wrong* with Bodhi, but I also don't typically make it a habit to trust someone like this within three hours of our first conversation.

"What are you thinking about?" he asks after a minute of silence.

I laugh, shaking my head as if to loose the thought. My damp curls sway with the movement and stick to the exposed bits of my skin. "I was just thinking about how crazy I must be to have gotten in your car. We only just met a few hours ago." I arch a brow at him. "For all I know, you could be some psycho."

"Well," he says, "I just so happen to like my girls crazy." This time, his smug grin is accompanied by wiggling eyebrows. I roll my eyes at the cocky idiot, though his gaze is fixed on the road ahead.

"Your *girls*, huh? So I'm just another one of the crazies you pity with bookstore trips?"

"Nope." He hitches a thumb in my direction. "You're the only one crazy about books."

This time, he sees my exasperated eye roll.

Bodhi spends most of the drive listing off random facts about architecture or the establishment dates of the few small towns we pass by. He tells me about a diner that's been around for nearly a hundred years and points out the exit for a zoo, explaining why he prefers this one over the one in Phoenix. He shares so much that I know I won't be able to remember most of it, but the noise fills the time easily, and we arrive before I've really felt much of it pass.

When he parks the car and I open my door and swing my legs out, I find that I've made the first mistake of the evening.

"Get back in," Bodhi insists from the driver seat. He unbuckles his seatbelt and hops out.

Confused, I watch him quickly walk around the car to my side. I don't see the bookstore, but I assumed that, with the car parked and shut off, we had arrived.

"What? Why?" I ask as he approaches. But he only ushers me back inside, closing the door once my legs are out of the way before reopening it and looking at me expectantly. I take a hesitant step out.

"The hell?" I mutter.

"You don't touch door handles." He grins. "That's my job."

My jaw drops, heavy with bafflement, and hangs agape. "Did you seriously just make me get back inside the car so that *you* could open the door for me?"

"Yes, ma'am."

I make the argument, "I thought this kind of treatment was supposed to be dead, or whatever," though from the stupid grin on his face, I know that it's useless. It seems I've met someone more stubborn than me.

"I brought it back just for you," he teases before extending an arm out to me, waiting for my own to loop through it.

I take one look at his arm and, knowing the deal I made with myself earlier, decide that this is the most opportune moment for me to make my intentions clear. So, instead of taking his arm, I swivel on my heel and walk away. I stand a little taller until I hear him from behind me.

"The bookstore is this way," he calls.

I swivel again, heading in the opposite direction, and ignore the arm that meets his side as he moves to step in time with me. I can't be certain, but after a few right turns, it feels like we begin to head in the direction I had originally started walking. I shake my head, but before I can decide if I'll let him have this small retaliation or point it out, he stops in front of a door whose hinges are attached to an old unidentified building.

I falter in my step and look over at him, confused. He merely offers a smug smile and gestures to a storefront—if you can even call it that.

"We're here," he says.

The interior of the building is dimly lit, if at all; it's difficult to tell from the outside with the thick layer of built-up dust pressed against the windowpane. The exterior of the building is no better. The rails around the windows sit askew, and the bricks in the building's walls sit loosely in place. Pieces have broken off and been left on the sidewalk, forgotten.

The only sign of invitation is the unlocked door that Bodhi now holds open.

If I had been walking alone, I wouldn't have given this place a second glance. The rubble of the building's exterior suggests this place is due for a demolition, and it doesn't so much as display a faded sign to advertise the books it allegedly sells.

Bodhi tilts his head toward the open door, indicating a growing eagerness for me to walk in. If he wasn't already holding it open, I may have reached for the handle myself, earning another scolding from him.

As I step through the threshold, I am not surprised by what I find.

The interior is no more impressive than its counterpart. The store is small—too small to operate and make enough profit, even if it were stocked and properly taken care of, which it isn't.

The walls are loosely covered in sun-bleached wallpaper that peels every which way, leaving it to the imagination to piece together what it once looked like. Bookshelves line the room, most with broken shelving, and are laced with a coating of the same thick dust that sticks to the storefront windows. They are lightly littered with the tattered carcasses of books, most torn, aged, and caked in dust.

The store is a ghost town. There's not a single soul to be found, even behind the ancient checkout counter where a clerk should be.

"Umm, not to be a drag," I say, "but this place is kind of a dump."

A soft chuckle sounds behind me. His reaction makes me turn, driven by the need to see what he could possibly find so funny when nothing truer could ever be said about this place.

"This way."

Bodhi saunters over to an isolated bookcase in the back of the small room. I follow, and it only takes seven steps to find a single book sitting at eye level, perched on its shelf.

I lean in to read the book's title: *The Secret Garden* by Frances Hodgson Burnett. The book appears to be in the same condition as the rest of the place, but with a little less dust coating it, like it had been touched not too long ago—placed here recently, maybe. Its sage-green cover and tan spine appear untouched by the time that has tarnished everything else in the store. Its colors, although dull, stand out in the space filled primarily with shades of grey. The novel sits upright, perfectly straight, waiting for someone to pluck it off the shelf and deliver it from its dreary halfway home.

"Congratulations," I deadpan, "you found the one book in this store that might be sellable. Let's get out of here before we have to fight someone for it."

The spine of the book fits easily into my palm, its binding firm against my skin. But when I go to pull it off the shelf, the weight doesn't follow my grip; instead, it stops after only tipping about forty-five degrees. Something mechanical whirs within the wall, and I don't have time for my jaw to drop before the realization hits me.

The bookcase swings slowly into the wall, revealing a hidden doorway.

My eyes shoot wide open. Bodhi laughs.

"What in the—?"

"Follow me." Bodhi steps into the opening, but only once he's walked a few steps into the passage do I manage to shake off the shock enough to force the muscles in my legs to follow.

The secret hallway is painted a grey hue to match the first room, but vintage sconces installed into vertical wood paneling softly light up the space. They stretch out the height of the hall with their lines, contouring it in a kinder way.

We walk a short distance until we reach a tall grey door with no handle. I wouldn't have known it was a door at all if Bodhi hadn't knocked on it. He looks back at me with a coy smile before doing so, rapping his knuckles against it once, twice quickly, then once again.

I instinctively doubt the secret knock is real, but then the door slides open to reveal an older gentleman, maybe in his late forties, sitting at a small barstool table. He wears a white tee with black joggers and tennis shoes. A pair of glasses too small to frame his face sits comfortably balanced on the edge of his nose. Wrinkles dig into his face in all the places where smiles pull and tug, and his hair is peppered with similar signs of age. Stitched on the breast of his shirt are two names: ReadEasy Bookshop and Tony.

"Welcome in, you two. First time here at ReadEasy?" he asks us.

"Yes, sir. We have a first-timer right here." Bodhi's hand lifts to graze my elbow. His touch is no more tangible than the breath in a whisper, but I feel it as though he grabbed me, every nerve he touched buzzing with life.

"I can tell," Tony laughs. "You've got that stunned look on

your face. Well, assuming you've been here before"—he motions to Bodhi, who nods—"I'll let you show yourselves around. Enjoy!"

We walk through the second secret door of the day past Tony, whose sole purpose, it would seem, is to man the idle entrance and play tour guide to any customers. Both seem excessive to me, and a little over-the-top, but I only make it a few more steps before I'm completely paralyzed.

Now I understand why we might need someone like Tony to show us around.

I turn slowly to take it all in. Walls at least sixteen feet tall with vaulted ceilings loom above us, enhanced with wood beams stained in a rich woodsy brown. The length of the walls stretches even further than the height. The vastness of the space pulls my gaze along its length, and I can't tell where one side of the room ends and another one begins. The smell of fresh paper and pressed ink hits me next and draws me in, enticing me to step further into the most incredible place that might exist.

And it's all books—every single inch of it. Clear to the top of the vaulted ceiling, the shelves overflow with literature. Each shelf's corner is rounded, creating both a harmonious flow in the room and additional space for rows and rows of volumes. There are books in *literally* every corner of the room.

"What do you think?" Bodhi asks.

"This place . . . this place is absolutely ridiculous," I marvel. As I turn to him, I can't help but grin. It has to be the first genuine smile I've given him. "I love it."

That lopsided grin appears on his face again. "So, it was worth the trip, then?"

"More than worth it."

He nods at this, seemingly satisfied, and wanders deeper into the room. I follow behind him, unable to make my own decisions at the moment.

"As I told you, this is my treat, so go on and find you some books. Get whatever you'd like."

"Seriously?" I ask him.

"Go nuts," he says in that sarcastic way a person only uses when such words are below them and their vocabulary, but I don't care. They are the last thing I hear before I dash off and begin to explore the expansive collection.

I start with the shelves closest to us on the left. The first aisle is full of nonfiction titles relating to science, and I quickly glance through them, not interested in spending too much time here. I walk through the history, self-help, and religion sections, picking up a few interesting titles before I reach the back wall. My view of it was obstructed by the tall bookcases before, but now, standing in front of the blockage, I can see it in its entirety.

It is completely covered in books, just like most of the rest of the room, but this wall is different. No visible shelving holds up what can only be described as a true *wall* of books. They seem to sit one on top of the other, stacked up vertically, the spines supporting each other to create a solid structure.

Thousands of titles must sit before me. Each one has been strategically placed to create a beautiful gradient, the shade of each binding just slightly different from the one next to it. Deep reds turn into brilliant pinks and continue to morph into fervent purples. From left to right, the transition is so smooth that at a glance, it would be impossible to distinguish the individual colors.

It feels wrong to look away from it too quickly. Almost disrespectful.

After giving the massive wall an appropriate amount of attention, I continue walking down the rest of the aisles. I take my time in the thriller and romance sections, grabbing books from each, and look around the room through the gaps in the shelves until I spot who I'm looking for.

Bodhi stands over at a tiny coffee bar I didn't notice when we walked in.

I watch as he orders something at the counter and sits on a stool to wait for his purchase. His back is straight with perfect posture. His fingers dance rhythmically on the countertop, not with impatience, but something else. Although we've been out for the better part of the day, Bodhi still looks completely put together. His hair sits in the same place it did when he bumped into me at the coffee shop, not a single strand out of place. His clothing still looks freshly pressed.

He is the total opposite of me in every way.

My hair, on the other hand, curls with a mind of its own, the frizz expanding its spirals without rhyme or reason. My clothing wrinkles freely, though, to be fair, I don't iron my shirts to begin with. I can only imagine how my light layer of makeup has already smeared and smudged, leaving dark traces below my eyes.

I've been trying not to notice things about him, especially in the car when there wasn't much else to do but notice. I don't want him to see me taking note of his traits, like his perfect smile and the way his thick eyebrows pull together in displeasure, especially in the lulls in our conversations.

I tell myself I don't notice these things out of interest. I convince myself it's just innocent curiosity. That I didn't want to take his arm when he offered it to me outside the car. That when my arm brushed up against his as we walked, I didn't feel the stinging sensation it left on my skin. That his flirtatious comments leave me unaffected.

But it's hard to keep believing all of this when I'm currently watching him through the gaps in a bookshelf like a total creep.

After internally chastising myself for my stalker-like behavior, I continue to roam around the store, leaving Bodhi to wait for his order without my gaze accompanying him. Eventually, my arms are so full of potential purchases that I have to find an empty table to set them on while I look through the last few sections. When I come back with the last of my finds, Bodhi is seated there chaperoning the ones already on the table.

He hands me a coffee cup. "Here, I got you this."

I thank him, and my eyes widen after I take a sip. "Is this a vanilla frappé?"

Bodhi nods. His green eyes remain cool, making me wonder if I mentioned liking this specific drink earlier and forgot, but he answers my question before I can give it a voice.

"I wasn't sure what drink I spilled all over you earlier, so I asked them for a white frappé with whipped cream and no coffee. They made that." He juts his chin toward the cup.

"Oh, well . . . thank you."

He nods again, just once like before, and I begin to sift through the books on the table, organizing them into piles of yes, no, and maybe. All of the books pique my interest, but I narrow it down the same way I do every time I go book shopping: I grab everything that catches my eye, and then I pick a few that intrigue me more than the others.

"What are you doing?" Bodhi asks. He glances between the piles of books I'm creating, eyeing the unsteady and ever-growing pile of nos, no doubt questioning its structural integrity.

Seeing his gaze, I realize he probably didn't expect to spend this much time at the bookstore with some stranger. I've been rather rude, taking my time perusing each aisle like I have all the time in the world.

"I'm so sorry," I say, flustered. "Just give me a minute to finish going through these, and then we can get going." I grab the next two books in the stack and place them in the "no" pile without so much as glancing at the synopses to speed up the elimination process.

Bodhi looks at me with a confused expression. "Go through them?"

I nod. "Well, yeah. This is how I normally shop for books: I grab whatever looks good and then put back the ones I don't want."

"Why would you grab them if you don't want them?" The confusion stays etched in his brow while his eyes graze the books I've collected.

"I mean, obviously I *want* them, but I can't very well get twenty books, can I?"

His eyes never leave mine, still stuck on that perplexed look as he studies me. "Why not?"

A short, sharp laugh escapes my lips. My head tilts with the threat of more laughter, but then my brain registers the sober look on his face, causing me to stop short. "You're joking, right?" I scoff when his face doesn't falter. "You can't be serious."

The sound of his chair scooting back quietly across the carpet is the only response. He picks up the two largest piles of books in front of me, scooping them up with little effort. He cradles them in one arm, making my two trips to get them all here seem comical.

"No!" I exclaim.

He turns to me, brows scrunched together as though *I'm* the one who's doing something completely mad. "No?"

"No," I say firmly. "This is too much! I have to put some back." I reach for the last pile, determined to eliminate some titles, but Bodhi slides it away from my reach with his free hand.

"You don't *have* to put any of them back." His words are just as stern, yet somehow they don't lose their vigor on the way to my ears like mine did to his. "If I only wanted to buy you three books, I would have told you so. I told you to get whatever you wanted. So," he continues, grabbing a few books from the final stack, "I will be getting you whatever you want."

I sit there with my mouth hanging open like a moron. "This is going to cost over—"

"Delilah," he says, cutting me off, "I'm not changing my mind." There's some finality in his tone, something teetering on the verge of annoyance. Not quite anger, but almost there, like refusing to let him buy me a small mountain of books is some kind of deep offense.

Then he shoots me a wink, a sly smile pinned to his freshly shaven face. "Grab those last few, will you?" And with that, he walks toward the checkout counter, taking with him any trace of uneasiness I felt about his tone.

I trail a few steps behind, holding both of our coffees and three books.

When the cashier says the total, I give Bodhi a furtive look as if this proves my point. Even with a handful of the books discounted, it is an absurd amount to spend. I wait for him to realize how ridiculous this is and agree to let me drop a few of them.

But he doesn't.

Bodhi pays in cash, and soon after, we walk out of the store with seventeen books. He carries the four heavy bags of literature and refuses to let me help.

"I don't know what to say," I confess as the crisp air greets the silence that spreads between us. He pushes the exterior door open with his hip, not letting me touch it even with his arms full.

"A 'thank you' will do just fine."

"Thank you!" I blurt out, cringing at not having said it already. "Thank you so much—really. You didn't need to get all of these for me."

"I know." I catch the quick curl of his lips, and we keep walking.

The sound of our feet on the concrete and the swish of the bags between us is all the noise we hear for the next few moments—that is, until the insanity of the outing finally registers in my mind and I begin to shake with laughter. I slap a hand over my mouth, trying to contain the sudden burst of giggles so loud that I can't even hear if he asks me why I'm laughing or not, but between breaths, I force myself to explain.

"Who buys seventeen books for a girl they just met?" The question comes out choppy and clipped, each word infected with giggles. "I'm starting to think *you're* the crazy one, Bodhi," I tease.

His steps falter, and a woman jogging behind us nearly plows straight into him. She jukes out of the way just in time and shoots him a threatening glare before running past us.

It occurs to me that maybe he meets everyone in his life by accidentally running into them, and though it isn't *that* funny, I nearly double over in another fit of laughter. But I stop when I look over at him once again.

Bodhi doesn't seem to notice the near collision. Instead, his lips are spread in a wicked smile. His eyes dance with some secret delight, and the look is so unexpected, I think something must be wrong. I touch my hair on instinct to feel if I somehow managed to get food in it.

"What? Why are you smiling at me like that?"

"You haven't called me by my name before." He pauses, but only for a heartbeat. "I like it."

My eyes widen as I take a step back from him, crossing my arms to put some kind of barrier between us. I wish I could appreciate the warmth my rosy cheeks provide on a cool after-noon like this, but I'm too flustered to think.

"Well, stop it. It's creeping me out." My feet carry me forward a little faster this time.

He chuckles behind me and catches up with little effort, his long steady strides moving him further than my quick short ones. I don't have to look at him to know his smile has not faltered; I can feel the smugness next to me in the same way you can feel the hum of a car engine.

I'm sure he's this way with a lot of other girls. He has a routine down and knows exactly what to say or not say to encourage a blush or coax out a shy smile. I may not know him very well, but I don't find it hard to imagine that women gravi-tate toward Bodhi. At first glance, he's everything most want:

he's attractive, funny, kind, and seems to have his life together. I imagine those crinkles around his eyes and the way he shakes his head and leans forward when he laughs have caught the attention of many women.

Have they all had these same conversations? Did the slope of his grin, the intensity of his stare, persuade them to delve into the details of their dreams the same way they did mine? Did he treat every one of them to these kinds of grand gestures, or does he cater each breath to his current audience? Am I just another name to be forgotten in a long list of contacts?

Do I even care?

Unsurprisingly, he opens the car door for me again. What's more surprising is my heart rattling against my ribcage once I'm alone with the question.

I shouldn't care. I don't . . . right?

I nibble on my lip and dare to consider the possibility. Would it be that bad to let myself do something a little reckless, like living in the maybes instead of dreading the what-ifs? Could I be someone who lets this be something that might— no, *will* hurt me?

I survey his profile once he settles in the driver's seat and pulls away from the curb. The shade of his dark brows brightens his eyes in contrast. The straight line of his nose points the way down to lips set in a firm line. I think of the dimple concealed in his cheek and wonder if it would disappear completely if he grew out his facial hair. I draw in a breath, and a sweet mix of wood and cinnamon stains my senses.

No. I can't be that kind of person.

I can't let this be anything that will hurt me in the end. Can't let it be anything permanent. Because if there is one thing I know for certain, it is that all things end, and with endings, there is pain. Why would I willingly dole out more of it if I can help it?

So, this is the only thing I can let this be: finite.

As I push away the thoughts swirling around in my head, Bodhi hums, seemingly thinking to himself.

"What?" I ask. Somehow, I know that look in his eyes means he's cooking up some other way to extend this evening. It's not a surprise when he parks again without answering my question, glancing at the time before he shuts off the engine and gets out of the car.

"Come on," he says when he walks around to open my door. He slips the bags of books into his large hands, and we begin walking to what's caught his attention.

Directly ahead is a park. Its square footage is no bigger than the surrounding lots, but it opens up with strategic landscaping. Life-size versions of Jenga, checkers, and chess litter the perimeter, crowded with families that give life to what little space there is. There aren't any open games, but that doesn't seem to bother Bodhi. Instead, he leads us toward some modern-looking metal chairs with built-in tables in the center of the park, places the bags on one of the tabletops, and settles into a seat.

Cautiously, I do the same.

"This park used to be a post office," he comments, "but back in the sixties, the foundation rotted away, leaving it to cave in on itself. Instead of repairing the damage, they cleared the rubble and filled in the hole. Built this park on top of it." As he looks around, his gaze lingers on the family playing Jenga. The youngest child takes out a block, making the tower teeter for a moment before it settles back into place. "I thought we could read here for a little bit."

"Oh," I breathe, having already suspected that was why he carted all of the books out here. I'm still imagining what this place looked like before its ruin when he speaks again.

"Unless you don't want to . . ." Mistaking my daze for reservations, Bodhi begins to shift his weight forward, threatening to stand.

"No, no. I—" I study his face for a heartbeat. "I'd like that."

And the scary thing is, I really would.

I tell myself it's just because I'd get to read—not because the inevitable end of this outing would be on life support for just a bit longer. I tell myself that agreeing to this is not the same as waiting to pull the plug. It's not a commitment.

So what if this is another ruse? Another tactic he uses to reel in the ladies? I can let this play out for a little longer. I can let him "play" me, I tell myself, as long as I'm the one in control.

He sits a little straighter and then settles back comfortably in his seat. Bodhi's focus returns to the Jenga game, almost subconsciously. I turn that direction too, curious what about the happy family keeps drawing his attention there.

The father takes out a block, and the tower topples over with a noisy ripple of wood colliding with concrete. The mother clasps her hands together while the father bellows a laugh. The two of them don smiles laced with innocent humor while their child frowns and begins to collect the pieces, wanting to get their turn.

I smile and turn back to the books. My hands dig through the bags purposefully, looking for a specific trio.

"What are you going to read?" he asks.

I smirk. "I was just going to ask you the same thing."

He tears his gaze away from the family, his brows once again pulled together in a bundle of confusion.

"I got you some books, too," I explain. "You didn't give me a chance to ask what you would be interested in, so you, my friend, have some options." I proudly place three books in front of him, happy that he didn't examine the covers while checking out.

He gently touches each cover as though they're made of glass. His breath hitches. "I—I don't know what to say."

"A 'thank you' will do just fine," I echo his earlier response, mimicking him as best I can. A small voice whispers something in my head, its words too quiet to make out, so I ignore it.

"Thank you." He looks deeper into my eyes. "Really. Thank you for these."

I tilt my head, letting a curtain of curls fall forward. "Well, you paid for them. I just picked them off the shelves."

"That may be true, but I wouldn't have gotten them otherwise. So, thank you."

I shrug. "You're welcome, I guess."

I start sifting through the rest of the books, deciding which to read first, but I mostly watch Bodhi out of the corner of my eye, curious to see which one he'll choose.

The first book is titled *Led Zeppelin: The Biography*. I figured he would enjoy not just listening to their music, but also learning more about the band he loves, though he seems to know everything about everything already. The second book I grabbed for him is *The Great Gatsby*. For some reason, the way Bodhi talks and carries himself reminds me of Jay. Plus, Bodhi seems like he would appreciate classic literature. The final book was supposed to be a joke, but he ended up buying it.

He looks up from the cover, disgust in his eyes. "*Twilight?* You saw *Twilight* on the shelf and thought I might like to give it a read?"

I smirk. "I think Edward Cullen's character will really resonate with you."

"Hmm." He flips through the pages. "Are you suggesting that I'm some homicidal monster?"

"No, I was thinking more along the lines of a mysterious man who takes a strange interest in the new girl in town." The sentence leaves my mouth before I can take it back, and a blush immediately spreads over my cheeks. "I mean, I—you know what? I think, I–"

Bodhi says nothing and cracks open the book with a smug look, choosing it over the classic and the specifically curated biography, and that effectively shuts me up.

I stick my hand into a bag, grab the first spine that meets my palm, and end up with *The Book Thief*. I turn the first few pages and begin to digest the words permanently pressed in ink, trying to erase the last few seconds of my life.

Curious, I take a peek up at Bodhi, only to find his eyes already on mine. We share a small smile and go back to reading our books.

CHAPTER SEVEN

"We should probably get going if you want to be back for dinner." The sound of Bodhi's voice makes me snap my head out of my book. I take a look at my phone.

Five o'clock? Have we really been sitting here for an hour?

"Oh. Yeah, we should."

We pack up our things in silence, not wanting to disturb the fragile calm between us, or maybe we're both just unsure how now that we've settled into it. It should feel awkward, this silence between two strangers, but for whatever reason, it's just . . . natural.

As we start to walk back to the car, I half expect Bodhi to offer me his arm once more, but he doesn't. He does, however, insist on carrying all of the bags again, not letting me carry a single one even after I offer.

When we get to the car, I remember to let Bodhi open my door, and he does. I hop in and wait in its still air while he puts the bags away. I wish I could pause time and live these last few minutes on a loop. It's been so peaceful. Bodhi's door soon opens, and I soak up the last few seconds of this limbo we've found ourselves in, knowing the end is inevitable.

But the engine starts, the blinker signals, and we begin to drive. The calm lives on for a little while longer, and when I look at Bodhi, an accidental smile spreads on my lips. Before he can see it, I turn away.

I soak in this extended moment until we're out of the city, the only view left of it in my side-view mirror. The words "Objects in mirror are closer than they appear" bounce around beneath it in sync with the bumps of the freeway. It's then, with this distance, that I finally take a breath and break the silence, pulling us out of the alternate reality we allowed ourselves to exist in.

"So, what did you think of your book?"

"Well . . ." Bodhi's eyes stay fixed on the road as he talks. "How would you like to be the proud new owner of a lightly used copy of *Twilight*?"

"It can't be *that* bad," I laugh.

"Oh, it most certainly can be. I can't understand why anyone would want to read something so far-fetched." His brow furrows as he stares ahead. "Vampires are fictitious. Why waste time reading about nonsense?"

"Because it's fun."

"Fun," he scoffs.

"Yes, fun! Don't you ever do anything just because it's fun?"

"Not if it's a waste of my time." He glances over at me. "Why don't you just take the copy home with you? Add it to the pile."

"Nope. Sorry, sir, but I've had a copy since junior high, and two would just be redundant." He sighs, and I let out an easy laugh. "You'll just have to give it another shot."

"Very well," he grumbles half-heartedly.

It surprises me how sophisticated he sounds when he talks. Like he was born in the wrong century. He carries himself in a way that's more synonymous with a politician than a twenty-something-year-old man. I study his face, hoping it will hold a clue as to why he speaks this way. I notice the small nick in his cheekbone, the sharp edges of his jawline, the way his eyes are paler from the side. This catches me by surprise, only because they're so brilliantly green when he's looking right at me.

As if he can hear my thoughts, he turns, and I'm met face-to-face with those two emeralds. I quickly turn to look out at the road ahead, pretending I wasn't just caught openly staring at his face.

"How did you enjoy *your* book?" I can hear the smile in his voice.

"It's alright. Kind of slow." I run my fingertips over the pad of my thumb, not even attempting to fight the blush.

"Hmm, sounds to me like someone else isn't loving their book, either."

I scoff. "Yes, well, you see, the difference between you and me is I don't give up so easily. I'm not a quitter."

"I'm not a quitter, either."

"Pshh. Tell that to Stephenie Meyer."

Bodhi rolls his eyes before checking his blind spot to get over one lane. "Oh my—if I say I'll give the damn book an actual try, will you shut up about it?"

I smile. "I just might."

"Good."

Turning back to him, I add, "I'm also going to pretend you didn't just tell me to shut up."

"I didn't tell you to—I never—"

"I'm just messing with you," I interrupt with a laugh.

Bodhi shakes his head, and I notice the way his curls drift with life at the movement. "You'll be the death of me, Delilah."

"What an odd thing to say to a girl you've only known for, like, five hours."

"You are entirely ludicrous."

"And you are *entirely* too serious."

"On this, you may be right."

I find myself searching for that singular dimple on his cheek, and without meaning to, I reach up and rub my own cheek, hoping to find a divot there.

"Can I turn on the AC? It's blazing in here."

Bodhi looks at me like he's just now realized he spent a good chunk of the day with a crazy woman. "It's December. How are you even remotely hot right now?"

"I'm from Utah, *remember*? I haven't acclimated yet, so this" —I gesture to the world outside of this tin can we're rolling around in—"is paradise. Or at least it would be with the air conditioner on."

Bodhi shifts uncomfortably in his seat, but before I can tell him to forget it, he turns the climate control dial to cool and shuts the vents on his side.

"Your hospitality is greatly appreciated." I adjust the vents facing me. I'm not certain, but I think he grunts in response.

Surprisingly caveman-ish for Bodhi.

The good ol' lug keeps driving while I talk his ear off about everything. Now that we've broken the earlier silence, I seem to have had my fill of it. I tell him about Utah and the cold winters there, how I once had to drive in a foot of snow to get to school because it wasn't enough to call a snow day. I tell him about Boss and how she puts ketchup on everything. I tell him a little bit about my family and how close we are. I tell him about some of my favorite books and the ones I'll never read again. I tell him a lot more than I care to admit.

"So you moved here for your dad's work?" he interrupts.

Guess I'm not leaving him much room to talk.

"Yep. He builds homes. Well, I guess he doesn't really build them, but he is—*was* one of the main developers back home. The big guys called him up, saying they needed him in Arizona, and here we are."

"What does your mom do?"

"She just started a business with my brother, Kayden. She

cleans houses and he details cars. They aren't super busy, but I think they're mostly doing it out of boredom more than anything, so it doesn't really matter if they have clients or not."

"And Collin?" he asks. "What's he do?"

I laugh a small inane laugh. "Collin's in a band. He doesn't have a job or anything right now, but he doesn't need to while he's living at home, I guess. They rehearse all day, every day, so he wouldn't have time for a job even if he wanted one."

"Are they any good?"

I lift a shoulder. "Not sure. Collin doesn't play anything for us, and they rent out a storage unit and practice there."

"What?" Bodhi asks, surprised.

"I know, it's crazy, but it's also super convenient. Once they're done, they leave all the equipment there, and it's ready to go the next day. Collin said one of the guys bought some cheap furniture and stuff for the ladies to watch." I wiggle my eyebrows, and he laughs.

"Huh, so they're *that* kind of band. Doing it to get some chicks."

"Ohh, Collin doesn't need any help in that department. I'm pretty sure he's doing it solely for the love of rock 'n' roll."

"Well, if they're influenced at all by Led Zeppelin, I'd be willing to give them a listen."

I open my mouth to reply, but stop myself. Does he think he'll get that chance?

A sinking feeling makes itself known in my chest, and all at once I remember what we're doing. I remember who I am, who he is, why we're here, and how this is only supposed to be temporary. I remember my original plan of making this the worst date ever so we wouldn't go out again and wonder when I threw that idea out the window of this luxurious vehicle.

Thinking back on the whole evening, I'm sick to my stomach. I've been leading him on this whole time—maybe not intentionally, but I have. First when I agreed to go to the bookstore, then when I let him drive me there, when I let us read in the park, and now, this entire drive, I've been babbling nonstop about my life like some lovesick puppy.

I fold my arms and face rigidly toward the road as I take complete control over my body, no longer letting it run on autopilot. As great as this day has been, I can't let anything else come of it.

"I wonder if the sunset was pretty tonight" is the only thing I can think of to say. Darkened clouds dot the sky, and in all honesty, most of the color has already dissolved, but it's something to say. Something unimportant.

Bodhi clears his throat, not missing the sudden change in my tone. "I don't notice the sunsets anymore. You get so used to them."

"Really?" He nods, and I shake my head. I can't imagine something like this becoming less beautiful just because it became more familiar. "I think I would cry if I stopped loving sunsets."

"You like them that much?"

I nod. "I try to watch them every night. I love that there aren't any mountains to block it out here, so the whole entire sky can light up with color. Sometimes I sit outside and watch the sky fade until the stars are out"

My gut clenches. I'm doing it again—saying too much, sharing things that aren't so trivial to me. How does he convince me to blurt out everything on my mind even when I *just* said I wouldn't?

Bodhi nods as he takes the exit. "Did you know that Arizona has some of the best stargazing places in the country?"

I shake my head.

"Some of them aren't too far from here, actually, maybe an hour away. But the best is the Grand Canyon," he shares. "Thousands of stars litter the sky there every night. You have to see it at least once in your life."

"Sounds incredible," I say, imagining the starlit sky.

"That, it is."

Soon, I start to recognize our surroundings and feel the tightness in my muscles begin to unravel. *Just a few more minutes.*

"When did you go there?" I ask.

"Where?"

"The Grand Canyon."

"Oh." He shifts in his seat again. "I used to go up there a lot when I was younger. I haven't been for quite some time now, but I imagine the stars haven't changed much since then." A faint smile turns up his lips for a moment before we find ourselves pulling into the restaurant parking lot.

I'm about to reach for the door handle when some voice in my head reminds me to stop. I know I should get out and do it for myself, should let this be the final nail in the coffin, but for his sake, I allow this one last mistake.

Everything starts moving in double time, and before I know it, Bodhi has everything transferred from his backseat to mine until all there's left to do is part ways. "Thank you for everything. You really didn't have to do any of this, especially the books," I say, nodding toward my backseat.

"I know," he says, matter-of-fact. "Thank you for letting me."

We stand together awkwardly, neither of us evidently knowing how to end this, but I know this is the part where it's better to just rip the Band-Aid off. I have to do it now.

"Well, it was nice meeting you, Bodhi. Thanks again." I can barely meet his eyes as I try for a quick escape.

He smiles at the sound of his name, and I curse myself for saying it.

"How about we do it again sometime? Say, tomorrow evening?" He leans onto my car so casually at the suggestion, just like earlier when he brought up the bookstore. Like he's so confident in how I'll answer.

I almost say yes right then, but for what reason, I don't

know. Maybe there is no reason other than wanting to see that dimple one last time, but I know I can't. It wouldn't be right—it wouldn't be fair. I don't want to hurt him, but if I don't do this now, it will only happen later.

"Bodhi." I flinch when he lights up again. "I really, really appreciate everything you've done today. I had an amazing time, but . . ." I trail off, stumbling over my words. *Damn it, why is this so hard?* "I'm—I'm not looking to date anyone right now. Everything is still so new since we moved, and I just got into a good routine. I don't want to mess that up. I'm so sorry." I cautiously meet his eyes. "I hope you can understand."

He's still leaning on the car, but nothing about his body language carries that same careless sort of confidence. Every inch of muscle in his body has gone so rigid that I worry he can't get enough air into his lungs. I worry he might freeze like this, the same way adults tell kids their faces will get stuck if they keep crossing their eyes.

He's frozen like this for a minute, an hour, an eternity—I'm not sure, because I'm immobilized, too—until he lets out a breath and smiles. But the smile doesn't quite reach his eyes the same way it did before. Chills trace their way down my spine, and I shake them off.

"I completely understand, Delilah. Have a good rest of your night, and thank you again for your company today." He starts to walk to the driver's side of his car but stops, turns around. "I hope to see you around."

And just like that, he's gone.

I don't remember starting to breathe again. I don't remember getting into my car or starting it. I don't remember the drive home and pulling into my driveway, or bringing in my books and setting them on my bedroom floor. I can hardly remember having dinner with my family. Everything is a blur up until this moment.

Because now, as I stand in my room staring at the books I just unpacked—all of them stacked neatly, each patiently waiting to be shelved—I find I'm not paying attention to those books at all. What I'm staring at is the large black book I found in one of the bags. The two hands caressing an apple on the cover stare right back at me.

That little brat.

CHAPTER EIGHT

"You're an idiot."

"Boss!"

"What? You are." She scoffs as if it's obvious. "You have done so many idiotic things in your life, Delilah, but this really takes the cake. If I ever questioned your stupidity before, I'm certainly not now! It's incredible, really. I don't understand how you could be so—"

"You've made your point," I interrupt. I've been avoiding this call since I got home last night. Glad to see it wasn't for nothing.

"No, I don't think I have! From what you've told me, this Bodhi guy is not only attractive, smart, and kind, but he is also interested in you—or at least he was. Who knows, after the stunt you pulled?"

I let out a groan. "It wasn't a stunt, Boss. I just told him how I felt."

"I can't begin to comprehend why you would do such a thing."

"Because."

"Because why?"

I don't respond. I let the silence between the miles that

separate us drift on, imagining a lifeboat out at sea with no one to rescue it. I certainly won't attempt to.

Boston lets out a weary sigh. "You guard your heart like you can prevent yourself from ever getting hurt, but let me tell you something: the longer you do that, the harder it will be to let people in when you eventually realize how *dumb* it is to live this way.

"Do you think I wasn't scared of getting hurt when I met Max? I was terrified, especially when I started to like him, but I didn't let that stop me from trying. You're going to regret not doing things just because you were scared, Delilah. Sure, there's always the chance you'll get hurt when you start dating someone, but there's that chance with anything you do! I can guarantee you that if you don't, you'll look back and think about all of the what-ifs, and there will be nothing you can do about it."

She's right. She's always right—but I won't tell her that. Because even though she's right, my decision is made, and I'm not changing my mind. The only person on this planet more stubborn than Boston is me. And the only person more stubborn than me might be Bodhi, but

Agh!

"Let's just not talk about this anymore," I finally respond. "What are you and Max up to tonight? Happy anniversary, by the way!"

She lets out a long, exaggerated sigh to let me know she's not happy with the sudden change in subject, but it's a futile effort. Her smile soon makes its way through the line.

"Well, if you must know, he's taking me out to this fancy new restaurant, and then he says he has a surprise for me afterward. I can't say for sure, but . . ." I move the phone away from my ear just in time to save myself from the screech about to come from the other end of the line. "I think tonight's the night he asks me to *marry* him!"

"Why do you think it's tonight?" It shouldn't be tonight, I think, but I don't say anything.

"I don't know, he's just been acting funny! It's just a hunch, though, so don't get your hopes up, D. I don't want to have to console you if I have to break that news to you."

I roll my eyes. *Like I would be the one to need consoling.*

"Uh-huh. Well, hey, call me later tonight and let me know how it goes, regardless of whether there's a ring or not."

"I will! Goodbye, D!" Her singsong voice echoes in my ears until she ends the call.

Once she hangs up, I'm alone again. Well, not completely alone.

It's just me and the silence, drifting off at sea.

I close my eyes and breathe in as much air as my lungs can take, and then I force in more. After a moment, I release it as slowly as I can manage. It's painful at first for my body to switch over and give way to such control, but after a few breaths it gives in, and I relax.

Maybe I did mess up with Bodhi . . .

My eyes snap back open, and I stand up quickly. I can't let myself think like this.

I make my way over to my bookshelf and stare at the same book I haven't taken my eyes off since last night. That same stupid book that Bodhi said he would give a second try is now sitting awkwardly on my shelf with no place of its own. It's alone, and my heart tugs in my chest at the sight, but I make no move to find a place for it. It doesn't belong here.

Work, my biggest and only real distraction, still isn't for a few hours, so I do whatever I can to keep myself occupied until then. The clothes around my room find their way into my full hamper, scattered shoes soon sit neatly in their pairs, crumbs are sucked up into the vacuum, the bathroom countertop and toilet are wiped down, the mirrors return to their glistening prime—and after all of that, I still have a couple of more hours to kill.

I rearrange my bookshelf three times, each time managing not to touch Bodhi's copy of *Twilight*, before putting them back how I originally had them. I go through my clothes and only end up with three shirts in my donation pile, so I put them back. I straighten and dust all the frames on my wall. I take out the trash in my bathroom and organize the drawers, and finally, when there is nothing left to clean in my room, I clean out my phone. I go through and delete old screenshots, organize my playlists, and arrange the apps on the screen by color, then in alphabetical order. For hours, I do everything and anything to keep my mind off my conversation with Boss.

Because as much as I try to fill this hole with anything and everything else, it's all I want. I want that person I can always call when I'm sad, bored, or lonely. The person who's always the first to hear everything I want to share, the person I still choose even when I can't stand them. I want to fight with someone, to do nothing and anything with them. I want the Tuesdays, the late-night calls, everything. I want to know what it feels like to be loved. Fully. Truly.

I want it more than I'll ever admit. But there's one thing I know I couldn't handle.

Losing that.

I'm afraid to give someone every part of me and then watch them walk away. Watch them take pieces of my heart and leave the rest shattered in my chest, unable to be fixed while part of it remains missing.

There's too much that can go wrong. Tomorrow isn't promised to anyone. I could fall in love just for life to rip them out of my desperate grasp. Or I could put my trust in one person only for them to wreck it over another woman and leave me unable to have faith in another person's love ever again. Or they could just leave, for no reason at all. No huge arguments, no "other girl"—just gone. Say they decide they don't love you anymore—how do you even cope with that? In that case, you're left loving someone who didn't think you were enough.

Nope. I don't think I'd survive any of it.

So instead, I choose to live my life in complete ignorance.

Pretending for as long as I have to that I don't need love. And I'll continue until I find the one person who would make risking any of that pain worth it. Until that creeping feeling of doubt doesn't seep into my bones the minute someone gets too close.

Finally, with nothing left to distract me, I grab my bag and throw on my Hawaiian shirt. *Might as well go to work fifteen minutes early.*

But just before I leave, I take one last look at the lonely book on the shelf and take it with me.

Molly meets me as soon as I walk through the door, and one look at her eager face makes me wish I spent these last fifteen minutes doing anything other than coming into work early—doing drugs, even.

"Tell me what happened with that—that *model* that spilled your drink all over you yesterday!"

I give her a blank stare. "Are you telling me that you saw that entire spectacle go down, and you did nothing to help?"

"Of course I saw, but I also saw the man's face and thought, 'Hmm, the sinks in the back really could use a good scrub,' and left you two to do your thing. So, tell me"—she leans in conspiratorially—"what's his name?"

"I am *not* talking to you about this." I was hoping to never talk about it, in fact.

"Why not?" She pouts. "My life is so boring—I need you to spice up my day with all the details! How was the restaurant? What did you wear? What's he like?"

"The restaurant?" I turn an accusatory gaze her way, and my next words are laced with venom. "Oh. My. Gosh. Molly, were you listening to our conversation?"

She shrugs. "I may have snuck behind the counter once scrubbing the sink anymore would have been considered abuse." I scoff, but it goes ignored. "I'm telling you, Delilah, my life is so dreadfully dull! You can't blame me for needing to listen in on a little drama." She follows me over to the counter as I clock in. "Please tell me everything. Please, please, please! I'm not going to stop asking you until you give in. Trust me, I perfected the formula of annoyance as a child and you're going to give in eventually, so you might as well tell me now."

"How many cups of coffee have you had today?"

"Just three." She grins. "Stop deflecting!"

"I told you, I'm not discussing this. Now move your caffeinated tush over, I need a lei."

With a gasp, she says, "Oh my gosh, he's a terrible kisser, isn't he?"

I roll my eyes. "Why don't you go talk to Rachel and Dennis? I'm sure they can keep you entertained." A couple started working here recently, and Molly has been obsessed with them.

"I already did, and their lives are just as boring as mine. Maybe even more. Absolutely nothing going on with them, which is not only odd, but very inconvenient for me."

"Maybe you should leave a note in their suggestion box telling them to stop having such a consistently happy, noncontentious relationship."

She points a stern finger at me. "If they had one, I would have already filled it to the brim. But they don't, so that leaves you. *Spill.*"

The door chimes, and I smile at Molly. "Aww, dang it!" I give her a fake pitiful look. "Looks like I need to go do my job— which is what you should have been doing this whole time, by the way. Guess we'll have to talk about this some other time."

She glares at me. "I'll never forgive you for not helping me in my time of need, you know."

I roll my eyes and go to the coffee bar. *So dramatic.*

The lunch rush keeps me so occupied, I don't even remember to forget about Bodhi. I make beverages at record speed, throwing in pineapple spears and tiny umbrellas like it's nothing. Our new monthly special is especially popular today.

The coconut cold brew is served in an actual coconut with a huge colorful bendy straw, made with coconut water, coconut shavings, one pump of sugar-free coconut flavoring, and a bit of maple syrup, all mixed in with the coffee. I'm told it tastes amazing, but honestly, it sounds horrible. Plus, I would never spend $12.85 on a coffee.

As the orders pile up one after the other, I dance around the counter effortlessly, glad to be kept busy. I'm in such a groove that when I reach to grab another receipt, it's jarring to find that there isn't another order to make.

"I'm on break!" I yell behind me. One semi-secluded table near the counter catches my attention. The rest of the room is littered with people on their laptops or with books, and I'd prefer to have as much space as possible. I notice Molly grabbing her bag before making my way over and ask, "You off?"

"Yep, and as much as I would love to stay and hear about your fiasco yesterday, I'm getting a headache from the smell of coffee grounds." It certainly couldn't be from the five cups of coffee she's had today. "Don't think I won't be interrogating you tomorrow, but I understand now."

My brow furrows. "Understand what?"

"You need time to process. Of course spending time with such an attractive man would take a toll on you—I imagine you're still trying to wrap your head around the hellos! I'm thinking by tomorrow, you should be completely recovered and ready to discuss." She pats my shoulder. "This means I forgive you, by the way."

"There's nothing to talk about!" I shout at her back, but she walks away so quickly that I'm only left with the breeze she leaves in her wake.

I shake my head. *A problem for tomorrow.*

I've just started to dive back into Jane Austen's world when Molly comes rushing back in with a huge shit-eating grin on her face.

My brows scrunch again. "Forget something?"

"No, I was just walking out when I remembered the sinks in the back could use a good scrubbing." Her eyes are wild, but before I can ask anything else, she slips behind the counter and into the back.

"What a weirdo," I mutter under my breath. As I turn back to my book, my eyes snag on the man making his way toward my table and my stomach drops.

The next words I say under my breath are not so kind.

"What are you doing here?" I ask in disbelief when he approaches my table.

"Hello to you, too," he says.

"Hello."

"Hello, Delilah. It's nice to see you again."

I curse to myself when my heart flutters at the sight of that dimple. "Well, I do work here, so the odds of you seeing me were pretty high."

"Still, it's nice to see you." He invites himself to sit across from me, ignoring my blatant rudeness.

I sigh. "Bodhi, I already told you—"

"Nope," he cuts me off. "Yesterday, I listened to what you had to say. I thought about it, and now I want you to listen to me for the next minute."

My mouth drops. "And what if I don't want to?"

He considers this. "Then that would be an absolute shame."

We stare at each other for what feels like a long time, both of us waiting for my answer. I'm not sure which of us is more surprised when I finally speak up.

"Fine. One minute."

He slips in a smirk before sobering up. "I had a great time with you yesterday, and I don't think I'm going out on a limb when I say you did too. I enjoyed our time together so much that when you said we shouldn't spend any more with one another, I was hurt, quite frankly." I try to interject, but he holds up a hand to stop me. "So, the reason I've come here today is to offer you a proposal."

My eyes narrow with slight curiosity.

"You've just recently moved here and have no friends yet. I've lived here my whole life and don't have many of my own, either. What I propose is that we be each other's friends. Nothing more." He pauses for a moment, letting that sink in. "I'll show you around and tell you everything there is to know about these parts until you're practically a local. We can keep each other company. No funny business."

Satisfied, Bodhi folds his arms and sits back. I pause, waiting for something else. ". . . That's all?"

He raises a brow. "Were you wanting more?"

"No, it's just—are you serious?"

"As a heart attack."

"Friends?"

"Nothing more."

I study the features of his face. How calm and collected he seems. No lines or wrinkles disrupt his expression—the total opposite of when he left yesterday. No rigid muscles make up his composure, and as he waits for me to respond, he's perfectly still. Content. He is all things patient while he lets me process. If we weren't sitting in a coffee shop debating my decision from last night, I think I could find peace in just watching him wait. But there's one thing bothering me.

"Why?" I ask him, wanting—no, needing to know.

This time it's him who takes a moment to reply. "Why what?"

"Why go through all this trouble? Why not make friends with one of your coworkers or some random dude on the street? Why me?" The questions won't stop flowing now. "Why go out of your way to be friends with me?"

He thinks for a moment, silent. Though I don't mind him giving it serious thought, my heart rate accelerates while I wait for his answer.

"I've never met anyone who listens the way you do. Never found a person who cares to hear what I say. You make me feel seen, Delilah." He looks down at his hands, clasps and unclasps them. "You make me smile, and I mean *really* smile. I haven't done that in a long time." He admits the last part so softly, I'm not even sure I've heard him correctly. "So no, I don't think I'll go make friends with someone at work or a random dude on the street, because none of them would be you."

He finally meets my eyes, and I swallow the dry lump forming in my throat. Bodhi sits exposed in front of me, his honesty opening him up and leaving him vulnerable, yet he doesn't try to cover it up or take it back the way I know I would. He just waits for me to say something. Anything.

I find myself full of respect for him at that moment. Not only did he come to talk to me after I rejected him yesterday, but he's left his feelings unguarded for me to see.

I clear my throat. "Okay."

". . . Okay?" He looks at me hesitantly.

"Okay. Let's be friends," I say with a shrug.

"Friends . . ." he trails off, as though the idea that I would agree isn't something he ever considered. Then he smiles the biggest, goofiest lopsided smile I've ever seen, flashing that dimple at me once more, and it feels like confirmation that I made the right choice.

"But there's one more thing." I get up and go to my bag behind the counter, pulling out the other book I brought with me today before I return to the table. "You have to take this back and finish it."

Caught off guard, he throws his head back and closes his eyes. "I can't believe you found that thing. I thought you wouldn't notice it with the hundred other books you got."

"Of course I did, and you, sir, are such a liar! You said you'd read it." I set it down in front of him with a *thump.*

"I most certainly did not," he says, pointing a stern finger at me. "I asked you if you would stop pestering me about it if I *said* I'd read it. I didn't say I'd actually read it."

"Uh-huh. And I'm pretty sure you're leaving out the part where you told me to shut up."

Bodhi blanches and blurts out, flustered, "I did *not* tell you to shut up."

"Oh, I'm just messing with you." My lips tug to the side in a smile when a thought occurs to me. "You know, now that we're friends, I'm going to have to find something to call you."

"Why? Bodhi works just fine."

"Because. How about Bodster?"

He cringes. "No."

I smirk at his contorted face. "Odhi?"

Bodhi runs his hand roughly over his face. "These are terrible nicknames."

I laugh. "They are not!"

He tilts his head, an exasperated look on his face. "One rhymes with toaster, and the other is something you'd name a cow."

I throw my hands up. "Well, I'm open to suggestions."

"Might I suggest you call me Bodhi?"

My eyes narrow as I cross my arms. "I'll think of something."

"That's what I'm afraid of." His green eyes dance with humor, and I find myself caught once again in the glass-bottle hue.

"I should probably get back to work." I hitch a thumb toward the counter.

"Of course," he says with a smile. "I won't keep you any longer. I'll see you later, Delilah."

We both stand to leave, and for a second, I'm scared there will be an awkward exchange of hugs, but he just turns and walks away. The book is in his hands.

I stand there until the door chimes and he rounds the corner, out of my sight.

Friends. Why didn't I think of that?

I start to walk back toward my station in a daze when

someone pops up from behind the counter. A yelp escapes me before I can stop myself.

"Holy shit, Molly! You scared the living daylights out of me!"

She jabs me in the shoulder, her face anything but teasing. "You, missy, have some explaining to do," she spits.

"Me? You were the one ducking behind the counter! Why don't you explain—" Our whole conversation from earlier suddenly comes flooding back to me. "You snake! Did you just eavesdrop on that whole conversation?"

Mischief flashes in her eyes. "Not the whole thing. I missed the beginning because I was crawling over from the back, but everything after the part where you told him you didn't want to spend any time together, I heard crystal clear." She folds her arms, mimicking my stance. "Explain to me why you would ever turn a man like that down."

I look around for someone to save me, maybe Dennis or Rachel, but I'm on my own. They're probably in the back, sneaking kisses or bickering. You never know which until you accidentally intrude.

"I cannot believe you, Molly," I reply, shaking my head. "You know what? You're cut off."

"Cut off? From what?"

"Coffee. Caffeine. Sugar. All of it! You've gone crazy, it's not even funny."

Her eyebrows scrunch. "You can't do that."

"Well, I sure am going to try." Molly rolls her eyes at that. "Besides, I thought you had a headache."

"Believe it or not, it was cured by this mini soap opera thing you had going on." She gestures to the table Bodhi and I sat at.

I shake my head at the ceiling and sigh, "Go home, Molly. Before I have to get a restraining order on you."

"As if I would ever stalk *you*," she snorts.

I look at her like she's psychotic and hold my hand out to

the very counter she was eavesdropping behind just moments before.

Molly rolls her eyes at me again. "Okay, so the *one* time. Well, two times if you count yesterday—but trust me, if I were going to make anyone go through the trouble of getting a restraining order, I would make it worth their time." She gives me a wink.

"I *so* don't want to know what you mean by that."

"You *definitely* don't." As she leans in to tap my nose, I wonder if she's somehow gleaned that I hate when people do that. "I do want to go home now, though, so tell your *friend* not to make any more surprise visits. I think I pulled a muscle running back in here."

She walks out of the shop again, but I don't fully trust that she's finally left until I see her car pull out of the parking lot. Once she's gone, I'm left alone with my thoughts once again.

And I actually don't mind it.

CHAPTER NINE

Be ready in 15 minutes.

That's all the text said. No meeting place, no explanation. Just 15 minutes to get ready.

The text came in ten minutes ago, and I'm fairly certain I'm going to be late. I still need to find my shoes, change my shirt—because this one now has mouthwash all over it—and do my hair. I take a look in my bathroom mirror at the frizzy mop on top of my head. Wearing it naturally these past couple of days has left it a mess. With a sigh, I start throwing it up in the only thing that will pass as presentable in this short amount of time: a messy bun. A clean enough shirt from the floor makes it onto my body before I start booking it down the stairs to find my missing shoes.

I don't have to look far. They're lying in a discarded heap on the first step, nearly tripping me.

I'm already two minutes late at this point, and I still don't know where we're meeting. *Probably the restaurant or the coffee shop.*

"Where are you going?" my mother asks as I snag my keys

out of the dish on the kitchen counter. She's whisking away at something in a bowl, making some delightful-smelling treats. Probably cookies.

"I'm not sure yet . . ." I trail off, not sure how to tell my mother the events of the last two days without giving her a minor heart attack.

"Not sure, huh?" She tastes some batter and gives a single nod of approval. "Are you going out alone? I can come with you if you want. I'm almost finished here."

"No," I say a bit too quickly. "It's okay, I'm going out with a friend." My voice tumbles over the last word, and I hope she doesn't notice. But it is the truth.

"A friend from work?" she asks.

"Uh, yeah, from work." *Technically not a lie.*

She smiles. "Okay. I'm assuming you won't be home for dinner?"

"I'd say that's a safe bet."

"Have fun! Don't do anything I wouldn't do." She gingerly kisses my cheek, and I roll my eyes as I walk out of the kitchen. There isn't much my mom wouldn't do when she was my age; she just knows I'd never do any of it myself.

Throwing on a jacket, I rush out of the house to start my car but freeze at the sight of another car in the driveway. The same one I rode in to Phoenix the other day.

Bodhi hops out of the car, but I still can't seem to move.

"What are you doing here?" I manage. "I thought—"

"Get in," he says. "We don't have much time."

"Don't have much time for what?" I ask, making my way over to the passenger door he's holding open.

"Now, Delilah." He smirks. "Patience is a virtue."

While I would normally protest until I got an answer, I can see the urgency in his face, hear it in his voice. So, I hop in. Bodhi shuts my door and hurries back around to hop into his seat. Once we buckle in, he turns to reverse out of my driveway.

"How'd you know where I live?" I watch him settle back in his seat as he speeds away from my house. *Geez, we must be pretty late.*

"Oh . . ." He shifts in his seat. "I asked some girl from the coffee shop. She was extremely helpful." He doesn't look at me when he answers. "I hope that's okay."

"That's alright," I say, but as I look away, I frown. *Molly.* I'll have to have a word with her next time we work together and figure out how she even knows my address. So much for her not being a little stalker.

"We're grabbing some fast food on the way," Bodhi tells me. "Would you prefer salads or subs?"

"Ew. One hundred percent subs."

"Ew? What's wrong with salads?" At that, he finally looks at me.

"Nothing, except that they're tasteless and disgusting."

Bodhi's face scrunches in confusion. "How can something be both tasteless and disgusting?"

I think for a second. "I think they're disgusting *because* they're tasteless."

"That doesn't make any sense." Bodhi shakes his head a little. Strands of his hair threaten to escape from its perfect shape to dance to the beat.

I shrug. "It makes sense to me."

"Well, it sounds like you've had some pretty boring salads in your life." He lifts his cheeks in a grin. "And as your newly appointed friend, I think it's time we change that."

I groan.

"Sorry, Delilah. My mind is made up."

I give him my best attempt at a glare. "Fine. But when I'm extremely hangry because I didn't eat, there better be no complaining. You'll just have to deal with the repercussions."

"You'll love it."

"Or I'll be starving all night, and you'll end up feeling guilty about the girl who sits desiccating beside you." I let my head loll against the seat but take a peek at him. "I accept apologies in the form of sandwiches, by the way."

He rolls his eyes. "Don't be so dramatic."

"I think my reaction is appropriately tuned for the situation."

Bodhi looks over at me before turning back to the road, concern etching his forehead.

"What?" I ask.

"I'm just thinking we might have to cancel tonight's plans and take you to a shrink. You clearly aren't right in the head if you think this is an appropriate way to react to not getting what you want."

It's my turn to return the eye roll. "Now who's being dramatic?"

His shoulders bounce in a silent laugh, stretching the fabric of his button-down. It's a perfectly fitted dark-blue one today paired with equally tailored grey slacks. I can't see his shoes, but I imagine they match just as perfectly as his outfit did yesterday.

"Do you always dress so . . . so posh?"

He takes a quick look at his attire. "I came straight from work."

"You didn't want to change?"

A pause. "Is there something wrong with what I'm wearing?"

"No, it's just . . . I don't know." I search for the right question. "Like . . . do you even own a T-shirt?"

He shakes his head, letting humor pull it side to side. "Yes, and I even own a pair of sweatpants, if you can believe it. But I like to dress nice when I'm out and about, even if I'm not at work."

I absently nod but turn my attention to my own clothing. The shirt I found on my floor is not only wrinkled but has a deep stain on its sleeve, my jeans have faded well past the point of fashionability, and my Converse reached their expiration date ages ago. Clearly, I don't hold myself to the same standards. I wrap my arms around my torso as though it might mask the differences between us.

As Bodhi drives, we fill the idle air with chitchat. Nothing we say is of real substance, but we both seem to enjoy it all the same. I think of how nice it is to have someone to talk to again. Eventually, we pull up to a salad restaurant with a drive-through, and my head lolls in his direction.

"What kind of place has salads to go?" I mutter.

"The best kind," Bodhi answers.

I let him order something for me and get a drink to help me choke it down; for all my talk, I don't care for wasting food. After a few minutes, we get our meal and start driving off.

"Do I get any hints?" I peek into the brown paper bag with our salads in it, and I'm surprised to see mine doesn't look too bad. It's covered in berries and nuts with a pink dressing.

"About where we're going?"

I nod.

"Nope. We'll be there in ten minutes. You can wait." He winks at me, and for the first time, I don't have to fight back a blush. It's easier to label his flirtatious behavior as teasing now that we've decided to be just friends.

I smile to myself, finding that I could get used to this easy, relaxed feeling.

Bodhi starts to tell me about the cities we pass through, when one was founded, and why they chose to name it that. He tells me about the White Tank and Camelback Mountains and explains where their names came from. He tells me about the animals that live on each one and about the plants that grow there. He tells me everything, and I love listening to every word.

"You know a lot about a lot of things." I sip my lemonade and look out the window, trying to spot the javelinas he's just finished telling me about.

Bodhi shrugs in response and checks his blind spot before getting over.

"How do you remember it all?" I wonder aloud. "I lived in Utah my whole life, and I couldn't name more than one mountain if I tried."

Bodhi glances at me, perhaps debating how much to reveal. "When I was a kid, I was always bored—not a lot of other children were where I lived. So, to occupy my time, I'd teach myself whatever I could. I would read anything I could get my hands on: books, maps, newspapers, cereal boxes, you name it. I loved documentaries, too, and would watch them whenever I could. Everything has just stuck with me all these years, I guess."

"So you just remember everything you've ever read?" I say jokingly.

"Everything."

I blanch at him. "*Everything?*"

"Yes." His eyes slide toward mine. "So you can see why I'm not too eager to read my copy of *Twilight.*"

I laugh, "Not too eager to remember that whole book for time and all eternity?"

"Not really, no. But I promised you I would, so I will," he says nobly. "My only regret is that I couldn't finish it all yesterday and get it over with."

"How far did you get? Halfway?" I joke, but as Bodhi nods, my jaw drops in disbelief. "I gave it back to you yesterday!"

"You did."

"And you've already read that much?"

"I have."

I let out an impressed whistle. "And I thought I was the only one capable of such atrocities."

"I don't mean to belittle your . . . *gift,* by any means, but it's not *that* hard to read, Delilah. It only took me the better part of my evening to get that far."

"Still, I'm impressed."

He huffs. "The bar must be very low for you to be impressed by basic skill."

"Well, I've found that if you set the bar low for everything, life gets a whole lot better." Before I can say anything else, we pull into a winding parking lot. I read a sign as we pass. "Papago Park?"

Bodhi just smirks while he parks the car. Taking the bag of food from me, he grabs a blanket from the back seat and gets out of the car. Once he walks over to open my door, we stand together facing the park.

"Um, are we hiking up . . . that?" I point to the mountain. It's not huge, but I definitely didn't wear the right shoes, and I'm not really in the mood for some blisters.

He laughs. "Just to where those people are sitting." A cluster of people are gathered near a hole in the mountain. "It will only take us five minutes. Super easy. We'd better hurry, though—I don't know if we'll even get a good spot this late."

"A good spot for what?"

Bodhi's lips spread until that same dimple I've grown so fond of reveals itself, and he stands a little taller. "To watch the sunset." He starts walking toward the hill and I try to move toward him, to take a step forward, but I stay where I am, frozen. In shock.

Turning back, Bodhi stops when he sees he's left me behind. "Did you forget something? We're already missing it."

I blink a few times before I shake off the shock. "Sorry. Yeah, I'm coming." As I make my way toward him, I can't help but be a little surprised that he remembered such a seemingly insignificant detail about me. I don't feel like a very memorable person, but I don't mind that; in fact, I prefer it most of the time. But to be remembered is something so . . . foreign. I'm not sure what to make of it.

We walk around the back end of the massive rock jutting from the earth, and Bodhi leads me up a fairly easy trail. When we reach the top, we step through the hole I saw from down below to see a crowd of people scattered throughout, chatting and sipping on their waters. Bodhi leads me to the right, and there we find a small alcove where he lays out the blanket for us to sit on, its checkered pattern distorted by the bumps and divots of the rock. I take a seat and start getting the food out while Bodhi tugs at his side of the blanket, stretching it to its full width so he can fit.

I hand him his salad bowl and a fork. His is covered in all sorts of vegetables, some of which I never would think to put on a salad, and no dressing. Just lemon juice.

"That"—I point to the bowl now in his hands—"looks disgusting."

His head shakes back and forth. "It does not."

"It's too healthy! It needs something sweet in there. Like cheesecake bits."

He grimaces. "Now that, I *would* consider disgusting."

I push around my bowl's contents with my fork. "I could kill for an Oreo cheesecake right now."

Bodhi's mouth is already full with his first bite. "Try it," he says once he's swallowed.

I try to get away with eating an entire bite of strawberries without him noticing, but of course, he does anyway. So, I find the smallest piece of lettuce and hold it up to Bodhi sassily before popping it in my mouth. I chew carefully and wait for it to taste awful, and horrible, and all things bad, but I'm surprised to find that it's . . . fine. Better than fine, actually.

"Well?" Bodhi looks at me sideways, waiting for me to either spit it out or let him say, "I told you so." And I'd do just about anything before admitting defeat.

"The strawberries are delicious, and I'm considering running off to Vegas to marry this dressing, but just like I told you: the lettuce is tasteless."

He rolls his eyes. "I wouldn't doubt that's due to the fact that the piece of lettuce you ate was no bigger than the buttons on my shirt."

I make a face at Bodhi and turn to look at the sky. It's nothing special right now; most of the clouds are still white, and the sun isn't fully behind the horizon yet, but it is a spectacular view nonetheless. No trees or buildings block the sky from up here. I can only imagine how incredible the sunset will be.

I continue examining the sky while Bodhi chews on another bite of food. He clears his throat, and when I turn to face him, I find him watching me as intently as I was watching the sky. I fight back an embarrassed blush as he speaks up. "Who do you normally watch the sunset with?"

"No one," I say. He looks confused by my answer. "What?"

"Nothing, it's just . . . what do you . . . do?"

I raise an eyebrow, confused myself, and slowly respond, ". . . Watch the sunset."

"Do you listen to music or read while you watch?" he asks.

"Sometimes. Not always. Mostly, I just think." I take another bite of my salad.

"About?"

I shrug. "Whatever. I don't really have an agenda."

"Why do you always do that?"

"Do what?" Now, I'm even more confused.

Bodhi mimics my shrug. "Shrug everything off. You do it all the time, like you're trying to make less of what you said."

I sit back, throwing up a defensive wall around the faint twinge of hurt in my chest. "Do I need a reason?"

"No, but it sure is annoying as hell." He must notice how my eyes are about to pop out of their sockets, because he continues to explain, "I just think you shouldn't belittle what you say. If you mean it, own it. Don't do it around me, at least. I happen to think rather highly of you."

I scoff. He hardly knows me. How could he think anything of me? "Why should I care what you think?" I ask with feigned indifference.

Bodhi ponders this as he takes another bite of his salad.

Somehow, he's almost finished with it. "You shouldn't," he finally says, matter-of-fact, "but I'm still going to tell you what I think anyway, and it would do you some good to listen to what I have to say."

"And why would that do me any good, listening to you?" I shoot back.

"For one, I'm always right."

I roll my eyes at him.

"And *two*, you keep forgetting we're friends now. And friends only have each other's best interests at heart." He cups a hand over his chest and gives me a teasingly endearing look, like it's all a big show. Maybe it is.

"Hmm" is all I say before going back to my salad.

We're both quiet for a while to take in the golden rays. Slowly, they fade into the light oranges and faint pinks that come with the setting sun. The peaceful view gives me a tiny moment of clarity in which to think.

Mainly, I think about Bodhi. How strange it is that I've been so willing to give him any of my time or attention. I keep thinking about how he doesn't know me, but I also don't know him. I hardly know anything about the man, yet I have allowed him to seamlessly slide into the rhythm of my life in such a short time. We met not even seventy-two hours ago, and already I'm letting him whisk me off to secret locations. What is wrong with me?

I feel so out of sorts. This isn't who I usually am. Maybe I'm being reckless—suffering from a quarter-life crisis, if such a thing exists.

If you looked up the definition of "careful" in a dictionary, it would show a picture of me. The same goes for wary, doubtful, and guarded: I'm the type of person to lock my car doors three times before putting my keys away. The type who takes pepper spray with me on the walk to the mailbox. The type to delegate my work, but then do it all myself because I know I'll do it exactly how I want it. I don't trust easily, and certainly not quickly.

So why am I now?

It's frustrating when you aren't acting like yourself. Even more so when you don't quite know why.

As I return to the present, Bodhi looks out to the horizon with such concentration that I want to reach out and tell him the point is to enjoy it, not to analyze it to death. But although I barely know him, I think that's just the type of person Bodhi is. He looks for practicality in everything. Does nothing without a specific reason. Says everything with intent.

Still, I wonder how much thought he puts behind what he says. Does he just make sure what he says is the truth, or does he carefully construct each sentence to mean exactly what he wants it to?

If you looked up Bodhi's picture in the dictionary, I imagine it would appear under *intentional, perplexing, mysterious . . .* and probably *magnetic* as well.

His broad shoulders are firm, with his elbows locked behind him to prop up his body. Every part of him is perfectly frozen in this moment. The seconds tick past him unnoticed, not interrupting his state of tranquility. There isn't even a breeze to lift a single hair on his head. The only movement in his form is the slight rise and fall of his chest, the flutter of his eyelashes lapping against his skin. But in those moments between each breath and blink, there is a perfect stillness to his being. It's both unnerving and inspiring to witness such stability, but there's also something calming in watching someone exist with this level of composure.

I take another bite of salad and watch the orange above us slowly bleed into the pink. The sky is almost like cotton candy now. I want to reach out and touch the soft tufts of clouds that line the entire sky.

I get so lost in the expansive beauty, I forget where I am. What I'm doing. Who I'm with. My mind is taken hostage by my wandering thoughts as I stare at the glittering horizon. The light sky-blue backdrop is dusted with a rose-quartz haze, the hues impossible to definitively distinguish. Their edges fade perfectly together—a seamless pair. It's magical.

Every time I blink, it's like I'm looking at an entirely different canvas. The small changes are imperceptible, but still, they are there. It's something I both dislike and admire about sunsets. Although I can't properly appreciate every second the way it deserves, I admire it specifically because the quick death of each tiny moment is what makes it special. It wouldn't be beautiful if it didn't end.

Bodhi's food is long gone by now—I'm not even sure when he finished it. Now, he sits in peaceful stillness and lets the sky's soft glow kiss his face, illuminating it in all the right ways. His sharp features soften, making his serious expression blend into something a bit more reflective, and I wonder if he indeed found something practical in the fading sun.

It's then, as the clouds begin to grey, that he finally breaks the relaxed silence.

"I see why you like them so much." His chin juts toward the western sky, and though he doesn't look at me, I know I have his full attention.

"I told you. Everyone loves a good sunset."

The yellowish-green tint in the sky seems to signal that the show is over, as the people surrounding us begin to gather their belongings. They start toward their vehicles soon after, eager to get on the road. Usually, I watch the sky until the stars pop out, waiting for the canvas to morph into colors so muted no one can really appreciate them, but I'm not going to make us sit out here longer. So, I stand and begin collecting our trash.

I let Bodhi gather the blanket, not mentioning that my favorite part has yet to come. The part where viridian gathers beneath denim for just a moment before it blackens completely. I stretch my neck to memorize whatever I can of the sky when a whoosh of air drags my attention away. I look back to Bodhi, who is spreading out the blanket once again.

"What are you doing?" I ask.

He pulls at his side of the blanket, making it as flat as possible on the rock. "I didn't realize we weren't done yet. My apologies." He must have noticed my head still turned toward the horizon. He pats the spot on the blanket where I was moments ago, next to him, telling me to sit back down.

And I do. Only inches separate us, and it's probably too close, but neither of us moves.

"We really don't have to stay; most people just leave right about now." I look at the few strangers still around us packing up their blankets.

"We aren't most people," he says as he playfully bumps my shoulder with his own.

I laugh. *What an understatement.*

We start to talk as the background slowly loses its colors, only glancing skyward as it morphs into my favorite shade. For the first time, I have something else to pay attention to.

"You've never had a pet?" I ask.

"Nope," Bodhi replies. "Not a single one."

"Not even a rock or something?"

He scrunches his nose. "A pet *rock*?"

I squint at him, thinking I must have misheard. "Who hasn't heard of pet rocks?"

He only tugs his lips to the side.

A short laugh escapes as I shake my head. "You baffle me, Bodhi."

"Just with my lack of knowledge in domestic pets and pebbles, or with everything in general?" he asks as a grin slaps itself onto his face.

I can't help but grin like an idiot right back at him at the sight of that dimple. "I'd say everything in general. You're very . . . different."

"Different how?" He looks at me both like he's been stung and with a little curiosity.

I shrug. "I don't know. There's just something about you that's different from everyone else." I only mean to look into his eyes for a moment but have a hard time looking away. Something in our gaze snags and keeps me there a bit too long, but no explanation comes out. How can I express what I don't even understand? "Come to think of it, though, it might be the way you buy strangers lunch and truckloads of books." I let out a light laugh, and his low chuckles follow.

"Yes, I can see how that might make me a little . . . different." He stares deeper into my eyes, and I feel the pull to stay there for a minute or two more. Maybe see if—

No.

I clear my suddenly dry throat and look away. "What do you think? Ready to head back?" I can still feel his eyes locked on me, but I don't let myself look at them. Not even when he grunts in response and stands to pick up our things. It's only when he folds up the blanket that he finally speaks again.

"You know, you're different, too."

I whip my head to him before I realize it, taken aback. "Different how?"

As he faces away from whatever light remains in the sky, a sinister shadow contours his smile into something unsettling, like it prevents it from reaching his eyes. Like the curl of his lips is too heavy to naturally lift beneath the weight of the darkness.

When he speaks, I nearly flinch, ripped out of the trancelike state.

"Just in every possible way," he answers, turning back to me. "Of course, I mean that in all the good ways." Then he winks.

And then he's walking away from me again. Leaving me behind. Again. But before he has time to turn around and catch me in another stupor, I put one foot in front of the other until our paces match.

I don't acknowledge his comment about me being different in all the right ways, and neither does he. I don't tell him it's an odd thing to say to a friend. I don't tell him that the way his face looked a moment ago frightened me in a way I don't understand. Only children are afraid of shadows, the things in them. I know better than to call something a monster when it is really just a trick of the light.

We just walk to the car with our arms full, the air between us silent and empty.

CHAPTER TEN
AFTER

The door swings open. I don't look as the sound of steps grows closer. I pay them no attention. I just keep staring at the same crack in the wall I've examined thousands of times by now. I know each jagged edge as deeply as I know how to spell my name. When I close my eyes, the image of the wall with its melancholy paint and lonesome crack is still there. It won't leave me.

"I brought you some food." The *clink* of the plate as it meets the table rings in my ears. It's the loudest noise I've heard in—I don't know how long. Since I stopped screaming, I guess. "It's teriyaki chicken."

My attention stays focused on the wall. I'm pinned here, gaping at the crack, and I don't want to move. It's unfair that the wall's wounds are visible. I slowly run my fingertips over the pad of my thumb, making sure to feel the sensation in each nerve ending. Trying to ground myself while my mind slips away.

I wish that the cracks on our skin revealed our pains. Our demons. Our aches. The ones we've already felt, and the ones that haunt us. Maybe then, I wouldn't be here.

My thumb traces circles on my index finger.

Maybe I wouldn't be here.

"Delilah, you have to eat something."

The crack is embedded about three feet up the wall. Its jagged reach stretches seven or eight inches wide. The dull paint around it is peeling, leaving flakes of cream carelessly at its feet. I trace the crack in the wall once more with my eyes, and for the hundredth time, I wonder how it got there. Why should this relic permanently haunt these walls? "What happened to you?" I want to ask it.

"Delilah."

I finally look up at my visitor's face. Giving him the attention I'm sure he thinks he deserves. Is entitled to, even. I study each feature. Notice the stubbornness in his tight brow, the placidness that settles on his lips, his hollow, empty eyes. He's not asking, but telling me to wake up. To be here. To be the person I once was.

But I don't think either one of us can be called that—a person.

Not anymore.

Just ghosts of ones.

But even ghosts remember who they once were.

The memories I have been carefully holding at bay begin to leak through. Emotion claws at my throat, threatening to suffocate me if I don't let it spill out. I don't want it to, though. To let it escape is to accept this. To give in is to lose.

My throat burns and tears prick willfully at my eyes. I'm weak, I realize. I'm weak, and I always have been.

I turn my head back to the wall, hoping my unwelcome visitor won't see how close I am to the edge. "What happened to you?" The four words are nothing more than a throaty whisper. A question asked but never to be answered. I don't even know if I meant for the plea to come out; I don't even know who the "you" in question is. My captor? The wall? Me?

Tears begin to fall quietly into my lap, and I'm shocked when a smile almost twitches across my lips. Because even though this is defeat, a small sliver of my pain is visible. My own cracks are forming. But like the wall, no one else can see the cause. They can only see the break.

Maybe he will turn and leave me. Let me be. Allow me to crack in peace.

But he never leaves me. Not really. And why would he, when he has all the control? My cold, empty, frigid companion can have anything he wants, it would seem. All he has to do is move the chess pieces to the perfect spot, and everyone will play right into his hands.

I did. And what's worse is, he didn't use fear to lock me in this cage. I gave him the key. Let him tuck it in his pocket. Let him break me.

I did this. It is my fault. He was my best friend, and I thought I could trust him. That's what hurts the most, I think.

My tears fall because there is only myself to blame for all the hurt I've caused. To myself, to everyone else. I should have known better—I *did* know better—and still I let this happen.

"It doesn't have to be this way." The words spill out of a stone-cold face. Nothing could move it. Nothing could change it. I've already tried.

My monster steps closer, and I try so hard to hold myself together. To tape the pieces back into place. I try to freeze every muscle. I tell myself I'm fine. I tell myself to stop shaking.

"It doesn't need to be this hard." Another step toward me. "Just eat the food." Two more steps.

Inches separate us, and it's too close, much too close. The wall blurs behind the tears that teeter on the edge of my lashes. Tears I can't contain.

What happened to you? What happened to you? What happened to you?

I blink, and some of the liquid races down my cheeks.

What happened to me?

My eyes slide shut, but it does nothing to stop the tears

from running. They betray me, escaping in warm trails down my sullen cheeks. The only warmth I've known in this prison.

My captor's rough hand cups my shoulder. It's so similar to what being held once used to feel like that I almost start screaming again. Sobs beg to escape at the sound of his icy voice.

"Delilah." A whimper makes its way through my trembling lips. "Eat. *Now*. I won't ask again."

My eyes slowly lift to meet those staring down at me, and I try so hard to see something, anything to tell me that this is all a façade. A glimmer of hope that this is just a nightmare. A joke. But all I see are hollow sockets. No warmth, no comfort.

Just empty eyes.

Something is messing with my head.

Something is horribly wrong with my mind.

"What's wrong with me?" I croak out.

He tilts his head then, and it's such an innocent, curious gesture that my lungs nearly collapse. It's almost enough to assure me. To comfort me. To make me forget what I know can't possibly be true. To make me think he might be human.

It's not true. I'm not here. I'm losing my mind. I'm losing my mind.

"It's okay." His calloused fingers swipe at one of the traitors still falling from my eyes, as if he might care. "You'll be better soon." But that is not true. Even when he says this, I can't believe it. There is no life in his voice, no personality. Just a void. How can I ever go back to the girl I was before?

My hollow playmate stands up to leave, and before I can stop myself, the question leaves my lips in a rushed whisper. "Am I crazy?"

My visitor pauses, his back to me.

"Just eat the food, Delilah."

And then I'm alone once again. The only difference now is the plate of food. I don't eat it. I don't want to get better, even if that is what he demands. I just turn my attention back to the wall and trace the crack over and over and over again.

Please let me be crazy.

Please let me be insane.

Because if I'm not crazy, if I'm not insane, then this is real. The man I love is a monster. The man I love is doing this to me. The man who put me together is the same man who is tearing me apart.

A final tear escapes, trailing slowly down my face and onto my neck. It rests on my collarbone for a moment before it bleeds into the fabric of my worn shirt.

"You are going to get out of here," I whisper. "You are going to get home."

I don't know why I say it.

I don't believe it.

I know it isn't true.

I died eons ago, and I'm still trying to convince myself there are reasons to be alive.

CHAPTER ELEVEN

Work feels different today. My shift is flying by, and not in the way it typically does. It's not measured out by the quick breaks where I get to read, but instead, I find that the morning has slipped by without me even realizing it. There's some kind of energy in the air, something electric.

It feels like excitement.

I texted Bodhi between making cups of coffee this morning, asking if he wanted to grab some lunch. I'll be covering Molly's afternoon shift, but with a bit of time between shifts and a new friend to spend time with, I thought, why not?

Within minutes he responded, saying he'd love to. He always talks like that, expressing his emotions. His responses are never a quick yes or no; they're always filled with something more. He should be here in a few hours.

Maybe I should care a little more about the coffee splashes on my shirt, or the pieces of my hair that have somehow escaped the low-hanging bun at the back of my head, but I don't. I don't have to worry about things like that when there's no one to impress.

It's a relief, honestly.

"You're Collin's sister, right?"

I look up from the counter I've been wiping to see a familiar blond guy standing in front of me. He shifts his weight from one foot to the other, a habit I know better than to attribute to nerves—it's pent-up energy just begging to be expelled. I don't know him well enough to say for certain, but I doubt he could hold still for longer than a couple of minutes at a time. I imagine it would pain him.

"Yes, I'm Delilah. It's Jett, right? How are you?" I flash him a brilliant smile, and though I don't need the confirmation, I ask just to make him feel better about not knowing my name. It's hard to forget the messy mop of shaggy blond hair and chronically mismatched clothing that the lead singer of Collin's band dons. And if that wasn't enough, he's also one of the tallest people I've ever met; at six feet six, maybe even taller, it wouldn't be difficult to identify him by his height alone.

His face relaxes a bit. "I thought that was you," he says, still moving from his left foot to his right, then back again. I don't ask him how he recognized me when the one and only conversation we've ever had was pretty unremarkable, but I want to. Really, I find it odd that he recognized me at all.

"I was just coming to grab my coffee when I saw you," he explains. I turn to see the to-go cup waiting to be picked up and feel some secondhand embarrassment for the name he chose for the order: Ozzy. If he had known I'd be the one to hand it to him, I doubt he would have chosen the name of one of his idols instead of his own. Jett, however, doesn't seem to care one bit.

"Oh, here," I say as I pick it up, but before he takes it from my hand, he asks me something else.

"You wouldn't by chance have Collin's new number, would you? I can't get a hold of him."

I smile at him again, and once I pull out the contact information for my brother, I write it on the coffee cup for him. "Here you go."

"Sweet!" he says, fist pumping the air. "You're a lifesaver,

Lilliana!" He grins and saunters toward the door, leaving without another word.

I'm not sure if he heard me wrong or just thought Lilliana was a good nickname for Delilah, but I shake my head and roll my eyes as he leaves, a small smile permeating my lips.

I'm just about to discard my dirty rag when a familiar mop of perfectly combed chocolate hair moving through the tables catches my eye. I glance at the clock to see if another hour has slipped by me without my knowledge, but it's only been five minutes since I last checked.

Bodhi finds a table and sits down hours earlier than he's supposed to be here. Even more surprising, though, is that he came in accompanied by a book and a newspaper—a legitimate *paper* newspaper. He places it on the table and opens it up, eyes immediately scanning the ink and stealing its contents.

A coworker, whose name I couldn't tell you, rounds the corner holding a few empty coconut mugs. "I'm taking my break. I'll be back in fifteen." I give her a nod in acknowledgement but don't meet her eyes. She shrugs in my peripheral vision before leaving.

Other than a wave hello and a broad smile when I caught Bodhi's gaze, he doesn't address me. My fingers dig anxious circles into the pad of my thumb, and my teeth trap my lip between them. *Something's off.* I feel it.

Though the tables all shine, I grab a new rag and slowly work my way to his table. I pass Molly on her break and she shoots me a mischievous wink.

Bodhi doesn't look up until I'm right next to him.

"Delilah! Hello, how are you doing?" he says, almost surprised.

"Oh, um," I stammer, "I'm—I'm doing pretty good. You?"

"Fine, thank you." His eyes and smile are a mismatched pair, like they're being forced to coexist. "Care to join me?"

"Oh, I, um, already took my break this morning . . ." I trail off. The clock reads 9:25. Nowhere near the time for the lunch we were supposed to be having.

"That's a shame," he says. "I just stopped by to catch up on the news"—he holds up the paper in his hand like evidence—" and to let you know that I sadly won't be able to make lunch today."

My heart sinks to my stomach, and the uneasy smile fades from my eyes. "Oh," I start lamely. No other words will find shape in my mouth.

"I sincerely apologize, Delilah. I wish I didn't have to cancel, but something has . . . come up. You understand, don't you?"

Of course I understand. This is how things like this always go for me.

"Oh, um, of course! It's no problem." A weak smile appears on my face as I fight to hide the deep dejection. "I better get back, but it was, um, nice seeing you."

"You as well." He seamlessly transitions from his polite smile back to reading the paper like this was nothing more than pleasantries exchanged between strangers. And maybe that's all it was.

If I really stop to think about it, we don't know each other *that* well. I shouldn't be this bothered, and yet I can't help but wonder what came up. Or, more accurately, what I did wrong.

With nothing more than a clean washrag and a muddled spirit, I return to the counter and start making a coffee just to keep myself occupied, afraid that if I don't, I'll walk right back over and make a fool of myself. It isn't until I finish that I realize I've made the coffee the way Bodhi likes it.

I leave it abandoned next to the filters.

The door chimes and, reluctantly, I look up to greet the customer with a welcoming smile. But instead of a new face, I find the back of a familiar man walking out to his car with a newspaper in hand. A man who didn't say goodbye.

"What was all that about?"

I nearly jump out of my skin at the abrupt question. "Geez, Molly! Do you always have to sneak up on me like that?"

"You didn't answer my question."

"It was nothing." I turn away and make myself look busy.

She flips her dirty-blonde hair over her shoulder and shoots a skeptical look my way. "Didn't look like nothing to me, babe. I sensed some serious tension between the two of you. Pretty sure the whole place felt it, if I'm honest. That was painful."

I scoff. "Gee, thanks."

Molly rolls her eyes. "Delilah."

"I—" I meet her serious gaze and sigh. "I really have no idea what just happened. He came in here, barely said hello to me, canceled our lunch, and acted like I was some person from high school he hoped to never see again. I don't know, it just felt so weird."

Molly scrunches her nose at some sour thought. "Did he see you talking to that guy? Who was he, anyway? I was about to finish my break to come up and ask you, but then I saw Bodhi walking in. Are you dating him, too?" she says, the words coming out in a flurry. "I have to say it would be a major downgrade, but that's just me; crackheads aren't really my thing."

It takes me a minute to catch on to her train of thought. The idea that *that* could be the cause of any sort of turmoil makes me want to bust out laughing. "You think he was jealous?"

She shrugs. "Looked like it to me."

"But that's ridiculous! That was a guy from Collin's band, who, by the way, is not a crackhead—or at least I don't think he is. He just needed Collin's new number. But even if he didn't, that wouldn't matter, because Bodhi and I are just friends."

"Maybe," she says skeptically, "or maybe not." Molly flips her hair as she walks away, leaving me to scoff at the now vacant space beside me.

There is *no way* Bodhi was jealous. There isn't any reason for him to be—we're friends. Nothing more. It's more likely I just did something to upset him. Ruined this friendship like most of the others in my life.

I could count on one hand how many friends I've had. First, there was Cedrick. We met in middle school, and were joined at the hip for two years until he started having feelings for me I just couldn't reciprocate. He spread some awful rumors about me, and after that, we never spoke again. Then I met Jessica in an art class my sophomore year. We sat next to each other every day, ignoring the assigned seating. Junior year came, and when we didn't have any classes together, we lost touch. I could have reached out. Tried harder. But I didn't.

The only friendship that has ever lasted for me is Boss. Somehow, even when we clash, we find a way to make up. We always come back to each other.

Interrupting my thoughts, Hank, a regular, comes in and orders his same coffee: black with three extra shots of espresso. He tells me about his wife and kids, how his youngest child just lost a tooth and his oldest is graduating early from high school this semester. She'll be attending Harvard next year after doing a service trip in Africa, he says. I ask how work is, and he tells me, "It's work." He asks me how my day is going and I tell him it's been great, even though that's a lie. Finally, I smile and hand him his coffee, and he leaves three dollars in the tip jar. Always three dollars.

And that's it. Just like that, Hank leaves, and it's just me and the smell of coffee again. And some stupid feeling that I'm sinking through the hardwood floor.

"Your boyfriend left this," says Molly as she walks closer. She hands me the book Bodhi had with him.

"Thanks," I mumble, too bothered to correct her.

I turn it around in my hands and assess the cover. It's a picture of a girl and a boy in Greek clothing, tangled in each other's arms, but the girl is looking off into the distance like she's trapped instead of being held. I flip it over and find it's a fictional romance—not something Bodhi would read, which confuses me. As I flip open the cover, I find a note written in perfect penmanship.

Dear Delilah,

I'm truly sorry I had to cancel our lunch plans today. I found this book and thought you might like it. Consider it the beginning of my apology. I promise to make it up to you over dinner. Just tell me when and where.

—Bodhi

I move the book closer and then further from my face, studying the letters again and again until I accept that their shape won't change.

Bodhi bought me a book. Again.

Warmth spreads through me, and I tuck the book close to my chest. The grin that overtakes my face is not one I could hide even if I wanted to. *I didn't mess this up. Not yet.* I run my fingers over the smooth spine over and over again. Even though I haven't read it yet, this just became one of my new favorite books.

Maybe he did get just a little jealous . . .

But maybe I don't mind if he did.

I'm shocked I'm not more scared to admit that.

And I'm more shocked I'm giddy over a dinner that hasn't even been planned yet.

The blades of the ceiling fan spin too quickly to keep track of just one, and yet I try anyway. A headache hijacks my skull after a minute and I close my eyes, hoping to clear it. The whir of the fan fills my head with its white noise, and I let it consume me. Let it wash away the ache. I let every part of me submit to the sound—every crack and crevice in the recess of my mind. But then I remember something.

I pull the book out of my back and read Bodhi's note again, this time focusing on the scrawl instead of the words. It's perfect—I don't think I've ever seen such perfect handwriting in my life. Mine isn't horrible, but this? This is immaculate. Every letter is sized perfectly, every space equal. Not a single one is bigger or smaller than it should be. It looks printed, not written.

But even looking at it, I can't shake the sick feeling that's come back to haunt me. Slowly, the belated joy from earlier has dissipated into this recognizable spiral of anxiety. I don't know if he wrote the note before or after coming in. Before or after he started acting weird.

This is ridiculous!

I snatch up my phone, tired of letting myself mope around when there's no real reason to nosedive into a sea of worry. My fingers jab at my screen, and before I can think to change my mind, I hit Send. If he's mad, he can tell me right here and now. If he's not, then I can stop acting like this.

> Makeup dinner tomorrow?

My shoulders feel lighter as it sends, but then it says "Delivered," and my chest fills with panic.

Maybe I said something I shouldn't have. Or maybe I *didn't* say something, and that's why it felt weird between us. I check our texts, but there's nothing unanswered and nothing out of line. Not even a missed call. I rack my brain for anything I could have done, and even when I come up empty for the umpteenth time, I still send myself further into the abyss.

"Why do I overthink everything?" I mutter to myself. Of course, there is no answer, so I roll onto my stomach and hope I'll sink through the bedding, where no one will find me and no thoughts matter. Where there's just emptiness.

I trace cursive letters into the pillow as I wallow. I write all the reasons you shouldn't romanticize life, all the reasons you should never get your hopes up, and why you shouldn't want or hope for anything. And then I write the reasons why you should never fall in love. The reminder is good, but it's not necessary. I've repeated this list in my mind so many times, it's just how my brain is wired at this point.

At the top of every list is the same thing: no matter what, in the end, you'll be heartbroken. Because love always boils down to pain.

You accept a person for everything they are, including the hurt they're capable of inflicting. You love your parents despite the fact that doing so will make it hurt insurmountably more when they eventually pass. You love your kids even though one day they grow up and don't need you in the same ways they used to, in the ways you crave being needed. You love your friends even though that love fizzles when you go to different colleges and marry the first, and hopefully only, love of your life. And then you love your spouse even though one of you will inevitably leave the other. Through death or by choice, the leaving happens all the same.

Why would I choose to add more pain to my life?

How poetic to have another set of opposites in tandem: the sun and moon, laughter and tears, hot and cold, and love and pain. But I don't want poetry in my life—I want to be happy. Pain is a daughter and love is a mother. They skip hand in hand, nothing and everything alike, inseparable from one another.

The cover of the Greek book opens noiselessly. Of course, I read Bodhi's familiar scrawl before anything else. I tell myself I do it because I have to read every written word.

But I'm pretty sure I do it because I'm scared it might be the last of him that I'll get.

The phone rings, and I shoot for it so fast that my eyes haven't readjusted to looking beyond twelve inches in front of my face. As the caller ID glares in my face, I'm shocked at the cold disappointment that rushes through my veins.

The conversation with Boss is quick. Updates are given, items are added to my ever-growing to-do list until Max gets home, and we hang up. Her laughter echoes through the phone and leaves me feeling empty once it's gone.

I'm happy for her—really, I am—but that pesky feeling won't go away. It's so insignificant, yet it sits there on my chest, making it hard to take a full breath. A thousand-pound thumbtack is piercing my heart so pointedly, I don't know how I've never felt it before. I place a hand on my chest and close my eyes, willing the pain to disappear. But it's a stubborn and unyielding thing, this pain.

When I open them again, the first thing I see is the book I tossed aside in my haste to pick up my phone. I see the two figures on the cover in each other's arms, but this time I don't see a girl trapped in a man's grasp, looking for an escape. I see a girl being held. Being loved. Being *wanted*.

Tears prick at the corners of my eyes. I don't let them fall, because doing so would mean I'd have to acknowledge this discovery about myself, and I don't think I'm ready to rewire the way I function completely. But I do pick the book back up again. I flip through the pages and find my place.

Once I begin losing myself in the story, that horrible feeling of loneliness slowly begins to creep off of my chest. There's still no word from Bodhi when I finish, but I do find that my initial assessment was correct: turns out the girl was trying to escape the boy after all.

But who knows? Maybe they fall in love in the sequel.

CHAPTER TWELVE

At 5:00 p.m. the next day, I'm not dressed presentably or ready in any sense of the word. I chose to call out of work this morning and spent the better half of the day sulking and the other half pitying myself. When I wasn't doing either of those things, I was just mad at myself for feeling that way at all. I looked as bad as I felt.

It's also at 5:00 p.m. that I open my front door to find not the pizza I ordered, but Bodhi. And despite probably looking like I died and came back to life, I'm pretty sure even Bodhi could see the relief and confusion on my face.

We both stand there in silence, taking in each other's appearance, equally lost.

"What are you doing here?" I finally ask.

"Uh . . . dinner?" he responds uncomfortably.

My brows knit together. "What do you mean, dinner?"

"You texted me."

I shake my head. "You never responded."

"Of course I responded to you," he says definitively, as if the contrary simply isn't fathomable. I only shake my head and grip the door a little tighter.

He takes his phone out of his back pocket and, after some

scrolling and tapping, curses while slapping his palm to his head. "You wouldn't know that, though, would you? Not when I never pressed Send." Bodhi tilts the screen toward me to show me the proof, and right then and there, I'm met with the one explanation that soothes all of my worries.

"You . . . didn't hit Send?"

He lets out a frustrated sigh. "I swear on my life, I thought I did. Gah—I'm an idiot! I should have looked when you didn't respond, but I just assumed you were able to because you had texted me. I made us reservations and everything, but we can reschedule—"

"No!" I exclaim before he can finish the sentence. "No! It's fine, really." My smile drops when I look down at myself, though. "I need a few minutes to get ready. I'll meet you at the car."

He smiles and says warmly, leaving no room for doubt, "Delilah, you look perfect."

I shoot him a stern, half-hearted glare. "Three minutes."

The door shuts with a slam, and only afterwards do I think briefly about how I should have invited him inside before darting up the stairs.

It takes me five minutes to change into a dress, brush out my hair, and slap on some mascara. It's a wonder how my shoes match when I run out the door. I don't look great, but I could at least pass as presentable now. Bodhi is there when I walk out, leaning against his car with his hands in his pockets. And when he smiles, it doesn't feel real.

"What?" I ask, raising a brow.

He shakes his head, perhaps trying to get rid of that pesky little dimple. "Nothing. Just thinking about how beautiful you look and how envious everyone at the restaurant will be, thinking you're my hot date."

I scoff as he opens my door for me. *Maybe when all you've seen me in is coffee-stained Hawaiian shirts, this would seem like an upgrade.* "In your dreams," I tease.

Maybe it's just my ears playing tricks on me, but when he shuts my door, I swear I can hear him say something about never waking up.

The dress I chose isn't nearly fancy enough for this restaurant, but at this point, I should just be used to being underdressed whenever I go out with Bodhi. Although, something about the way he looked at me through dinner never made me feel anything less than perfectly in place. His attention never strayed from me, not even when the busty waitress leaned down to ask for his order. He watched me and listened intently to everything I had to say, and apologized again and again for the miscommunication.

"Bodhi," I finally intervened, "if you apologize to me one more time, I swear I will huck this deliciously buttered roll right at your face. And then I'll really be mad at you because I really, *really* want to eat this roll."

We laughed and laughed and then talked and laughed some more. It was truly a perfect meal. After he paid the check, we took a stroll around the neighborhood with no real destination in mind—until we both saw it at the same time. Without a word, we headed toward the only empty game, and we've been playing ever since.

"Checkmate!" I yell as I take his last piece on the board.

"You say 'checkmate' when you play chess, not checkers," he points out before putting the pieces back into place.

"I'll say whatever I want as long as you keep letting me win."

He quirks a brow. "What makes you think I'm letting you win?"

"Well, it's either that or you suck at checkers. You could have taken the win multiple times, but you didn't." I start to put some of the pieces on my side away.

"Sounds like it was *you* who was letting *me* win."

"No, I just really suck at checkers."

Bodhi tosses his arms up in the air, speechless. "Maybe I suck at checkers, too."

I firmly shake my head. "No way. I definitely peg you for the type of kid that loved this stuff growing up."

"Well, you got me there. But it isn't fair; I was distracted by my beautiful opponent." He winks at me.

"As long as you aren't going easy on me," I say back. My chin dips to my chest before the blush shows on my cheeks.

I know very well the agreement I made with Bodhi was to just be friends, but that doesn't mean his compliments mean nothing to me. There is this hollow part of me that I've learned to live with and even forget, but it's always there, even when I'm surrounded by people. My family and friends can't do much to fill the heavy emptiness in my chest.

The thing is, I don't realize a part of me is bereft of warmth until I'm with Bodhi. When I'm with him, I notice that feeling is harder to find.

I won't do anything to ruin it.

As the sky starts to darken, we decide to walk around for a bit, letting the even pavement, cool evening breeze, and city noises guide us. "What's your favorite thing about this place?" I ask.

"About Arizona?" he replies. I nod.

Like most of his answers, he takes time to consider his response. "I love the deserts. Not because of their grandeur, but because they're harsh and unyielding. It's just like people, in a way. If you respect it and give it time, you'll find beauty. Underestimate it, and you'll regret it one way or another. I love the desert because most don't know how to."

I smile. "You've thought a lot about that."

"I've had the time to think."

I hum in response.

"What about you? What did you like most back home?" he

asks, bumping softly into me. From his tone, I can tell he genuinely wants to know.

"I liked that everyone there was close, like *really* close. We knew all of our neighbors and their families, and we would go to their daughters' dance recitals and their sons' baseball games, bring soup over when someone was sick." My fond smile falls a bit. "But I also kind of hated that about there, because it wasn't genuine. Most of the time it felt close enough to caring, at least, even if they were judgmental behind closed doors.

"Here, everything is more private. I couldn't tell you if our neighbors now even have kids. But in a way, I kind of like the distance." I start to shrug but stop myself, remembering what Bodhi said about my habit. Instead, I let the short silence linger.

His eyes grow distant as he scans the sidewalk. "I don't think you'll find too many judgmental people here."

"No?" We round the corner to find statues littering the area.

He shakes his head. "Everyone is too self-obsessed. They're too worried about how they'll be judged to have time to judge anyone else."

I think that over for a moment. "Don't you think that happens everywhere, not just here?"

"Perhaps. But I think it happens especially so here. Look." He points to a couple walking directly across the way from us. "Look at that couple and tell me what you see."

The girl is younger, maybe twenty. She's thin, like she hasn't eaten in a few days, and wears revealing clothing, yet her slim body somehow allows her to maintain some semblance of modesty. The man accompanying her is a good decade or so older. He wears all black and has narrowed eyes. Long pieces of raven hair threaten to impede his vision, but he occasionally jerks his head to move them out of the way. He holds himself tall and confident as he walks, making the sickly woman next to him seem to shrink in comparison. He has one arm slung around her waist, but it's stiff. They exchange clipped responses and nods, never looking each other in the eyes. They don't look unhappy, but they don't look content, either.

"I see a couple on an awkward date, and by the looks of it, he'll have her home by nine."

"But what do you notice about them individually?" he asks.

I know he's urging me to see something else, but I'm not sure what. I throw my hands up. "I don't know."

He moves closer and sighs. "Look at the girl. See how she's holding her arm over her stomach like that? She's most likely trying to cover it up. To hide it. She likely thinks she's fat."

My jaw drops. "But she's so thin!"

"She doesn't seem to think so." Bodhi leads me to a bench facing a statue but that still gives us a clear view of the couple. "See the way she quickly looks at her reflection in the windows they pass by? She's checking out her appearance, making sure she looks fine."

I watch for a moment, and sure enough, the girl's eyes drift to the windows. "I would have thought she was just looking into the stores."

"Maybe. It's more likely, though, that she's subconsciously looking at herself. And look at the man—look at the way he holds her like a prize. He makes eye contact with everyone he passes. Almost like he wants them to notice the girl on his arm."

We watch them for a moment longer, and when a stranger passes them, the man greets him with a cocky smirk. His grip on the young girl tightens as he approaches and relaxes after he passes. "It's his way of showing off," Bodhi explains. "He probably wants to come across as incredibly successful, and maybe he is. But he isn't hanging around that girl because he likes her. He hasn't looked at her once this whole time."

"I noticed that," I say quickly, half because it's true and half because I'm proud to have made the same observation.

This time as I watch the pair, I see something else. Instead of an awkward couple on a date, I see a girl trying to hide her insecurities and a man trying to show off what he claims as his.

I'd have to agree with Bodhi—they don't seem to like each other.

"I wonder why they stay with one another when they seem to be so miserable," I mumble.

"I imagine they do it out of fear, mostly. The girl fears rejection, or maybe being alone, so she settles for a man who placates that fear. The man fears being unseen, so he keeps a young attractive woman in his arms, and he dresses like that to stand out. He makes her feel wanted, and she makes him feel seen." He turns to me. "People do things out of fear all of the time, Delilah. It's just that some people learn to tolerate the consequences more than others."

"Everyone does things out of fear?" I ask.

Bodhi nods.

"Including you?"

He hesitates. "I used to."

"But not anymore?"

"I try not to."

"And how did you stop doing that?"

"I stopped caring," he says simply.

I laugh, a smile crossing my face. "That easy, huh?"

"It can be."

A girl rounds the same corner the couple just disappeared behind, and I take a moment to examine her, hoping to make some smart observations before Bodhi can take them all for himself. She's blonde and pretty, but not in an obnoxious way. She walks with her headphones in and her face tilted toward her phone—maybe switching songs, since her fingers aren't jabbing at the screen like she's typing. The girl has this stiff look on her face, but it feels like a default expression. Like an automatic setting for walking around in the city to ward off unwanted interactions. She seems determined; her stride is strong and lengthy, like she's just left work and is eager to get home.

"I think that girl right there is kind, but I don't think she likes showing it," I share once I've made my deductions. "She probably puts on that face to avoid talking with strangers. She makes herself unapproachable. I wonder why." I think about what Bodhi said about fear. "I wonder what she's scared of."

I look up to see why he hasn't yet chimed in only to find him gawking at the blonde girl. Not like he's taking in details and coming up with a conclusion, but something entirely different —something I can't place. He freezes, his whole body tensing up, and rigidly shifts his weight.

The girl glances up from her phone, looking in our direction but not really noticing us at first. But then, as though her thoughts have just caught up with her vision, her eyes snap back to me and Bodhi.

She suddenly loses her footing, just barely catching herself as she trips over the air, and there's no mistaking the utter panic in her eyes. The blonde scrambles to gather herself and darts down the closest street, but before she completely disappears behind a grey building, she takes one last look back at us, burning her horrified features into my memories.

Behind us, there are only statues. Nothing that would instill such fear in a person.

I look to Bodhi, and for the first time, I feel a little bit less than comfortable at his side. "Bodhi . . . why was she looking at us like that?"

Bodhi's gaze stays trained on the street corner, but whatever I saw in his gaze before is gone. Now, he wears the same mask of confusion I do. When he responds, it's with a quiet hesitation, like he's searching for the answer as he speaks.

"I . . . I have no idea. That was . . . so odd. She probably mistook us for someone else," he offers with a shrug. A light, airy chuckle escapes him. "My professional observation is, that was really weird."

I hesitantly laugh, too, because I don't know what else to do. "A lot of crazy people in the city, I guess."

Bodhi lets out a stifled breath. "I'll say."

Ignoring the tension still in his muscles, I finally look at the statue we're seated in front of. A man and a woman are arm in arm mid-walk. Their heads are tilted in toward the other, their bodies close. Everything about their body language screams love in every way but one: they're crying. Tears fall from the eyes that their smiles don't quite reach. The two look straight ahead, no life in their gazes. It's practically morbid.

Afraid I might cry, I look away. "Let's look at another statue," I suggest. We stand up and leave the odd concrete carving behind, along with the unusual encounter with the blonde lady.

The next statue is a child playing with broken dolls. Her clothes are tattered and worn, her shoes are mostly made of holes, and her hair is in knots, but on her face is a brilliant smile.

"I'm starting to think this artist is bipolar," I say.

Bodhi's eyes trace the mess of a statue. "The artist's name is Jack Polteck. These are replicas of some of his more famous works. I believe this series is called 'Love in Everything.' I haven't read much on it, but I think it's meant to be contradictory to itself. It's supposed to show the emotion in all of its forms."

"I swear, you know everything."

The next statue, which is really two statues separated by about ten feet of space, is less haunting. There's a girl on the left lying on a bed with a phone held up to her ear. She's grinning broadly, giddy over some nonexistent conversation, and on the right a boy leans up against a wall, smiling just as big with a phone to his ear as well. I look between the two a couple more times, deciding it's one of my favorite pieces, before moving to the next one.

This statue depicts a girl looking at herself in the mirror, only the image is distorted to look like she's smiling at herself. She's prettier in the reflection, happier even. It's like seeing her own opinion of herself expanded in the reflection. I like this one even more.

We reach the end of the collection just as the street lights flicker on. Only the final piece isn't a statue—it's a wall about six feet high constructed of some smooth dark glasslike material, covered in layers upon layers of different handwriting. Some parts are clear, while others are too faded to be legible. Each states a different way that the author of the sentence feels love. Some are positive, like kisses goodnight or walking someone home, but others are sad, like saying goodbye. As a whole, it's kind of beautiful.

"Want to write something?" Bodhi asks. He holds up a marker he must have grabbed from the bucket on the ground.

"Sure." I take it from him and hover my hand over a mostly blank space.

I look for some inspiration in the other writings, but nothing sounds right. Images flit through my mind of sunsets and conversations, but none of them scream being worthy of memorialization, so I choose something easy even though it feels like cheating. The marker's translucent tip meets the surface, and the ink turns into a solid line with every flick of my wrist. I wonder how long it will be until the writing disappears forever.

"Where's yours?" Bodhi asks as he moves closer from where he was writing his own, and I point to my vandalization. He reads it and gives a nod. "Hmm. I like it."

"And where's yours?" He points to his spot, and I smile at his neat scrawl. "I like yours, too."

Bodhi smiles back at me and holds out his arm. I don't hesitate as I loop my own through his. "Let's blow this popsicle stand, BoBo."

His brows shoot up, either momentarily shocked that I've taken his arm or confused by the nickname I've given him.

My nose scrunches. "Still working on it."

"Thank God," he sighs.

I giggle before I meet his sea-glass eyes, brilliant even in the dying light, and he breaks out in a full-blown smile, dimple and all. Then he laughs, deep and hearty, like he's never laughed before. My own laughter mixes with his in a magnificent symphony, and I don't know why, but it makes me think of the wind chime that hung on the porch of my childhood home.

We head back to the car arm in arm, me listening to him and him taking a walk with me, each of us doing exactly what we wrote on the wall.

CHAPTER THIRTEEN

"You can't truly believe that."

Bodhi points to his cheek, letting me know that there's something on mine, and I move to wipe it off. A bit of cocoa powder dusts my fingertips before I wipe my hand against my pants.

"I wholeheartedly do," I reply.

Bodhi scoffs, grabs a napkin, and leans over to wipe the cocoa I seem to have missed. I don't blush at his touch when the soft cloth grazes my cheek. That is the luxury I get from having our friendship firmly established.

But my stomach does do a small backflip that I ignore.

"The Olympics won't start a war," Bodhi argues. "Isn't that the point of them? World peace?"

"Mmm." I swallow the sip of coffee already in my mouth. "Technically, they were created in honor of Zeus way back when in Greece, but now, yes, one of the reasons we still have the Olympics today is for *world peace*," I say, the last two words filled with the verbal equivalent of an eye roll. "But I've seen how men let college sports dictate their moods, and you're telling me there isn't *one* country so invested in some Olympic sport that they'd start a war over it? I guarantee there's some president, king, emperor, or whatever who loves curling so passionately that if they lose to someone—like, I don't know, Bermuda?—they'd start sending off the nukes."

Bodhi seems to consider this, weighing the possibility. "Maybe," he muses. "I suppose it could be possible. But that's why leaders have advisors."

I wiggle my eyebrows at him, the grin on my face slowly growing. "They have people to advise them on not starting wars over losing curling games to Bermuda?"

"Amongst other things, I'm sure."

"Alright, maybe it won't start a war, but I would be willing to bet it's *almost* started them."

"Let's just agree to disagree while you eat your donut." He pushes the napkin toward me, which acts as the donut's plate, and I smile at the shiny maple glaze sitting before me, rubbing my hands together in anticipation.

"Agreed," I declare before digging in. I can't see the glaze that falls onto the napkin after my first bite because my eyes dramatically roll to the back of my head at the sheer heavenliness invading each and every one of my taste buds. "You always bring me my favorite things. I needed this today. Thank you."

"Bad day at work?" The question seems to die on his lips as he glances around at the tables covered in coffee cups and plates strewn with the crummy remains of pastries.

"Ohhh, yeah, you could say that. It'll be okay, though, once the new hires are trained to—"

I turn to look for the girl I've spent the day training. Her chin dips to her chest, and though her hands are hidden behind the counter, I know she's scrolling on her phone. I've caught her four other times in the past two hours sitting there just like that instead of clearing off the tables.

"—not sit on their phones the whole shift."

"You should file a complaint."

"Eh, what good will that do?" I shrug in the way I know sometimes bothers him, but honestly, I don't care to make a big deal about this. "It will work itself out. And if it doesn't, I'll do something about it later. Maybe the girl just needs a little break."

Bodhi examines the girl behind the counter, his gaze taking in everything about her, and then does the same to me. He's likely comparing how clean her work attire is compared to mine, and how perfect her hair sits around her shoulder in flawless curls. "Or maybe she's spoiled rotten and doesn't want to work," he says, unamused.

"I—" I begin to say something in the girl's defense, but I quickly pull my lips together and think about what he's said. It doesn't matter why she does or doesn't do her work. To see it from his perspective, I've been picking up all the slack, over-working myself instead of putting my foot down. "Maybe you're right," I sigh in mock defeat.

"Probably am," he says arrogantly.

My eyes narrow at him, but he shoots me a quick wink, and a sloppy smile tugs at the corner of my lips.

"I need to get going, but I'll pick you up after your shift tomorrow. Does four fifteen work?"

"That's perfect, but, um . . ." I wring my hands and trip over my words. "My parents want to . . . meet you?"

It comes out more like a question than a statement, and I bite the inside of my cheek as I wait for him to answer. It's not a big deal, but for some reason, my parents meeting my new friend feels more monumental than it should. *Probably just because I've never had many friends for them to meet.*

Eventually, my parents were bound to notice my growing absence from the house, which I knew—expected, even. But something was exciting about the way I had Bodhi all to myself. I liked being home before dinner and telling my family about my day, never lying about my whereabouts, but never telling the exact truth either. When I'd leave while they were home, I'd tell them I was meeting a friend from work. What I didn't tell them was that it was a boy who was a helpless flirt. A boy I hardly knew, yet allowed to whisk me off to one place and the next.

I liked having a part of my life that was just my own. I wasn't ashamed, wasn't hiding it—it was just mine.

It was last week, when Bodhi picked me up from the house while Collin pulled in at the same time, that I knew our harmless rendezvous had come to a halt. I'd never asked my brother to lie to my parents about something like this, but I was bummed the rest of the night, and whatever remained of my relatively good mood was killed by the onslaught of texts and missed calls I'd received from my mother. Each message demanded to know who the boy was picking me up and to immediately call her back with every juicy detail.

I stayed up pretty late that night, forced to begrudgingly rehash the details of how and when Bodhi and I met and what had happened since. Never mind the fact that I had the morning shift the next day.

Despite my nervousness, Bodhi grins, flashing me that devilish dimple. "I'll be there at four."

———————

"Uh, Bodhi, how exactly did you find this place?"

His smug face swivels toward me. "What? Done calling me Bodster already?"

I roll my eyes, and he chuckles.

Stress was eating me alive before Bodhi showed up at the house today. My shaky hands wrung themselves over and over in anxious spirals. But then he came in and met them, and my parents loved him. Of course they did—how could they not? But still, my nervousness must have been apparent, as my mother was soon shooing us out the door.

"We'd better let Delilah go, dear, before she has a mental breakdown," Mom said.

"Tonight's a surprise, huh?" my father asked, deducing what had me so jumpy.

Flustered, I threw my chin up in the air and retorted, "I do *not* hate surprises that much."

Mom snorted while Dad gave me an unimpressed look, but before either could say a word, Bodhi said, "You most certainly do."

My eyes bulged. I scoffed, "If you know I hate them so much, then why in the world do you always keep what we're doing a surprise?"

Bodhi grinned a small but mischievous grin. A grin that made me wish I hadn't asked the question at all. "Because you're cute when you're mad."

I've gotten used to his harmless flirty comments when it's just us. But in front of my parents, it was simply mortifying—especially when the two of them bent over laughing at the furious blush spreading over my cheeks and neck.

And I was worried about my parents being the ones to embarrass me.

I stalked to the door and threw it open, my parents' laughter only growing behind me with each step I took. Turning around, I shot a glare at Bodhi. "We're leaving."

He followed me out the door, but as he shut it, I heard him quietly say to my parents, "Just like I said." Their second fit of giggles told me they found it just as funny as I'm sure he did.

I glared at Bodhi once more before catching myself and neutralizing my face. Then I shot back the only thing I could think of.

"I'm calling you 'Bodster' for the rest of the night."

It turns out that was very short-lived, however, because nothing has ever felt so wrong. Bodhi is just Bodhi. No nickname fits him like his own name.

As we head toward some mystery location, he pulls off the side of the road and takes the car over the bumps and divots in the barely trodden dirt. We've only been driving for twenty-five minutes, but it feels like an eternity when the destination is unknown. I've kept my angst under wraps until now, since he's decided to bring us onto what could be the set of a horror film.

Bodhi answers the way he always does in the car: both eyes forward, focused on the direction of the vehicle, and speaking like it's an afterthought. "I found it when I was looking at prop-erties a few years back."

"Properties?" What puzzles me more is the "few years back" portion—he's only twenty-three—but I remain quiet on that front. "Why were you looking at properties?"

Bodhi lifts a dismissive shoulder. "Just because."

"Hmm . . ." I trail off. "Nothing but desert for miles out here." He says nothing to my muttered words but shifts his gaze as if assessing the land for himself.

We make it to the end of the dirt road, if you can even call it a road, and park next to a dismal shed bleached by the Arizona sun. I look around to locate the reason we came all this way out here, looking for any landmarks, really. But there's nothing to indicate that other people have been here. Nothing but the abandoned shed.

"Okay, now I'm starting to think you might be a homicidal murderer."

"That's a redundant statement," he mutters.

"How so?"

"All murderers are homicidal."

"Huh," I think aloud. "I guess you're right."

Bodhi turns the key in the ignition, hops out, and, as usual, comes around to open my door for me. I put my folded arms on the roof of the car once I'm out.

"Just thought I'd let you know, if you're planning on killing me here, in the middle of nowhere, you went about it all wrong."

"One," Bodhi says, opening the trunk of the car and rummaging through whatever he has stored in there, "I did not bring you here to kill you. And two"—he looks up at me with puzzlement in his eyes—"what could you *possibly* mean by that?"

I grin at him and roll my eyes like it's the most obvious thing in the world. "Well, everyone knows you don't go shaking hands and looking at gun collections with the father of your soon-to-be victim. It's, like, rule number four in the book."

"Rule number four?" Bodhi leans behind the open trunk, disappearing from my view. "What other rules are there?"

"Well, obviously, don't eat forty-five minutes before you commit your crime—that's rule number three."

"Obviously."

"Then rule number two is making sure you stretch."

"Wouldn't want to pull a muscle," he adds.

"Exactly. And rule number one is to get a good night's rest."

His head pops out from behind the trunk. "Quite the extensive knowledge you have there. You sure *you* aren't this homicidal murderer everyone seems to be so worked up about?"

"Even if I were . . . I didn't get a good night's rest, so you're in the clear." I send him a little salute, and his head goes back behind the trunk.

"Well, thank God you're a stickler for rules, then." Sarcasm oozes from each word, as we're both well aware he could probably take me down one-handed without a second thought. I let out an airy laugh and look over the top of the car out at the desert.

Nothing but hardened dirt and dry plants for miles and miles. It's beautiful, the way the earth has hardened and yet still holds so much life. *Scary how easily you could get lost out here, too.*

Realistically, I know we just drove here and that there are homes, shops, towns, and paved roads within reach. But if you forget that for a moment—forget that just beyond the hills and horizons are people and buildings and smog and noise—it all seems so endless. Terrifyingly peaceful, in a way.

Bodhi pulls something out of the trunk, and I hear plastic,

or maybe metal, connect with the rough floor. "What are you doing?" I keep examining the expanse of the empty desert, knowing he won't let me help even if I offer.

"Setting up."

A bird swoops down in the distance, probably spotting its next meal. Perhaps a mouse or a small snake. "And what exactly are you setting up?"

Bodhi moves back, a lax grin on his face as he sweeps his arms behind the car, signaling for me to come look. I take a couple of steps toward him until I'm by his side, looking at the little setup.

A couple of camping chairs and a small folding table are neatly placed to face the western horizon and the soon-to-be setting sun. A miniature griddle, plugged into some portable power bank, sits on the table beside some dinnerware and a container of what looks like some premade mixture. Accompanying that are a couple glass bottles of lemonade.

My jaw drops as I look to Bodhi, whose mouth is stuck somewhere between a proud smirk and sly grin. "Dinner is served," he says with mock graciousness.

"I . . ." I look back at the table and chairs. "I . . . I don't even know—is that a *tablecloth*?"

Bodhi laughs and ushers me to sit in one of the seats. "Yes, that is a tablecloth. You murderers must be a few more notches down the uncivilized belt than I thought."

"Funny," I say, still taking it all in. "What's that for?" I point to the griddle.

"My specialty, and one of the only things I can make besides toast and grilled cheese." He picks up the container filled with the batter-like mixture. "Pancakes."

I balk at the audaciousness of it all. "This—this is too much." I look at every little thing laid out before me and think of the planning and prep that must have gone into this. This wasn't some outing taken on a whim; he thought this all out. Bodhi packed up these chairs and that griddle, he made the pancake mix (and kept it in the cooler I'm just now noticing in the trunk), charged the power bank, and bought some lemonade—lemonade he knew I would drink because it's my favorite.

"It's too much. You—" I cut myself off, finally looking at him again. I can't explain it, but something shifts in me. I still see Bodhi, but it's as though one tiny pebble has been removed from the carefully crafted stone wall around my heart. One pebble has been evicted, and something other than detachment is getting through.

He's here, and he's looking at me. He's looking *right* at me. And it doesn't feel like he's going anywhere.

His shoulders lift in a very Delilah-like shrug. "It's not too much for you." One side of his mouth tugs up in a subtle smile, and I look down as a blush I don't try so hard to fight heats my cheeks.

"So, what will it be, then?" He moves to the table and starts opening bottles and grabbing utensils. "A lion? Big Ben? A box of popcorn? What crazy pancakes am I whippin' up for ya?" he asks goofily, his tone emphasizing the slang so foreign to him that I can't help but release the breath I've been holding since we last locked eyes.

"Let's see you try a Mickey Mouse pancake before you degrade national monuments and theater food," I tease.

Bodhi clutches a hand to his heart, wounded. "Do you think so little of my artistic skills?"

"I just think it's important to set realistic goals for oneself."

———————

At some point after the crimson-steeped skies faded into a haze of maroon and bled into a bleak cover of black, we end up sitting on the hood of the car, lying up against the windshield and staring up at the night sky. It's still warm enough out that I don't need a blanket, but if a chill did creep up, Bodhi thought to bring one of those too.

"I'm not saying you don't have talent; I'm just saying you may be overselling your pancake artistry a bit." My stomach hurts from the laughter pulling at my ribs, and I rest a hand on the ache.

"How could you say such a thing?" he demands. "Did I or did I not make you a Mona Lisa pancake?"

"She was missing her eyes."

"Well, I remembered the important parts," he says in retort.

"Like what?"

"The smile, obviously! That's what she's known for."

I laugh and roll my eyes. As our laughter dies down, I look down at the hand on my stomach that rises and falls with each breath. It's peaceful here in this moment, staring at things that don't matter but do: my hand on my torso, the stars in the sky, my friend next to me.

I sneak a glance at Bodhi but find he's already looking at me, and our gazes snag on each other. I want to stare a bit longer, but we both turn away and look back up at the stars. I'm suddenly painfully aware of the proximity of our bodies on the car. *Inches*—that's all that separates us. To the dust in the air, it's an eternity away, but to our fingers it's just a small twitch. A moment away from touch.

I clear my throat. "Tell me something." Our conversations always come back to this. It's a comforting routine at this point, something to fall back on, but also into.

Bodhi shifts comfortably in the direction of our conversation like he's relaxing into the cushions of a couch. "Let's see . . ." he trails off as he usually does, not needing to fill the air with needless words. I've never met someone so comfortable with silence. Although he always chooses what to say with meticulous detail, never just speaking for the sake of it, I've noticed that the more time we spend together, the more he has to say.

Sometimes, when I prompt him with this demand, he lists off facts. One time he just read me the back of a cereal box in a grocery store aisle. Other times, he tells me stupid things that have no meaning behind them, like that I'm pretty, and I just roll my eyes. But sometimes, when he says things about the way I look or how I make him laugh, I let it sink in. Just a little bit.

While Bodhi mulls over the memories and facts stored in his mind, thinking of something to tell me, I peek over at him. He clenches his jaw in thought, the line sharp all but for the place where it meets the skin beneath his ears. His soft curls are gently tossed by the dry breeze, and with it comes the fresh scent of his shampoo. His nose, which I had assumed was perfectly straight, houses a small dip in the bridge that's only noticeable this close. I've only seen it on one other occasion about a week ago, when I accidentally elbowed Bodhi on the forehead. I pulled his head down to me to examine the damage, and only then did I first notice the ever-so-slight dip in the middle of his nose.

With his eyebrows relaxing after such intense concentration, he speaks up again, finally landing on some thought to share. "Humans are the only living things that experience embarrassment."

I smile, comforted by the stability in his extensive knowledge of fun facts. "And why is that?"

"It's too complicated an emotion for other animals to have. They would need to have an awareness of others' opinions and care about them." Bodhi looks at me, the remnants of my smile still lingering and the beginnings of his just forming. "We are also the only living creatures to blush, you know." He taps my nose with his finger. "And you have that one down pretty well."

I shove his hand away and roll my eyes, ignoring the soft red hue that is no doubt already sweeping my cheeks. "Oh, please. Give me a break."

I feel Bodhi's stare for a moment longer. He's about to say

something—I can feel it—but then he stops and redirects his words. "You tell me something."

"Like what?" I always ask for clarity. Always. Even if I ask him first and he sets the tone, I ask what he wants to hear, if there's anything he wants me to say specifically. You never know the motives behind a person's words unless you ask.

"Anything."

Even then, sometimes we are left in the dark.

I don't think about it for long, just saying the first thought that jumps out at me. I'm not so careful with my words the way he is. "I'm scared of swing sets."

He sits up and looks are me curiously. "Swing sets?" I nod. "Why?"

"I told my friend to jump off one in the third grade, and she broke her wrist." I shrug. "Guess that was enough to make me retire from my swinging days."

"Even still?"

"Even still."

"Huh," he says thoughtfully.

"What about you?" I bump my shoulder against his. "What are you afraid of?" It's hard to imagine Bodhi being afraid of anything, but still, I ask.

"Hmm." He slightly purses his lips. "I'm scared of rabies." I laugh, but his face freezes with seriousness. "Delilah"—he leans forward, getting a clearer view of my face—"it's a serious condition. You can *die* from it."

"It's also treatable," I point out. "And extremely rare."

"Extremely rare does not mean nonexistent. If you aren't careful, a bat could swoop down at any moment and bite us. It's prime time for it, too."

I nod at the somber sky enveloping us. "You do have a point. Conditions are ideal for contracting rabies."

"Exactly!" Bodhi exclaims before realizing I'm pulling his leg. He leans back against the windshield in defeat, arms acting as a pillow for his head. "You don't get it."

"No, no, I think it's sweet that you're afraid of little puppies."

He makes a noise of protest. "I didn't give you any shit about the swings, and if we're being completely honest, that one is exponentially more pathetic."

"Debatable. I watched a girl *break* her arm."

"You're twenty-one and scared of playground equipment."

"Better than being twenty-three and scared of pups."

"It's not a competition."

"Only a loser would say something like that."

Bodhi just shakes his head. "How the boys in Utah were able to put up with your stubbornness is beyond my brain's ability to comprehend."

A laugh, leaning toward a scoff, leaps from my lips. It's a dry sound, full of a kind of humor only the butt end of a joke would understand.

"What's so funny?" he asks.

"You say that like there *were* boys back home."

Something in Bodhi's eyes fizzles with newfound confusion. "Well . . . weren't there?"

My teeth find the insides of my cheeks again, biting into the soft flesh. I've gotten so comfortable around Bodhi, I sort of forgot that we don't already know everything about each other. Forgotten that there are some things I barely admit to myself, let alone talk about. Some things that the people in my life just know because they've been there for so long.

"No," I answer. "Not really, no."

He sits up as though it'll help him hear me better, his jaw now hanging heavy with disbelief. "Seriously?" When I nod, he asks, "Why not?"

"Guess I was just scared of that, too," I laugh, but it feels like molasses coming out of my throat. Any trace of humor dissipates when I catch the intense look on his face. This doesn't feel like a joke anymore. It's too serious—too much.

"Want to know something else?" I slap my hands on my

thighs and sit up straight, finally facing Bodhi again but not looking at him. I look toward the sky instead in an eye roll, then close them while I talk. "I have no idea where that came from. That was awkward, and totally ra—"

Bodhi's touch frightens me. Not because of the strength of his grip on my arm, not because he's rough or hurting me—no, his touch is warm and gentle. Welcomed. It's what his touch might do to me that sends a jolt of nerves crashing into my stomach.

With this one touch, I just might let him in. With this one touch, I feel another stone fall free from that steadfast wall surrounding my heart.

"Tell me," he says, knowing no other words need to be supplied. Two little words can hold so much power if you let them. And with him, I always seem to be letting them.

But this part of me? Being so vulnerable with something like this—getting into why I don't let anyone in when I myself have only just barely begun to uncover the answers? It's such a simple question to ask, but a complex one to answer. I could tell him about every little experience growing up that made me believe I was better off this way, but it's easier to simply boil it down to its brittle bones. Easier in the way that it makes it feel less important, makes it acceptable to give fewer words to the feeling.

"I've always been too scared of getting hurt." Predictably, I shrug. "That's really all there is to it. Stupid, I know. But if I'm being honest, then that's why."

I've learned to love the silence in my life. Its familiarity is welcome in every spare moment. I let it accompany me while I read or while I sip my tea; I invite it to linger while I watch the stars flick on in the distance. It tickles my ears with its deafening white noise and fills my head with a stillness that is otherwise unattainable. But this silence is hungry.

It eats at me and holds my heart in its famished grasp. Years fit themselves into seconds, and seconds divvy themselves up into hours while I wait for him to speak. Now, the silence between us hurts—it holds something vulnerable between it, a naked truth so few others have seen.

When he finally does break this stuffy void, he clears his throat to try to cover up whatever emotion threatens to break it. "It's not stupid."

My throat itches, threatening to let something real through. And that something catches on the words that leave my lips in a whisper. "You don't think so?"

He shakes his head, his lips pressed in a firm line. So tight that even if they wanted to betray him by letting something loose in the air between us, they couldn't. His glassy eyes search my own, but I don't know what they're looking for.

"What?" I whisper.

"It's just—" The lump in his throat bobs as he swallows hard. "It's just that I can't imagine anyone more deserving of love, and . . . and you're too scared to let yourself have it."

I shrug once more—I can't help it. "If you have something . . . you can lose it. And . . . and I don't think I—I can't lose something like that."

Bodhi shakes his head, seemingly unable to accept this explanation, and whispers, "Some people stay, you know. There doesn't always have to be a leaving."

"I don't want to get hurt."

"You wouldn't," he says, so sure. And his answer surprises me.

The typical response to such a childish wish would be "Everyone gets hurt." You can't avoid it in life, and yet still I wish I could.

Sighing, I shake my head. "You don't know that."

"I do."

"How?"

He places his gentle hand on my arm, and when I don't pull away, he lets it settle. "Because I would never let that happen."

I freeze. Each beat of my heart louder in my ears than the last.

"I'll never let you get hurt, Delilah. I promise you, your heart is safe with me."

Salty tears well in my eyes as his words knock through another layer of that impenetrable wall. It's like he knows exactly what to say—knows exactly what's been missing in me. A kind of kindness I cannot show myself. A kind of acceptance I have not earned. A kind of love I would never allow. And yet here he is, offering it to me. All I have to do is take it.

The familiar dull tug on my heart now threatens to yank the thing out of my aching chest. It slams its fists against my ribcage, begging for me to open up just this once. To let this happen. Just *once*.

The salty streams trace my cheeks as Bodhi reaches to cup my face, covering the tears with the warmth of his palm. It feels so much like home that more tears begin to spill.

"Delilah? Are you alright? What—"

"No, no. It's . . . I—"

My bleary eyes seek some sort of answer in the depths of those two emerald pools. Looking into his eyes, all I can think about is the walk in the park where we talked about fear. How people let it drive them and bind them. How I've let this fear root itself so deeply in my life that even now, when the universe is screaming at me to let this happen, I'm too scared. Fear has kept me from wanting this for so long that the thought of these walls around my heart crumbling to dust terrifies me.

For so long, I've told myself that I can survive without being known. I can survive not being loved. But now he's sitting here, he's looking at me, and the walls are too shaky for me to push out the thought that I might be able to survive like this—but I don't know that I can live with it. If I can live with never *really* being known. And it petrifies me that this fear exists in me, that he's still able to make me *want* for something like this.

I've come face-to-face with this fear, and now I have to decide: do I let it control me, or force myself to make a change?

"What if there didn't have to be a leaving?"

"I'll never let you get hurt, Delilah."

"I promise."

Could he really mean it? I look at him, *really* look at him, and it instantly settles enough turmoil in me that I wonder what it is that frightens me so much. This is *Bodhi*—the boy who brings me maple donuts on my breaks and happily answers every single one of my unimportant questions while we drive somewhere. The boy who spilled my drink and bought me two bags of books to make up for it. The boy who tells me I'm beautiful and makes me smile even when I do everything I possibly can to keep him from doing so.

And for what? For me to ward off something I'm too much of a coward to let myself have?

The last stalwart wall around my heart tries to remind me that if I let this happen, it will only hurt me in the end. But then I'm hit with another thought: one so volatile, so unacceptable, that I'm stunned. Right then and there, like a car wreck and a butterfly kissing my cheek, it hits me. All at once and oh so softly, the thought comes to my mind. And it *terrifies* me.

"Shit," I whisper, dropping my chin to my chest. *Shit, shit, shit.*

"Delilah?" Bodhi turns my face back to him. "What's wrong?"

"I . . . I don't think I want to, I—"

I scramble for the words, the courage, the syllables—anything to help me make some sense right now.

"Delilah?" Bodhi pleads, panic swarming his features.

I lean into the warmth of his palm, scared that this might be the last time it'll be like this. That I'm about to mess this up. And even though I'm scared that everything will change right now, even though I don't know what comes next, I just say what I probably should have said weeks ago. I say it scared, because after this, there really is no going back.

Because if Bodhi left now, my heart would already break. I'm already going to get hurt if this ends badly. And there isn't anything I can do to stop it.

"What . . . what would you say if I said I didn't want to be just friends anymore?"

He freezes for a fraction of a second, and in that second, my heart drops to the bottom of my gut. But before I can take it all back, he grins so big that that pesky little dimple appears.

"I'd say it's about damn time."

Then he pulls me close and kisses me.

CHAPTER FOURTEEN
AFTER

"Tell me," he says in that cold, lifeless void of a voice. He watches me watch the girl reflected in the coffee mug, saying nothing else. Lets the silence drag on in the way he knows I once hated, and still sometimes do. It tugs at the strings of my thoughts and causes them to unravel in unnerving spirals.

Tell you what?

How often I think of death as an escape?

How I sometimes still dream of the you from before all this?

How I wake up with the ghosts of your arms still wrapped around me?

How I'm so lost, so far gone, that if you told me this was some messed up joke, I'd break out in tears of joy just because I'd have you back?

Tell you what?

Once the silence has been wielded to his liking, my thoughts a dangerous mess, he speaks again.

"Tell me what it was like. For you." Curiosity gets the better of him, it would seem. Or maybe he is just permitted these kinds of thoughts. "What did it feel like?"

"What was it like for me . . . ?" I trail off. Can I ever really know?

Our minds like to forget. To deem certain memories useless and paralyze the neurons that fire and allow us to recall what once was. We live each moment never knowing if we will look back and remember *exactly* what it was like to live in it.

Was it really magical to catch that snowflake on your tongue while your nose shone red and tingled from the cold? Or did you forget that your socks were soaking wet from trudging through the slush, and that you couldn't stop coughing for weeks from the pneumonia? Do you remember the depth of the sigh that left your aching body when the pain pills kicked in, or is it the tightness of your eyes trying to shut out the pain that stuck with you? What did you forget?

How grateful we should be, then, to remember things.

It's never an exact science, though, remembering. You cannot influence remembrance, and I think that is why it is so maddening. Trying to force yourself to remember something is a vain attempt. It is not something we can control, let alone trust ourselves with.

And maybe that's why you've asked me this. To drive me mad.

I stare at the reflection in my mug and question the girl looking back at me.

Did getting every one of those books make your grin grow in a way that melts even the coldest of hearts?

Did admitting that you felt the things you tried so hard not to feel, feel like breathing that first breath of clean air after sitting in smoke for decades?

Did watching the sunset truly not compare to listening to the strings of words woven from the person next to you?

Was walking around with coffee-stained shirts and messy hair while eating a donut as perfect a moment as you remember it being?

Was kissing him for the first time like coming home? Was it the first time you felt alive after realizing you were letting yourself die from the inside out?

Or is none of this the way it was?

Am I forgetting that the socks were soaking wet?

Tell me, I demand from the girl in the reflection.
What was it all really like?
What am I forgetting?

Because I see books and poetry and think of the green in the sunset and cry having to learn how to live with what grieving for you feels like. Because I don't know if what I remember is really how it happened.

I know I'm forgetting something, that the socks were soaking wet. That the sickness was coming. I just don't know how they came to be this way.

My eyes lift weakly from the reflection in the mug to trace the memory of him.

There was a time when his voice was filled with warmth and life and love. A time when he made promises and wishes. A time when I felt so safe, so sure, with him that he resurrected me in a way. And I don't remember what it was like to realize that I would never roll my eyes and smile at him again.

I don't remember the moment where the before and after met. I don't remember what it was like. All I know is that there was a then and there is a now, but I don't know what it was like to get here.

"I just remember being promised that I would never get hurt," I mumble.

He tips his head. Picks up his coffee mug. Sips from it. So methodical. So precise. "I have found that promises are the easiest things to break."

Lifeless. Loveless. Empty. That is all he is now.

All I want is to forget what he was to me back then. But memory is a torment I must suffer, and forgetting is a mercy I will never know.

CHAPTER FIFTEEN

I once carpooled to school with an unruly Catholic girl named Samantha. Her mother, the complete opposite of her, only spoke when spoken to and softly smiled in the mirror at us junior high kids. Samantha's mother was always someone I admired. Soft and beautiful. Direct and loving.

I once asked her about confession—what it was like, and how you feel after.

"You can find the mechanics of the whole ordeal anywhere. I won't talk off your ear about that," she said, "but the feeling you get after is nearly indescribable. It's an overwhelming sense of peace if you do it truthfully." She looked back to face me in the back seat. "You could never feel a greater sense of relief. It's like being set free."

To this day, I have yet to experience confessing in a Catholic manner, but I have experienced a confession of my own.

And she was right—it's the greatest relief one could ever know.

Bodhi lies beside me, propped up on his arms. His outstretched legs far surpass the length of mine and he wears only a swimsuit, giving me an unapologetic view of his muscular build. His skin is tanned from the harsh Arizona sun that kisses it on all of his shirtless runs—runs that I've tried to join him on but can never keep up. Even riding a bike, it's a chore to maintain the same steady pace as him, so once my breaths become too shallow, I head back to the house and let him finish the workout alone. If he wants to kill himself with excessive endorphins, that's his prerogative.

"I'll be leaving for Utah in a couple of weeks," I state simply to Bodhi.

"Oh yeah?" He faces me with a smile. "And what exactly will this trip entail?"

"Well, there will be lots of prep, of course—tons of errands to run, the setup for the bridal shower, and putting together the bachelorette party, which I'll need to finish planning soon." Bodhi raises an eyebrow at me, and I swat his shoulder with my hand. "Nothing crazy, of course."

He lets out an exaggerated sigh. "*Bor-ing.*"

I roll my eyes and continue, "I think she'll want help with the dinner as well—"

Bodhi wraps an arm around me and interrupts with a kiss, smothering any protests with his lips. I quickly abandon all thoughts of talking and return the surprise show of affection. He draws it out, savoring this moment like he has all the rest, finally able to do so now that I've taken back the former restraints I put on this relationship.

He moves to leave a trail of kisses down the line of my jaw, stopping to kiss the lone freckle that resides just above it in the middle of my cheek. "You're distracting me," I try to say, but it comes out more like a gasp of breath.

"Is that what I'm doing?" he murmurs under my ear, right where he knows I'm ticklish.

"Stop that!" I giggle as I do my best to fend him off, but he only pulls me closer, now dragging me half on top of him. My hands push against his chest so that I can smile down at him. "You're impossible."

He lifts a helpless curl from my face and tucks it behind my hair. "You can't possibly blame me. I don't want you to leave."

I lean into the hand now cupping my cheek and grin at him, already hoping that the conversation would steer this way. "Then why don't you come, too?"

A devilish smirk crosses his face. "To the bachelorette party? Delilah, they have men you pay for those kinds of services—"

"No, you pig!" I laugh and slap him playfully. "To the wedding."

I wait for that feeling of anxiety to root its way into my bones the way it always has, but I haven't felt that way in weeks. Bodhi has made trusting him almost easier than breathing. He's been perfect.

His smile grows deeper, solidifying in place. "Are you asking me to be your date?"

"I know how much you love your Arizona desert, but it could be fun—don't you think? Then you can meet Boston, and I'll show you all the places I'd go growing up." I raise my eyebrows and give him a serious look. "You can finally try real fry sauce."

"You should have led with that."

"Seriously," I say, "you could come up a few days earlier and make a trip out of it." I wiggle my eyebrows playfully. "C'mon, it'll be fun!"

Bodhi sighs, but he can't hide the tilt of his lips. "Fine, I'll come." He rolls me over onto my back so swiftly, you'd think I weigh nothing at all. The sound of my high-pitched laughter fills the warm, dry air. "But only if you promise not to spend *all* your time doing wedding stuff."

I give him a quick peck. "Who else would I want to spend my time with if not you? You just better promise not to forget about me after realizing how amazing fry sauce is."

His lips quirk up, but quickly resign themselves to a more serious look I've grown so used to. He memorizes my features like he still can't believe I'll be here tomorrow, afraid he's dreamt this all up. I want to tell him he isn't the only one afraid of being pinched, afraid of it all being ripped away, but I don't have to. He knows.

"How could I ever forget you?" he whispers.

The same affection I was once so scared to accept and show comes so naturally to me now. That fear no longer plagues me the way it once did, because even though I realized there was no going back from the inevitable hurt this would cause, hurt doesn't seem like such a certainty anymore. I'm not so focused on the what-ifs; I'm focused on him and me and us *now*. I want to be here in his arms, and I don't want to imagine anything other than the familiar safety of being wrapped up in them. It's been two months of this, and I still want more.

A loud splash sounds behind us, and we're promptly drenched by a wave of chlorine water. I gasp and pull away from Bodhi, wiping my face as I look for the source.

Kayden's head pops out of the water. He casually whips his hair out of his face, not acknowledging that the two of us are gaping at him like a couple of fish. I don't know when he got home or how I didn't hear him open the back door and come out here.

"Hey, Bodhi!" he unnecessarily shouts from the water as if to announce his presence. "You coming over to watch the play-offs tomorrow?"

"Wouldn't miss it," Bodhi answers through gritted teeth made to imitate a grin. I stifle a giggle behind my hand.

"Can't wait!" Kayden lies back to float in the water. "You guys should really consider getting a room," he adds with disinterest, as if he's saying it looks like it might rain today.

"Thanks for the tip," I snap back. All I receive from my brother is a thumbs-up while he floats atop the water's surface. I look back at Bodhi, who is still dripping with pool water, having taken most of the impact. "Maybe we should go somewhere else."

He nods. "We probably should." But a devilish grin takes

hold of his lips before they meet mine. I kiss him through my smile and laugh just before another splash of water hits us.

"Oh, go clean a car or something!" I yell at Kayden with absolutely no real conviction, grinning as I wipe the water off Bodhi's scowling face.

———————

Bodhi and Collin's girlfriend, Emma, arrive at the house at the same time. When I open the front door, they turn to face me in unison.

"Hey!" Bodhi steps over the threshold and greets me a bit too eagerly with a quick peck. In his arms, he holds a small bundle of flowers neatly arranged in a delicate white vase. Daisies—my mom's favorite.

"I'm Delilah," I chirp as I turn to Emma. "Come on in!"

"I'd shake your hand or give you a hug or whatever, but . . ." She glances down at the bags of chips and dips in her hands.

"Let me help you with those." I take the containers of dip off her hands and lead her toward the kitchen.

Collin pops up from the couch in the adjoining living room. "Hey, babe," he greets, draping a lazy arm around her shoulders as he guides her to the kitchen, where Bodhi is looking help-lessly at the island for a place to set down his vase.

"You weren't kidding about me not needing to bring any food," Bodhi says. He scoots a tray filled with frosting-covered brownies over toward the bowl of ice for the drinks. "I'm just going to set these here."

Emma's shoulders slump, her eyes widening. "I didn't real-ize . . . I would have brought something else." She looks to Collin with accusatory eyes, and he takes his arm off her shoul-ders to scoop the chips up out of her arms.

"Well, I'm glad you didn't. We seem to be fresh out of chips in the Collymore household." He grins, trying to make her feel better about something she should feel no guilt for in the first place, but her cheeks are still tinged with embarrassment. Collin—in a manner not nearly as careful as Bodhi—shoves aside a plate of cookies and stacks of cups, then throws the chips down onto the table with an effective *smack.* "See?" He beams. "Perfect."

"You two," I say, pointing at the boys, "get started on the burgers. Us girls are going to get the game on." I loop my arm through Emma's and lead her toward to couch.

She gives me a grateful look, and behind us I hear Bodhi exclaim, "*More* food?" Collin only scoffs, wordlessly questioning my ability to complete the task.

Emma and I both giggle and take a seat while the boys begin rummaging through the fridge looking for the hamburger meat. I turn to her and warmly say, "So, tell me about yourself. Where are you from?"

Even if Collin was one to overshare, which he isn't, I've hardly seen him at all these past few weeks. I know next to nothing about the girl he's decided to bring home.

Emma clears her throat. Though she seemed grateful for my gesture of acceptance by bringing her over here, she seems to of reverted back to her timid manner. "Um, here."

I smile. "That's cool. Have you lived here your whole life?"

"Uh-huh."

I nod at her to go on, pausing to allow for an elaboration I slowly start to realize will not occur. It appears that Emma is just as forthcoming with information as my elusive brother. "I see. Well, we moved here just over two months ago. I don't know if Collin mentioned it."

"He did."

I shift in my seat. "Right." I pick up the remote and press some buttons, and the screen flashes to some static that I've never seen before. "Crap. I don't know what I just did," I confess. "Do you, um . . ." I begin to hold the remote out to her, but she declines the offer with a single shake of her head. I press a few more buttons and the screen goes blue.

I'm about to give up when Kayden walks into the room. "Kayden!" I exclaim, holding up the remote. He walks over without a word and takes it from me, presses two buttons, and hands it back. Commentators appear before us mid-conversation, both bald and suited in grey wool.

After thanking him profusely, I turn to face Emma. "This is our younger brother, Kayden. Kayden, this is Emma."

He walks over and extends a hand out to her. Emma gingerly accepts the gesture. "I wasn't aware that Gray had any friends," he says.

"Oh, no. She's, uh . . ." I pause to allow her to label herself, which she does not. "A friend of Collin's."

Emma nods once in agreement, and Kayden does the same. Unfortunately for me, I'm sandwiched between the two people on this Earth who refuse to add anything more than the bare minimum to a conversation.

I look to Collin and Bodhi, who are now outside on the patio grilling the burgers. Bodhi is explaining something to Collin and shutting the lid. He points to the circular thermometer, and Collin nods, taking the information in. "Don't tell Collin you had to help me, please."

Kayden shrugs and walks into the kitchen, bringing back a plate of cookies. He plops himself into the chair next to Emma's and, without a word, holds the plate out to her. Crumbs tumble to the ground when her calloused fingers pick one off the plate. When he doesn't offer them to me, I lean over to snatch a cookie off the plate.

I start to rummage through my brain for any kind of conversation topic that could lift this awkward tension surrounding us, but I'm saved before I have to.

Mom and Dad walk in from the garage at the same time that Collin and Bodhi come in the back door. "Sorry!" my mother exclaims. "I completely forgot to get some seasoning for the burgers and had to run to the store to grab some." My dad shakes his head behind her, exasperated. I know for a fact that we have seasoning in the cupboard; it probably just wasn't the exact one she wanted.

"Perfect timing. The grill is warming up now," Bodhi chimes in. He walks up to take the bags from my mother, and Collin grabs the bags from my father.

"Looks like more than just some seasoning," mutters Kayden.

"Bodhi!" Mom exclaims as she crushes him with a hug. "How are you, dear?"

"Well, thank you. You?"

"Just busy, busy, busy."

Bodhi chuckles at the minefield of food on the table. "I see that."

Dad gives Bodhi a clap on the back and begins to unload the grocery bags.

They happily converse about the day and the traffic and all of the normal things, bumping into each other and reaching to place food in the proper spaces. Collin cracks jokes while Bodhi helps my mother place a bag of flour at the top of the pantry, even though she's more than tall enough to reach. Dad shuffles around and smirks at the exchanges around him, but doesn't do much more to let anyone know he finds humor in it.

It's all so perfectly natural. I can't help but admire how seamlessly the four of them move about the kitchen. It's like a planned-out dance, but with chaotic choreography.

"This is Emma, by the way," Kayden says, hitching a lazy thumb toward the girl in the chair next to him.

My jaw drops and my mouth hangs agape, horrified that I forgot she was on the couch, let alone in the house at all. "Yes, this is Emma," I say too quickly. I shoot Collin a look that goes ignored as he speaks up.

"Emma, this is my mom and dad. You met Bodhi, and I'm assuming you and Kayden have been introduced?"

My mother drops her purse and rushes to the living room, and from the look that haunts her face, she, too, is feeling ill-mannered. "Oh my goodness! I am so sorry, dear—I couldn't see you sitting on the couch from over there! Emma, was it? I'm Scarlett, it's so nice to meet you," she says, fussing over Emma, but there's no time to warn Mom of her timid manner.

Emma does her best to give a warm smile, but behind the attempt at warmth, I can see she's fighting the urge to vomit. I've never seen someone so nervous in my life.

"Nice to—to meet you," she stammers.

Collin saunters over and cups both her shoulders in his hands as he takes his place behind her.

"Emma here is going to be a rockstar one day. Did she mention that?" He grins down at her, and she returns the gesture with an embarrassed blush.

"No," I pipe in, "she didn't."

"Well, I wouldn't say that," she murmurs.

"Don't be modest. Seriously, I've never seen anyone shred the guitar the way she does. It's actually *in*sane!" Collin takes his hands off of her shoulders and begins shredding on an air guitar, contorting his face and bending his knees slightly, getting super into it.

Emma laughs at his ridiculousness, and looking at her now, it's like meeting a whole new person. She's comfortable next to him. Her smile reaches her eyes now, no longer forced by a need to be polite or make a good first impression. She playfully punches Collin's arm, and he feigns hurt and rubs the spot where her fist made contact.

"I'm sure you're a lovely guitar player," Mom coos, using an adjective I'm not entirely convinced describes her kind of play-ing. "You met through the band, then, I'm assuming? Collin likes to keep all the details to himself." She shoots him a glare similar to the ones she would shoot me after finding out I'd been spending so much time with Bodhi.

Emma explains how when she tried out for the band, she had confused the ad with another one looking for a guitar player. Collin's band was looking for a drummer, but they wanted to hear her play anyway. With a small smile, she describes how she only played for a few seconds before Collin stopped her and told her she was in. He gave her his spot as the guitar player and began playing the drums instead, quickly perfecting his rusty skills.

"We started hanging out after practice and would meet up for lunch or dinner before or after sometimes. I thought he was full of himself," she confesses as a vandal-like grin spreads over her lips. "And he totally is. But I guess it's kind of cute," she laughs.

Collin returns her grin with one equally as mischievous, wiggling his eyebrows up and down. "I am pretty cute, aren't I?"

She gives Mom a serious look. "See what I mean?"

As Mom laughs at the two of them, I excuse myself. Dad walks by and I leave a phantom kiss on his cheek, saying hello. Bodhi leans against the sink, propped up on his elbows, as he watches everyone gather around Emma, hearing stories about the band and her life.

I sidle up next to him and bump his shoulder with my own. "So, what do you think of Emma?"

Bodhi mouth twitches as he quickly glances at her. "She seems . . . nice."

"So she wasn't a big talker with you, either, huh?"

He relaxes and leans in toward me, gripping the sink's edge. "Oh. My. Hell. It was insufferable. I thought *I* was difficult to talk to." He's already speaking in a tone low enough that my family won't hear over their chatter, but he whispers even lower, "It was like talking to a *wall*. An *actual wall*. I offered to carry some of her things, and she just looked down and walked to the front door. I thought, 'Whatever,' but then I tried talking to her while you came to answer the door and ended up talking her ear off about investments."

I giggle while imagining that exchange and then whisper, "I *know*. It was just one one-word answer after the other. I thought she was just shy, but . . ." I trail off, looking at the now-sociable Emma. She's not even blushing now; she's just leaning into Collin, talking like a normal person.

"Maybe she's just more comfortable around Collin," he reckons.

The group suddenly bursts out in fits of laughter, and the jarring change in tone makes me flinch ever so slightly. Looking at them gathered around talking reminds me of watching the group in the kitchen moments ago, but this version feels too boisterous. It's happy, but almost like a dress rehearsal. Not yet natural and lived-in the way Bodhi and I interact with my family. It reminds me of bringing him over for the first time to meet my parents.

Everything was so new and unexplored then, so loud. Like they were trying to make those moments stick. I don't necessarily wish to be back at that point in our relationship, but it's bittersweet to look back on, yet I can't quite pinpoint why. It isn't nostalgia weighing down my heart; it's something that feels more like jealousy. But I don't understand why watching Emma meet my family would make me feel this way.

Bodhi grabs my chin with his thumb and pointer finger and turns me to face him. "What are you thinking about?"

I look into his eyes and soften a bit, letting out a sigh I hope sounds happy instead of confused, and give him a smile I hope looks content and not lost. "I was just thinking that it was nice to see you getting along with my family so well earlier, in the kitchen. I like having you around," I confess.

His lips pull together in a smile, but his eyes seem to be searching mine for an answer I don't have. I lift onto my tippy-toes and quickly kiss him, not wanting to delve into my confused thoughts any longer.

"I like being around," he says simply, pulling my body into his own. His clean scent engraves itself in my mind, and I try to memorize this moment. Try to remember what it's like to be held in this exact grip, the warmth of his body temperature to the precise degree. It's one of those moments you're in and you know is finite, but you do everything you can to commit it to memory. I want to catalog this feeling and bring it back out again when I need it, or even just when I want it again.

I peek over at my family once more and see Emma laugh at something Collin said. My mother and father join in, and I even see Kayden shaking his head on the couch, not wanting to give Collin the satisfaction of making him laugh.

It hits me like a brick, this yearning for this moment—even though I was there when Bodhi met my parents, *I* haven't been through this myself. I haven't met anyone important to Bodhi, let alone his family. Bodhi never talks about them.

I asked about his father once, in the beginning. We were looking at the stars when he mentioned the Grand Canyon again. He said he'd take me there one day. I asked if he had ever gone with his dad, thinking maybe they went on little father-son camping trips there. I smiled at the thought of them being so close when he was younger. He just grunted and very swiftly changed the subject to something that I can no longer recall, but that moment left an impression on me. I haven't brought it up since, thinking he would eventually, but he never did.

I pull away just enough to look into his eyes, searching for the answer as to whether asking this would be too much. "What?" he asks. He seems so relaxed now, so content. I don't know if there will ever be another time when it will matter enough for me to ask, or another time when I'll have the courage to do so. "What is it?"

"Why don't you talk about your family?" I prod as gently as I possibly can, stepping on a pressure plate and hoping nothing detonates. Hoping that if I soften my words enough, he'll answer through muscle memory. Or maybe I read too much into our other conversation; maybe the reason he doesn't talk about them is because I never thought to ask again before now.

His whole body stiffens in place. "My family?"

"I just saw Emma with everyone and wondered if I'd get to meet your family someday. But you never talk about them, and I . . . well, I was wondering why you don't talk about them."

After what feels like a solid minute of him staring at me, frozen in a cold sweat, I begin to wonder if I've crossed some line, asking this question. But he looks away and releases a heavy breath.

"Your family is good," he says, nodding to everyone gathered around the couch. The game has just started, and they're settling into their seats. But the distance in his eyes tells me he isn't really looking at them, but something else entirely. His voice is just as distant. "Not everyone has that." He shrugs then, and it's so unlike him, it makes my heart sink into my chest.

"Bodhi?"

"My parents were just not good. Not like your family."

"What do you mean?" When he doesn't answer, I ask, "Do you still talk with them?"

"No," he says stiffly.

"Why not?"

Bodhi's hair sways with the soft shake of his head. "Now is not a good time to get into this."

"Get into what?" My soft hand wraps around his rigid forearm, and the feel of it turns my stomach into sick knots. "Bodhi, you can talk to me. Why don't you talk to your family?"

The muscles in his jaw tighten, holding back words he doesn't want to part with, but when he looks at me he lets them free. "Because bad people do horrible things to people that don't deserve it. And I refused to watch them hurt anyone else."

His voice only carries far enough for me to hear, but still his eyes flicker to the family behind us—the "good" people who are yelling at the television and exchanging plates of baked goods and snacks. All I can hear is the sound of my pounding heart in my eardrums, muffling everything else.

"What horrible things?" My voice wavers, but I keep my focus on him.

"Delilah," he groans, pulling his arm away from me to drag his hands up his face and through his hair. "Can we not talk about this *right* now? This isn't exactly 'get-together' conversation." He earnestly looks over to the couches again, reminding me that we are, in fact, not alone.

"Yeah, of course. I'm sorry," I say, the pit in my stomach growing deeper and deeper as I wonder what he means.

"Don't apologize," he insists, grabbing hold of my hand to keep my fingers from running circles over the pad of my thumb. "There isn't anything to be sorry for." Bodhi's eyes look deeper into mine, begging me to accept this as truth until I nod. He kisses my forehead before lacing an arm around me to rub my back. "Let's go watch the game, yeah?"

I nod again and take a deep breath to steady myself. *I'll never meet his family. I'll never laugh with his mother or joke with his father.* And I hate myself for being so selfish. For feeling sad that I won't have that when it seems he is missing so much more.

We walk over with plates so full of food that they nearly topple over, and luckily for me, everyone is so involved in the game that all they notice is our bodies blocking the television as we walk in front of it.

"Move it!" Kayden demands.

Bodhi hesitates like he might say something back at Kayden, but I tug on his arm and lead him to our seats. It was probably shocking for him to hear Kayden speak at such a volume when he usually adopts a monotonous, almost robotic tone.

We take the only two seats left on the edge of the large couch next to Emma and Collin. I sit closest to Collin, who is staring at the screen, chanting, "Come on, come on!" The moment I sit down, however, the screen goes black.

"No, no, no, no, NO!" My two brothers begin to curse and shoot accusing looks around the room.

I grab the remote from under me and begin pressing away. "You gotta put the remote on the coffee table next time."

"Give me that," Collin demands. He reaches for the remote, but I move it out of his reach.

"I got it, I got it."

He rolls his eyes. "Why don't you just hand it to Kayden now and save us the time?"

I glare at my traitorous brother but make no such move to hand over the remote. Instead, I press another promising button.

"Just let me—" Collin reaches for it just as the TV flashes with life. My chest flares with a quick prick of pride only for it to die out immediately—because now we're staring at a breaking news headline.

"—was biking the Grand Canal Trail when he stumbled upon what is believed to be the body of the missing woman Marcy Mae Thomas."

"Wait!" Dad exclaims. "Turn it up."

The boys protest with groans, but I press the one button whose function I know for certain until the volume is high enough.

"Reporting at the scene: Daniel Striker." A slender, cocky-looking man appears on the screen, standing in front of a taped-off area crowded with men in black-and-blue uniforms. "This is Daniel Striker, and I'm standing only yards away from where, early this morning, a biker named Richard Jones stumbled upon something he found suspicious."

The camera cuts to a man in a tight spandex shirt and sunglasses. He holds a helmet at his side, his hair—a sweaty mess—poking out in odd directions. "I bike this trail at the same time every single day, real early so it isn't as busy, you know? But today I thought I saw something in the water, like something big, which is kind of odd, you know? And I got this weird feeling, you know? Like something just wasn't right. I thought maybe someone threw a large thing of drugs or something in there, you know? And I thought I better check it out."

"If this dude says 'you know' one more time," mutters Collin.

"So I got off my bike to check it out, but once I got a closer look, I whipped my phone out and called the police immediately."

The svelte Daniel Striker takes up the screen once more. "What Richard saw was something indescribable: the body of twenty-two-year-old Marcy Thomas lying crumpled at the edge of the canal, dead. He states that he didn't leave her until the police arrived."

"I was supposed to get to work, but I couldn't leave her alone like that, you know? So I waited," Richard says. He begins to rub his upper arm, no longer making eye contact with the camera. "They got there fast, and I felt bad because, well, I did lose my breakfast near the scene, but it was just so horrible to see her like that, you know?"

My eyes stay glued to the screen, and I feel a similar urge when they flash back to an image of the taped-off crime scene.

"Police do not have any leads at this time, but they ask that if anyone has any information that could aid in catching the person responsible, please come forward. If you were near the address below between the times of midnight and two a.m., please get in contact with local law enforcement."

A familiar address flashes below before the screen goes back to the original news reporter.

I pivot slightly in Bodhi's direction and say quietly, "Don't you work close to there?"

He swallows hard and nods in my peripheral vision. But before I can turn to him, a face flashes on the screen that holds me in place.

"If anyone has any information that could aid the officers and detectives working this case, please come forward. Even the smallest bit of information could help."

Shoulder-length blonde hair and faded hazel eyes are the first things I notice about Marcy. Delicate freckles kissing her nose and cheeks, and her infectious grin with strikingly white teeth, are what I notice next. Bile rises in my throat at the knowledge that this smiling, happy, beautiful girl is *dead*, but also because there's something too familiar about her.

I tug at my memories, trying to place her face somewhere that makes sense. "I think I've seen her before," I say to no one in particular.

"Did she come to the coffee shop?" Dad asks.

I shake my head a tad and say unconvincingly, "Maybe."

I place a hand on Bodhi's arm and flinch. Tight muscles, rigid as stone, are all my fingers meet—there's no trace of comfort to be found. His face—glued to the screen, captured in a dark, icy trance—is frozen. A bead of sweat collects on his temple.

"Bodhi?" I prod, but Marcy's face is the only one he'll look at.

"Well, that is just depressing," Kayden says.

"It's horrible," Mom adds.

Dad just shakes his head, and Emma holds on to Collin. I will Bodhi to look back at me, to hold me tightly, or to let his thoughts trail to a place I can pinpoint, but he doesn't tear his eyes from the screen. Even after Collin changes the channel back to the game, Bodhi sits there like he's still looking into those light-hazel eyes.

My family quickly forgets the sad interruption, and soon they're back to watching the game and eating too much food, as planned. My brothers occasionally make some dumb jokes that everyone laughs at—everyone but Bodhi.

I continue to watch him, wondering what's going through his mind, and when the game ends, he leaves quickly with some excuse about having work in the morning. Mom hands him some baggies of food to take home, then he kisses me goodbye —quick, almost strained.

As Bodhi's car pulls out of the driveway and speeds off, I'm left trying to imagine what would push him off this ledge, what would make him so cold, so quickly.

The lump in my throat chokes me as I slink to my room, not offering to help clean up the mess we left behind.

CHAPTER SIXTEEN

Bodhi doesn't know that I'm sitting in my car outside his work, trying not to throw up at the sight of the forgotten police tape that once acted as a perimeter for Marcy Mae Thomas's body. We made plans to watch the sunset together tonight since we've seen so little of each other this week, but little does Bodhi know, I also made time to surprise him with lunch the way he so often does for me. Though knowing I'm across the street from where they recently recovered a dead body does dispel my appetite a bit.

I hadn't realized Bodhi worked this close to the canal until the strip of yellow tape clinging desperately to a shrub flicked in my peripheral vision. Oddly, Bodhi hasn't brought it up despite the minimal time we've spent together the past week. But that's why I'm here.

The news about Marcy had to have brought up some things with his family, and seeing now that he has a daily reminder of the tragedy, I'm not sure my little pick-me-up will be so effective. I hoped a kind gesture might smooth things between us, lay a path for Bodhi to feel more comfortable in trusting me with this part of him. I hoped it would remind him that I'm simply Delilah and he is simply Bodhi, and that what happened before doesn't change that. But that bit of tape complicates things. Because every day now, he's reminded of whatever memories this flash of yellow drags out of the recesses of his mind.

What horrible luck that they found her right there. That someone left her here.

It's been a week of us only spending time alone together during the seven-minute drive to Lava Java. A week of him getting emergency calls for work and leaving while my family is still there, acting as a buffer. A week of wondering if all of this is really a coincidence or if it's just him avoiding having a real conversation with me. A long, painful week.

It's been tedious, dancing around the one thing that's constantly on my mind. Letting everything else spill out in conversation while I grow more and more anxious to ask him about his past. But waiting for the right time feels vital. I don't want to jeopardize the relationship we've built.

Despite that . . . I miss him. And bringing him lunch can't hurt things.

Five bone-grey stories reach up toward the clear denim sky. *The First Choice Trust Group* is displayed in large sleek black letters across the top corner of the building facing the street, just waiting to be noticed. Windows reflect the landscape, but the tint prevents anyone from seeing what they contain, giving me no indication of where Bodhi might be inside. Luckily, four beige walls inside house a beige lobby filled with beige furniture and a security guard who embodies the same mute shade.

I approach the desk and attempt to liven the room with a smile and chipper tone. "Hi, I'm looking for Bodhi Williams. Do you happen to know where I could find him?"

Ledger, as his name tag says—a man who would be easily overlooked without his uniform—points to a plaque on the wall and answers me without a smidge of inflection. "That will tell you what floor to go to."

I look at the plaque he's pointing to and bite my lip. "Here's the thing," I chuckle. "I'm trying to surprise him with lunch"—I hold up the bag of to-go salads—" and I don't know *exactly* what branch he works in, but I do know he works with investments. Sorry."

Ledger looks pained by the weak smile he musters with incredible willpower. "Floor two. Jen can redirect you if needed."

I sigh, relieved, and thank him.

He nods, smile dropping before I've even stepped away.

Four elevators greet me in an inlet of the building. One is taped off with a cleaning cart sitting inside. The yellow divide sends a shiver down my spine. I quickly press the up button a second time, impatient to leave. Once inside an empty elevator, I'm slammed with the sweet smell of citrus chemical that leaves my nose tingling.

Compared to the lobby downstairs, the second floor is lively. Rather than muted colors and a quiet atmosphere, this floor is made up of complementary blues and greys, and a hum of energy permeates the air. It feels almost systematically clinical in the way that banks often are.

A dozen or so desks in the main area, behind the desk that I assume is Jen's, are separated by dark-grey dividers, giving the illusion of personal space. Men in white dress shirts sit rigidly in their dark swivel chairs, some with ties too tight around their necks and some with sleep still clinging to their eyes, but all are focused on their work. Along the back wall, panes of glass and wooden doors lead to smaller offices. If I had to guess, I would say Bodhi is in one of those. Probably one of the two with the blinds angled *just* perfectly so I can't see who's inside.

The plaque on the reception desk displays the name Jennifer in dull bronze letters, as though they're worn with age. When I approach, the woman holds up a finger, signaling for me to wait a moment as she ends her phone call. I nod distractedly and continue scanning the floor for Bodhi.

Jen hangs up the phone and smiles at me with brilliantly

white, perfectly straight teeth. "Sorry about that. How can I help you?"

"Hi, the officer downstairs said that you would be able to help me find one of your employees. I'm a little lost, not sure where to go," I laugh.

She maintains the same smile as she nods. Her hands lift to the keyboard in front of her, and her fingers begin to dance atop it. "What's the name?"

"Bodhi Williams."

She purses her lips. "Do you happen to know his position here?"

"No," I admit, "I just know he works with investments. Sorry."

"No problem." Jen continues typing. "The name doesn't sound familiar, and I know the staff on this floor, so it's likely he's just in another department. I'll look him up real quick for you."

A frame with fancy white swirls sits on her desk, sporting a photo of two smiling children wrapped in her arms. "Cute kids."

"Thank you," she says before her brilliant smile turns into a frown. "Are you sure you have the right place? I'm not seeing a Bodhi Williams listed anywhere."

My heart constricts even though I know I checked the address twice before coming in. "I think so." I hold my phone up to her to verify that I'm at the right place, but this only seems to puzzle her more.

"That's very odd." She pounds the keys a few more times. "Let me check that name with our other locations."

I nod, but I'm not convinced. I'm certain this is where he works. He pointed it out to me not that long ago.

She sighs. "Was he, by chance, recently hired? Or maybe just transferred? That could be why I'm not finding his records."

I shake my head. "I don't think so. Could you look again? I'm sure he works here."

Jen gives me a doubtful look, fueling the confusion building up in me. "I'll cross-reference all of the analysts and associates again for you, but I think you have the wrong place, hun." After checking again, she simply shakes her head, unable to provide me any answers. Her phone rings and she looks at me in apology. "I have to take this. I'm sorry, we don't have anyone by the name of Bodhi Williams here."

My mouth hangs agape, and I can't find it in me to put my jaw back in its place.

Bodhi doesn't work here.

Jen motions for me to scoot aside for the delivery man waiting to drop off a package, and I mumble an apology before reluctantly shuffling back toward the elevators. One last glance at the semi-cubicles and offices gives me nothing.

What in the hell?

I hardly register the potent smell of citrus in the elevator on the way down, the space filled with the steady stream of confusion running through my mind.

The elevator opens up, and I leave its mechanical whirring and citrus smell behind. The same goes for the bland security guard in the bland lobby, though the blandness now makes for a more fitting blur.

I don't process anything at all until suddenly I'm sitting in my car, hands in my lap, unable to even move. I know I should reach for my phone and text Bodhi, just *ask* him about it, but something seems wrong to me. I don't quite understand what I'm missing, but I know I'm missing something.

Maybe I went to the wrong place, like Jen said. It's the only thing that makes sense. But as I look back up at the massive black letters strewn across the side of the building, it keeps me from fully believing this explanation. I *know* he said he worked here.

The phone chimes, knocking me out of the trance that had me staring out my windshield. On the screen, a notification pops up.

. . .

Excited to see you tonight.

The phone's cool metal digs into my palm. *I should respond to him right now. I should call him and let him explain. I should ask so that I can laugh and feel dumb for this sick feeling in my gut.* But when my thumb moves to the Call button, I hesitate. Something doesn't feel right, but calling feels like overreacting.

There is no reason to flip out.

There is a completely rational explanation for all of this, I tell myself. Maybe he did recently transfer or was recently hired. Maybe his records are still being moved over. Whatever it is, there is an explanation—I'm sure of it. I'll just wait and ask him tonight.

Excited to see you, too!

I hit Send, and although I am excited, the acid in my stomach won't stop turning.

There is no reason to flip out. There is no reason to flip out.

CHAPTER SEVENTEEN

The blanket on the car's hood slips ever so slightly under us, probably trying to vacate this awkward moment like I almost want to. I watch him leaning back onto the windshield and staring out at the skyline while we sit next to each other in silence. Not the comfortable kind we so often share, but the kind when there's something that must be said hanging heavy between two people.

We both halt here, having already danced around the question for as long as we possibly could. Our days have been good, the weather is nice, and it looks like it should be a good sunset. These are the things we've used to fill the silence while I wait for the courage to ask him what I really want to know.

Fear gripped me by the throat and kept me mute when I tried to bring up his family earlier. I tried to say the words quickly, just to get them over with. But instead of words, it was nothing that came out of my mouth, and I let it stay that way. Because too many things have become dangerous things to talk about. Too many landmines could blow up what we have. One wrong step, and this selfish curiosity might wreck us.

Facts and logic come more easily to him—this, I know. He's analyzed life and the world around him down to its marrow and recites the knowledge the same way water so easily slips through our lips. Every time the conversation drifts toward something too real, he finds a way to maneuver the syllables back toward the unimportant. The facts.

Most every conversation that I can recall has been about something other than himself: the science behind the clouds in the sky, how and when the monsoons come and go, the length of the roads that stretch across the valley, the migratory patterns of a butterfly whose name I can no longer recall. All of it made it seem like I was getting to know him, but now it feels like I've been getting to know the things that he has gotten to know.

But just because something is more difficult to discuss doesn't mean it should be off the table. How can you know who someone is without first knowing who they once were, who they were raised to be?

How can you feel like you know someone so well without knowing much of anything at all?

I clear my throat. "I feel like I don't know that much about you," I confess, this broad admission feeling like the easiest of segues. The hesitation in my voice echoes off the hard-packed dirt surrounding us. It's better to start with something vague than to jump right to the two questions burning a hole in my esophagus. Better to build up to those slowly than feed this suffocating anxiety.

He shoots a glance at me, eyebrows scrunching. "Of course you do."

I shake my head and pick at a scab on my arm.

"You know a lot about me," he states.

"I know you grew up here." I gesture to the dry Arizona landscape. "I know you like classical music and that you have an eidetic memory. I know you have one dimple on this cheek." I run my thumb over the smooth part of his left cheek that sometimes caves when he smiles big enough. He smiles slightly underneath my touch.

"But I feel like everything else you've told me isn't about you." I look at him, hoping for some kind of answer. When I don't find one, I let out a heavy sigh. "I just feel like I should know more about *you*."

Bodhi looks at me then, *really* looks at me, and I wonder if he knows how to interpret that crease between my eyebrows or if he's just now learning. We've only really had the good parts of a relationship up until this point; we haven't hit any bumps or left bruises on one another with our own baggage, but somehow that makes everything we've shared seem so disingenuous. Almost shallow. Like we have avoided the very things that give relationships depth.

Was this by intention? Or have we unknowingly veered from the realness? I don't know. But I've made the decision to steer straight into the barrier we've been avoiding and hope that the crash doesn't leave us too broken. You always build things better the second time around, right? I'm just fearful that there won't be a way to repair things together.

He must find some sort of guidance in the flutter of my eyelashes, or the length of my short breaths, because his face softens as a small smile tugs at the left side of his mouth. "Have I ever told you how I got this dimple?"

A petite shock jolts through my body, taken aback by where he's steered the conversation. "You haven't always had it?"

Bodhi smiles and shakes his head, the soft brown locks swaying with the movement before once again finding their perfect place when he stops. "No. When I was little, I had a fixation with chewing on pen caps. I'd chew on them while I colored or worked on my homework." He gets lost for a moment in some memory, perhaps the drawings he'd spend his time creating, or maybe a time when he punctured the cartridge and the ink spilled over his lips. His green eyes shine as he plays it back, and I wonder how often he thinks of this.

"It drove my father crazy," he laughs. "He eventually told me I needed to stop. That he wouldn't buy me more, and that they would dry out if I kept ruining the caps. So, every time I'd go to put the pen in my mouth, I'd remember what he said, and instead of chewing it, I'd push it into my cheek. Odd? Yes. But I stopped chewing them. I did that for so long that eventually a dimple formed." He beams, and his smile is just big enough for me to see the imprint left by the pens he once used to chew.

The sweet story of my favorite feature of his turns my anxieties into something softer, something more at ease. I don't know how he does it—navigating his vocabulary and constructing a sentence with such influence. Words carry too much weight to toss them around without delicate care, but his words carry a perfect tranquility.

"So there," he says, "now you know how I got this dimple. What else do you want to know? I'll tell you anything, Delilah. I'll tell you anything you want to know. I don't want you feeling like there's something off or wrong or missing. Just ask." He places a reassuring hand on my knee and rubs his thumb back and forth, the motion so soothing that I want to melt into the moment and forget that anything was bothering me before. I practically do, but the first question sits there impatiently tapping its foot against my skull.

"Your parents?" It's hardly more than a whisper.

Bodhi nods like he knew this is what I would ask next. "It's not a good story," he explains. "It's not one you probably want to hear."

I reach over to place my hand on his own, running my thumb back and forth over it the way he did to mine.

He lets out a breath and looks back at the sunset, looking for stability in the tangerine-tinted clouds. "I don't believe in regrets. I own up to my decisions and make no apologies for how I got to where I am now," he prefaces. "I haven't seen either of my parents in years. I left home when I was fifteen because at some point, being alone out here was better than being with them in that house. I just—" He swallows hard.

"Most parents shield their kids from their shit. Mine didn't.

I kept to myself, stayed in my bedroom, because if I came out when they were all out there, their 'friends' and them, they'd—well, they just weren't great people." Though he stares off straight ahead, he isn't looking at the tract of land before us. He's somewhere else. Somewhere I wish he'd never been.

"So, I got on a bus and took it south until I hit the city. I'd sleep on park benches or curbs, wherever I could find, until I finessed my way into getting a job at a gym. It worked out well enough. I had a place to shower and a forgotten utility closet I could sleep in."

After a moment that feels like hours, he continues. "They never came, my parents. They never thought to look for me. I knew they wouldn't, but a part of me wondered if I might be wrong. If my parents might come down from a high long enough to realize their son up and left. That the kid they'd scream at to grab another bottle of beer wasn't there to hear it anymore. That there was no one to pick up the broken glass. A part of me wanted to be wrong, and the rest of me hated that part of myself." His glassy eyes find mine, brimming with similar emotion. "But when I was young, it wasn't so bad. That story I told you is true. I used to ask my parents for things like pens."

Tears spill from my eyes, and I have to focus to keep my breath from shaking.

"They were still parents to me then. But with youth comes a certain blindness. I'd say that being young is to be oblivious, but that isn't accurate—you aren't ignorant of the sins of your parents, but rather the small things outweigh the bigger things. It was so easy not to see it then, the harm they were causing, because my father was once a father who bought his son pens for his drawings. It was simple, then.

"But once I left, I made myself forget. All of it. I worked tire-lessly. I got a second job, I took care of myself. I grew up. I made a *life* for myself," he says, each word enunciated with pride as if this alone separates him from the people who were supposed to raise him. "It wasn't until a couple of years ago that I really thought of them again.

"I was at the mall—I don't remember what for, but when I got to my car, a man shoved my face into the hood. I had no idea anyone was following me. I had stopped looking behind my back long before that day. When he flipped me around, I froze. I froze because I knew that face." Bodhi paused, his eyes lost in recollection. "I recognized the man who used to sit and count cash out on our coffee table. The man who put his cigarettes out on the couch I'd watch my cartoons on for days when my parents disappeared." As he shakes his head at the sky, I, too, find myself disappointed in whatever maker failed Bodhi so, so miserably.

"He asked me something that confused me. He asked me if I knew where my parents were camping out these days. But I knew they didn't have enough money to get another place— they hardly had enough to keep the one we had. And then it clicked: they were homeless. I should have felt bad. At least a part of me should have. And I waited for that feeling to come— the pity, the guilt, the remorse, anything. But it never did.

"I convinced the guy he had the wrong person somehow, and he left. I just sat there with a broken bleeding nose for a long while before I did the same."

He fidgets with a button on his cuff and takes a long pause. I want to say something, to comfort him or hold him, but moving right now feels like treason. This story feels unfinished. I don't dare betray him with words when I begged him for this.

After a deep breath, he continues. "'So, this is the man you are,' I thought. 'You're the kind of man who leaves his parents to live and die on the streets and can't bring himself to feel even a little bit bad about it.' But you have to understand." He turns to me and grabs me by my arms, gently enough not to hurt but firm enough to implore me to comprehend the depth of what he's about to say. "They weren't my parents then, Delilah. Those people had stopped being my parents long before that.

The life I built for myself was not due to them—it was *despite* the nothing they gave me that I became this. I could not allow myself to ruin it all for two people who simply gave me life. That miracle didn't warrant my mercy." His chin dips down. "I know that makes me a horrible person."

"Oh, Bodhi," I whisper. I cup his face in my hand and wonder how he isn't crying, telling me all of this, because I can't seem to stop. "You didn't do anything wrong."

He nods into my hand. "I left them even though they weren't ever there. I never heard of them or thought of them long enough to remember to forget them again. I never want to see those people again. There is nothing left in me for them.

"I think they're dead, which sounds terrible, but I think they are. One day I woke up, and that was the first thought in my mind: *My parents are dead.* I couldn't possibly know, but I did." He takes a deep breath in. "I tried to find something online. I allowed myself one single hour to wonder, but it was pointless. Even if they were found dead on the street, they'd just be John and Jane Doe. Part of me was grateful for this, because it wasn't something I would have to feel guilty for. They were either gone or they weren't, and I didn't have to know. They could die as Jane and John Doe because they were better off being that than the people they were. And I could live with giving them this one small bit of compassion."

Bodhi's eyes return to mine. "I'm sorry I didn't tell you about them before. It's just . . ." He desperately searches the features of my face. "It's just that from the moment I met you, it was as if I had met the one person on this Earth who was everything they weren't. I ran into you, and the first thing you asked was if *I* was alright," he laughs, and it's like hearing that sound for the first time.

"You asked me if I was alright, and my world stopped for what felt like forever. Here was the most beautiful person I had ever seen, and you cared more about a total stranger's well-being than your own. You were kind before you knew if I deserved it. And—and I suppose I *wanted* to deserve it. I wanted to prove to you that I wasn't a monster before I told you I was raised by them. I didn't want you to think of me as the horrible person I know I am. I'm so sorry, Delilah."

"Bodhi," I whisper, my voice rough against my throat, "you have nothing to apologize for. I'm so sorry you went through all of that. I understand why you don't talk about it. I can't—I can't even imagine what it must have been like to grow up like that. I—" I swallow the lump in my throat and reach out to grab his hand in mine. "But I'm glad you told me."

"You are?" Bodhi asks, and I nod.

"You did what you had to do. If you hadn't, who knows where you would be?" He doesn't let tears fall, doesn't even allow them to gather, but his mask is slipping. He's looking at me, and I say the words he's probably waited his whole life to hear. "You are not a bad person, Bodhi."

At this, he pulls me into his chest, and he breaks.

I don't know how long we sit there, crying into each other's arms, but I promise myself right then that I'll sit here holding him until the sun rises if that's what he needs. The occasional surge of emotion shakes up the breaths that leave his lungs, and I cling tighter with each one. He doesn't talk, and neither do I, but I think it's okay to just be with someone sometimes. Words can't always say what silence does. Sometimes just being there is enough.

His breathing is even, his shirt soaked from my tears when we finally pull apart. The vivid colors have leached themselves from the sky, leaving only a whisper of the fading green-blue sunset draped across the horizon.

"Are you okay?" I ask, still close enough to feel the warmth radiating from his body.

He nods, eyes red. "Thank you," he whispers.

He searches my eyes, and without words, I know this is it— the moment that everyone spends their whole lives waiting for. It crept up on me so slowly, so silently, and then all at once.

I couldn't pin it until now, sitting here with him holding me like this, like I'm the only person in the world he's ever cared about and ever will care for. In his arms, at this moment, I finally understand what they mean when they say "When you know, you know." It took this entire time for me to comprehend, but every single bit of it has been leading up to this realization. Every glance, every awkward pause in conversation, every bit of shared laughter, and every moment of anxiety I've felt is just a part of what made up this feeling. *I love him.*

Bodhi pulls me in and kisses me then, and I keep this epiphany tucked safely away in my chest, not yet ready to voice it. His kiss is gentle yet earnest, soft but intentional. He pulls away suddenly, caresses my face in his hands, and holds me there with what feels like urgency, and I know he feels it, too.

"Don't ever leave," he pleads. "Promise me you'll stay." The look in his eyes is something crazed, almost manic, and I understand it.

I nod. "I promise."

He lets out a sigh, and I can feel the relief that replaces his anxiety over the reality of how devastating it would be to lose what we have. The tension in his expression melts into adoration, and he pulls me into him once more.

I find it difficult to imagine anything in life that could be better than this.

Too soon yet also an eternity later, he stops and we eventually settle, lying against the windshield. Bodhi tells me more stories about his life, but most of what he tells me is what I've heard before tonight: random facts, statistics, and knowledge that he has stored and collected. But now it feels like I've finally listened. I see why he doesn't talk about the life he had before, and I understand that this is who he is. He is made up of everything he has ever known, and him sharing this is him sharing himself.

I tell him stories from when I was younger, too, and we spend the rest of the night in each other's arms, looking up at the stars, stealing kisses, and laughing at how I spent all of second and third grade with a chip in my front tooth and the time I fell in the pond at my grandmother's house and cried thinking I stepped on a koi fish.

He takes me home, and when he kisses me goodnight, it isn't enough. Now that I know what it feels like to be so certain about someone, being anywhere but with him feels criminal. I don't want to leave his side after we've had such a beautiful night.

But good things begin and end. I used to think this as a cynical thought, but they don't just end—they also begin. Tonight is not the end, I must tell myself. This is just the beginning.

Nothing but tonight plays on repeat in my mind as sleep somehow finds me. Even in my dreams, I feel my grin permanently etched on my face.

CHAPTER EIGHTEEN
AFTER

He does what he can to make this place the perfect environment to collect his data. He has filled the room with the things that supposedly make up me. Apparently, you can boil a human down to some tangible items. There is a bookshelf filled with books. Some I've read. Some I have not. But there are none that I care to touch. I tried pushing the shelf over to block the door and keep him out, but it's bolted to the wall.

There is a rack of clothing as well. Each item is an exact match for something in my closet, but some articles of clothing are missing. My favorite hoodie from a trip to Bryce Canyon—before everything happened, of course—has no twin, nor does a pair of vintage sweatpants I thrifted. I tried to dismantle the hollow bars, but they are so light that even if I were to get a piece loose, it wouldn't be any good for bashing his skull in.

The bed frame looks the same as the one in my bedroom. The sheets and comforter are a perfect match as well. The only thing missing is a throw pillow. I wonder if he thought the beads sewn onto it would have been dangerous somehow, or if that was simply unattainable. The bed frame is too solid to even dream about using a piece of wood in any way. There is no way to cut through it, at least not in any timely manner.

The bathroom is just like the rest of this place: a hazy carbon copy. A falsified relic of my past. A taunt of what life once was, made to mimic and to mock. Decorations and paint match as much as this cage could allow, though anything that could be weaponized has been replaced with something safe. Something useless. Not even the lid of the toilet will detach.

But it is not these imitations that bring burning hot tears to my eyes. No. It is the lone, pointless window that sits above me day in and day out. Taunting me. I used to think it might mean a chance at escape, but I have had time to realize it is just another variable in this controlled environment. It is not a risk to have it here since it is completely useless.

I have mostly stopped looking at the window. Sometimes at night, when the fuliginous light comes through and a small rectangle of it paints the floor, I like to pretend I am looking at the stars I looked at before. That it is the same moonlight that lit up my bedroom floor. But I also try not to wish for these things, knowing I will never see them again.

And there is also that same crack in the wall. The only thing that has oddly been left though it resembles and represents nothing from my life. I've traced it a million times, wondering why it is there. Why didn't he patch it up? A little spackle, and it would cease to exist. Its life is an easy one to extinguish. It has been through enough; it would be merciful to end it. But, for whatever reason, he has chosen to spare it.

A kindness he has not offered me.

He sits here now, seated across from me at a table like so many times before. But this table is bolted to the ground, unable to move or be utilized in any way other than its intended purpose. His hands sit clasped on the table between us. He doesn't write anything down because he doesn't need to. My captor remembers everything. His face is the same as it almost always is. Blank. Emotionless. Cold. Sometimes he contorts it to reflect emotions he cannot possibly feel—fear, guilt, remorse—but does so only to mimic the face before him. He does so, I suspect, only to practice.

Today is a question kind of day. I know the man I used to know has some kind of routine in place, but since I don't know what day of the week it is, I cannot say for sure how his schedule would lay out on a calendar. I have just listed the days as numbers, one through seven. Today is day four.

On day four, we sit at this table after breakfast and he asks me questions about my old life. Observing it could only tell him so much, you see. He likes to get inside my mind and compare my answers to his assumptions. So far, according to him, he has been entirely correct.

"When did you first know something was off?" he asks so casually, you would never suspect the topic to be something as cruel as my boyfriend devolving into a psychopath right before my eyes. You would never think he was asking me about how I got trapped here in this chair.

"Right when we started dating." I have found that answering as honestly as possible is the only option. It is better to rip the Band-Aid off. Sometimes it hurts, being forced to be vulnerable with someone I once willingly confided in. Yet as messed up as it sounds, sometimes it is comforting, too. Like an old habit.

It is muscle memory, talking to him this way. Like we used to.

He narrows his eyes, not believing the words that slip from my numb lips. Telling me without words to try again, to be more specific, truer to the story.

I put myself back in those rooms. The real ones we took up space in, not this mockery I inhabit. I think about my answer for a moment before adjusting the theoretical lens of the camera he was using to photograph my life. "I mean, it isn't the exact moment I knew. How could I have known then?" I stare at my useless hands. "But I think that is when I should have known something was wrong. I should have put some distance between the two of us then . . . asked more questions. Given myself room to think. To breathe."

He tilts his head. "Why did you not?"

"I was scared of crossing some made-up line. But even if I hadn't been, why would I have suspected something so dark as the truth? I—I never would have thought something could be so wrong when everything *finally* felt so right. We were so good. I thought the two of us were so good," I croak, my voice giving out. Although it has been what seems like eons since I've come to accept this as reality, as my fate, I hate remembering the good. Because even in the good, there were things I should have picked up on. Even in the good, there were times he showed me who he was.

"But you already know that," I say, my words softer than a whisper.

He nods slowly, digesting yet another bit of the story he already surmised. Not caring that he is making me relive the first of the truly horrific moments in my life.

I should have known from the beginning. From the moment we met, I should have seen. *I* should have known there was an ulterior motive. *I* should have *seen it*.

I should have known, I should have known, I should have known.

And it is this unwillingness to forgive myself for this transgression that has slowly eaten me alive. It is my fault that I'm in this prison. There is no one else to blame.

"You were in denial," he simply states.

I nod and get myself a drink of water. The drink brings relief to my throat, now hoarse with emotion, and I wish it would burn. But he'd never gift me something as humane as poison.

I used to be afraid to move while he was sitting here. I did not know what he wanted from me. Was it all a test? If I touched a book without his explicit permission, would I be foregoing my right to a meal? If I stood up to get some water, would I receive less the next day? Did every action made result in punishment?

It took me a long time to realize he just wanted me to be organic. To be myself as much as possible. I am a subject to be studied, an animal being observed. The key to survival in this place is to act as though I am not being held against my will. I have to act like everything is normal. Like every day in here is just any other day. I have to be me so he can watch.

I do not know what he will do with me once he has learned everything there is to learn from the girl in his cell.

"It was like I was a crab in a pot on the stove. I couldn't feel the temperature of the water rising until it was at a boil." I shrug and continue, "But once I saw the bubbles, I was able to look back and realize I felt it getting hotter all along." I stare at the crack on the wall. "I just didn't want to."

"So, you did *not* know something was wrong, then," he says. "Tell me, when was the first time you thought to yourself, 'Something is not adding up'? When did you think there was something wrong? When was the first time you realized you were possibly holding hands with a con man?"

I let out a short harsh breath. *Con man.* What a perfect word to describe the man before me. And somehow, I've never thought to name him this despite all his deceit. I've seen so many of his faces before, but this blank mask he dons is the one I now know him by.

Gone is my friend. Gone is my companion. Gone is any trace of humanity. He has become someone so strange to me that I can no longer even call him by his name. A name holds too much tenderness. It's too personal. A person doesn't choose their name; they are given it, and every time someone uses it, it reminds them of the gift they have received.

I have taken his name from him.

Robbed him of the only thing I can.

"We were alone, talking. I remember the smell of cinnamon" *How could I forget it?* I wonder absently "and your face, it felt . . . wrong." His eyes narrow, encouraging me to elaborate. But I see it, the same moment playing in his mind too. "I suspected something was deeply wrong then, but I ignored it. Ignored the tight knots lining my gut. Tried to pretend they weren't there. I should have seen it before the wedding . . . that without a doubt, something was wrong. It was right there in front of me." I swallow hard. He nods, seeming satisfied with my answer. "But you know that. You were there for it all."

He nods again.

"Well," I sigh, "that was when I knew. We were fine until we weren't. I had no idea I was holding hands with a liar until it was too late."

He scoffs, the closest thing to a laugh he ever conjures. "Seems to be the way these things go."

"Seems to be." I pinch my arm enough to feel pain, but not enough to bruise. He doesn't respond well to me harming myself.

This is the only punishment I can get away with. Because even though I am not the one who set these events in motion, I did not stop the dominoes from falling. I let them cascade one into the other. Each one fell because of something I let slide. Something I missed. And for what? Because watching it happen was beautiful?

Meeting him was the force that collapsed into me, changing who I was and crashing into Marcy being dead, into him avoiding me, into the fight, into Andy, into the wedding, into what happened with Luca, into being taken, and into me ending up at this very table staring at this lifeless gaze.

All the dominoes came crashing down, and all the while I turned a blind eye.

I was shown what was going to happen, and I squinted to see a different picture.

There is only myself to blame.

"Seems to be," I repeat in a whisper.

"So, then, tell me. How did you know? What gave it away?"

CHAPTER NINETEEN

"Two weeks is too long," Bodhi grumbles, my head lying in his lap as we relax on my bed.

Despite my early call and last-minute invitation for him to come over, he managed to find the time to shave. His signature scent of sandalwood and cinnamon drifts up from his clothing, and if I breathe deeply enough, there's also a hint of fresh aftershave. I let the mixture of them seep deep into my lungs, praying it stains. Even at work, when I dust a coffee with cinnamon, my thoughts drift to him. Oddly enough, he can't stand the taste of the sweet dust.

His face is sharper from down here—more defined, almost unnaturally so—and his eyes are darker from the shadows cast by his eye sockets, the shade of them such a deep shade of green. I find it rude I've never seen them like this, so dark and yet still so brilliant. This hue reminds me of the pine trees I'd see back home when I was floating on the lake in the mountains. It reminds me of the winding curves of the canyon road, the smell of smoke, and the things I hadn't realized I missed until I found them here, in his eyes.

I wonder if he sees home in my eyes the way I do his. If the brown reminds him of the rough dirt or the Joshua trees that litter the desert floor. If he looked at me from this same angle, would the shade of them grow so dark, he'd think of those reckless monsoons he admires? When the sun hits them just right and they shine a brighter amber, does it remind him of the last rays of sunshine before it sinks beneath the horizon?

"You should push your flight," he suggests as he tucks a piece of my hair behind my ear. It wasn't in the way, didn't bother me at all, but he reached for it anyway, like he always does. Like he needs to see every bit of my face. Like he can't stand to miss memorizing any part of me.

"I can't. I've already pushed it as much as I can," I say. "I should have left weeks ago to help Boss more." I run my hand through his already perfect hair. "Why don't *you* change *your* flight?" I lightly poke him in his broad, muscular chest and smile up at him. He's so beautiful. *Why have I not realized this more often?*

"I have to work, or you know I would."

"I know, I know. I—" I trip on my words at the mention of his work. Last night, I got so completely swept up in the moment with Bodhi that I spaced on bringing it up. It feels so trivial to even bring it up right now. It hardly bothers me at all, the whole work incident, if you can even call it that.

It's hard to bring myself to care about anything other than his fingers running through my hair. Hard to care about anything other than savoring every second we have left together before I leave.

"What?" he asks.

My cheeks heat, for whatever reason, and Bodhi smirks. Runs his hand through my hair again.

"You know, I miss how much you used to blush when we first met. It was so addicting to see your face fill with this very shade of scarlet. I would do pretty much whatever I could think of to get your face to do exactly what it's doing now."

I feel the heat spread to my hairline and narrow my eyes at him. "Oh, I remember. You would always tease me and tell me how beautiful you thought I was. I always thought you were just trying to annoy me."

"Maybe sometimes," he says, smiling softly down at me, still letting his fingers brush through my hair, "but I always meant it. You have always been beautiful to me." His voice softens, hovering above a whisper.

I look at him through my eyelashes, a smile growing on my lips. "Even when I was drenched in my drink?" I tease.

"Oh, especially then. You simply exist, and you take my breath away."

I sit up a bit, ready to roll my eyes and debate this with him, but knowing what I'm about to do, Bodhi presses his lips to mine, smothering the words before they can surface.

I lean into the soft and simple moment, letting whatever I was going to say fizzle out of my brain as my lips melt into his own. He moves his hand back up to hold my head, but what feels like much too soon, he moves it to cup my cheek and pulls away. He keeps our faces close, separated only by a breath. His eyes search my own, trying to instill some certainty in me, it seems.

"Want to know something?" He whispers the question like the answer is a secret he doesn't want anyone else to overhear. Like it's something only the two of us should share. "You're my best friend."

He says it with certainty, like he does everything else, but I know that this means more to him than it might to anyone else. He means it in the same way I would, had I said it: that he is the first person I think of when I wake, the only person I look for in a room, and the one person I want to tell everything. He's the kind of best friend who both complements and completes me. The kind of friend I love more than my own self.

My smile spreads beneath his palm. "Yeah? You're my best friend, too."

He grins and leans in to kiss me again. I smile against his

lips and try to memorize this moment, knowing it will be all I have left until he gets to Utah.

"Looks like my plan worked," I say when we finally pull away.

Two lines of confusion burrow themselves between Bodhi's eyebrows. "What plan?"

"You know, to get you to fall for me."

He picks a piece of lint off my shoulder. "Pardon me?"

"You heard me," I say in a mock-serious voice. "I planned this whole thing out. Even timed that little coffee spill so you'd buy me all those books over there, then got you to beg me to be friends until you were ready for all this."

"Because that's definitely what happened," he mumbles, shaking his head at me.

"Well, what else would you attribute it to?"

"Um, a hell of a lot of patience on my part," he says, exasperated.

My lips tug to the side, trying to suppress a smile. "Hmm, that could have had something to do with it, too, I guess." I move so I can lie down. "But I'd say it was mostly my scheming."

Bodhi shakes his head, and the mattress dips as he lies next to me. "Like you'd have planned this." I move his arm to fit it around me, and his eyes slide shut as he shuffles to get comfortable, mumbling, "I was the one planning."

"What?"

He peeks out of one eye. "Delilah, did you seriously think for one minute I *just* wanted to be your *friend*?"

"For a little while, maybe."

He shuts his eyes again and lets out a sigh from deep within his chest. "Well, then you see? It was *my* plan that worked out. I knew that if I showed up at your work and could get you to agree to be friends, you would eventually cave. I just had to be patient."

"I—" *Work!* How many times am I going to forget about it?

"What?" he asks. His fingertips dance along my forearm, but his eyes stay shut while he breathes evenly, in and out, in and out, in and out. It's so methodical, I nearly forget again and let myself drift to sleep.

I laugh, still feeling a bit silly for bringing it up now. "I completely forgot to ask you something last night." I know it unsettled me in the moment, but lying here, admiring Bodhi while he rests like this, I can't remember why.

"Ask away," he encourages in a mumble, sleep tempting him as well. His fingers trace invisible patterns across my skin, and goosebumps threaten to break out against his touch. Electricity runs through my veins.

I have to ask before I'm pulled into a nap or get distracted. Again.

"Did you get transferred at work recently? Or move offices, or something?" The question leaves my lips so carelessly, it's hard to believe I was ever scared to ask him in the first place. *What is the point in worrying when he'll tell me anything I ask?* The answer is just one question away.

He stills for a moment, the muscles in his face flexing so that his eyes can snap open. "No. Why do you ask?"

"Oh," I breathe, a little confused now too. "Did you, uh, get a new job?"

Bodhi's brows cinch together in puzzlement. "No—Delilah, why are you asking me this?"

I wiggle around, uncomfortable but not sure why. His outstretched arm still holds me close, but there's this undeniable distance between us now. Not physically, but separating us nonetheless.

Suddenly, I *do* feel nervous. I *do* feel a pinprick of that uneasiness I felt when I left the First Choice Trust Group. The bile in my gut sours, but I can't say for certain why.

This was so much easier when I thought he would easily write off my worries with one of the explanations the secretary offered me. When I thought he'd say, "Oh yes, I forgot to mention it, but I did get transferred to a new office!"

"Oh," I start, my voice wavering with the weight of treading lightly, "well, I tried to visit you yesterday, and the lady at the desk said she didn't have anyone by the name of Bodhi Williams in the system."

I sit up and face him, my face turning a little red; I don't know which of the many emotions banging against my ribcage is the cause. For some reason—maybe the confusion in his eyes shifting to something sharper—I don't think he finds this scarlet hue quite as endearing as before. "She said you might have transferred recently, or that I was at the wrong bank?" I add.

He tries to hide it, but Bodhi's whole body goes cold next to me. Every muscle in his body freezes up like he's been caught in some lie. Like a child whose mother just found a stolen candy bar in their backpack. He stiffens like he's desperate not to let out an emotion he can barely contain.

I search my memories for something, anything else I'm forgetting. Some memory that helps me paint this reaction brighter. Something more forgiving. Something kinder. Something more like the Bodhi I know. But when he speaks again, his voice is not as easily restrained.

"What do you mean? You came to my work? Yesterday?"

It's hard to dismiss the feeling that I've said something I shouldn't have. Like maybe I'm the one who's spilling secrets.

"I—I did, yes. I was trying to surprise you with lunch." My words stumble out quickly, trying desperately to rectify whatever I've broken. To figure out what I've done wrong. To locate a misstep or recall something he told me that I ignored. Was I not supposed to visit? Had he told me it wasn't a place I could go? Am I forgetting something?

How did I mess this up?

"Why would you do that?" he snaps, and I flinch.

It feels like he's slapped me across the face.

His words are so cruel, so forceful, that I can't help but sit back and check that this is the same Bodhi I walked in here with, because he would *never* speak to me like this. But that mouth with that sneer just did. I find my blood starting to boil the same way his unjustly seems to be.

"I—I was just trying to surprise you." I tilt my head again as if it'll knock my thoughts into place and help me understand. When a curl falls into my face, he doesn't try to fix it.

Bodhi breathes in and out, not so methodical now as it is controlled. He doesn't so much as utter a word or an apology. I wait for him to soften into the man I know, to relax and laugh and tell me he's joking. To tell me he did transfer recently. But instead, he clenches his jaw tighter, his stare boring into me like it's the only means of control he has.

"What is your problem?" I snap. "Why are you pissed at me right now? You come to see me all of the time!"

"That's different," he says lowly.

"How?" I scoff at him, wide-eyed and baffled. Does he not see the hypocrisy?

Bodhi closes his eyes and breathes in and out through his nose two times before my blood boils over. I can't contain it. "*How. Is. It. Different*?!" I demand.

"DAMN IT!" He bellows so loud, it almost hurts. "It just *is*, Delilah!" He jumps off the bed and begins to pace the space before me, only taking three steps in each direction before he meets a wall.

My eyes track his movements across my room. Back and forth, back and forth, I watch as each of his steps pounds a nail into my heart, breaking it as the love I have for him becomes tainted by this moment, by this *fear* growing inside me. I want to jump up and shake him by the shoulders and tell him to knock it off. I want to reach over and pinch my arm to wake myself from this sick nightmare I've found myself in. But I can't move.

I'm glued to the mattress like a child hiding beneath their

covers, and I wish I could hide under them and make this go away. I wish I could go back to when I was so innocent that being covered by the bedsheets made the scary things disappear. But it doesn't work like that. The only thing that can remedy this is the same thing that's breaking it.

And right now, he does nothing to make me feel better.

My best friend does nothing to fix this.

He just paces the room, angry with me but not telling me what I did wrong.

"I think you should go," I manage to voice, so shattered that the words leave painful claw marks as they leave my throat, but they are steadier than they have a right to be. I just watched someone I love flip a switch and turn into a stranger—how could my voice do anything but tremble?

Bodhi stops and looks right at me like he didn't hear me. I repeat myself. "You should go."

A new wave of panic seizes him suddenly, and he moves to step closer. "Delilah—"

"Go," I say sternly, scooting back on the bed. I don't want to be anywhere near him. Not right now. Not when he just actually *yelled* at me for something like this—for doing what he does for me all of the time. Yelled at me for something as trivial as a *surprise*.

"No, Delilah. I'm sorry. Please—"

"Holy shit!" I laugh, coming completely unhinged at the sheer absurdity. My voice shakes now, but not out of fear. He isn't the only one who gets to be angry. "I said get. *Out.* You are not going to yell at me over something as stupid as *a salad*! Get out of my house right now. I won't be treated like this. You're being ridiculous."

"*I'm* being ridiculous?" he scoffs. "You won't even let me say an—"

I jump off the bed and march out of the room. Luckily, no one else is home right now. An audience would only make this worse than it already is.

"Where are you going?" Bodhi demands. "Will you just listen to me for one second?" He follows me through the hallway and down the stairs, badgering me with questions and demanding I stop. I don't until I've reached the front door and held it open for him.

"Thank you for helping me get packed," I say through gritted teeth, and though my words are kind, my tone is anything but. I'm doing everything I can to hold back any emotions threatening to spill over the dam.

"Delilah, please. Let's talk—"

My lips form a tight line, and when his pleading eyes meet my glare, he quiets. Stills. As if he's just now noticing I'm upset. I don't look at him as he walks past me and out the door.

"Delilah, don't do this," he begs as he turns around.

I slam the door and then, just because I know he'll hear it, I flip the deadbolt. I back away from the closed door and hear my name on his lips on the other side, but I don't reach for the handle or turn the lock. I turn and run to make it up the stairs in time, because me breaking is not something he gets to hear.

The rage dissipates with each step as pools gather in my eyes, but the first tear doesn't fall until I've shut my bedroom door. I slip uselessly down the frame, and with each shudder, my shoulders make soft hollow noises against it. I gasp for air and try to tell myself that this is not the end, but my mind can't seem to understand it.

You are not dying, I repeat. *You are not dying*.

But somewhere in my mind, I hear my own voice argue, *Then why does it feel like it?*

Each time I try to collect myself, I remember the feeling of his arms tightening with anger while still wrapped around me. His jaw clenched, him pacing. The sound of his yell echoing against the eggshell walls. And then I fall back apart.

I replay the moment he snapped over and over again and find a part of me breaking with each tear that falls. Because for the first time since I've known him, I was scared of Bodhi. And I can't figure out what the hell just happened.

CHAPTER TWENTY

I remember it was Valentine's Day when I looked up at the clouds and decided that that was Heaven. This much, I remember. My great-grandmother had passed away, and I decided that was where she went. To the clouds. To Heaven. At eight years old, it's so easy to think you have it all figured out.

I remember hopping on an airplane for the first time and being so excited to fly next to the angels and look for my great-grandma up there. I wanted to ask her if she got to keep the hat I made her for Halloween or if she wasn't allowed to have those in the clouds.

We took off, and I wasn't scared because I was going where the angels lived. Up and up and up, and the cars and the buildings and the mountains shrank smaller and smaller and smaller. Once we neared the clouds, I held my breath. *This is it!* I thought. *I'm going to see all the angels!* We entered the white expanse, and for a moment, that was all I could see out my window: the center of the dove cloud we were in. But after a few seconds, we broke through the other side and—AND—!

Nothing. There were no angels with harps or waiting great-grandmothers. It was just the tops of the clouds, which looked remarkably like the bottoms. I stared in shock as the whole belief system I had developed as a child collapsed. I could not bring myself to believe the angels weren't up there in the clouds —every single painting I had ever seen had them atop the clouds. But after a few minutes of staring out my window, disappointed with the lack of Heaven, I began to appreciate the golden hues the clouds reflected. It wasn't what I wanted, but it was still beautiful.

I believe that was the first time I experienced that peaceful feeling while looking at the clouds. My first sort of sunset. My own version of Heaven.

I smile at the clouds as we make our final descent and still feel that childish urge to reach out and take a piece for myself, to feel the tufts between my fingers and steal a piece of it even though it's absurd. A part of me still hangs on to my youth, I suppose.

The mountains soon come into view, and a handful of city lights gleam through the last few hours of sunlight. I take in the shapes of the roads and the curves of the mountain ridges and sigh. I memorize the snow that frosts the peaks and the green that infests the valley. It's one of those feelings you don't realize is within you until it's left, but once it's gone, you realize you carried it with you all along. That you know every letter of its name.

I've been so homesick.

And I'm finally back home.

"I'VE MISSED YOU! I've missed you, I've missed you, I've missed you!" Boss's screams crash against me just as fiercely as her hug. For how petite her figure is, she is *incredibly* strong. Somehow, the headache I had the entire flight has disappeared with her familiar volume.

"I've missed you, too," I wheeze. "Let up a little, will ya?"

"Absolutely not!" she refuses, somehow managing to pull

me in closer. There aren't many people who can hold you like this, in a way that recenters every atom in your body, but Boss is one of them. Her hugs always have that effect on people. She makes everything feel better, even when everything is alright.

Just one hug from her and I'd forgotten for a moment that anything bothered me in the first place. But only a moment.

"Oh, I don't want to let go!" she squeals before she pulls away and holds me at arm's length. "But we have no time to waste. Let's get a move on. I want to finish that checklist of yours! I know you're hiding it somewhere."

I give her my best "I'm so innocent and confused" look.

"Not buying it!" she chirps, tapping the tip of my nose.

"Alright, alright. You caught me." I pop the trunk of her car and toss in my suitcase. Considering I'll be here for the next three weeks, it's pretty light. Friends like Boss come with the perks of free-range closets.

We each climb into the car and buckle up. "We do need to get a lot done today, though," I say. "There's the dress fitting for both of us, finding the rest of the vases for the reception, putting together the wedding favors, moving the—"

"Oh my gosh, if you don't stop talking, the rest of us aren't going to have enough oxygen to breathe! There's a reason you have it on paper." She taps the list I'm reading in my hands. "Take a breath. This is supposed to be fun!"

"Aren't you supposed to be stressed out of your mind? You should be grateful for this thing," I retort, waving the checklist in the air.

"Of course I'm grateful." She gives me a fake sneer and returns her attention to the road, pulling away from the curb. "I just also know it's going to turn out absolutely perfect no matter what," she sings.

"Oh my, you're making me nauseous. Where's Max?" I ask. "I thought he might tag along to help tone down your chipperness. You know, keep you in check."

She scoffs. "Keep me in check? D, please, you know there is not one person alive that could 'keep me in check.'"

I sigh. "We miss you, Heath." Boss giggles at my remark. "'Boston Ledger' would've had a nice ring to it."

"It sure would have." She nods.

"Sadly, it looks like you'll have to settle for Boston Saunders."

"What a shame."

"Hey, at least your babies will be cuter than if you had them with Heath."

"Max does have a nice nose."

I nod. "And with your eyes?"

"We are going to make so much money off of those little babies! I've already got a few modeling managers interested in working with us."

My eyebrows shoot up. "Have you, now?"

"Oh, absolutely," she teases.

We both laugh in our seats, and I end up having to reach up and jerk the wheel when the car begins to veer onto the shoulder. "Boss! We'll never make it to your wedding with you driving like this!"

She laughs like we didn't almost just crash into the barrier and returns her hands to ten and two. "Oh, and that would be a shame, wouldn't it? Because I am *so* looking forward to meeting this Bodhi of yours. When is he coming up, by the way?"

My heart drops as the blood drains from my face. I can't think about him right now—not when it's still so fresh and I haven't sorted my thoughts. I can't think of it at all, but especially not right now.

"Oh my gosh!" I exclaim, changing the subject as quickly as I can. "I completely forgot to give you . . ." I dig through my backpack. "This!" I present a Tupperware container filled to the brim with her favorite treat.

"Ah!" Boss swerves toward the shoulder again. "How did she know? Your mother is an actual angel! I have missed Scarlet's scotch-a-roos so, *so* much. Gimme, gimme," she begs, and I place one in her palm. She instantly pops the entire chewy peanut butter crispy rice bar in her mouth, smearing some of the smooth chocolate-butterscotch topping across her lips. "Ohmygaf," she groans. "Dif is *so goof.*"

"I have no idea what you're saying," I laugh.

She holds up a finger while she chews. "I said," she says after swallowing the last bit of it, "hand over the rest of those if you wish to remain unharmed."

"You are so dramatic," I complain, but a smirk finds its way onto my face as I hand her the container.

She nods in approval. "Wise decision. It would've been such a shame to have to pay the photographer extra to photoshop your face to look normal again."

I shake my head at her. "First stop: the seamstress."

"Yef, ma'am," she mumbles through a mouthful of scotch-a-roos as she merges into the next lane.

I fling myself on top of the perfectly made bed in Boss's guest bedroom and allow the exhaustion from the past six hours to drain out of me. Four vases are still needed for the reception, but after the wild-goose chase we went on searching every craft store in the valley for them, we put a pin in that task for now.

Tiring as it was, running around with Boss wasn't the worst thing. Far from it. Searching for elusive vases is the most fun activity in the world if you do it while laughing with your best friend, and I forgot just how much I love laughing with her. It's sad that something as precious as your favorite person's laugh can be distorted through a phone speaker.

The strain in my muscles loosens as I stretch, allowing me to sink further into the mattress. It's nearly ten o'clock and the house is silent. Sleep should meet me here, but I'm alone now with nothing to distract me from my thoughts.

I check my phone for the hundredth time. *Nothing.* Bodhi has not called or texted once. He hasn't reached out to explain, say he's sorry, or even pretend like nothing happened.

From the moment I kicked him out of the house, it's just been radio silence.

Is this what it's like? One catastrophic blowup, and it's over? All of that time together is just what, then? A waste? Was this all for nothing and bound to end?

My fingers itch to click his name and dial his phone number. I want to hear his voice and let it erase what happened. I want to snap out of this and let it all be a dream. I want it to be him that makes me feel better, even though it was him that made me feel so small.

It's a complicated thing to want the cause of your pain to also be the end of it.

I was so scared in the beginning when we first met. Scared of the hurt. But somewhere along the way, we just fell perfectly together. Seamlessly, he became a part of my life, and without knowing it, I began to want him there. Life without him became such an odd thing to imagine, and imagining life with him in it felt like seeing the finished puzzle after years of trying to make the pieces fit. He felt like something that had just simply belonged in my memories. Something I had simply forgotten, something I could easily remember despite having never known it.

His presence in my life had opened me to a kind of vulnerability I had never allowed myself to experience before, and it was exhilarating. I don't believe there is anyone else I could have met and felt this same way with. I think a piece of me would have always remained tucked away in my heart, a failsafe to preserve the parts of me I could not bear to lose. I would've hidden how deeply and easily I care, concealed the books and things I hold closest to my heart, and kept the people

I love out of their reach. But with our friendship came this sort of bridge to that gap I would have made with anyone else.

I slipped into this rabbit hole of wondering how his day went or how the drive home was. I cared to know about the dull things, like the traffic he drove in, and I did nothing to hide this from him. I loaned him annotated copies of books I've read over and over again, freely offering up little tidbits of my brain and what I found noteworthy and loved. And, almost without realizing it, I allowed him to find a groove within my family in which he fit so perfectly.

Him being in my life felt like having the answer to a question I never asked.

So how can the person who tucks the stray hair behind my ear say nothing now, when I need him the most?

With every other potential person not already in my life, I've held them under a microscope. I examined every little action and comment and formed hypotheses on what it meant and where it led until I came to the same conclusion each time: nowhere. Every other boy who has entered my life did so without regard for where it would head. So, I would take matters into my own hands. I'd snuff out the life of what was between us before it could even take its first breath.

And, for whatever reason, I never saw that inevitable end with Bodhi. Not that I decided we were soulmates or anything, but getting hurt just didn't feel like a cold certainty like it had before. This time, it felt more like something of a whisper of what could happen. Like that fleeting moment when you start your car and imagine getting in a wreck. You know it's just anxiety, and that it is a possibility, but you don't give it a permanent residence in your mind once the thought has come and gone. You drive along the pavement and leave the thought behind.

Perhaps I would be better off if I had allowed the thought to linger. Just for a moment.

Maybe then we wouldn't have gotten to this point, and I

wouldn't know what it's like to be the girl staring at her phone wanting so desperately to reach out, but knowing this isn't a mess she can allow herself to clean up.

Tears fall for a few minutes before I bottle it all back up. I used to hate myself for being so good at compartmentalizing my feelings, but right now it's necessary. I need sleep to wash over me, and to forget that a plane ride away, there's a man who weaseled his way into my life and then walked out with my heart in tow.

There's too much to worry about here with the wedding to be thinking about whether or not Bodhi will be reaching out again, let alone tonight. But I'm still at a loss about what to tell everyone when they ask something as innocent yet hurtful as how we are or where he is.

Great, I will tell them. *Stuck working*, I will lie.

And I'll live with these temporary fixes until the definitive damage is no longer concealed by my little white lies. Until I can no longer pretend to believe them.

I check my phone one last time, and that small bit of hope that resurfaces each time I grasp the device dies like it has every other time. It takes a little piece of me every time I'm let down, and soon there won't be much left to take.

CHAPTER TWENTY-ONE

"How am I supposed to know who I'm meeting up with?" I ask, exasperated. I'm sure I sound annoyed, but I know she's too flustered to pick up on it.

Boss came running down to the basement kitchenette early this morning to inform me that not only did her measurements get lost, but the custom backdrop she ordered needed to be picked up today. Seeing as I can't get fitted for her dress, I got backdrop duty. But without a vehicle to transport it, Boss had to call in a favor with one of Max's friends.

She didn't even have a chance to calm down before rushing to get to the seamstress, let alone have time to notice the smell of coffee beans or the questionable mocha concoction in my glass mug. Sleep never found me, and I spent most of the night tossing in the sheets. The bitter drink passes through my lips more easily than it used to before. Smothered in milk and sugar, I welcome its sharp bite.

"Just look for a black truck. I told Luca you're in the old family sedan, so he'll probably come park by you," she reassures me through the phone. I sigh and scan the parking lot of the home improvement store we decided to meet at. I have to pick up some hinges and screws for some of the other displays we're putting together tonight and figured I could grab them after Max's friend, Luca, drops me back off.

A truck pulls in, but it's more of a deep grey than black, and an older man exits it. *Not Luca.*

"Okay, I have to go. I'm sorry, he should be there soon! I'll have Max send you his number in case you need it, but I'm walking into the seamstresses now."

"Sounds good." I hang up and go back to examining the vehicles coming in and out of the parking lot. A few trucks are already parked, but the only one that looks even kind of black is the older gentleman's.

I've never met Luca, but I have heard of him. I think Max met him in college, but that's really the extent of my knowledge of the man. And it does nothing to help me identify him now.

Two minutes go by when a black truck enters the parking lot and slowly passes each row before turning down my aisle and making its way toward me. I get out of the car, certain that this is him.

The truck parks in a stall next to me, but the windows are completely tinted, so I don't see the man's face until he gets out and steps toward me. "Delilah?" he asks.

"Yeah. You're Luca?"

He nods and extends his hand, a brilliant smile plastered on his face. "Nice to meet you." I shake his hand and accept the formal gesture.

"You, too." We stand there awkwardly for a moment before I clear my throat and tell him I have the address for the place in my phone.

"Well, alrighty, then, let's get going," he says, hopping back into the driver's seat. I walk around and climb into the passenger side. When I close the door behind me, the vehicle's interior is so dark, I wonder why anyone would want their windows tinted to this extreme. It would drive me crazy to have this little light in my car. I'm the kind of person who opens up all the windows in the house when I wake up to let the morning rays in.

For a while, we exchange awkward small talk, and only my directions, telling him where to turn or what exit to take, interrupt that. It feels like one of those awkward dates you go on when you're being set up, where you don't have anything in common and know nothing about the other person, but you're forced to be near and speak to one another. This time, it's without the actual date part. I just get to experience the awkwardness all on its own.

He seems like a nice enough person. He isn't outright rude or annoying, which is something. I could be stuck in a car with a guy who goes on and on and on about his truck or someone who doesn't bathe, so I'll count my blessings.

Luca's appearance is rather average, but not in a bad way. He has plain brown hair and plain brown eyes, both lighter than mine. He's tall, but not so much so that he sticks out, and he dresses rather normally, just jeans and a tee. I guess by "average," I mean he's someone you wouldn't necessarily pick out in a crowd. Other than his smile, which is painfully perfect. He's objectively attractive, sure, but not the kind of attractive that walks around like he knows he is. He's the kind of attractive that grows on you.

"So, have you been dragged into running a lot of wedding errands?" Luca asks.

Internally, I thank the universe for a question about something other than the weather and how our days are going, since it's barely past nine o'clock and there isn't much to report on.

"I just flew in yesterday, so not a ton. But I'm sure most of the next couple of weeks, I'll be helping with a bunch of stuff like this," I laugh.

"Flew in? Where from?"

"Arizona."

"Cool. I've never been. Did you grow up there, or . . . ?" His sentences are clipped, tumbling out one after the other so quickly that I wonder what his rush is.

"No, my family just moved there at the end of last year. I grew up here."

"Sounds exciting," he says with a grin. "Must be nice getting away from the winters up here."

"Yeah, it's not so bad. What about you? Been running a bunch of errands for the wedding?"

"Just whenever they need someone with a truck," he laughs and slaps the steering wheel. "So this is my first official wedding errand."

"Wow, you got off easy, then."

"I'll say. You're the maid of honor?" I nod, and he lets out an exasperated breath. "Hope you weren't planning on any sight-seeing during these next two weeks. I'm sure you'll be swamped with things to do."

I open my mouth to tell him I do have plans after the wedding to show Bodhi around, but stop myself short. I don't have those plans anymore.

Still nothing from him. The thought, so sudden, hurts my heart just enough to make me turn toward my window as if I spotted something interesting until I can get the moisture to leave my eyes. I do my best impression of a laugh, half filled with humor and half with sarcasm. "Wasn't planning on it."

I hear Luca chuckle softly in return and realize I'm probably getting too used to pretending everything is okay. Too good at omitting details and speaking in selective truths.

"I'm from here," Luca says. "I've never lived anywhere else. Travelled for work some, but didn't stay in one place long enough to call it home."

I turn to examine him for a moment now that my eyes have stopped tearing up, and I wonder how old he is for a moment before realizing I can simply ask. "How old are you?"

"Wow, getting to the real deep and personal stuff, huh?"

"Oh, did I cross a line just now?" I ask sarcastically.

"Uhm, yes. However, I will allow it, seeing as it appears we have time to kill." He nods at the cars beginning to slow ahead of us, and I groan. This will definitely put a kink in today's to-do list.

"I'm twenty-four," he says. I look at him again and find that the age fits him. He could probably pass for a couple of years older or younger, but twenty-four would be right in the middle of where I'd guess. "I'm guessing you're twenty-two?"

"Just about," I answer.

"I figured, since you're friends with Boss and all."

"Astute observation, there."

"So, you got yourself a boyfriend, or what?"

My jaw drops, and my eyes pop wide open at his sudden question.

"What? Did I cross a line?" Luca asks with a chuckle. "I told you, we've got time to kill. Might as well skip the part where we politely avoid certain questions out of some kind of odd respect, when it's just 'uncomfortable' or whatever." He does air quotes with one hand and keeps the other on the wheel.

I stare at him for a moment, still stunned and confused, but I think I see where he's going with this.

"What?" he asks innocently.

"Are you—are you hitting on me right now? Like *right* now?" I finally say.

"So what if I am?" he says huskily. Luca wiggles his eyebrows at me, and the look of magnified shock on my face sends him into a fit of laughter. It's deep and hearty, and I am not at all amused. "Delilah, I'm so sorry, truly I am. You are a very pretty woman, but you should see your face right now!" The last bits of laughter die out on his lips. "I'm not hitting on you. I promise I'm asking out of genuine curiosity."

I quirk up a brow, unconvinced.

"Honestly. I have a girl, you see."

"Oh!" I exclaim. "You do?"

"Yes, ma'am. We met a year ago while I was on a work trip to Philly. Her name is Ali. She's beautiful and funny and smart, and the one for me." He grins with those perfect teeth like a perfect fool, and I laugh because I've never seen someone be so openly sweet about someone they love. Other than—

I push the thought away. Throw it off a cliff and into a river to drown.

"You sound like a lucky guy," I say with a smirk.

"That, I am." He grins. "So, you see, Delilah, you have got nothing to worry about. Do you have a boy back home or not? This is going to be a long outing, and I'd prefer we skip the rest of the small talk." He's enthusiastic to the point of absurdity, but despite his questionable strategy, I do loosen up a little. The tension in my tired body is lessening.

"Are you on something?"

"You're not answering my question," he says, peering over at me. "Trouble in paradise, then?"

I go to my arsenal of one-liners to bring out during the trip. *Yes, he's stuck at work. Yes, I wish you could meet him, too—next time. He's sorry he can't make the trip.* But for whatever reason, being stuck in this car with this practical stranger, I feel the need to confess. I don't want to play pretend anymore. I'm exhausted, and it's only been a day or two. "It's complicated," I confess.

"So, there *is* a guy."

"There is a guy."

"And . . . ?"

"And . . . I don't want to get into it." I shrug.

He frowns. "That's disappointing."

"Is it, now?" I scoff.

"Well, yeah. I was hoping we could open up to each other and swap advice or whatever. I thought that would be a great way to make this car ride go quicker and—"

"I don't need advice," I interject.

"Well, good for you, Delilah. Glad your life is just fine and dandy and not complicated at all," he says sarcastically. "Did you stop for a minute to think that I, however, might be the one who could use some advice?"

My mouth presses into a thin line. "Then why don't you just ask for it?"

He rolls his eyes dramatically. "Well, typically when you have what is called a 'conversation' with someone, you ask questions and they answer, and then you build what is called 'rapport' before you jump right into something like asking for a favor."

"You don't seem to have issues with jumping into things," I mutter.

"Not sure I like that tone." Luca tilts his head toward me in mock chastisement.

I scoff at his audacity, my sleepless night eating away at any manners I should have when talking with a stranger. "I can't tell if you're just full of yourself or if you're mental."

"Some people would call my personality 'charming.'"

I nod slowly. "Full of yourself, then."

He smirks. "Did you consider the possibility that I am simply hilarious?"

"Wouldn't I be laughing if that were the case?"

"Depends on how bright you are." He turns to me with a quizzical look on his face. "My witty material may be too complex for you. Do you happen to know if you're of average intelligence? Or should I start to dumb down my material for you?"

Anger flares up inside my chest. "Did you consider the possibility that you're simply *rude*?"

"I have not," he says, "but I'll take it under advisement." Luca drums his thumbs against the steering wheel and makes an exaggerated thinking face. "Yeah, that's not it. I'm just a very funny guy."

"You sure are something," I scoff.

"You can't just say that."

"Sure I can."

Luca shakes his head definitively. "No, you can't just be *something*. You have to say the *something* that that someone is."

"Well, there just aren't enough words in the English vocabulary to describe you," I huff.

Luca grins and gives me a devilish look. "So what you're saying is, I've left you speechless?"

"What? No, that's not—"

"Delilah, calm down. I have plenty of experience dealing with these situations. You aren't the first, and you certainly won't be the last to endure these symptoms. Just take a few deep breaths with me. Come on, now—in through your nose, out through your mouth."

I just sit and stare at this guy for a moment before I shake my head and give up mentally. I'm pretty sure he's just being funny—or what *he* thinks passes for funny—but it's exhausting trying to have anything that even remotely resembles a conversation with this man. My coffee hasn't even had the chance to kick in, and I'm starving.

"What?" he asks after a beat of silence.

"I give up. You are impossible."

"You give up? On what, the conversation?" he exclaims. I nod, and he considers this. "I may be impossible, but I'd put money on it that all this time, you haven't thought about that boy situation back home that you so totally *don't* need any advice on."

I instinctively open my mouth to rebut whatever sentence has left his infuriating face, but unfortunately, I find that it's true. We've almost made it to our destination, and for the first time in days, my mind has not been on Bodhi. It's actually been quiet, all but for the annoying chatter coming from Luca.

I shake my head again and point ahead. "Take a left there," I sigh. I decide to let him keep that stupid smirk on his stupid face; I don't have the energy to attempt to discuss whether or not my mind has indeed been taken off of Bodhi. Then I would have to think about him.

I could *kill* Boss for making me chaperone this idiot to pick up the backdrop.

This is going to be a long couple of weeks if we need the truck for anything else.

CHAPTER TWENTY-TWO
AFTER

These walls have heard screams that only broken people can make. How intoxicating it must feel to contain such a thing. Deep within the paint, these cries of mine are held and kept secret from others. Not even the owner of these walls knows the exact pitch at which their echoes rang. My own two ears could not fathom what they sounded like, the sound distorted by muscle and bones. No, only these walls and this crack know what it sounded like when this young, naïve girl broke. When her world was ripped to shreds.

I stare at the wall and wonder if she will remember everything forever. If I am a permanent part of her story. I wonder if those screams will last for as long as the foundation stands. Would my silent agony die if the wood burned? Or would they live on as whispers in the ashes that drift off with the breeze? Would the pain scatter and taint the Earth with its haunted soot? Or would the memories cease to exist once I am no longer here to remember them?

I stare at the wall instead of remembering how it used to feel when his knee would bump into mine. I stare at the wall and ignore that there was a time when this simple act brought a warm color to my cheeks and stirred a soft, safe feeling in my chest. I stare at the wall and refuse to remember. Because remembering the what-wases or the what-could-have-beens is a solely destructive act.

He bumps his knee into mine as we sit side by side on this couch. I've become a shell of the girl he brought in here all that time ago. I know that he notices, but I don't know if he cares. The point of my being here, I once believed, was for him to hurt me. To watch me die from the inside out or torture me in more ways than I could fathom. But he doesn't gain any sort of gratification from this.

I now know I am here to be studied. It is the only explanation that fits. He observes my every blink and breath and dictates what they mean. But what is there left to watch?

I have unraveled and lost the parts of me that made up any real semblance of a person. I blink and breathe and eat. I am here, but that does not make me a person; it simply makes me someone who happens to be alive. They unplug people for less than this. I am a husk of someone who once was, barely going through the motions. And yet, miraculously, I am still here. He still allows me to be here.

My thoughts tend to lead in this pessimistic direction on day seven—the day I spend the most time with my captor. My version of Sunday is the day that I am expected to participate in some sort of activity that, in any other setting, would be normal. But here, it is just another angle at which I am tortured by the faint whisperings of what life used to be.

Board games remind me of Kayden throwing his last few bills of fake cash in my face. Puzzles remind me of my mother and father cowering over a thousand little pieces of a brilliant forest. Music, playing lightly in the background, reminds me of the notes that would seep through the walls while Collin perfected his technique. The shuffling of cards reminds me of the castle that Boss and I once built on a camping trip. It all reminds me of something, because it all used to mean something to the girl I was.

Today, I am reminded of a time when watching a movie with the person next to me was something I looked forward to. I'm reminded of the popcorn we'd throw into each other's mouths while waiting for the internet to start working again. The posters we'd pass as we walked into the theater and the stickiness of our shoes after we walked through the soda spills.

I'm reminded of watching a film not with my captor, but with my friend.

Now, we watch people and cars and animals dance against the wall. The small projector is all he brings in here. A television would be too difficult to transport in and out of the room, I imagine, and I am not permitted to have one installed—a wire could be confused for a noose, you see. Instead, like always, he has found a suitable substitution for this part of life. The miniature projector poses no threat. The bulb doesn't even heat to a temperature dangerous enough to cause anything more than a borderline first-degree burn. It emits a terribly fuzzy and deafeningly muffled sound that is always slightly behind the picture. The strain to make out the words is enough to give me a headache, and that's without ignoring every weak bone in my body quietly pleading with me to scoot even just an inch away from the man beside me.

I never do now. Not anymore. Whether it's self-preservation or a symptom of giving up, I do not know, but I've stopped. I no longer listen to that bit of hope that used to tell me to fight. I've learned there is no point. I understand now that whatever God exists wants me here. The universe didn't conspire against me. This isn't bad luck; this was simply the way my life was meant to be. I was meant to be kept tucked away. My life was never mine to live. I am not a part of something greater, only this harsh fate.

The movie drags time slowly along with a leash. Perhaps it would go quicker if I paid attention to the images projected instead of just the wall they are painted onto, but instead, I just think of the screams lost inside of it. This is when my thoughts are allowed to get a little darker. To roam just far enough to come back the moment that I call.

And I do just this when he shuts the projector off. He makes no move to leave and instead stares at me with a curiosity in his eyes that I don't often see. In the beginning, I remember clinging to this look. I thought maybe this was some part of humanity I could tap into and exploit to get me out of here. I was desperate then. I am more realistic now.

"You don't ask questions anymore," he states. I shrug in response, surprised I can even muster up the necessary care to do so. "Why not?"

It may have been an eternity before I spoke, but he waits perfectly, frozen, until my lips form a response. "I guess I don't see the point."

"Hmm," he muses, mulling something over in his head. Even monsters can think and ponder. I wish someone could go back and tell the girl who once was not to think much about this or try to find something human in it. "I'd like you to."

"I'm alright. Thanks," I spit without any real emotion.

"You will ask me questions," he insists. Something about his posture and the way he tilts his head should alarm me, but I no longer care. The way this man used to carry himself used to make me feel safe. Later, I feared it. Now I am indifferent. What could he do now other than put me out of my misery, saving me from this fate?

"Why?" I ask. "Why do you care?"

He tilts his head the other way. One soft strand of hair falls ever so slightly with the shift in its gravitational pull, and he narrows his two brilliant eyes at me. These things once made him beautiful, but now they only make him cruel. "I don't," he says. "I don't care."

"Then what? Are you getting bored?" I ask flatly. "Is it not enough to keep me locked away in here? Do you need to know every little thought in my head? There isn't much left that you don't already know."

He stares me down, and I can feel that this isn't the point he wants to make. I'm not sure if there even is one, but he is nothing if not meticulous and calculated. If he wants me to ask him questions, there is some twisted reason for it in his corrupt mind. He just may not care if I'm privy to it.

"You know how my mind works. You know *everything* about me. Why don't you just deduce the questions I supposedly have in this hollowed-out skull of mine and answer them yourself? Cut out me, the middleman, and get to the point. What do you need me for, anyway?"

The words leave my lips carelessly, and I realize I've just asked an awful lot of questions for someone who is insistent on not asking any at all. Rhetorical or not, this is what he wants.

"Why I need you doesn't matter. You just need to ask me questions when I'm here with you."

I scoff. "Like what?"

My visitor shrugs. "Whatever comes to mind. Whatever you think of. Even some of the things you've asked me before, if you'd like. The answers may differ."

"Why? Because they were lies before?" I ask. He stares emotionlessly at me, and I know that this is all the answer I will get. My eyes narrow into snakelike slits. "Are you asking me to get to know you again?"

"I only mean that you do not know me. You don't ask questions anymore, and you should."

"I . . . don't . . . know you?" I sound out. I repeat myself a couple of times before—for the first time since my life was truly stolen from me—I laugh.

Not once since my life was taken and squished to conform to the mold of these four walls has real, actual laughter escaped my lips. It's sick and messed up, it feels almost criminal, but it is real. I bend over and clutch my stomach, begging it to accept the air I'm barely taking in between the fits of twisted, demented giggles.

"*I don't know you,*" I laugh again. Tears prick my eyes, and my lips crack from the smile they haven't felt for eons. I laugh and I laugh and I see him staring at me, lifeless as ever, and it makes me laugh harder. For a moment, I think maybe I should stop—that maybe this is going to result in some punishment—but this only makes me spiral further.

After some indeterminable time, I calm down and let out a breath. He sits in the same position I left him in. It's seeing his face like that, empty, and feeling this utterly deranged bit of joy in me that illuminates the atrocity in his statement. It's infuriating, the thought that such a sentence could leave his lips and he would not find it amusing.

"Of course I don't know you," I sneer. "You were the person I trusted most in this world. You were someone I thought cared for me."

I don't choke on the words like I once did. The sadness that once plagued me is long gone. Now, if ever I feel at all, the only emotion I can conjure is anger. Misplaced as it may be, it is typically directed at myself. But somehow he has said what is perhaps the only thing that could shift that focus onto him.

"You were the person I wanted to have by my side for the *rest of my life*. Of course I don't know who you are. Why would I want to know you now?"

He shifts in his seat slightly, and I find myself almost hoping he hits me. Slaps me across the face or gives me a black eye. This would be so much easier, I think, if he would hurt me like that, though I know that is not true. That wouldn't make this more real. It is still happening now. I am breaking and hurting all the same, though it cannot be seen.

He gets up and collects the empty bottles near the door. I stay seated, silently watching his muscles move beneath his tight T-shirt. His arm flexes at something he's thinking and his eyes scan the room, looking for some sort of answer, perhaps. The door creaks open, but just before he leaves, he pauses. Looks me in the eye.

"One question," he says. It is not a question or a request. It's a statement. A demand said with nothing to back it other than the ominous threat of what he will do if I don't ask.

And for whatever reason, I do.

"You knew you were going to take me here one day." The cotton shirt feels tight across my chest, threatening to smother whatever life is left in these two lungs of mine. "But why did you take me when you did?"

He nods, and it makes me think that he knew this would be what I asked.

"I saw you getting close with him, being *friendly* with him, and I knew that it was time. You were getting too attached. I had to move when I did or I might have lost you."

I do not respond. I've given him what he asked, and now I just want him to leave. To let me and the wall and the paint sit in silence and decay.

"You got what you wanted," he says. My eyes drift to trace his outline, his broad back to me, and for a brief moment I can pretend he is who he used to be.

"And what is that?" I ask, giving him one final question.

"You get to spend the rest of your life by my side."

He shuts the door behind him, turning the lock inside the solid frame.

One last wry laugh leaves my lungs like a dying breath, because it's true. It seems I got my wish.

"I did, didn't I?" I say to no one but the wall, who now has heard the sick laughter only broken people make.

CHAPTER TWENTY-THREE

"You know, I'm getting real tired of this attitude of yours."

Unfortunately, we *have* needed the truck for a lot more than just the backdrop. It took only four hours after Luca dropped me off two days ago for Boss to send me on another errand that required his assistance, and today we've been out picking things up since seven o'clock this morning. It's been great, aside from the fact that I've been annoyed by his presence for pretty much every minute of it.

"I haven't even said anything," I mutter.

"Exactly my point. You've hardly tried to converse with me at all over the past 282 minutes." I lift a surprised and questioning brow at his words. "It's been four hours and forty-two minutes," he clarifies. My brow holds steady, and he merely shrugs in response. "You've given me a lot of time to do the math. You are missing the point, though—I've been patient. I think it's time you get to know me a little bit."

I scoff, "I didn't realize the word 'patient' even had a place in your vocabulary. I also *highly* doubt you are capable of being so."

Luca frowns. "Okay, and how would you know such a thing? You've been quiet all morning."

"Do you consider yourself a patient person?" I ask.

"No, not really," he responds matter-of-factly.

I throw my hands up in the air. "There. Happy?" My stomach emits a low growl that I ignore.

"No, Delilah, I am not *happy*. You know that isn't what I meant." The sarcasm in his voice irritates me in a way I know better than to acknowledge. We've already spent enough time together to let me know that this will *not* be the last last-minute errand we have to run together, and if I address the fact that his arrogant voice gets to me, there's no way I'll be able to sit in a car with him again without losing it.

If I weren't such a perfectionist when it comes to this wedding, I would let him run these errands by himself. I get the feeling, however, that if I let him pick up the sparkler machines and sparklers on his own, they'd be all used up before the wedding.

"You'd like me if you got to know me," he says before he laughs his stupid, hearty laugh. "Hell, we might even become friends!"

I let out a huff of humorless air, and he turns as much toward me in the passenger seat as he can while still maintaining focus on the road. "What?"

"I think it would be in our best mutual interest if we didn't speak. You know, so that we can remain civil," I say casually.

"Civil? I'd say we've been pretty civil."

My face lights up sardonically. "Ah, see? And we haven't spoken! Let's keep it that way."

"You see"—he points a finger at me—"*this* is the attitude I was referring to. It's tiring, Delilah. I'm sure you are exhausted pretending not to find all this," he says as he gestures to his whole self, "absolutely charming."

"Being around you is quite exhausting, yes." Honestly, I've never been an upfront person, let alone a rude one, but I can see through him. I find him completely cocky, so entirely smug, to the point where I question how Max can tolerate him enough to make him his best man.

Luca flips his blinker on and slows the vehicle at an upcoming turn.

"Whoa, what are you doing?" I ask. "We stay on this road for another eight miles." He ignores me and continues on his little detour. "Luca, are you listening to me? Get back on the road!"

He pulls into a small complex and parks the truck. Without acknowledging a single one of my protests, he gets out and shuts his door behind him. I sit stunned in my seat, confused by what's happening, and jump when my door opens unexpectedly. I didn't even see him walk around to my side.

"Luca. What are you doing?" I ask, staring at him. I'm not staying in this vehicle any longer than I have to. "Get back in the car. Let's go."

"Did you eat breakfast this morning?" he asks unexpectedly.

I sit back. "What?"

"Did you eat this morning before I picked you up?"

"No, but what does that h—" I begin to say before he steps back, holding the door open for me.

"Get out. I'm not talking to you until you've had something to eat. You're like a hangry old hag," he huffs.

My jaw drops, and my words nearly lash out and whip him with the anger contained in them. "You do *not* know me well enough to be talking to me like that."

"That's. My. Point." He bangs the side of his head softly against the door with each word. "Will you please just come and eat some street tacos? I promise they are heavenly—life-changing, even. Please."

I go to protest—I'd rather get going and check this task off my to-do list than extend this errand with a meal—but then I catch sight of the small restaurant sign and stop short. My stomach growls again, louder this time, at the sight of my favorite taco place. I used to come here every single Tuesday for about two years before we moved. Well, not this location, but this same chain. They'd do two tacos for a buck on Taco Tuesdays, and I would eat as many as I could. My record was twelve.

"Fine," I relent. "But we're making it quick." I don't tell him that I love this place and their tacos, or that I am, in fact, starving, my mouth watering just at the prospect of eating here. Somehow, that feels like letting him win. Getting out of the car already feels like defeat.

Luca bends his knees and fist pumps in the air, and I know he feels like he's just won as well. "Yes! We'll be quick, I promise."

He shuts the door behind me, and I just shake my head.

———————

"I can't believe this place does street tacos for fifty cents a piece on Tuesdays," Luca mumbles through a mouthful of chicken and tortillas. "This is incredible—I'm coming here more often."

I swallow the bite I'm currently chewing before speaking up. "I thought you'd been here before? You said the tacos here were heavenly," I say, echoing his earlier claim.

Luca shakes his head and waits until he quickly swallows to answer, and then stuffs his face once more. "Nah, I just said that hoping to get you in here. I pulled off at the first food place I spotted. I've spent enough time around toddlers to know when they're moody, you need to feed 'em." He shoots me a wink, and I roll my eyes. "Oh, come on, Delilah! You were acting childish. Admit it," he insists.

I fold my arms across my chest and sit back in my seat, but I realize this in itself is a childish act. Instead, I grab my taco and take another bite. "Whatever," I mutter.

Luca snickers to himself and downs another whole taco in

one bite, and we finish the meal in relative silence. Once we're back in the car, I pat my tight abdomen and sigh. "Well, that was delicious. I haven't been there in forever."

"So you've been before?" Luca asks.

I curse myself for some reason and shoot him a "Yeah" that lacks the spitfire my words possessed before, but out of pride, I try to still maintain some semblance of it. It's somehow embarrassing to admit that my irritation was not entirely caused by his presence and voice, but rather my forgetting to make time to eat something before he picked me up this morning.

"So . . ." Luca trails off. "Is it still in our 'best interest' to remain silent in each other's presence, or can we chitchat now?"

I let out a deep sigh. "Don't get used to this, because I won't be saying it again, but I'm sorry," I say a bit reluctantly, "for being rude earlier."

Luca nods as a slow, stupid, smug grin begins to spread across his face, and his shoulders give way to shakes of violent laughter—laughter so large, it takes over his whole body.

"What?" I demand, scrunching my brow.

It takes him a moment to stop laughing just enough to speak again. "I should have fed you something two days ago," he chuckles. "You're so much more pleasant when you've eaten." He goes back to laughing and I shake my head, fighting the grin that forms on my face.

"You're impossible," I sigh, my tone much gentler now without the venom it possessed pre-tacos.

Luca just laughs again and shakes his head, his messy mop of hair jumping around with each chuckle. "Ohhh, Delilah. I have a feeling you are just as stubborn as me."

"Now *that*," I say, "is the first funny thing you've said."

"Yeah." He grins a stupid lopsided grin. "That one may have been a stretch."

"Oh, one hundred percent," I laugh.

We both sit there lightly laughing for a little moment, and I don't entirely hate it. I don't hate it so much that it actually reminds me of laughing with Bodhi over stupid things, like the copy of *Twilight* that seems to keep traveling back and forth between the two of us. The memory flashes through my head like I hit the fast-forward button, but I know it so intimately that I see every breath and blink. Every eye roll and chuckle is etched perfectly in my mind.

"Delilah!" Bodhi calls from the car. He must have rolled down his window as I was walking up to the front door.

I turn and, as if looking at Bodhi simply results in such a thing, a smile grows ever so slowly on my face. The sweet, safe feeling I get when my brain registers the two of us are near spreads through my whole body, and when I walk back toward the car, it feels like I'm floating.

I lean down to the open window and tilt my head to the side, my soft curls tickling my upper arm. "Yes?" I sing.

"You forgot something." He turns around in his seat and searches the floorboard with his hand, and before I can remember what exactly he's searching for, he brings his arm back up with his find.

"No," I warn with a sternness that could not possibly be taken seriously with the smile still permanently pressed to my lips. "No, no, no."

"Yes," he says, holding it out to me. The book is only a few inches away. It would be so easy to take the pages tattooed with a story he cannot stand and put them on my shelf.

"Bodhi, you promised," I whine. The endearing look in his eyes seems to hold me here in this frame. I want to drag this moment out for as long as time allows and barter for even more of it. I could look into these green eyes for eternity. They are the exact hue of what this feeling inside me feels like.

"I promised to read it. I did. Now, the book is forever in my mind. I'll die with the beginnings of a far-fetched, awkward love story memorized. I did not, however, promise to keep the damn thing."

I wrap my fingers around the spine's edge and take it from his grasp with a long, exasperated sigh. "I guess you're right," I groan. I tilt my head the opposite way, giving him a teasing look, and Bodhi brushes away the curls that invade my face.

"I often am." He smirks.

I lean further into the car, and our lips meet through the smiles still spread across them. His hand that moves those mischievous curls back into place slides down to hold me at the nape of my neck. He kisses me softly, like he's savoring the moment too, like he's bartering with time for just a little bit more of her.

My heartbeat picks up, and I know his fingers feel this change in my pulse. It flips a switch in him. He suddenly becomes more eager for this moment, more eager for this touch. It's a feeling that you can't possibly understand how it exists until you just do.

Too soon, I pull away, knowing it's getting too late. These nights together seem to inch further and further into the late hours despite us both knowing there will be a tomorrow. Though we both know we'll see each other again, each parting is painful nonetheless.

He pulls me in for one more quick kiss and finally lets me go.

"Goodnight," he whispers with that love-drunk look in his eyes.

"Goodnight," I murmur with the same look in mine. I turn around and begin walking back to the front door when I hear his confusion at finding the book back on the passenger seat.

I wiggle my fingers goodbye at him, but before I can turn to keep walking, I see a devilish grin take over his face.

"Not so fast," he taunts. He opens his door, never breaking eye contact with me, and gets out.

"No, no," I laugh. "Don't even think about it. That book is yours—I got it for you." I step backward toward the house and hold up a finger to him, which does nothing to ward off his advances.

"Well, if you want to get technical about it, I purchased it."

"Still yours," I say, stepping closer to the house as he works his way toward me.

He laughs that laugh that makes me wonder if I've ever actually heard laughter before or if all the other times were just horrible imitations of this one. "Well, I'm gifting it back to you."

I put a hand to my chest and feign horror at what he's just said. "You're regifting something I gave you? That is so incredibly rude, Bodhi." He steps dangerously close, so I turn to dart toward the door. "Don't even think about it, Bo—ahh!" I scream as Bodhi wraps his arms around my waist and lifts me in the air as if I weigh nothing at all. He spins me around while I scream at him to put me down through fits of laughter.

"Never," he says even as he sets me down. I turn to face him, still inside the circle of his arms, and catch my breath a bit.

"You are impossible," I murmur up at him.

"Says the one who won't take this stupid book," he murmurs back. He leans down to meet my lips once more, and it feels like maybe time listened and gave us this moment to keep. Here with Bodhi, I've never felt so completely seen. I've never felt so *known*. Like I could never say anything to mess this up. Like he already knows everything. I don't question any of it.

He's simply mine, and I am simply his. Nothing has ever felt more right.

"Delilah?" Luca's soft voice rips me out of the memory.

I jerk my face to look at him, confused. I was just laughing with him. *What happened?*

"Yeah?"

"Are . . . are you alright?" he asks carefully.

"Of course I am," I claim, forcing a laugh, but I wonder if he can somehow see the memory of Bodhi still lingering in my gaze. "Why wouldn't I be?"

Luca stares at me for a moment and quickly looks back to

the road, and for the first time, I see some unselfish emotion in his eyes: concern. He says something so gently that the softness in his voice distracts me, and I can't register the words. I didn't know he could speak so kindly. I didn't know he could care about anyone else.

"Huh?" I question.

"You're . . . you're crying, Delilah."

I swipe my hand across my face, and sure enough, it comes back smeared with moisture. "Oh." I didn't feel the tears glide down my cheek and make their soft landings on the spot on my T-shirt that rests atop my collarbones.

Feeling bad for having made a scene in front of Luca, I force myself to laugh again, which only seems to deepen the pitiful look in his eyes.

"I'm sorry. I . . . I don't know what came over me. Sorry!" I try to wipe the rest of the tears away quickly, as if removing them will erase the embarrassment of letting my facade crack in front of someone.

"Don't apologize," Luca says. It's quiet for a moment before he hands me a napkin from the taco place. After I dab my cheeks and neck and blow my nose, he speaks again. "Do you . . . want to talk about it?"

I shake my head.

"Okay," he murmurs. "But you can. If you want to."

"Thanks." I lift the corner of my lips and give him a real smile—the first one since we met. We sit together in silence for a little bit. "Don't tell Boston, please," I add. "Or Max."

Luca looks at me with a curious glint in his eye, but mostly he just looks concerned.

"Please," I beg.

"Alright, I won't say a word. Cross my heart and hope to die." He smiles softly at me, and I shake my head at him, but I know he can tell I'm grateful for this kindness.

"Turn here."

CHAPTER TWENTY-FOUR

Even though we've been staying in the same house, I've hardly spent any real time with Boss. When I'm here, she's off meeting up with her photographer or grabbing lunch with her mother-in-law, and when she's home, I'm picking something up with Luca or—let's face it—avoiding her just enough to avoid a conversation with questions I don't want to answer.

So far, most of our conversations have been about the wedding, which is a relief. Bodhi has only come up twice, but both instances were in passing, like Boss listing off the people who will be at the dinner and what table to have them at. I've yet to mention that I haven't heard from or spoken to Bodhi since the day before I left to come here, and that saving him a seat at a table is likely a waste.

"Ugh," Boss groans, "I feel like I haven't sat down all day." She splays herself on the couch across from me and lifts her foot, wiggling her toes in my face. She juts out a pouty lip, trying to earn sympathy she won't be getting from me.

I push the sock-covered foot away with the pen in my hand. "I am not massaging your sweaty feet. That's what fiancés are for."

She drops her foot to the floor and groans. "But Max won't be here for another, like"—she glances at her phone—"ten minutes!"

"Ten minutes?!" I gasp, sarcasm lacing each syllable. "Well, had I known that—"

She holds her foot up again and I shove it playfully away, which only results in more dramatic groans.

"Hey," she says with more seriousness, "when does Bodhi fly in again?"

Well, so much for that.

I do my best to hide the way my whole body jolts at the mention of his name. It's the same feeling I had when I was ten and my mother asked me where the cookies she made for my school's bake sale went. The crumbs were still on my face, plain as day, and I knew I'd been caught.

"Oh," I respond, dragging out my words and stalling for time, "he's supposed to fly in on Thursday." Which isn't technically a lie. "He, uh . . ." I start before the familiar creak of the front door stops me.

"Max!" we both exclaim, and I hope they can't tell that I may be more enthusiastic about his arrival than Boss. I've never been so grateful for an interruption in all my life.

"Hey!" Max drops his gym bag to the floor and catches a jumping Boston in his arms. He gives her a sweet kiss hello and puts her down. I've seen her like this before, happy and in love, but there's something different seeing the two of them together now. They look at each other like they know forever isn't too far away. Like it's so close, they can taste it.

"Hello, Delilah," Max greets me when they finally tear themselves apart.

"Hello, Maxwell," I return. "Nice to see you again."

"You, too." Max walks over and gives me a quick hug. "Sorry I haven't been by to see you yet. How was your flight?"

We catch up for a little while, and it turns out that Max's side of the family has been a little crazy with the wedding getting closer. He's an only child and the youngest grandchild in the family, so apparently they've been going all out for the wedding, wanting everything to be perfect. So many unnecessary tasks have been undertaken by the Saunders clan, like having all of Max's outfits fitted, including clothing he's owned for quite some time already. He's had to meet with his mother to go over specifics for flower arrangements that are so detailed, I don't even understand the intricacies of it all.

"My mother is trying to import camellias for the wedding because there is supposedly a very significant difference between those and peonies, and peonies 'just simply won't do,'" Max imitates in a high-pitched posh voice that I assume resembles his mother's. "She keeps asking me if we would prefer the stems cut at forty-five-degree angles or if we want to request them to be cut at a steeper thirty-five-degree angle."

Max pauses, sitting in disbelief at his own story. "I keep telling her who the hell cares, but she's insisting I give her a real answer, and when I finally choose one, she gives me this disappointed look and *hmm*s to herself until I ask her what's bothering her, and then she tells me that 'it really would be better to request a steeper cut on the stems of the flowers because one of her friends' daughters did that at her wedding, and her arrangements held up oh-so-much better,' and then I—" He throws his hands up in the air and lets out a breath so full of annoyance, I can practically feel the steam of frustration roll off of him.

Boss bites her bottom lip, trying to suppress a smile, and I clear my throat to cover the short chuckle that I can't hold back.

Max's brows shoot up, and his voice grows stern. "This isn't funny, you guys. I don't know how much more I can take." With a look between us, he can tell we still find his plight amusing. "They altered a T-shirt I bought from the grocery store. The *grocery* store!" he exclaims.

And without meaning to, Boss and I burst out in laughter together. Max keeps trying to tell us it isn't funny and that we're acting like children, which only adds fuel to the fire. At some point, Boston rolls off of the couch and lies on the floor clutching her stomach, the both of us laughing so hard that no sound comes out. We sit there doubled over in slight pain, laughing silently, and I can only imagine how insane we look. Max is sure to tell us, though.

"Oh, babe, I'm sure they're just excited. Let them do whatever they want. Send them a couple of my clothes to alter while they're at it!" Boss jokes, but her smile falters when she sees the serious look on Max's face. "What?" she demands.

"Don't be mad . . ." Max looks to me but finds no reprieve. "But they had me bring over a few of your dresses and outfits for the party this weekend. They're in your room. My mother—"

"WHAT?!" Boss screams.

"—had them altered. I didn't—"

"Ohhh boy," I say quietly.

Max's words and mine both go unheard as Boss gets up and fervently makes her way to her bedroom. He turns to me, and I slowly shake my head. "You are so screwed."

He just groans.

I start laughing again, and Max throws one of the couch pillows at my head. "Stop!" I beg. "It's just—look, she was bound to explode sometime. I'm just glad it wasn't at me." Another throw pillow comes at my head, and I dodge it.

"I should . . . check on her." Max hesitantly gets up, but I motion for him to sit back down.

"She's stopped freaking out, so I'm guessing she's tried one on and doesn't hate how it looks. She'll be fine." I wave my hand dismissively and Max sits down without hesitation, grateful for the permission to not walk into the belly of the beast that is his fiancée's temper.

"You're probably right," he quickly agrees, but I think he's just happy not to have to go after her.

I laugh at him once more. After a few minutes, Boss comes

downstairs with a stone-cold look on her face. As Max looks to me, I can hear him yelling at me from inside his head that he shouldn't have listened to my advice.

She crosses her arms and glares at Max. "How did they get my measurements?"

"They called the seamstress altering your wedding dress to get them." Max shifts in his seat, and I do everything I can to not bust up laughing again at how nervous he looks answering his soon-to-be wife when she so clearly does not hate how the clothing turned out.

Boss nods slowly and walks over to plop herself onto the couch near him. She swivels in her spot and places both feet in his lap, wiggling her toes at him. "I'd like a foot rub," she deadpans.

Max immediately grabs her feet and starts massaging them without question. I make eye contact with Boss long enough for her to shoot me a wink and a sly little smirk. After a little bit, she clears her throat. "Okay, you're forgiven."

"So I can stop rubbing your feet?" Max asks.

"What? Nah-uh. No way, mister." Boss cozies into her spot on the couch and grabs the remote off the armrest. "But we can watch a movie while you do," she offers, grinning cheekily.

She flips the television on and goes straight to the news channel, telling us she wants to check the weather for the week and see what it'll be like for the bachelorette/bachelor party. Max tells her to use the app on her phone, but she insists the weatherman is more accurate. Both of us know that Boss just has a thing for the nightly weatherman, Jack Breeze.

"This guy is so dumb," Max grumbles. "His name isn't even real."

Jack moves swiftly across the television screen, pointing at various cold fronts and explaining wind patterns and whatnot. In all honesty, Jack and Max share a lot of physical traits. Their facial features aren't exactly alike, but they share some kind of echo—enough that it wouldn't be far-fetched for someone to point out that they share a resemblance, but not enough for them to be confused for one another while walking down the street. Jack's hair is neatly cut and parted to the side, whereas Max's hair is wavy and has grown out a bit more. They both have a very similar facial structure, but Max is rounder in the cheeks, and his eyes aren't as narrow as Jack's. Max also prefers a clean shave, but if he let the scruff grow out, they'd have that in common too.

I don't pay much attention to Jack otherwise until they show a seven-day forecast. It will be partly cloudy tomorrow, but the weekend will be sunny. *Perfect for the party.* I wait for Boss to change the input and put on a movie, but she doesn't move. When I ask if she's going to change the channel or what, she tells me to wait a minute.

"I want to see if they have any new updates on that missing girl."

"Missing girl?" I question.

Max nods at the television, now more interested in its content since his archnemesis's departure. "She got drunk at a college party a few nights ago and left early. She and her boyfriend got in an argument and she walked home by herself. It was only a five- or ten-minute walk, but her roommate said she never came home."

"A *ten-minute* walk. She was just down the street . . . it doesn't make any sense." Boss shivers in her seat.

"How awful," I murmur.

"Oh! Wait, this is it!" Boss grabs the remote and turns it up.

Two reporters sit at a table with their hands clutching the papers in front of them. They both face the camera, speaking about the case, but from the sounds of it, there isn't any new information. Their words are rehearsed, nonurgent. There's a dark-colored sedan that they're suspicious of, but that's it.

The two reporters rehash pretty much everything Max just said, showing a street view of the house where the party was held and the missing girl's apartment complex. Andy is her name. The reporters relay the information so professionally that it feels wrong, like they should be the ones relaying the weather forecast.

The photo onscreen changes from the apartment complex to one of Andy smiling brightly. Boss says something, but I can't hear her. My heart is pounding so hard, it's filling up the space in my ears.

"Delilah?" Boss asks, and I realize I must have gasped, but I don't remember doing it. My jaw hangs open as I stare at the girl's photo. Her blonde hair, cut just short enough to barely graze her shoulders, and her pretty face dappled in freckles tugs at some memory in my mind.

"What? Delilah, what is it? Do you know her?" Boss moves her feet off of Max and turns toward me.

"It's just—it's just—" I stammer, "it—she looks *exactly* like this girl who went missing in Arizona a couple of weeks ago, I . . . it's like looking at her twin, but she looks a little younger?" I try to take a deep breath. "I don't know, it's crazy, but I mean . . . look at this." I pull out my phone and type in Marcy's name, and in an instant the screen is filled with articles on her murder.

"She was *murdered*? Oh my—did they catch the guy who did it?" Boss's voice teeters on the edge of panic. I shake my head, and when I scroll down to show them her photo, they both let out a gasp of their own.

"They could be sisters," Max murmurs.

"They *have* to be related," muses Boss.

They both scroll through the article, reading each word like it's some kind of compulsion. Other than the girls' appearances and both being taken while they were walking home, they don't share any other commonalities.

Boss's eyes go wide. "That's insane."

"Crazy coincidence," Max says.

The two of them mull over how strange it is that these two girls share a similar face and possibly a similar fate, but in what feels like a blur, we're all sitting on the couch watching a movie. They move on so quickly, no longer bothered by the girls with the same faces, that I miss the part where we get over the unnerving feeling. I miss the part where we stop being so shaken up by this.

Their commonalities can't just stop at facial features and disap-pearances, I think. Not when they look *this* identical, separated only by age. I want to dismiss this as easily as Boss and Max have, but their blonde hair and brilliant smiles burn themselves into my retinas, and I rack my brain for a memory I don't know if it possesses. *Why do I know their faces?* And what about this familiarity unsettles me so completely?

I don't know how to explain this nagging pinch in my chest, telling me there's something else here. The same pinch I felt when Marcy's photograph flashed onscreen for the first time. Her smile haunted me in a way I was certain would stir up a memory, but it never did. I chalked the ghost up to some girl I may have seen in the coffee shop even though it never felt right. I wrote it off with some easy, convenient explanation though it never felt correct. Maybe I should have given the blonde girl they found in the canal a second thought.

What about Marcy makes me think we've met before?

The thoughts whirling around in my mind cause the evening to go by in a flash, and without even realizing it I'm suddenly in bed, drifting off to sleep with only an eagerness to remember keeping me company.

That night when I dream, I picture Andy in a wedding dress, watching me as I walk the streets of Salt Lake City. Every time I turn a corner, I see her on the other side of the street screaming without words, trying to tell me something. She jumps and silently yells, pointing behind me, but I just keep turning street corners without so much as a glance at what's coming for me.

CHAPTER TWENTY-FIVE
AFTER

This is the moment, I think. The moment it all makes sense. The moment it all comes together and everything before now adds up.

You seamlessly move around the kitchen, throwing together ingredients for this surprise meal you're putting together. Between the peppers you're cutting up, you check on the pot simmering on the stove, tossing your hair out of your face now and again. You need a trim, but you haven't let me cut it since the last time, and I don't blame you. There's a reason I don't cut hair for a living.

I offer to help, but you insist I have a seat and relax. You pour me a glass of red wine, and I curl up on the barstool to admire your work. A few shared glances and soft smiles keep us company while Frank Sinatra plays lightly in the background. I've asked about your day, and you mine, and now you let me watch as you dance around the kitchen, grabbing spices and adding food to the pan. I don't know what you're making, but I don't care. I just like watching you cook.

Even though it's only just after six, I've already gotten ready for bed. But I don't mind you seeing me like this: all undone. My loose sweats and matching long-sleeved shirt will be the same clothes I probably fall asleep in. I don't feel insecure when your eyes look over me. Your gaze is not one of judgment; it holds a fondness only you have ever been capable of showing me. I realize that this is the feeling I've been missing out on my whole life—no, it's the feeling I've been waiting for. The feeling I have been looking forward to my whole life.

I get off my stool and walk around the island to where you're still concocting some undoubtedly unbelievable meal and wrap my arms around you. My face presses into your strong back, and you relax at my touch, leaning into it. I close my eyes and breathe you in. The fabric softener and laundry detergent are faint after a long day at work, but it's still there, just barely overpowering your cologne still lodged permanently in my senses. I breathe in again, deeper, and memorize you: the feel of your muscles against my cheek, your woodsy scent. I memorize the sizzle of the pan and the sting of tears the cut onion brings to my eyes.

You turn around in my arms and wrap your own around me, forgetting for just a moment what you're doing. You take a deep breath, and I wonder if you can smell the conditioner from when I washed my hair this morning. I pull away and look into your pale, pale eyes until smiles slowly form simultaneously on both of our lips. The evening glow refracting through a vase filled with this week's flowers softens your features in my favorite way. You lean down, and our smiles meet one another. You kiss me so softly, so gently, it's like a whisper. Nothing else outside of this moment is loud enough to exist. We are just two people in love. You are just a boy, and I am just a girl in the kitchen. We've grown so much from the day we met, and still, we are here, together.

This is what happiness is, I think. This is what it is. This is what my life was always supposed to lead to. I was made to make it to this exact moment.

I throw up on the floor next to my bed.

I don't get up. I just lie there on the mattress facing the

vomit below, sobbing. I can't see much of anything through the tears. My vision is blurred from the memory of the dream. My body shakes from the feel of phantom limbs still holding me. Tears steadily stream down my face, and I know that if I weren't crying, I would be able to hear them collide when they meet the floor. It's so silent here.

This dream, although loosely based on reality, isn't real. We never experienced it, never got to that point. But I thought we might. I imagined it before when I would lie awake at night, dreaming what my life might look like five or ten years from then. He was in it. He was always there.

I cry out some inhuman sound and clutch at my chest. This kind of pain is new. It is jagged and sharp, and I can't breathe underneath the weight of it—the pain of what could have been. The pain of what I thought we would be. Who I thought I was. Who I thought you were.

I cry until my eyes are no longer shut from the agony, but from exhaustion. I cry until there is nothing left inside of me. I cry until I am empty and there is nothing left to feel. I haven't cried like this in what seems like years, decades, or eons, maybe, but I also haven't let myself remember the before. I haven't allowed my thoughts to drift to what our life used to be like. I haven't allowed him to be anyone but the villain in my story. Because it's only when I remember that he was not always so cruel that I break all over again.

"It's not real," I tell myself in a scratchy whisper when the image of us smiling in the kitchen flashes in my brain. "It wasn't real. It's not real. It isn't real."

I leave the lights off and grab the chemicals from the bathroom. I don't want him to find out I'm awake, though he probably already knows. He always knows.

The mess is quick to clean. I am thankful my hair was in a braid so I don't have to wash that as well. I just need sleep, I think, but the thought of seeing a version of him that I don't hate again keeps me from rushing too quickly.

I tie the garbage sack shut, hoping to staunch some of the odor. When I go to place it near the door, my gaze snags on the small rectangular window. "Useless," I whisper to it. I place the cleaner back in its spot and curl into myself on the mattress.

I haven't felt this spent in so long. There isn't much to physically drain me in this room. I can't exactly go for a jog, and I see no real benefit in doing jumping jacks. But emotionally? Every day would be this taxing if I didn't block it all out. If I didn't wake up every day and force my mind to be elsewhere, to think of nothing, I would never make it off this bed. But I can't force my mind to veer away from the not-so-ugly thoughts of him while I sleep. I can't make myself forget then.

How long can a person survive like this? Theoretically, I could live like this forever, I suppose. I have everything I strictly need to keep breathing. But how long can I *survive*? Before I give up?

One day, I will become so weary with this new life that I'll stop going through the motions. And then what will he do with me?

I look to the crack in the wall and hold back the bile threatening to come up once again.

If I don't get out of here soon, I may just find out. But there is no way to leave. Not one that I can find.

I would need a miracle, and I haven't believed in those for a very long time, if I ever did.

CHAPTER TWENTY-SIX

I use a set of keys to cut through the tape of the third package to arrive this morning. Although I was cutting it close ordering playing cards from China and then sending them off to some lady from Etsy to customize them, these thankfully made it in time.

Once the box is opened, I pull out a deck of cards and splay them out in my fingers. All of them have been refinished in the wedding colors with the party's theme, "All In," printed on the back. The face cards were replaced with Boss's and Max's faces, and the aces have been swapped with mildly inappropriate cartoonish body parts instead of the traditional spades, clubs, hearts, or diamonds. I hand the deck over to Luca, who, as usual, won't leave me alone.

"I've been stressfully planning this for months," I say. "Just show up and I'll let you take some of the credit."

He holds up one of the explicit cards like a piece of moldy cheese. "No one in their right mind will believe I had anything to do with this."

"Not my problem." I begin to repack the box, and Luca sighs rather loudly. The more time I spend with him, the more sarcasm I pick up on in his dramatic antics.

"Delilah, please, I am quite literally begging you. I can't have done *nothing* for the party. I'll be the worst best man there ever was!"

"I told you, you could help bring everything to the Airbnb."

Luca rolls his eyes. "That is hardly contributing."

"Well . . ." I shrug. "I've already got everything else covered. What did you expect would need to be done"—I peek at the time—"four hours before we need to leave?"

"There's always something that needs to be done."

"I've made the list and checked it twice." I gesture at the boxes organized before us.

"How very St. Nick of you," Luca grumbles. "What about food?"

I point to the two coolers behind him while I go over my list one final time.

"There is no way you have *everything*. There's something you've forgotten, I'm sure of it." Luca snatches the paper out of my hand. I try to retrieve the list, but he holds me back with one hand and extends the other out of my reach.

"Cards, poker chips, tables, tablecloths, decorations," he mumbles as he reads. "Holy—do you have *every* decoration listed in a subcategory below 'Decorations'?" He turns slowly to give me a bewildered look. I sneer back at him and try to use this distraction as a segue to get my list back, but he keeps his hand out of my reach and continues reading it off. "Cookies, chips—"

"I swear if you rip that, Luca—"

"—scotch-a-roos, whatever those are. Oh—hey, look, you listed . . ." He mumbles as he counts, "Eight, nine, ten different kinds of drinks." Luca turns to look at me, one brow raised. "Delilah, why the hell do you have *ten* different kinds of beverages listed?"

"That's how many we need."

"For *two days*?" He lets out an exasperated sigh as I nod, which seems to loosen his muscles enough to bring me slightly closer to the list in his hand. "I'm pretty sure if you had two different kinds of soda and water, that would be plenty," he says, moving just close enough for me to snatch the paper back.

"We need ten," I state firmly.

"Uh-huh." Luca walks over to the coolers and peeks into both of them. "This is all the fridge and freezer stuff?"

"Yes." I shut the lids. "And I would appreciate it if you didn't let the food spoil before we've even had a chance to get there."

Luca nods and pulls his lips together in amusement.

"What?" I grumble, annoyed.

"Oh, nothing. It's just that I found something you forgot on your list."

My heart drops for a millisecond before I remember that that is entirely impossible with how much preparation I've put into planning this. "You're lying."

"Am not."

I cross my arms and narrow my eyes at him. "Okay, I'll bite. What could I have possibly forgotten?"

Luca takes two steps toward me and places one finger down on the paper, pointing at something that isn't there. "Ice."

"What? No, there's—" I go to point it out on the list under the Food category and realize he's right—it's not on there. I remember thinking we would just grab it on the way there, but I didn't write it down. Without the reminder, I likely would have forgotten.

I shake my head at myself. "I'll just grab it on the way—"

Luca steps back as if I've just personally offended him. "Um, no. *I'll* be grabbing the ice."

"It's no trouble, I'll just grab it real quick."

"Delilah, please." Luca gets down on his knees, clasps his hands together, and contorts his face to form the most pathetic pleading look I have ever seen. I can't help but let out a semi-shocked laugh at the picture before me.

"Now *this* is quite literally begging me to let you do something," I laugh.

His tone is grave. "Woman, I beg of you: let me grab the ice for this party tonight."

I roll my eyes and Luca grins, knowing that I'm about to cave. "Fine. You can get the ice. Geez . . . now get up. You're embarrassing yourself."

Luca's cheeky grin stays plastered on his face as he hops up off the floor and fist pumps in victory.

"Oh my. You'd think you just won Super Bowl tickets," I deadpan.

"This is better than the Super Bowl, Delilah! Actually, this is *my* Super Bowl. Without this ice, I would have contributed nothing to this party. I needed this." Luca's hand shoots up to his forehead in a salute. "Delilah, I promise I will not let you down."

"Oh, I have complete and total faith you won't screw the ice up, Luca. I'm convinced even you can handle this," I reply with a smirk.

Luca shakes his head, unable to believe that I'm trusting him with such a task, it would seem. "Everyone is going to talk about the ice. Just wait!"

"Sure," I say cautiously before going back to checking things off my list and packing up the custom playing cards. "I do need you to bring up some of these in your truck, though. The tables, for sure, and the bigger totes. I think I can bring up the rest in the car."

"Anything you need," he beams. I look at the pride oozing out of his every pore and give him a look halfway between disgust and concern. If he truly wanted to help with the party, he would have probably offered before now. But for some reason, helping with these two small tasks seems to have him overjoyed.

"Ooookay," I say slowly. With that, I help him put the poker tables and totes into the back of the truck, and we end up having enough room for some of the other boxes too. Luca leaves to grab his bag with his clothes and whatnot—and probably research the best ice or something—and I sit down to decompress after the exhausting encounter.

Although he's not as aggravating as before, he's still . . . a lot. I feel rude for thinking it, but I'm excited for the wedding to be over just so I don't have to hang out with someone who's constantly running on what has to be the product of several energy drinks. *Once the wedding is over, everything will be fine. I'll be headed back home and—*

I'll be headed back to Arizona, and what? Calling Bodhi? Or wallowing because there isn't anything left to distract me?

I pick up my phone and tap on his name in my text messages. It's been six days since he texted me anything. Six days since I last saw him. And every day since, I've tapped his name a thousand times, hoping to find something that isn't there. A message, a missed call, anything. Instead, I find nothing.

It feels like a slap in the face every single time.

The total lack of acknowledgment almost hurts more than the act itself. It would almost be better to be back in that room with him, being yelled at, than to exist in this nothingness. At least when I was in that room, I could pretend that there might be an apology to follow. That he might have felt sorry. At least in that room, there were words.

I wipe the tears from my cheeks, knowing that for a while, there won't be anyone else to wipe them, and get up from the seat that holds both the memory of my grieving and of me picking myself back up.

Today, I will be strong. Today, I will be a version of myself that doesn't know what it's like to be the version I have become. Tomorrow I will do the same, and the next day, and the day after that. I'll be this person for everyone around me until I'm alone again and the thoughts of losing someone can no longer be pushed aside. I'll be this person until I can make it home.

The only way I'll get through this without taking away from Boston is to pretend. So, I'll pretend.

I'll convince everyone I'm fine, and hopefully do it so well that I even convince a part of myself for a little bit. I'll find excuses for why Bodhi isn't coming anymore, and I'll pretend to be bummed about that instead of barely being able to hold it together. I'll tell everyone the things they want to hear and leave out the details I have to keep to myself. Because if someone asks me something and I let myself think too much about how the color green now makes me feel a bit sick if it reminds me of his eyes, I'll probably spiral, and that wouldn't be fair.

This trip isn't about me, so I won't feel any of it. Won't think about any of it. I'll just keep thinking about this wedding, making more lists than needed, and checking off all the boxes while this, at least, is still in my control.

CHAPTER TWENTY-SEVEN

I have officially outdone myself. Every single detail in this room came to be from my mind and my mind alone, and each one simply magnifies and complements the last. Our casino night is in full swing, and if it wasn't for the windows, random furniture, the smaller space, and the lack of cigarette smoke in the air, this could be mistaken for a little slice of Vegas.

Two poker tables are set up in the dining room: Texas Hold'em and blackjack. Behind them dealing out the cards are two of Boss's cousins, who spent some time dealing in Wendover—although they don't discuss that period of their lives, for some reason. But despite their shady past, it cut out the cost of having to hire someone to deal cards for the night.

One of Max's father's pastimes happens to be collecting old-school video game machines, and he just so happened to have a tabletop slot machine for us to use as well. He insisted it be used solely as a decoration to maintain its monetary value, and we've been keeping to that promise tonight; it's plugged in, but only to show off its flashy bright lights. Everyone has just been taking selfies with it instead.

The theme of "All In" has been incorporated throughout the

room. Flashy neon signs I found online are hung with Command strips on the walls, and in the kitchen are desserts with fondant and frostings spelling it out as well.

"I love your dress, Delilah!"

I turn to the shrill voice of one of Boston's work friends. For some reason, I can never remember if her name is Emma or Gemma, which makes things extremely awkward with how much she uses my name in conversation. I typically try to steer clear of her, but I knew it would be impossible tonight. We've hung out a handful of times on occasions where Boss has invited both of us—birthday parties and dinners, mainly—and each time, she finds her way over to me.

Gemma—whose name may or may not have a *G* in it— has the kind of nasal, high-pitched tone in her voice that typically accompanies an unauthentic compliment. She's pretty and can be kind, but she's also insanely jealous—to the point that it's obvious to practical strangers, including me. I'm nice to her because we don't have to see each other often, but it makes me wonder how she ever became friends with Boston.

"Thank you! You look absolutely stunning yourself," I say in a tone much kinder than her own.

Tonight's event has a formal dress code, and most of the girls opted for fancy cocktail dresses, myself included. I chose a simple black skin-tight dress. Emma, however—or Gemma— opted for a fuchsia floor-length gown with an obscene amount of itty-bitty ruffles. The sparkles that infect the gown seem to have been spritzed on with body glitter; they're unevenly distributed across the fabric and highly condensed in some areas. She's even left a snail trail of it behind her. Two large ruffles strap themselves around her shoulders and hold the heart neckline against her chest. I don't know if she already had the gown in her closet, but she's the kind of person who regularly wears statement-type outfits like this. Even with everyone else dressed up, she stands out.

Her little compliment means a lot less now with that smug look on her face.

"You did *amazing* on this party, Delilah . . ." she speaks in that fake voice of hers and leaves the end of her sentence unfinished. Her gaze flits around the room judgmentally, and I ignore the part of me growing increasingly vexed by her presence, telling myself to give her the benefit of the doubt.

"Thank you," I say tentatively.

"Especially when you consider the budget you must have been working with. You are a *miracle* worker, Delilah."

I open and then shut my mouth, unsure if that backhanded compliment actually just came out of her mouth or if she really meant it condescendingly. I wait for her to laugh or say something else, but she just blinks at me with seemingly innocent eyes and waits for a response. I don't need her to tell me that she wants to start some kind of petty bickering match with me. Without her saying a thing, I know she wants to upset me and cause a scene to knock me down a few pegs with Boss. She's the kind of person who thinks doing so will bring her up a few notches in return.

Whatever anger she stirred up in me dissipates. Instead, I just feel sorry for her. I can't imagine being so jealous of someone that I would try to tear them down to bring myself up like that.

"You're so sweet," I respond with the best smile I can muster. "I better go make the rounds and, you know, check on things and make sure everything is holding up with that budget of mine." I wink. "But it was nice talking to you for a second! Make sure you fill out one of the keno cards. We'll be playing that shortly." I leave without another word, and though I probably could have done without the budget comment, it was satisfying to let myself be a little petty.

As I turn, I catch a glimpse of her face filling with angry heat and hightail it out of there.

Other than Gemma, I don't know many of the other girls.

There are ten bridesmaids in total, and most of them are people Boss met during parts of her life I wasn't involved in, like college or her after-school sports. While she was kicking around a soccer ball with some of these girls, I was studying for a physics test. Other than passing in the hallways and maybe a hello or two here and there, these girls and I have not spoken. I recognize two of the groomsmen from Max's social media posts, but excluding Luca, the other seven are strangers.

The twenty-one of us pack the room up quite nicely. A few people crowd in the kitchen, talking with Max. One of the bridesmaids—I think her name is Katy—enthusiastically throws her arms around in the air as she tells a story to the group. They laugh, and some throw their hands over their mouths in shock at what she's said. Max rolls his eyes and shakes his head, laughing alongside them. I would imagine the story is about him in some way, and I wonder how Katy knows Max.

As I make my way around the room, I check in on the poker tables and collect a few discarded glasses. People tell me in a much more genuine way than Gemma that they love the party, but what no one can seem to shut up about are the stupid ice cubes. One person playing poker next to Luca even grabbed me by the arm earlier to tell me she had never seen anything so perfect in her life and how genius I was for adding that perfect touch.

Had I been given the chance, I would've redirected the credit to its rightful owner, but Luca was quick to rectify the false claim. "That was all me," he said with no hesitation, "and they *do* bring the whole party together, don't they?" Somehow, he had managed to finesse *dice*-shaped ice cubes. I had legitimately never seen anything like them before and have no idea how he managed to get them with less than four hours' notice. I would've asked, but there was no opportunity between all his boasting about it.

After completing my rounds, I take the glasses I've collected to the kitchen. Max's group has now left to crowd around the Texas Hold'em table, where Luca, Max, and one of Boss's friends stare each other down with their best poker faces.

I take a deep breath and use the space to relax a little bit. The party is going incredibly, despite Gemma–Emma's comments. Everyone is laughing and having a good time, the food turned out delicious, and the games are in full swing. Nothing is out of place, yet I still feel the need to be doing something, to keep busy somehow. My hands feel naked.

I start rinsing out the glasses and fill one side of the sink with hot soapy water. There are already a bunch of other dishes in here, so I start to work on those as well. I'm about halfway through when I hear someone come up behind me.

"What are you doing, D?"

Boss sits back against the counter, folding her arms over her chest. The short veil attached to her headband fans perfectly around her face, framing it like a piece of art. Without her makeup, she's gorgeous, but with it, she is something to be envied. I can see it in most of the girls' faces when they're near her. Their smiles and laughs and attempts at friendship are clipped, almost fraudulent, and yet someone as pretty as Boss is also too kind to cut ties.

I hold up a wet dish. "I feel like that's kind of obvious."

"Why aren't you enjoying the party?" she whines, moving over to lean against the counter next to me. "Now is when you get to enjoy your hard work." She bumps her hip into mine and wiggles her brows. "Come on, let's go play some poker."

I laugh, "You just want me to play so you can take all my money."

"Guilty!" she playfully confesses.

I muster a laugh but keep scrubbing the glass in my hands.

"Seriously, though, you should come enjoy the party," she says earnestly. "I think these can wait."

I keep scrubbing, the naked feeling in my hands still there, even when they're submerged in the scalding water, doing something productive. This task is not enough to keep my mind from reminding me of the things I'm supposed to forget. Being around everyone without a constant list of things I'm doing or planning on doing isn't something I can handle right now. "I'd rather get it out of the way," I explain with all the fake cheer I can manage, keeping my focus on the dish. I think I've scrubbed this same one twice now.

In my peripheral, I see Boss almost say something but stop herself. She watches me for a moment, taking in what she can before she decides to speak up again.

"Is everything alright?"

I let my hands and the soapy dish dip into the water and face her, confusion etching my face. She'll think I'm confused because nothing is wrong. She'll think I'm confused because I didn't see this question coming. She won't know it's because I'm wondering if somehow I let how I'm feeling slip through the cracks.

I want to mess up and tell her everything. She's the one person I should tell, but I don't want a bit of this trip to be about me. All of this time should be spent celebrating her and her soon-to-be husband. She'll kill me for it later, but I have to keep this to myself until after the wedding.

So, despite every instinct telling me not to, I lie.

"Yes," I tentatively say, "why wouldn't it be?" I put just enough of a lilt in my voice to convince her that the smile tugging at my lips isn't fake. I sound just humored enough by her question that for a moment I, too, believe nothing is amiss.

She tilts her head ever so slightly, confused for a moment before she brushes away the thought and returns the smile. "Never mind."

I bump her hip with mine and nod toward the party in the other room. "Get back in there and have some fun! I'll be in to kick your ass in a minute." I wink, and she immediately laughs because if there's anyone who's worse at lying than Boss, it's me.

She starts to walk away but turns quickly to face me again. "Oh. My. Gosh," she exaggerates. "I forgot to mention, these ice cubes?" She grabs the dice-shaped ice in the bucket next to her and drops her jaw in awe. Of course, the one thing I didn't provide for the party is all that anyone can seem to talk about.

"You should go tell Luca you love them. He's the one who brought them," I say in the verbal equivalent of an eye roll.

"He is?" she says, shocked.

"I'm surprised you haven't heard; he can't seem to shut up about them. He's been bragging all night to anyone that will listen." I move to grab another dish but stop short, the thought bugging me. "You know, you should have warned me," I say.

"About what?"

"That he is, like, a total narcissist! The guy is so full of himself, it's exhausting. What is his deal?"

Boss smiles in the way she does when she agrees with me on something. "Yeah, he can be a lot sometimes, can't he?" She pauses for a moment, thinking. "But he grows on you."

"How?" I nearly exclaim. *I seriously doubt that.*

She shrugs. "He can actually be really sweet, sometimes." I scoff, and she continues with a laugh, "No, really! You just have to get to know him better."

I tilt my head, and she holds her hands up in surrender.

"I'll try," I say, "but we might already be past that point."

Her brows knit together. "What do you mean?"

"Well," I explain, "I kind of told him he's exhausting to be around and that he should just shut up when he's around me."

Boss's jaw drops anew. "You did not."

I pinch my lips and shrug. First, her shoulders begin to shake, and then the rest of her body follows. She doubles over, howling much too loudly, and I try to shush her before someone overhears. I whack her with my still-soapy hand, telling her it's not that funny, which only seems to encourage her. I'm so busy trying to get her to knock it off that I don't hear the two girls approaching us.

"There you are!" one cheers. "We've been looking everywhere for you!"

"Hurry! They just went all in!"

The two girls drag Boston up, but before she leaves the room, she points a mischievous finger my way. "We'll be talking more about this later," she says through giggles.

I roll my eyes and turn back to the sink. Boss bursts out in another bout of laughter as they go, and I just shake my head.

"Talking about what?"

I jump at the sound of an unexpected voice. The spoon in my hands slips and lands in the sink, splashing my face with water and making me jump again.

I whip around to see Luca standing behind me, having just walked into the room. "What the hell, Luca! Where did you come from?"

"What was so funny?" he asks, his face alight with playful curiosity, like he already suspects he was the subject of our conversation.

"What? Nothing, just—" I heave out an exasperated sigh and start over. "Why aren't you out there watching the crazy poker game going on out there?"

Luca shrugs and comes to stand where Boss was just moments before. "Maddie has a royal flush. Max is lucky his folks are loaded or he'd be in a lot of trouble with the missus." He chuckles before he takes in what I'm doing. "And why aren't *you* out there?" he asks. "Can't these dishes, like, I don't know, wait?"

I shrug. "I'd just rather get them done now."

Luca pulls his eyebrows together, confused, and puts on a face of mock pain. "How can you say that when you know you would get to hang out with *me*? You're missing out, you know. I'm the life of the actual party."

"So I hear," I say. "You went above and beyond with the ice cubes, by the way—"

"*Dice* cubes," he interrupts.

I drop my hands against the lip of the sink and raise my brow at him.

"The people have spoken, and we must give them what they want, Delilah. 'Dice cubes' are their preferred term for what the masses are calling 'the most perfect ice on Earth.'"

I shake my head and swap the clean dish in my hands for a dirty one. "How'd you get those in time, anyway? You had, like, what, three hours before we left?"

Luca shrugs. "Maybe I'm just that good."

I shoot him a stern glare.

He relents and looks away from me, almost shy, and explains, "If you must know, I asked Boston to sneak me a picture of your party list so I could try to find something to help with. I noticed you didn't have ice on there, so I found these ice trays online and have been making them all week."

"You what?" I ask, my brows raised in disbelief.

"I know, I should have respected your privacy or whatever, and I'm sorry, but Boston said you've had this whole thing planned out for weeks now, and I just wanted to help." Luca digs the toe of his shoe into the hardwood floor. His hands conceal themselves in his pockets, and his shoulders drag themselves up toward his ears. He peeks up at me, checking to gauge my reaction, and there's no possible way he can correctly interpret the stunned look on my face right now.

It's as though I'm seeing a whole new person. Where once there was a jerk whose shrugs were conjured from a place of entitlement now stands the sweetheart Boss just described to me. It's like the fog has lifted, and suddenly I can see Luca in a better light.

"So, are you going to give me a hard time for interfering with your party or what?" he finally asks. His eyes squint in a teasing tilt, and I smile at the warmth that fills me at the degree of them.

"No, that was . . . that was very thoughtful," I say softly. "Thank you, Luca."

He simply huffs in response, dismissing any of the kindness I'm giving him credit for, but he softens too. His lips can't help but turn up at the edges, and he relaxes at a nearly imperceptible level. Luca steps closer and saddles up next to me with a hand outstretched. "You wash, I'll dry."

"What?" I say, taken aback. "No, go gamble or whatever! Go have fun. Enjoy the dice cubes before they melt."

"No offense, Delilah, but I'm not offering to help you out of the goodness in my heart."

"You're not?"

"Nope." He shakes his head. "I'm being entirely selfish. If I have to have another conversation with that one bridesmaid— Gemma? Emma? I don't know, whatever her name is—I'll actually start banging my head into the wall. You'd be doing me a real service."

I let out a surprising laugh and cover my face with my hand to try and contain it, but all that is effective in doing is splashing soapy water onto my face.

Luca laughs, "See, I *knew* I wasn't the only one to find her god-awful!"

"Luca!" I yell in a hushed tone. "Someone is going to hear you!"

"Oh, if only we'd be so lucky," he sighs. I slap his arm, and he ignores the splotch of water now seeping into his sleeve. "Maybe then she'd stop not-so-subtly suggesting that my dice cubes are tacky. Those things are incredible, and I will not stand for this kind of slander."

I throw my head back as I cackle, and for the first time since getting here, I've forgotten what it was that forced this feeling to the back of my mind in the first place. I forgot what it felt like to laugh wholeheartedly with a friend without one half of me fixated on another train of thought.

I laugh, and the crinkles near my eyes don't feel so foreign anymore.

CHAPTER TWENTY-EIGHT

The weekend goes by quicker than it has any right to. With last night's laughter still ringing in my ears and the smile creases in my makeup, it's evident as to why.

Once Luca finally dragged me into the other room and got me to stop walking around like a busy host, I actually did enjoy the party I put together after months of meticulous planning. For the first time since the day I arrived, I was able to spend more than thirty minutes with Boss. I won a game of Texas Hold'em, which was completely by accident—had I known I had a half-decent hand, my terrible poker face would have instantly let the rest of the table know.

I enjoyed the evening more than I might've deserved. But for a moment, it was nice to forget. Nice to let go of everything else and not feel like I was pretending. Nice to not scratch the itch of checking my phone every ten seconds.

When I got up early this morning to start cleaning, I found Luca already walking around picking up trash. With the two of us, we had everything spotless and put away in time to have breakfast made for everyone before they woke up.

I ended up riding back to Boss's place with him because— and I know her name for certain now—*Gemma* was trying to weasel her way into the passenger seat of his car, and he told her I was already riding back with him. Her pouty lip was so childish, I saw Luca forcing himself to not roll his eyes.

The ride back was quieter. We were both tired from the late night and early morning, so his usual enthusiastic way of deflecting was watered down. For the first time, I had a conversation with a much more amiable version of Luca. He was surprisingly open about anything I asked. I found out he runs his father's nonprofit for homeless veterans. He took it over after his father passed, and it was on one of his many work trips that he met Ali.

Luca had seen her walk by the window of the restaurant where he and a client were getting lunch, and he immediately left to catch up to her. He said he saw her confidence in the way she walked and had never seen anyone so captivating. In his own words, he was entranced. Somehow, he convinced her to meet him for dinner, and then somehow convinced her to meet him for breakfast the next day, and then to check out a museum after. After that, they never stopped talking. He flies out any chance he gets to visit her in Texas, where she lives now, and she does the same.

He mentioned he was very close with his parents growing up because he was an only child. He told me about traveling around the country and how he had been to almost all of the states. Three, including Arizona, were still unexplored by him. Outside of the US, he had only been to Canada. I found out that he used to ski every winter, but once he got older and took on more responsibilities at his father's foundation, he didn't have the time anymore. Instead, he resorts to watching competitive skiing in hotel rooms while he travels. I also found out he hates rollercoasters and is scared of the ocean.

I told him about my brothers, how Collin's in a band and how Kaden is incredibly smart. I told him about my parents, how my mother bakes too much and my father loves movies. I told him how close we all are. I told him about my life in

Arizona and how it's different than my life here. I found myself just unguarded enough to tell him about Bodhi, but I didn't tell him anything other than the fact that he exists. He let his unspoken questions weigh down the air around us but never gave voice to them, which I was extremely grateful for.

We talked openly like this until he dropped me off at Boston's. Together, we unloaded the tables and boxes, and once he left I flung myself onto my bed, where sleep overcame me so quickly, I didn't remember the part where you start to drift.

We talk just as openly now, riding in his truck again.

With Boss and Max both at work, the last-minute errands I'm in charge of have somehow also fallen onto Luca. He doesn't mind, though, as he took off work for the wedding. The two of us manage to get most everything checked off of my to-do list quicker than expected, and now we only have the groomsmen's and Max's ties left to pick up.

Luca made sure to grab some fast food before we began, so we pick at the French fries sitting between us on the middle console as he drives.

"Is Ali coming up for the wedding?" I ask.

Luca simply shakes his head until he swallows his mouthful of fries. "No, I wish. But she has a friend's wedding the same day." He shrugs. "We'll see each other next week, though."

"That's too bad. I would have loved to meet her."

"She would like you."

"You think so?" I ask, smiling warmly.

"Oh, yeah. She gets super ornery when she skips meals, too," he teases. I slap his arm. Luca simply chuckles, finding himself once again the most hilarious person in the room. "Seriously, though, I think you would like her. I most definitely am biased, but she's probably the best person I have ever known."

Luca looks over at me then, and my lips can't help but pull together in a similar soft smile, because I can see in his eyes how much he loves this girl. It's something straight out of a movie, the way I can feel how his every atom is drawn to loving her. It feels so sweet to be near someone who radiates so much emotion for another person, so much that you can sense it without them saying a word.

"Aw, Luca," I say, placing a hand gently on his arm in the same place I slapped him. "I had no idea you were such a softy."

"Okay, *way* over the line," he says jokingly, shrugging my hand off of him. I laugh while he parks in one of the stalls at the mall. "Get off your butt, you meanie head. We have things to do."

We grab the ties with no complications and decide we have time to grab some cinnamon pretzel bites on the way out. Eleven ties in the bag, all the perfect shade of baby blue, are kept as far away as possible from the sugar that falls from the doughy bits of heaven as we walk back to the car.

"Thank heavens Boston has had to work so much this past week," Luca says. "I would be bored out of my *mind* without all of these fun little errands."

"Ah, yes, who doesn't love picking up bulk orders of ties?" I say, my words laced with sarcasm.

"They do come with pretzels," he points out.

"Good point," I agree.

Luca pops another bite into his mouth and talks through his chewing. "Is that everything on your list?"

I pull out the paper from my pocket with my hand not covered in cinnamon sugar and look it over, scanning each written letter to see if anything was left behind. "Yep."

"Sweet. What day are we picking up the suits?"

I halt in the middle of the parking lot, letting my eyes bulge and jaw clench. "Luca? What do you mean?" He stares back at me blankly. "Do you not have your suit? We aren't getting suits, Luca. That's not on the list!" The words come tumbling out of my mouth, and my mind goes haywire trying to find a solution and keep myself from getting too furious with him. "Luca, we don't have time! The wedding is literally in three days, and we still have to—"

Luca's shaking shoulders stop me from listing off everything we have to get done before the wedding. Husky laughter starts seizing his body and rolls off of him effortlessly. If I weren't so confused, it would be contagious.

"What?!" I snap. "What is so funny?"

"Y-you," Luca wheezes, "you should see your face! Oh my, Delilah. Why are you so serious? Lighten up!" He nudges my shoulder.

I scoff at him. "*Not* funny."

"It kind of is," he laughs.

"No. It's not."

"Why? Do we not have time to stop and laugh for a minute? Did you not pencil that in?" Luca raises his eyebrows at me, and when I have to fight the smile starting to form on my lips, he claps his hands together in victory. "I *told* you I was funny. I knew you would come around!"

"That was so dumb," I say, but somehow the stupid joke gets through my cold exterior.

Luca shakes his head with a stupid grin to accompany his stupid sense of humor. "I made Delilah Collymore laugh!" he says triumphantly. I roll my eyes and pop another pretzel into my mouth.

For May, it's relatively warm out. It's my favorite time of the year, when the air sometimes betrays itself and you never really know what you'll wake up to. Yesterday was a bit chilly, but today you can feel the vitamin D seeping into your skin. Summer is creeping up on us, and in a way, it's bittersweet. As all summers do, it will fly by, and the slow-moving winter will be waiting to greet the lot of us once again with knowing and open arms. That is why spring is my favorite. The time does not creep or drag; it's the only season that stays for the appropriate amount of time. The only time that you can live in long enough to enjoy.

Luca, surprisingly, seems to agree with me on this.

"Ahh," he exhales, his eyes closed toward the burning star in the sky. "Do you not just love days like this? Screw summer, winter, and fall. Spring is hands down the best season." Luca opens his eyes, having appreciated the perfect warmth enough, it would seem, and points out a couple of trees that still have some lingering blossoms on them.

There aren't many trees left with flowers this late in the year, but with what would seem to be some kind of divine intervention, these trees kept a select few tucked safely away. They hold on with a dying breath to the remaining petals, and although it's a fruitless effort, the flower struggles to live on. It's sort of beautiful to see something so delicate trying to so hard to survive. I notice some dark clouds rolling toward us in the distance and hope that they'll make it through another bout of rain.

"What place that you've traveled to has the best springs?" I ask.

"Here," he answers without hesitation, "hands down. Although I guess I've yet to stay in any other place long enough to notice the weather. Unless, of course, it was awful—then I take note and do everything in my power to not go back."

"And what places have made the 'do not revisit' list? I would like to take note for myself."

"Florida in hurricane season is a definite no. North Dakota in a snowstorm is also very difficult to look past." His face takes on a haunted expression. "I kid you not, Delilah, there was twelve feet of snow on the road. I was snowed in for three days until they could plow the road to my Airbnb, and then I still had to shovel out my rental car."

"That sounds horrible." We get in the car and buckle up as the engine roars to life.

"It most definitely was. Let me see," he thinks, "Gilbert was probably the closest I've ever been to the depths of hell. It was hotter than Satan's—"

"Wait, Gilbert? Didn't you say you'd never been to Arizona?" I ask, suddenly confused. I swear he's mentioned multiple times that he's never been.

Luca pauses for a moment, so quick it's almost synonymous with a flinch, and just as quickly seems to catch on. "Nevada. Gilbert, Nevada," he explains. "Definition of a ghost town. I got a flat on my rental car and had to wait for a tow truck to pick me up there. It was a horrible experience."

"Oh," I say with a laugh, "I had no idea there was a city named Gilbert in Nevada."

"Calling it a city is simply too generous. The population is a whopping zero. Ze-ro," he dramatizes.

"Oh, a *literal* ghost town?"

"A literal ghost town."

I nod thoughtfully. "Huh, I've always been fascinated by those. I wonder what happened."

"Not a clue," says Luca. "Not too keen on stopping by to find out, either."

I laugh at the worn expression on his face, memories of sitting in the scorching desert probably playing through his mind. "I've only been to one ghost town in Arizona, but they had gift shops and a restaurant there."

He sighs wistfully. "I would have killed for a gift shop or two."

"They also had a zip line," I beam.

"A zip line! Oh, that is so unfair. Your ghost town was way better than mine," he groans.

I laugh at the absurdity of it all, comparing ghost towns, of all things. "I used to think that ghost towns were abandoned because they were haunted."

"The name is slightly misleading," he agrees.

"You're telling me. I was so upset when I found out. I had planned all of these ghost hunts, thinking I'd find the next hotspot for the ghost hunters I'd watch on TV at night."

"You *wanted* to see a ghost?" He blanches at the thought.

I nod at him quite enthusiastically.

"I freaking knew it," Luca says definitively. "You are psychotic."

I gasp at him. "What? Because I wanted to see a ghost?"

"Uh, yes," he replies matter-of-factly. "Who willingly seeks out paranormal activity?"

"Oh, I get it," I say. "You're chicken."

"You know I normally deny any and all allegations of being afraid of anything, but I am man enough to admit that spirits or ghosts, or whatever you call them, are terrifying. There is no way you would catch me messing with that stuff! No freaking way." Luca throws up a hand to hold in my direction, maybe warding off whatever bad juju I've brought to the conversation, and although he has that same joking demeanor about him, I can't help but wonder how much truth to ascertain from what he just said.

"Okay, okay," I relent. "I agree, it is pretty creepy. I actually gave up on those ghost hunts pretty much as soon as I decided I wanted to go on one, because I was also chicken about it."

Luca barks a laugh. "Not so tough, huh?"

"Guess not."

We continue talking so much and so comfortably that I hardly notice the drive go by. Our conversation and laughter stick to the leather of the truck interior so simply that sitting here seems to result in more of it. It's like muscle memory, laughing and talking with a friend like this, and I'm grateful to have it. There aren't many people in the world that you can fall into a rhythm with so quickly—especially when you may have made it quite difficult in the beginning.

I think it's a beautiful thing that human beings can connect and be brought together by something as random as two friends getting married. If Boston and Max had never met, then Luca and I would never have laughed while sitting on the leather of his truck seats. We'd never have become some odd kind of friends.

I'm digging through my purse looking for the key to the house, still laughing at the story Luca told me about Max back when they first became friends, when Luca interrupts himself with a confused chuckle. "Um, I think Boston has some serious explaining to do."

"What?" I say, still rummaging through my purse. How I can't locate a key in a purse with four things in it is beyond me.

"Well, it's either that, or this sucker has the wrong address," he says, pulling up to the driveway. I finally fish out the key and notice the amused look on his face. I follow his gaze to the front door, and I'm too stunned to speak, let alone move.

A man stands at the door with his back to us. He's dressed in clothing far too nice and holds a bouquet of roses much too extravagant. The man begins to turn around just as Luca says something along the lines of "Who is this guy?" but I can't trust my hearing, because the world has gone a bit fuzzy.

Everything is too confusing. Nothing is making sense.

My mouth goes dry when a pair of green eyes search the tint of the truck window.

"Bodhi?" I breathe. *I must be seeing things.*

As if he can hear me over the roar of the engine, he smiles, just enough to show that one dimple he knows I love so intently. And that's when I know I'm not.

This is real. Bodhi is here.

CHAPTER TWENTY-NINE

"Do you know him?" Luca looks between us, confused for only a moment before putting it together. "Is that? That is not who I—"

"That's him," I barely murmur. The realization that the only thing separating me and Bodhi is a pane of tinted glass has yet to hit me. I'm looking at him standing there with an absurd amount of roses, nervous and smiling like this surprise is welcome, and there is some kind of disconnect between my brain and my eyes. It won't compute, because how can it? He's standing there smiling like we haven't not spoken in weeks. Like I should be happy to see him.

Luca curses under his breath, and though it's the last thing I want to do, I unbuckle my seat belt. Surprise invades every feature on his face, but there's no point in delaying this.

This is what I asked for, isn't it? Every time I checked my phone, every night before I closed my eyes, this is what I wanted—for him to show up and try to make it right. Because even though he's the one who hurt me, who made me feel this way and forced me into this life of pretending, he's still the one person I want to fix it all. Despite everything, he's the only person who can say what needs to be said to make things right between us.

"I'll get the boxes from you later," I tell Luca as I collect the bag of ties and the trash from the pretzels.

"I can stay—"

"It's fine," I say with my most reassuring smile, and before I can think better of it, I pull the handle. In the minute space created by the car door hinging off the cabin of the vehicle, my eyes meet Bodhi's. His grin grows, but my lips don't so much as twitch to match his. All that goes through my mind is a single thought: *Twelve days.*

"Do you want me to walk you in?" Luca asks loud enough that Bodhi will hear him. He wants him to know there's someone else here.

Bodhi's lips twitch, threatening to cave from his fully formed smile, and his eyes harden while he searches through the tint for the source of the voice. I wonder if he assumed it would be Boss in the car with me. Though I know he wonders who I'm driving with now, he's doing his best to conceal whatever jealousy bubbles up in him.

"No," I say as I step down to plant my feet on the concrete, "it's fine, really." I give Luca another smile and find that it comes so easily. The act I've been putting on for everyone around me requires little effort now. Telling everyone I'm fine for so long when I feel anything but has been good practice for this moment.

Luca examines my face, looking for any reservations, searching for any hesitation. "Let me bring in the boxes real quick." His eyes strain with stress, willing for me to let him.

"That's okay." I see Bodhi shift from one foot to the other, and I wonder if his arms are getting tired from holding all of those flowers. "Come drop them off in a couple of hours?" I silently plead with every ounce of my being that he'll agree. I don't want to navigate how to tiptoe around the eggshells with him as a witness.

When he nods, I let out a small sigh of relief and step back to shut the door. It's not the biggest worry on my mind, but not having to do this in front of someone else is a small mercy I'll gladly accept. "See you soon."

Luca's smile doesn't quite reach his eyes, and before the tint obscures his face, I catch him shooting a worrisome look toward Bodhi. What exactly does he see when he looks at him? Because in all honesty, I'm not sure what I see, either, apart from memories. Most are good—almost all of them, really— but the bad memories, the most recent ones, find a place in the loop, too, louder than the rest.

One step forward.

Bodhi rips his gaze from the truck and drinks me in.

Two steps.

His lips turn up in a real smile again, any thoughts of the man in the truck visibly leaving his mind.

Three steps.

I take in a deep breath and muster up whatever courage I can to not crumble into tears right here in the driveway. How can someone who has caused me so much pain make me want to collapse into their arms and sob?

Four.

Five.

Six.

When we're separated by just a few feet, I stop. I don't trust myself to be any closer. I have to do what I can to put distance between what I'm feeling and what I need.

He stops when I do, letting the inches between us stretch to feet, then into miles. The silence pulls at the distance like taffy. We stand there, staring at each other, and I let the growing ache fill the hole he left in my chest.

Bodhi's gaze flicks behind me, and I realize the truck engine is still roaring in the driveway. I let out an exasperated sigh and turn to give Luca a final goodbye wave. It's much too enthusiastic to be credible, but it's enough to get him to leave.

I don't turn back to Bodhi until the rumble of the engine dissipates in the air. For some reason, the death of the noise does not seem to bring any sound to his lips.

"What do you want?" I ask. The question holds no malice. No anger. No hurt. The thirteen letters hold no emotion at all. I'm surprised to find any bit of control in them.

Bodhi opens his mouth to speak, but the words die in his throat. They claw against it, seeking purchase, and when they finally climb their way out, I want to walk away and forget that he ever showed up. "Who was that?" he asks, feigning nonchalance.

A scoff loud enough for the neighbors to hear leaves my lips, and though it feels anything but appropriate, a humorless laugh follows after it. "Unbelievable," I breathe. "You are just—unbelievable." I take a couple of steps to walk past him, and his hand reaches out to grab my arm.

"Delilah, wait—"

"No!" I boom, angrier than I've ever felt before. I rip my arm out of his reach, and the bag swings violently with the movement. Heat boils inside of me, rising in my throat and scalding the words that burst from me. "*No.* You don't get to do this. You don't get to show up here after not speaking to me for weeks and then get to act *jealous*." My muscles shake, having no other outlet for the building rage. "Do you realize how cruel this is? How *cruel* you've been to me? I can't believe that you—"

I choke on the words as all of the sorrow I've been feeling from our fight, all the pain from the weight of his absence, floods through me all at once. With him here, standing in front of me, I can't pretend anymore. I can't hide the hurt. I'm drowning before him.

And still, he says nothing.

I suck in a deep breath and look toward the sky, seeking strength anywhere I can find it, and force the tears to stop forming. I wait until the anger has fizzled out, not yet dead, but small enough that I can center my thoughts on the aching need for him to rectify this.

"Well?" I whisper to the sky.

"Delilah," he starts, but stops to clear his throat when my name slips through his lips too softly. He sounds as scared as I felt the last time I saw him, and it tugs at the part of my heart that is still his.

"Delilah," he tries again, finding better footing, "I messed up. I know I messed up. I was so horrible to you, and nothing I can say will take any of that back, but please, I'm begging you, give me a chance to explain. Please, Delilah, I don't deserve it, but please give me a chance. I–I can't lose you. I couldn't bear it if I lost you, Delilah. I love you."

He chokes on the fear that's been suffocating me every single day since I left for Utah. I've woken up with it smothering me and silently carried its weight everywhere I've gone, walked around with its fingers wrapped around my throat day and night, gripping tighter and tighter while I smile and pretend not to notice the lack of oxygen in my lungs. He's grappling with the same question I've asked myself over and over and over again: *Is it over?*

Only Bodhi is just now asking himself. Just now feeling a pinprick of what this ending would feel like.

"Bodhi." I choose my words carefully, letting them leach their way into his brain. Because even though he's here and all I want is to go back to before, even though I love him, his showing up now doesn't erase the rest of the hurt. "If you really couldn't bear the thought of losing me, you would have done something. You would have called or sent a text. If you actually couldn't stand to lose me, you would have done something, *anything,* before right now. You wouldn't have done *nothing.*"

"You don't understand—"

"Is your phone broken?" I cut him off. A raindrop falls onto my arm, then another onto my forehead.

"What?" His face scrunches together, confused by my words.

"Did you forget to pay your bill, and your calls wouldn't go through?"

"No—"

"Did someone steal it?"

"No, De—"

"Did you drop it in a lake? Lose your ID and had to wait to get a new one so you could get on a plane?"

The raindrops turn into a light sprinkle, but neither of us pays them any mind.

"Delilah, please."

"Did someone hold you hostage, or put a gun to your head for the past twelve days?"

"Delilah! Please, just—"

"Then what was it?" I demand. The words are hoarse, but still the anger holds tight. "Please. I would *love* for you to explain to me why I should forgive you for letting me feel so alone, so horrible, this whole time, and why you showing up here with that smug smile on your face like none of it even happened should result in my forgiveness." I hold his gaze with a simmering glare. "Because you hurt me, Bodhi. You hurt me, and I would like to know why."

"I . . . I," he stammers, and I want to laugh. I want to laugh right in his face, because he looks so caught off guard. He thought this would be easy—I can tell. He thought he would just show up here with roses, and maybe I would cry and tell him how much I missed him. He didn't think I would still be holding so tightly to this anger.

"If you can't explain it all, then tell me what I did," I finally say. "Tell me what I did to make you so angry at me."

"You did nothing!" he exclaims. "You did nothing wrong, I —I overreacted and lost it over something that should have been nothing. It should have been nothing, but—" He closes his eyes and lifts his chin to the sky. "I should have been happy about you visiting. Really, I am happy that you wanted to. It was a nice gesture."

I bite my lip to keep from interrupting him. He deserves a chance to speak, and selfishly, I want him to.

"But when you said you were asking for a Bodhi Williams? I panicked!"

"Why?" I shake my head, not understanding.

"Because, Delilah, when I met you, I didn't ever want to lie to you. When I met you, I knew that you would be the only person I ever wanted to share every part of me with. I knew that one day I'd tell you about my parents, and how I left, and I knew that I'd eventually trust you with every ugly part of myself if you would let me. From that very first day, sitting at the café and watching you walk around the bookstore like there was nothing that existed outside of it, I knew that you were it for me. So when you asked me my name, I told you. I told you *my* name. I told you my name because I didn't want this one thing to be taken from me. I wanted you to know the real me."

"I don't understand," I whisper. He's not making any sense. Our clothing begins to stick closer to our frames, and I wish for the rain to stop, but it doesn't matter what I want. It doesn't care that we're out here. It simply falls. It simply is.

His eyes plead with mine, shining with emotion. "Delilah, I told you my *real* name, but when I left, I had to change it. When I left home, I became someone else so that they could never find me. And if my employers found out that my name is falsified on every single document in that building?" Subtly, he shakes his head. "It would be reason enough to fire me. But it isn't even that—I don't care about the job. But if they somehow found me again—my parents or the people from my past—and they came looking, I'd have to leave. I'd have to leave, and I had just gotten you," he chokes. "I had just gotten you, and I was so scared to lose you."

He lifts a hand to hold my arm, and this time I don't pull

away. "I was so scared to have to leave you, Delilah. I wasn't thinking straight. I didn't realize how horrible I was being, and I don't deserve your forgiveness, but I'm begging you to believe me. I would never want to hurt you. I could never hurt you. I love you."

His voice goes from a hoarse declaration to a mere whisper, and the closer he gets, the more tangible his desperation becomes. Every part of him needs me to accept this. Every bit of him begs me to believe him.

I love you. Those three words, those eight letters, hit me softly in the chest, but it's not a surprise. I've felt it, and I know he did long before me.

I nod, slowly, and the desperate grip on my arms loosens with relief. I feel terrible for not having thought this was another thing tied to his past, and it makes sense. Of course it makes sense . . . *right?*

I tamp down the funny feeling out of my gut. Yes, it does make sense. There was always going to be something he needed to say for me to understand all of this—I knew he had the words. But there's still something I can't comprehend. Something that doesn't fit into this puzzle.

"I wish you had told me," I say carefully.

"I know, I should have. I should have, I'm so sorry." His features pull in agony.

"So why didn't you?" My words are sharp, hardened from the time spent sitting with this. I can tell they sting, but I make no move to smooth the hurt from his skin. Maybe I mean for them to cut the way they do. Perhaps I'm inflicting a little bit of what he's made me feel by making this apology so much harder than it needs to be. Or maybe I'm just sick of dancing around the point and want him to give me the whole truth.

Bodhi's lips part to make room for a sharp intake of breath, but I keep going.

"You let me sit here for days. *Days.* I was stumbling around with this empty feeling in my chest, just trying to get through one minute to the next, trying not to think about you long enough to remember the hurt I was hiding, and I didn't know if you even cared. You said *nothing*. How am I supposed to just forgive you for that? How am I supposed to forgive you for letting me hurt when all you had to do to stop it was call?" I shake my head.

This is too much for me right now. Luca will be stopping by soon, and then Boss will be home, and already I can feel the tears staining my face in red blotches. I'll have to get them all out and reel myself back in before they can see.

I sigh in frustration. "I just don't think I can do this right now."

Bodhi's eyes widen. "Delilah—"

"Just stop." I try to take a step back, but his hand still grips my arm.

"Delilah . . ." His hand desperately holds on to me, trying to keep me right here. His wild eyes flick around my face, looking for some solution to the problem he's created.

"Stop." I look at him, so mad and so hurt, and for whatever reason, he notices it for the first time. He senses the bitterness I feel toward him. It's a tangible thing to him now, this hurt that he's caused. I see it even more clearly now: how he thought he could erase it all with one simple apology, a bouquet of roses, and just by showing up.

But this isn't a reminder written with pen on my skin—it's a jagged hole carved out of my heart. You can't just wash this away.

"I understand why you were upset the day I was leaving. I get it," I continue, seething. "But I can't understand how you could just say nothing after. I can't wrap my head around it, and I think it's because I know that I would never do that to you. I would never be okay knowing you felt the way I was feeling."

"You think I was okay knowing I hurt you?" The roses fall slightly in his arms, and he looks even more pained than when I met his apology with something other than forgiveness.

I shrug. "Yeah, I guess so. That's what it feels like."

"I cared."

I laugh humorlessly. "You have a funny way of showing it." I shake my head, taking another step back. *I can't do this anymore.* How can he not grasp this?

"Delilah—"

"No!" I yell. "I don't want to hear anything else! If you cared, you would have called. You would have texted." Something wet falls and traces both of my cheeks, but it's warmer than the cold rain. Bodhi tries to step toward me, but I step back again. My voice trembles, but the words come out just as strong as I cry out what I wish he'd done this whole time.

"If you cared, you would have *come*! You would have come before today! Why didn't you? Why didn't you come?" My voice cracks, and I realize the wetness on my face is from the tears that blur my vision.

"I did!" he nearly yells.

"No, you didn't. You—"

"I came!" He drops the roses, and when he steps toward me and cups my face in his hands, I don't have enough fight left in me to move away. I'm so angry, I don't want to let him hold me, and yet the broken parts of me welcome his touch.

"I came," he whispers desperately. His crazed green eyes flare with anguish. "I figured things out with work and bought the first flight here."

"What?"

"I got here last week, Delilah. I came." His breaths come fast and hard.

"Last week?" I croak. When he nods, more tears form. *Last week.*

My head tells me that he could have chosen to take this hurt away sooner, could have spared me days of agony. My heart only says that he *came*.

"Then ... then why are you just now here?"

"I didn't know what to say." He runs a thumb across my cheek, wiping away a tear soon replaced by another. "I got on the first plane I could and planned to come straight to you, to make this right, and the whole way here I tried to piece together the perfect thing to say to you. I tried to find the right words, and nothing was good enough. Nothing I could say would be good enough for you.

"So, I went to my Airbnb, and I said I would know what to say tomorrow, but then tomorrow came and I still couldn't find the words. All I could think about was how if I messed this up, then that would be it, and I was sick over it. And I still don't have the right words, but I knew if I didn't just show up here, I would keep talking myself out of it, keep putting this off because I was scared to lose you." He chokes on the last words as his Adam's apple bobs. His hands still cup my face tenderly while I cry between them. Sobs threaten to escape my tight lips, but all that comes out is a whimper.

"Delilah," he croaks, "please tell me I haven't lost you."

My lips tremble, and I beg every other part of me to keep from doing the same.

Has he?

I blink away the tears that keep me from seeing him. His beautiful brown hair sits in messy wet clumps that I've only seen when we go swimming. His eyes are a more brilliant green than I've ever seen. The whites are tinged with red lines from stress, and I notice the dark circles beneath them. Has he not been sleeping? His jaw is clenched, trying just as desperately as I am to keep himself from falling apart. Lines crease his face in places I've never seen before. It's like he's aged since we last met.

My perfect boy sits before me, and I realize I was wrong earlier. He isn't just now feeling some of that pain, that fear I've been enduring—he's been feeling it this whole time. This whole time, he's been just as scared, just as sad, as I have. He's been hurting, but I'm just now seeing past my hurt. Only now can I see his.

We've both given so much of ourselves to the other that with one carefully crafted sentence, we can either destroy or repair one another. How can two people be both each other's destruction and their remedy?

He might not deserve it, but I *want* to forgive him. I want to go back to before. I want him to be the one to hold me and tell me it's alright. To take this all away.

"You came?" I choke.

He nods earnestly. "I came."

I nod, and I let it all go. I let everything I've held back escape, and when he pulls me into him, I don't pull away. He holds me, shushes me, and whispers apologies into my hair again and again. The sobs wrack my body, and I no longer try to hold myself up because I know he will. His strong arms support me, and I cling to him because this is what I've needed. I've needed him. I've been so angry and hurt for so long, but beneath it all, I just missed my best friend.

"I thought you were gone." I clench his shirt in my fists. "Don't do that to me ever again."

"I promise," he murmurs into my hair.

After a while, when the tears have stopped and the shaking has ceased, he finally lets me go. My eyes already feel too puffy to conceal, and I wipe at the makeup I know is streaking my face before I break the delicate silence.

"I–I, uh . . . still need to get some things done around here." I motion to the house.

"Oh," Bodhi says, a blend of hurt and confusion flashing across his face.

"But can you come by and pick me up at six?" I suggest softly. "We can talk more then."

His whole body relaxes at that, relieved I'm not pushing him away. "I'll be here."

Bodhi picks up the flowers and tries to hand them to me. I

tell him I don't want to have to explain them to Boston yet, and with a nod, he agrees to take them to his rental.

When we hug goodbye, it feels a little awkward still, like we don't quite know how to be us again after being apart for so long. But when he tells me he loves me again, it feels like a tiny piece is glued back into place. And it feels wrong not to tell him.

"I love you, too."

CHAPTER THIRTY

"Bodhi, you are too much!" Boss's voice carries a ring to it I've only heard on rare occasions, like when she first met Max and started describing him to me. Excitement invades the syllables, choking the proper nouns and sympathizing with the verbs. She's so happy to meet someone I've only ever described to her as perfect.

I told Bodhi I would forgive him if he promised me that he would be honest about everything from now on, even if it was hard. I told him he couldn't lose it like that again. That we could move past all this if he promised *this* would never happen again.

He promised me all of these things and apologized over and over and over, again and again and again. He told me I knew everything now, that he had just been scared. That it was no excuse, but he was still so sorry. He told me he loved me.

Whatever quip makes Bodhi and Boss throw their heads back in laughter falls on deaf ears as I'm lost in my thoughts. My lips still spread to muster a grin though it's separated from the giddy feelings freely floating around the room.

My knee bounces quickly as I watch them, and I force it to hold still.

He promised to do whatever I needed, and practically overnight he became the Bodhi I knew again. The Bodhi who showers me with flowers, books, and handwritten notes. The one who visits me at work, like he always has, and jokes around with my dad. The one who messes around on the guitar with Collin and pulls Kayden aside to talk about investments because he's the only other person who's interested in that kind of stuff. The Bodhi that Mom always sends away with baked goods and dotes on.

He holds my hand and runs his thumb over my knuckles. He smiles and tells me I'm beautiful. Makes me feel real. Tells me how much he missed me. It's as though none of it happened at all. He's the same person he was before.

I should be happy. I should relax. He's Bodhi, and since forgiving him for the crime of making a mistake, he is just that. After all, we're all human, aren't we?

But since seeing him blow up that night two weeks ago, I can't help but question all of his past actions. When he gave me gifts, some part of me wonders if it was meant to soften me up for a future apology he knew he'd have to make. When he visited me at work, I wonder if he was just keeping tabs on me. When he talked with my family, I wonder if he was digging his roots down deeper in my life to make it harder for me to leave.

He holds my hand, and I try to remember if his grip was always this tight.

Boston's hands flit around her enthusiastically as she tells some story, seeming to glow with excitement. Bodhi smiles fondly at her as he listens, but there's no divot. I don't necessarily miss it, but I do notice it's gone.

I've forgiven him, but it is not so easy to forget. My father once told me that our brains are wired to remember negative experiences, and it's much harder for us to remember a positive one. Some kind of survival thing, I guess. I think that's why his hardened face and angry voice still haunt me. I don't hate him for that night, but I'm struggling not to let that be the only thing I remember.

"I'm so glad you were able to take off work to come for the wedding!" Boss exclaims. "I feel like I've been there since the two of you met, and I've been dying to meet you." Her infectious grin and vandal-like eyes flicker my way, and in the width of her gaze, I smile shyly like I know I should.

I've been working my way back toward becoming the girl I was in the heat of the Arizona spring, but it's a slow process. Focusing on the little feelings, I have decided, is the best course of action. I know the love is still there, because I can feel its quiet warmth nestled softly in my chest. I can feel the way I gravitate to protect its delicate shape in my heart and move to shield it from the aches and the worry. It was the hesitation that I realized I needed to ignore, not this feeling.

I don't want Boss—or anyone else, for that matter—to know Bodhi and I have been fighting. It's no one's business, and I see no reason to involve anyone else in something we've moved past.

Because we *have* moved past this.

I'm choosing to.

So, I ignore the instinct to hesitate or add any unnecessary mess to this meeting. I smile lovingly when I should, lean in toward Bodhi, and hold tight to his arm. I do what I should and what once felt natural, because even though it seems foreign right now, it still is natural; I'm simply out of practice. Once I remember how to let myself let go and feel vulnerable, it will come easily to me once again. The hurt just has to exist a little longer. Soon, it will pass. Soon, these smiles will not be planted.

"I've heard so much about you," says Bodhi. "I've been told you are partially responsible for helping the two of us get together. Is that true?"

Having always dreamt of playing Cupid, Boss seems to shine, elated to be given any credit at all. I imagine she's drafting speeches in the back of her mind at this very moment in case the two of us get married. She'll want to bask in every matchmaking moment. "Yes, it's true!" she chirps. "D would likely still be trying to convince herself you guys were just friends if it weren't for me. I love her, but geez, she was *determined* to see you guys for everything but what you were."

Light laugh. Playful eye roll. Pull Bodhi just ever so slightly closer to me.

It's neither an act nor happenstance. It's just what I know I have to do.

"You're exaggerating," I argue.

"No, I don't believe I am. Though if it wasn't for you being so patient with my girl here," she nods toward Bodhi, "I don't think any help on my part would have done any good."

Bodhi smiles at me, not looking at Boston but still listening. Still paying attention. "I knew she was something worth waiting for," he says sweetly. Bodhi pulls my hand up to his lips and kisses the back of it, and there, in the emerald shade of his eyes, is love. Pure and simple. Impossible to mistake.

Would his feelings be so easy to express if I had hurt him the way he hurt me? If I had put him in the position I've found myself in, would his loving gaze be just as automatic? Or would he have to put some thought into it?

Or am I holding on too tightly to something I should let go of?

A slow-growing grin that reaches my eyes.

"Ah! You guys are just too perfect!" Boss coos. "You'll both be at the dinner tonight, right?"

"Yep," I answer quickly, not wanting myself to consider any other alternatives. Dinner will be good. A chance to pick up the pace toward normalcy.

"Perfect! Delilah has been helping with so much of the wedding planning—she's a lifesaver, let me tell ya—and every bit of it is going to be so beautiful." She sighs contentedly. "You have to see it all, Bodhi."

She talks with us for a little while longer, mostly with

Bodhi, and he plays the part of a loving boyfriend so perfectly. I wonder how he's never played it before. Though I'm sad not to get to do this dance with the people in Bodhi's life, I know I wouldn't have done so in such a gracious manner. He's poised. Perfect. Charming. He's everything you could hope for.

When Boss excuses herself, I find that I've lost track of time. I put myself on autopilot at some point and can't locate the reason she's leaving. She's happy for me, she tells me when she pulls me in for a hug. "I adore him," she says just loud enough for him to hear when she pulls away. Her approval and praise follow her out the door, and the silence between its closing and the sound of Bodhi's voice is a shapeless eternity. It's a walk in the desert with no mirage in the distance. It's forever and all at once. Somehow, that small instant stretches and snaps at the same time.

"She's exactly as you described," he says.

I nod and make my way back into the barely furnished home. Bodhi had already paid through the weekend for this Airbnb, so when Boss offered for him to stay at her place, he had to politely decline. I was grateful he had another place to stay. At least that meant I didn't feel obligated to constantly perform in front of everyone.

The four dozen red and white roses liven up the otherwise barren kitchen counter, despite some being smooshed from Bodhi dropping them on the cement, but aside from the hundreds of petals that curl around one another, there isn't much life in the room. The two of us stand here suspended in time, alive, of course, but stale.

"Are you okay?" Bodhi asks. The concern etched in his brow and fixed in his eyes is real. I feel it, and without him saying it, I know what he's really asking.

Are *we* okay?

"Of course." I give him a reassuring smile. If it's more for me than him, though, I can't say.

Our talk last night was rather uneventful. There wasn't

much more to be said than what was exchanged on Boss's porch. Although I hadn't given it any conscious thought—him still taking his flight and showing up just like we planned—I know deep down, I had hoped he would. Deep down, I had wanted him to show up and explain it all away. Deep down, I had wanted some grand gesture. So no matter how he apologized, I think I was always going to forgive him. Or at least try to.

I've seen and been told how all relationships have their bumps and bruises. No one is perfect; we all have to learn how to live in step with someone else. So how can I fault him for learning?

Part of me feels idiotic for not reaching out on my own. Maybe I could have avoided some of this difficulty had I simply spoken up, even if it was to yell and scream and just show how hurt I was. Maybe if I hadn't kept it all to myself, locked it up, and thrown away the key, we could have fixed it quicker.

There's one thought on repeat in my head that keeps me from throwing this all away: *Maybe this is partly my fault.* I don't know that it would have killed him to explain, but would it have killed me to try? If everything we've built together matters to me as much as I think, am I not also partially to blame for the past two weeks?

So, I decide to take some of the responsibility so that we can work it out. That's what we're doing.

We're working it out. It's working.

Bodhi seems to believe me—or at the very least understands my method of repair—and moves on. Together, we sluggishly go through the quiet morning. There isn't much to do for dinner tonight, or for the wedding tomorrow. Everything has been taken care of or assigned to someone else. Caterers have tonight covered, and the venue has the place set up. All I have to do is show up.

We. All *we* have to do is show up.

We watch television and I fall asleep, somehow exhausted

by midmorning from all the nothing we've been doing. When I wake, Bodhi isn't on the couch next to me anymore, which is both strange and a welcome chance to breathe. The TV is still blaring. Images flash across the screen, painting a scene of an eerie lake house, and I have no idea what's playing. I try to shut it off, but the remote won't work. I grumble to myself. Of course the batteries would die right now when, for whatever reason, we had the volume nearly all the way up.

I drag myself off of the couch and check the time on the oven clock. *Noon. Still a few hours before I need to start getting ready.*

With nothing better to do, I start searching the drawers for spare batteries, though if the rest of the minimalist home is any indication, I doubt I'll find any. Spoons, napkins, and can openers fill the first drawers I open. Next to the sink are some washcloths and sponges. Nothing helpful at all. A peek into the last drawer tells me it's empty. Annoyed, I shove it shut.

Thunk.

I quickly turn back to the drawer, unsure if the small noise was something I made up in my head. I allow my fingers to wrap around the skinny drawer handle and draw it closer to me, moving slowly.

Inside, a phone has slid toward the front of the drawer. It must have been hidden in the back and slid forward from the force of me shutting it. It's an old flip phone, one that slides up to reveal a keyboard. I pick it up and examine it, feeling a little wave of nostalgia. I used to have one just like it when I was younger.

The phone buzzes. Startled, I drop it but quickly scramble to catch it. I turn it over in my hands to see someone calling.

Someone must have left this here.

I click the green button to answer and step out the sliding back door, away from the noise of the television. The small fenced-off grassy area acts as a small sanctuary. "Hello?" I answer.

"Hello," says the low voice of a man on the other end of the line. The sound is a little fuzzy, and I blame it on the outdated cell clutched close to my ear. Hesitantly, his voice comes through again. "May I ask who I'm speaking to?"

"My name is Delilah. I, uh, I think this phone was left at this Airbnb by mistake. I just found it and answered, thinking maybe you were calling trying to locate it."

"Oh," the man says, disappointed. "No, I'm actually calling trying to get in contact with the owner of the cell."

"I'm sorry, they aren't here." I think of the time. "Is there somewhere I could maybe bring the phone? I have an event tonight, but I could drop it off or leave it on the porch for someone to come grab." I try to think of any other way to help, but with the owner without their cell, I'm not even sure how the caller would contact them to get it back.

"Well, it might be best to keep it there in case he comes back looking for it," says the man on the other end. "If you wouldn't mind, you could maybe put in a report with the local police station to let them know you have it. He may call to see if it was turned in. We just need to reach him as soon as possible to follow up on a case we're investigating."

I jolt back, not realizing I've been speaking with a detective this whole time. I thought they were supposed to introduce themselves as such—maybe that's just something they do on television. "Oh, I—is he a suspect?"

"I can't comment on an open investigation, ma'am. I just need to follow up with the owner of the cell as soon as possible."

"Of course." I nod even though no one can see me. "Whatever you need. I could drop it by a nearby police station, maybe?"

"No, no. I wouldn't want to put you out. If you file a report with his name and where to find you, I'm sure that would be fine. But if you're more comfortable dropping it off, that would work, too. I'm just hoping to reach him sooner rather than later. We are dealing with some time-sensitive stuff, you see."

I give another unseen nod. "I'll be here for another couple of days, so hopefully he'll come by before then. What's his name?" I pull out my own phone to write it down so I don't forget, but as it turns out, I don't need to.

"Thank you, ma'am. His name is Bodhi Williams."

CHAPTER THIRTY-ONE

"Ma'am? Hello? Are you there?"

The oxygen thins, and the world crumbles around me.

"I–I'm sorry," I stammer, "what was the name again?"

"Bodhi Williams," the detective says. "Did you get that?"

"Bodhi?" I say slowly. "Bodhi Williams?"

Please tell me I heard you wrong. Please. Please.

"That's correct. Just leave your contact information with the department, and hopefully we can get in touch with Mr. Williams. Thank you, ma'am. You have yourself a great day."

The man on the other end hangs up, leaving me in this strange trance between space and time. Everything moves so slowly: the fingers that come up to graze my lips, the phone lowering from my ear, the breath that leaves my lungs. Everything slows down as I try to piece together these awful, horrifying pieces laid before me.

Why does Bodhi have a spare phone hidden in the drawer? Even worse, why is a detective calling and trying to contact him about an ongoing investigation?

I realize that maybe I should have told the detective that Bodhi was here. I should have brought the phone to him, but the shock overrode every other thought in my mind. How can I think clearly when I'm staring straight into the face of what can only be another lie, another hidden truth?

There are no easy explanations for this. I would know if Bodhi had a work phone, and even if I didn't, there would be no reason for him to hide it in the back of a drawer. I've never even thought to go through the one I knew he had. There's never been a reason for me to question him about anything. Until recently, it seems.

It's then I realize I have no idea where Bodhi is in the house. The phone suddenly feels like evidence I'm about to be caught with, and I panic. *I need to put the phone back. I need to put it where I found it, and then after that, I can figure out what to do. I just need time to sit with this for a minute. I need time to think before I do anything else.*

I slide the door back open with the phone hidden behind my leg in case he's back on the couch, which is a terrifying three feet from me. My head pokes through the opening, every molecule in the air and in my body now on overdrive. The slowness I experienced before has passed, and now everything is too quick, too loud, too suspicious. If he finds me here like this, with the phone in my hand, I don't know what I'll do. I don't even know if I want to ask him about this yet.

He's not in here.

I leave the door open, not wanting to waste time closing it, and quickly tiptoe to the kitchen. It's unnecessary to do so with the television still blaring—no one could possibly hear a normal step over the noise—but I can't help it.

I'm at the drawer in seconds, but the adrenaline coursing through my veins makes me feel every ounce of it. It opens easily, but when I go to set the phone inside, I realize I don't recall how I found it. Was it placed on its back? Its front? I don't have time to try and remember, so I just place it as far out of sight as possible, thinking that's what I'd do if I were the one hiding a phone. I shut the drawer slowly as not to jostle it, then sigh with relief when it's done. And then my heart plummets to the floor.

"What are you doing?" Bodhi asks over the sound of the television.

Shit. When did he walk in?

My chest thrums from the blood pounding through my veins, but I do my best to hide it. With my back to him, I step toward the next drawer, opening it and pretending I don't already know its contents. Dish towels stare up at me dangerously, warning me to act normal. Something quiet in my gut tells me I have to, though it isn't Bodhi I'm afraid of—it's what he might say. Can I handle more than what I already know?

That's something I have to figure out before I ask. Or at the very least prepare myself for if I can't.

"Do you know if there are any batteries here?" I ask, and without the deafening roar of the television, I think he'd be able to hear the tremor in my voice as I try to find a convincing tone. I force the vibrato to smooth itself out of my words. "The remote died. I can't turn the volume down."

I can feel his stare drilling into the back of my skull, and I realize I need to be more convincing. Staring at these forks and knives isn't going to make him believe me. He needs to see that there's no hidden expression on my face. He needs to look at the face of a liar and believe it. Luckily, he has given me the opportunity lately to excel in this subject.

I look right at him with a face blank enough to be construed as innocent, maybe even a little naive. "Did you hear me?" I ask. "Do you know where any batteries are?"

Bodhi examines me for a moment before he spots the remote on the counter, picking it up and turning it in his palm. He doesn't break eye contact as he points it at the television, but he doesn't press anything. He just stares and lets his finger hover, as if giving me a chance to protest. When I don't, he presses down on a plastic button.

I hold my breath.

But nothing happens.

He walks up to the TV and runs his hand along the bottom. A second later, it shuts off.

"Why didn't you just turn it off?" His eyes narrow at me, and I can't tell if he knows. I can't tell if I'm just digging the hole deeper, acting like I didn't just find what he hid in the drawer.

"I didn't think about it," I answer. I open the fridge and conceal my face behind the door. "You should message the host and let them know about the remote. Do you have anything to eat here?" I pretend to scan the fridge for something edible. There's a half gallon of milk and some random condiments— not much to convincingly keep me here. *I have to shut it soon.*

"Did you open this door?" Bodhi asks. Confused, I turn and realize he means the sliding glass door to the small yard where, just a minute earlier, I was outside with his hidden cell phone speaking to a detective. *Do I confess now? Do I ask him to do the same?*

"I wanted some fresh air," I explain, turning back to the fridge.

He seems to accept this answer as he slides it shut. "There's not a lot to eat here. We can go grab something. We'll pick up some batteries on the way back, too." Any trace of speculation I detected in his voice earlier has dissolved, thinning into the sweet, easy sound I know so well. A sound whose integrity I'm beginning to question.

I let out a silent sigh of relief and close the fridge door. "That sounds great." I smile softly. "Do you think you could run and grab the food, though? I just want to make sure I have everything ready for tonight and tomorrow."

He hesitates ever so slightly. Had I blinked at precisely the right moment, I would have missed his glance toward the drawer—one that confirms what I already know to be true.

Though he promised to keep nothing else from me, there is, at the very least, still this.

"Of course." He walks over to me and leans in, kissing the cheek of a girl who has once again found herself in a position where she isn't sure if she's pretending for those around her or for herself. I tell him where he can stop for food, conveniently located a ways away, and he sits down at the table to put on his shoes. "Could you grab my keys and wallet for me? They're on the desk just in the other room."

I nod and smile, doing all the things I'm supposed to, just like before. Only now, there seems to be a more important reason for doing so. Now this acting is done with intent, to grant me a moment to breathe, to think. To get that phone back in my hands and figure out what to do with it.

Once he's out of the house, maybe I can see what else is on that phone. Once I know a little bit more of the story, maybe then I'll understand what I need to do. If I can just get on that phone, maybe I'll get the answers I no longer believe Bodhi will give me.

People don't hide phones for nothing. If I'm lucky, he has a second phone for a wife he hasn't told me about. Somehow, that seems like the best explanation right now. It would also explain why he freaked out on me for visiting him unannounced and, if he lied about his family, why I couldn't meet them. It would be awfully convenient for an adulterer if his family were out of the picture. That would be the smartest way to hide two lives—to keep them separated by something as permanent as death.

I find the keys in a bowl on the entry table instead of the desk, but I don't think much of it. Bodhi stands up from the kitchen table as I walk in, shoes laced perfectly. He's in the most relaxed outfit I've ever seen him in: a fitted white tee with jeans that fit a little too well not to have been altered.

"Thank you," he says. He takes everything out of my hands and kisses me quickly before walking out the garage door. The touch of our lips feels like a sin, not knowing what secrets the phone holds. *Am I kissing the lips of a cheater? A cheater who's part of some investigation?*

Bodhi pops his head back in with a bright smile plastered on his face, dimple and all. "I love you."

"I love you, too," I reply. The hollow words kill me as they escape my chest.

The door shuts, but it isn't until I hear the garage open, the car reverse, and the garage shut that I finally let my limbs sag. The past ten minutes have been utterly exhausting, and they crave a rest I cannot offer. There isn't enough time.

I head straight to the drawer, ready to figure out exactly what Bodhi is hiding from me: a family, a whole other life, whatever it is.

The drawer slides effortlessly. Without the noise of the television, I can hear the quiet glide of the hidden mechanism and the empty *swoosh* of air as the handle draws closer to my hip. The smell of new cabinetry and fresh cedarwood permeates the room. Things I hadn't noticed before take hold of my senses, and there's so much more here in this drawer than I could process before. There are smells and concealed gears and empty air. What is missing, however, is the cell phone.

My stomach drops. I don't know if he knows, or if he was always going to leave the house with it. I'll never learn what's on that phone, because the only chance I had with it is gone.

A sharp gasp accompanies the realization that he was smart enough to get me out of the room *just* long enough to grab the phone. He was smart enough to tell me the keys were somewhere they were not to delay me, and smart enough to say something just misleading enough that it could be overlooked through the lens of innocence.

What other tricks have I been naively blind to?

Or is this just another thing that will be explained away later?

The thought of waiting for the next unexplained thing to happen just for Bodhi to dismiss it when it's convenient for him makes me sick. If all this relationship will be is one story, one explanation, one excuse after the other, regardless of truth, can I handle that?

I don't know that I care to go down that path right now.

The wedding is almost over. The flight is already booked to go home. A few short days from now, it won't matter so much if all of this is brought up. In a few days, it'll be more manageable and only affect the people I want it to. I can control how this goes if I can just pretend for a little bit longer. A couple days of acting is doable. *I've been doing it this whole trip—what's a little longer?*

Because even though there's this bile rising in my throat, a sourness clinging to my insides, I know he isn't capable of doing something truly horrible. I know there has to be an explanation for this. One that will make sense, one that can placate me for a while. But even if that's true—even if he can explain this sick feeling away—I'll just keep wondering what else he's hiding from me, what other secrets I'll uncover.

I'll deal with this later, I decide. *I'll talk with him later.*

Right now, I just want to forget.

CHAPTER THIRTY-TWO
AFTER

He picks me apart, chews the pieces, and spits me back out. He has dissected my every breath and twitch as though they will lead him to some conclusion I couldn't possibly offer up with words.

And there is nothing I can do to defend myself from his gaze.

I am a piece of clay in his meticulous hands, forced to form whatever shape he sees fit, but somehow expected to remain untouched. I do not know what fate I might meet if I am perceived as anything other than the perfectly imperfect person his delusions have made me out to be.

Is it cruelty? A lesson?

Which does he believe himself to be: a sadist or a teacher?

Is it simply nothing? Perhaps it just is?

Either way, he knows what he does is objectively wrong.

Why else would there be locks on the doors?

I have been in the corner, curled in on myself, for hours. I do my best to block out the memory of the only thing I didn't realize was still mine being taken away from me, but the new nightmare scars. I know he is watching. Somehow. Somewhere. I know there must be cameras or a hole expertly disguised so that he can digest every single thing I do. I suspected it from the moment I arrived, but now, for the first time, I know this is a fact.

Because he caught me.

For the first time in a long time, I tried to escape. I saw an opportunity and thought to myself, *What the hell?*

A hole began to call the bottom of my shirt home. He nestled in and burrowed deep, nearly invisible when he first appeared, but he quickly made himself known. I looked down at my new friend, the hole, and glanced at the door. And before I could think to snuff it out, a thought entered my brain and planted a little seed of hope. A spark lit itself in my hollow chest, and like a fool, I fanned the small flame, hoping to feel something there once more. A lick of the flame, a burn of an ember—whatever I could sustain. I just wanted to feel something.

So, I tore the shirt. I tore at the cloth and eyeballed a piece just big enough, but not too big for the hole inside the door frame. The small hole that works with the lock to keep me trapped here. I couldn't risk him seeing it, but if it wasn't large enough, it wouldn't serve its purpose.

The measly scrap of cotton lay dangerously across my open palms, my only weapon in this forsaken room. The only time I have thought of an escape plan that might work. The only one that was not so easily smothered with reason. That had just enough merit to make me wonder, to make me hope.

I crumpled the piece in my hands, compacting the fabric into the size of a large ice cube. It would work. I knew it would —it had to.

I tucked my shirt into the waistband of my sweatpants, hiding the fraying ends, and formulated a plan that would get me close enough.

Because at this point, what did I have to lose?

A life is not something you have when it no longer belongs to you.

He came in at the same time as always on the fifth day, when the window lets in the most light. He sat at the table across from me, quiet. Some days it is like this. Some days he stares at me, watches me eat, and says nothing. I don't feel self-conscious as much as cautious when he does this, but in these moments, he gains something from the interaction I've never been able to interpret.

Today, though, he seemed different. He watched me with a curiosity that had worn off weeks ago when I became entirely predictable to him. He narrowed his watchful eyes at me, a wolf in nothing but wolf's clothing, and hid only his thoughts, but no longer his demons.

I ate the meal, a rather bland mix of chicken and vegetables, while he merely nudged the sliced carrots around with his plastic fork. I could feel the vibration of the gears grinding inside his skull. I could hear the silence of speculation, could feel the extra weight of his gaze. And I acted as I had many times before. I played the part and showed him that I was just the girl in his little box. The girl he keeps locked away until it is time to play.

When we finished, I picked up the plates and stacked them together as I was expected to. I gathered the utensils as he stood. Once he opened the door, he stepped through and took the cutlery from my hands, no longer interested in a further silent interrogation. He looked away just long enough for me to shove the balled-up cloth into the small hole in the frame. Just long enough for me to get away from the door so he thought I dropped the plates and left. So smoothly, he never saw me hesitate.

One swift shut of the door and I held my breath, waiting anxiously for him to yank it back open. For him to tell just by the shift in the air that something was amiss. I waited and waited with the anxiety choking me until I heard the most beautiful sound that has ever existed in this world.

The sound of the key sliding into the doorknob as he left.

I sat and stared at the door for what I perceived to be an hour. That was how long I imagined it would take for him to be far enough away. *Perhaps I'll be lucky and he'll be napping*, I thought. *Perhaps I'll be lucky and he'll have left.*

Some days, on the fifth day, he doesn't come back for dinner until long after the window shines a much duller hue. Some days, he's gone from the box for so long that I think that the only thing he could have done is leave this monstrous prison.

I hoped that today was one of those days.

When I could no longer take the nerves buzzing through my veins, when the window's light began to dim, I approached the door. I approached both my cage and my captor and prayed today it would be my savior.

One soft push did nothing. The door held firmly in place. I shoved harder and then a little more, my bony body not capable of much. Four, five, eight, ten shoves at the door, and nothing.

I began to hyperventilate as the hope died in my chest. *Feeding that hope was wrong*, I thought. *I'm going to die from the feeling of this loss.*

Desperately, I threw every bit of my feeble strength into the door—and was met with the floor. The floor of the other side.

I splayed my fingers across the ground. In a daze, I lifted my head. My body had only been on this side of the door one other time: when I arrived. Tears sprang to my eyes, but I gathered myself quickly and started to stand when something whirred by in my peripheral.

Then the world went dark.

I awoke in the box once more, attacked by this pounding in my head.

I brought a hand up to gently inspect my temple and found a tender bump. Confused, I tried to open my eyes but was met with agonizing pain. I rolled over to conceal them from the light and moaned. Even clenching my eyelids hurt.

Eons later, I was able to peek out. The light from the window had softened enough that it no longer hurt like before.

But when I opened my eyes, I knew a whole different kind of pain.

My captor had taken everything from me.

I was half naked. Strewn across the floor like garbage, clothed in nothing but a bra and underwear. Exposed. I threw my arms across my chest and instinctively reached for a blanket. When my hand only met a stripped mattress, I turned too quickly. The world swirled around me viciously, and I held back the urge to vomit. When the room stabilized, I slowly peeled my eyelids and looked toward the bed. The floor. The clothing rack.

Every last bit of anything that could be used to conceal my bare body was gone. I was left with nothing. *Nothing, nothing, nothing.*

Now I sit alone, curled up in the corner, skin enveloped in the cool air with tears streaming down my face. The one thing I had left was so easily taken away from me because he knew. He will always, always know. He knows what I'm thinking before I even do. That is what his careful watching has gifted him. He will always know me.

Time is a cruel, cruel punishment, and I will feel every second's sting.

There is no escaping this monster that has so seamlessly woven himself amongst the rest of us.

There is no outsmarting or escaping a man not restrained by morals.

CHAPTER THIRTY-THREE

"Delilah? Hello? Did you hear me?"

Boston's fingers snap in front of my face, whipping me back into reality.

"Sorry, what?"

"What is with you tonight? You're acting so weird," she complains. "I said where's Bodhi?"

"Oh," I say, distracted still by the lingering thoughts that plague my mind, "he's parking the car."

This seems to be all she needs to move past my momentary blip. Through the fog, I respond appropriately to her comments about being excited for Bodhi and Max to meet and mantras of plans for the four of us that I've heard repeated over the phone every time we've talked these past few months. She drifts like a hologram in front of my eyes, like I'm watching life play out on a screen. None of it feels real, but it is somehow familiar.

Eventually, the smell of a passing tray of some fancy appetizer brings me back into the moment, and I wish it hadn't. Because behind Boss, I catch the eyes of someone I've been avoiding. Someone I was hoping I'd be able to dodge at least until I had Bodhi by my side to keep from having this conversation.

He stalks over toward the two of us, right as Boss gets pulled away by a distant relative of hers. With no one to save me, I wait like a sitting duck.

"Hey—"

"Are you alright?" Luca asks in a tight voice, cutting through my attempt to act normal.

"Of course," I answer, much too chipper. "Why wouldn't I be?"

Luca tilts his head in disappointment at the obvious lie. If I had been given the courtesy of not knowing him to the extent that I do, I would ignore the blue seeping into his kind brown eyes, but I do know him. Enough to relent.

"I'm fine," I sigh. "Really. I know I rushed you out of there, but—"

"I am *not* worried because you got me out in a hurry," he says, cutting me off. "I *am* worried because the boyfriend you were too hurt to even mention just showed up—I assume without notice—and you haven't responded to any of my texts."

A large group of people begins to file through the door, but Bodhi isn't among them. I don't imagine we have much time left before he walks in.

"I know, I'm sorry. I've just kinda been busy with, well, with everything." I gesture to the room full of linens and greenery and shades of baby blue. "But I'm okay. It's just been a lot to figure out."

"So you figured it out?" he asks skeptically.

Luca is the one person on Earth who even knows a sliver of the stuff that's been going on between Bodhi and me. If I were to tell anyone, it would be him, simply because he is the most detached from the situation. After the wedding, I doubt we'll see each other again more than a few times, if ever, and that's only if the happy couple happens to invite both of us to something else. Because despite the considerable amount of time we've spent together, this is just a friendship of convenience.

Once we aren't forced into close proximity, it will almost certainly suffer a swift death. In a few days, Luca won't be someone I have to face anymore, someone to be embarrassed around. He'll be gone, and my secrets with him. If there was ever anyone I could tell, it would be him.

My mouth cracks with this temptation on my lips, the desire to confess and get this heavy thought out of my mind, to let him tell me what to do. It hinges open just enough to tease me with the possibility of putting this responsibility on someone else. It would be so easy to say it: *Bodhi's hiding something from me.* The five words could tumble out of my mouth, and then the rest would follow.

It only takes the beginnings of a breath filled with admission to tickle my lips before I let the sentence die in my lungs. Because then I see Bodhi walk through the door, and I remember myself.

Such a confession isn't so straightforward. There's no reason to involve a virtual stranger in something that doesn't concern them. I'll figure everything out when I need to. Right now, I just need to be a wonderful guest at my best friend's wedding dinner.

"Everything is figured out," I lie with a smile.

A small light dies in Luca's eyes, their brown hue turning from a deep honey to a dark walnut. He shakes his head almost imperceptibly, and I know I have not convinced him. Somehow, this stranger knows me too well.

"Excuse me," I say as I step forward and make my way toward Bodhi. He's looking around the room for me, and I'd rather go find him than give him the chance to join this conversation.

As I sift through the crowd, it isn't hard to sort people into the categories of "bride" and "groom." Maxwell's family comes from old money turned new. Oil rigs and thousands of acres across multiple vineyards leave his family dripping with wealth. Clothing sewn in designer factories I could never dream of pronouncing, let alone affording, is strategically draped around their bodies, pinned and pulled to perfectly accentuate their features in the ideal light. Jewelry perches itself upon the ladies' collarbones, and large belt buckles grip the men's waists.

Boston's family, though dressed well, stands out amongst the others. They're scattered around the room dressed in knock-offs and off-brands, but no one seems to care. Every smile in the room is accompanied by crinkles near the eyes and a sincerity in their laughter that can't be manufactured. Yet despite the differences, no one cares or seeks to compare; they are simply here to celebrate the two people they love who happen to love each other.

"Hi," I say as I slide up next to Bodhi.

His hand slips around mine, squeezing it gently in greeting. There's something in that tenderness that threatens to rip me to shreds, but there's a hardness in his eyes that holds me steady. Something curious lies in his gaze, like he's solving a puzzle. But the instant I recognize it is the same instant that it's gone.

We spend the next twenty minutes moving about the room with no real strategy. A few of the bridesmaids, including Gemma, approach us, intrigued by this mystery man I failed to mention. I feel an internal sting every time someone asks who Bodhi is—a pinching guilt for not having mentioned him once, even in passing. If Bodhi feels hurt by it, he doesn't show. He handles each exchange with a grace I've envied in every person I've found it in.

Perfect words and flawless jokes flow from his tainted tongue, and though my cheeks gather up in soft smiles every time, I suspect my eyes betray me. Their hollow gaze holds tight to the doubt steadily building behind the question they pose: *Is any of this real?*

Boss drags Max over, and the boys nonchalantly greet each

other the way men tend to do, but soon they hit it off. I watch the way they interact, and Boss does the same, but for her this is the beginning of something. She's watching the first of what she expects to be many conversations, while I only watch for another lie, for any scrap of proof. All I find is annoying perfection.

We drift through the dinner—or rather, I do. The meal, though carefully chosen and entirely too expensive, finds no place in my memory, forgotten before they even take our plates. My mind focuses more on the person beside me. Though I know I shouldn't let it, it snags on the face of the man from the coffee shop.

His lips—still so soft, still so gorgeous, that form warm smiles I get drunk on—now also seem to form lies and excuses I'm sick of. His full perfect eyebrows I used to envy now raise in surprised laughter, which only makes me question if we've ever shared a genuine laugh before. His eyes, the shade of a cool patch of grass in the summer, are still just as captivating, but now I wonder what secrets they hide.

What I wouldn't give for just a bit of the truth.

The toasts are finished by the parents of the bride and groom. My speech will be saved for tomorrow at the reception, so while everyone else tears up with emotion at the father's remarks about the bride, I let my mind leave the room. I don't come back until we stand to say our goodbyes.

"They're a lovely couple," remarks Bodhi.

I nod, and for one of the first times tonight, the soft smile on my lips is real. "Yeah," I agree. "They are."

We file through the short line of people waiting to hug the happy couple even though I'll be staying with Boss tonight. Bodhi congratulates Max, and they pull together to clap each other on the back. For a minute, my heart wants to swell at the image, something I've always wanted—for my and my best friend's partners to be friendly like this. It makes me think of those two little girls, giggling in a bedroom covered in boy-band posters and littered with flavored lip gloss, and how they dreamed of the day they'd be standing here together.

I don't think they dreamt one of them would be pretending the way I am now.

I hug Boss, telling her I'll be at her place soon, and move to hug Max.

"See you tomorrow, Maxwell."

He laughs, "See you tomorrow, Delilah."

Bodhi grabs my hand to lead me out, his rough palm foreign against my own, but we only make it halfway to the door before someone's familiar voice stops us.

"Leaving without a goodbye, Delilah? How very rude."

Luca's chastisement causes us to pivot in his direction as he makes his way in front of us. My heart quickens, hoping and praying that he isn't about to do something stupid. He may be feeling brave enough to cause a little tension, to bring up what little I've told him, but he's not the one who will have to sit through the contentious car ride home if he does.

"You must be Bodhi," Luca says, extending a hand. "Pleasure to meet you. I've heard so much. Nice to finally put a face to the name."

Bodhi hesitates but soon accepts the gesture, giving him a firm handshake. A gesture I imagine the two of them have religiously practiced in their own lines of work.

Bodhi's eyebrows pinch together despite the effort to neutralize his features. His eyes dart to me for just a second, probably wondering why this man already knows of him. "I'm sorry, who are you?"

Luca laughs and sends a fleeting glance my way. Bodhi reactively squeezes my hand, still held in his, at the sight. "Luca," he states, as though this name will dislodge some memory from Bodhi's brain, and when it doesn't, he tilts his head almost predatorily. "I'm the guy who dropped Delilah off when you were waiting on the porch."

"Luca is Max's best man," I rush to explain. "He's just been helping with a couple of the wedding errands and stuff."

"A couple!" Luca exclaims, his eyebrows lifting. "The two of us have had to drive around most of northern Utah picking up random shit—sorry, *stuff* for the wedding. You see that over there?" He points toward the back at a rounded arch draped in the artistry of the florist. "That took us two hours to pick up because they could *not* figure out how to break it down to fit in the bed of my truck. And that was just *one* of the many, many errands they roped us into running." Luca rolls his eyes, letting out an exasperated breath, like finally admitting all these errands were exhausting has lifted some massive weight off his shoulders. "Luckily, I think we should be in the clear now, with the wedding being tomorrow and all."

My eyes widen as I try to convey through a look alone that this conversation is better off concluded, but he stares straight at Bodhi, whose face has been transfixed into stone. I haven't seen Bodhi in any other social setting than the two of us alone or with my family, but from how he acted around Boss this morning and everyone else at the party tonight, it's odd to see him so reserved.

"They're lucky to have friends like you who will help out." The words leave Bodhi's mouth through gritted teeth. Luca narrows his eyes, picking up on the thick tension growing between the three of us.

"We better get going," I quickly pipe in. "Bye, Luca."

Before either of them can argue, I tug Bodhi toward the exit. He goes to grab the car and leaves me out front, walking away in a deeply unsettling calm.

A few other bridesmaids are loitering out here as well—waiting for a car, I assume—but we exchange nothing more than forced smiles. I wrap my arms around myself tight, regretting not grabbing a light jacket. This floor-length light-blue dress keeps my legs warm enough for the late spring chill, but the spaghetti straps do nothing to protect my arms. I sit there shivering for a moment before I feel the air shift to make room for someone behind me.

"Hey!"

I turn to see Luca once more, and I can't help but be slightly annoyed. I face the parking lot again, ignoring him. The fact that he—the one person I could *maybe* tell everything with no real consequences—keeps showing up and taunting me with an impossible temptation is something I'm quickly growing to resent. Not to mention the fact that he also just made the rest of my night with Bodhi immeasurably more difficult to navigate.

"What?" I snap more harshly than I intended.

Luca steps back, and in my peripheral vision, I see him lower something he had held out. "Geez, are you sure you ate in there?"

I don't answer, scared of what I'll say and angry about what I can't.

"Lighten up, Delilah. I just came out here to ask if this was your bag."

I glance at the clutch held in his hand and realize that I did leave it inside, but I don't remember setting it down. *Maybe when we said goodbye to Boss and Max?*

I sigh and take the clutch from him. "I'm sorry."

The silence between us grows steadily afterwards, each passing moment heavier than someone can reasonably be expected to carry. I spare a quick glance at him, trying to find some sign or signal that he's going to leave and spare us this burden, but when my eyes meet his, I find him already staring at me. My gaze snags on his, unable to look away.

Maybe it's the way the shadows contort the light around his eyes, but they feel like a safe place to store these heavy thoughts. *Are you okay?* they seem to ask, with no words necessary.

I can't be sure what my own eyes say, but the weakness I feel reflects in his, and I know he knows. Not everything, but enough. He has seen through every fake interaction tonight.

Just like at the bachelorette party, I know he saw every way in which I kept myself from being here—not literally, but metaphorically. I've focused my mind on actions and reactions, thinking only of making the world around me buy what I'm selling.

And he bought none of it.

A familiar black sedan turns into the lot, its tires turning toward the inevitable destination before my feet. A stranger behind the wheel, a naive girl on the curb.

I clear my throat to break whatever hold has been placed over the two of us, keeping our eyes locked. "Thanks," I say lamely as I hold up the clutch.

Bodhi stops the car in front of us, and I quickly turn forward and get into the passenger seat. The scent of the freshly detailed interior hits my nose even though he's been driving it around for a week now. Before the door shuts, Luca wishes us a good night. He walks inside as we drive away.

Too far away to share any part of what burdens me.

"I don't like that guy," Bodhi mutters after watching Luca hold the door open for a couple and disappear inside.

I scoff, immediately irritated. The night has been too tiring for me to play these stupid little games with him. I don't know what any of it means anymore. I feel the glance he shoots at me, but I continue to stare at the pavement rolling slowly underneath us. It picks up its pace once we turn onto the street.

I should care, shouldn't I? I should care how Bodhi feels, or how what I do or don't do will make him feel. I know I did before. But it seems the more we keep going at this pace, the further I get left behind. I'm sick of it.

I don't think I can fake another smile or craft another laugh. I'm tired of participating in life at the expense of my own happiness. I'm tired of living just to make it easier for everyone else.

Bodhi reaches for my hand, and I pull it away.

He opens his mouth before shutting it again, sorting

through his thoughts. When he finally speaks, his voice is low. "What's going on with you tonight? Where have you been?"

Had anything else been on my mind, anything at all, the question wouldn't have been so infuriating. I might've even softened at the sound of his concern and interpreted it as concern for me. But sitting here, listening to him now, all I hear is concern for himself.

I don't think he cares about what's plaguing my mind. Not really. He only cares how my thoughts will affect him, and I'm so sick of feeling used that I spit the question out before I can think.

"Why was there a phone in the kitchen drawer?"

It's a simple question. One that shouldn't have the potential to be so volatile. One that shouldn't carry a detonator. One that should never produce a look like the one that darkens Bodhi's face.

"What?" he asks, his tone hostile.

"Why was there a phone in the kitchen drawer?"

Every moment we've had together lately seems to involve some repetition of this demented cycle: Bodhi hides something, I stay quiet, and eventually, he comes up with some excuse. Dirty the dish, wash it, rinse it, dry it, and repeat. But although I'm hurt and confused, it's almost comforting knowing that the next part of the cycle is coming.

I just want him to explain. I don't know that I'll forgive him, but I do know that I won't be able to figure out the rest until something's been said. It's too much to have living in my head, especially in the midst of what should be a joyful occasion.

He's quiet, likely contemplating how much to divulge, and I give him the time. Though I'm not sure he deserves it, I give it to him nonetheless. It's the only olive branch I can offer.

All he says is: "I was wondering when you were going to say something."

And I feel like I've been hit by a bus. "You knew that I knew about it?"

"I thought so," he replies.

My arms cross as my nostrils flare. "And you wanted to . . . what? Not say anything about it?"

"I didn't think talking about it would do any good. You're still angry with me for how we left things in Arizona." Bodhi stares stiffly at the road, his grip on the steering wheel turning his knuckles white.

"You mean how *you* left things?" I retort, trying to stop my teeth from grinding together.

"See," he says, as though this is the issue worth discussing right now, "you still haven't forgiven me."

The blood beneath my skin begins to boil. "You know, I've been trying really hard to forget about everything else, the yelling and the lies, because you said it was all over. But then I found out you're still lying to me. You're *still lying*, Bodhi. Don't you see how that might upset me?"

He shakes his head, frustration building up inside of him. I'm doing my part to hash this out rationally, to give him a chance to defend himself, and yet still, he lets his anger grow. "And you keep jumping to these conclusions without giving me a chance to explain anything to you."

"By all means!" I exclaim desperately, sweeping my arms between us. "I would love *nothing* more than to hear how you explain the burner phone hidden in the kitchen of your Airbnb!"

Bodhi rolls his eyes, the tension between the two of us growing grossly thick.

"My God, Delilah, a burner phone?" He scoffs. "Who do you think I am?"

"That's just it, Bodhi! I'm starting to think I have no clue who you are, and every explanation I can come up with paints you out to be either a scumbag or a shady person, so which is it?"

"It sounds like you have all the answers," he retorts, his tone clipped, his lips flat. "Why don't you tell me?"

"I don't know anything, Bodhi!" I practically shout. "You won't tell me *anything* unless I confront you about it first or do something wrong, and I'm not trying to, but you hide something from me and then expect me not to step on the landmine! I just want you to tell me what's going on," I plead, hot tears escaping and sliding down my cheek. Doesn't he realize what keeping quiet is doing? Can't he see how much it's hurting me to have to beg him for the truth? "Please, Bodhi, just tell me."

He sits there silently, white-knuckling the steering wheel and working his tight jaw from side to side. *Is he weighing his options?*

Thoughts of a secret family tucked away in the Arizona suburbs run circles around my mind, and I wonder if they find a place to do so in his. Is he thinking that if he comes clean, I'll stay? Or is he just thinking of some lie that will fit snugly into the hole the truth has left? I don't know much, but I do know that if he doesn't tell me the truth right now, in this car, I won't be able to take anymore. If he tries to hide this from me, I'll never be able to trust him again.

He runs his tongue along his teeth—some tic I've yet to pick up on—and lets four passing street lights illuminate his face as he does his best to control his breathing. His sentences come out cold and precise when he finally speaks.

"It's an old phone. I've had it since I moved out on my own," he explains deliberately, each syllable somehow bringing both a sense of relief and impending dread. "I never told you about it, because for a long time, you didn't know about my past, and I don't use it anymore. It just sits in a drawer at my house, waiting for a call from my parents that it will never receive. It's pathetic and embarrassing, and I don't know why I brought it here—out of habit, I guess."

He turns to face me, anger and pain spilling from every pore on his face. "So which am I, Delilah? A monster or a liar?"

His words spark with fury, chastising me for jumping to

conclusions instead of coming to his defense. For assuming the worst in him when it's all he's shown me lately.

He's angry that I could ever comprehend a world in which he's not perfect. And I'm angry because this isn't the truth—at least not all of it. He's actively lying to my face, trying to guilt me into dropping this.

He doesn't know that I talked to the detective. That I'm well aware that he does, in fact, still use this supposed relic of his past, and for more than a provision of hope. It's not a reminder of history, but paraphernalia for deceit.

How many other times has he used my emotions against me like this? How many times has he ended the questions before they could be asked?

"That's it?" I ask quietly, every bit of me begging him to tell me what I already know. I plead with my eyes for him to confess. I beg the universe not to let him do something I won't be able to look past.

And once again, I am let down.

His Adam's apple bobs with a swallow. A rough hand runs over his stiff face. "That's it. That's the whole truth."

"There is *nothing* else you want to tell me?" I beg once more, but my face is already falling, going numb.

"That's everything," he says. "I swear."

This is the lie that pushes me off the edge. With those few simple words, I'm falling, stumbling off of a tightrope I've been balancing on for weeks. Hearing this final lie is the catalyst for all that comes next. Without this last nail in the coffin, I don't know how much longer I would have spent trying to convince myself that what has been dead wasn't dying.

There is nothing I can do to save this because there is nothing left to save. How can something built on so little character be redeemed by only one person?

The car is silent for the remaining twelve minutes it takes to get back to Bodhi's Airbnb. I make no move to stitch the seconds with forgiveness, and he does nothing to hem them.

The time stretches on and on and forces me to tread through every last moment of it. The hum of the engine and occasional clicks of the blinker are the only noises to drown out the silence. Each turn forces this swelling emotion to grow in my chest until it's too big to contain. It hurts too much to hold it all in.

I allow a single teardrop to collect in my eye and tear its way across my cheek and down my neck. It loses too much of itself along the way, and the moisture dissolves completely somewhere near my collarbone. Somehow I find I empathize, because I've lost myself, too.

Once Bodhi parks the car in the garage, he looks at me. Waits for me to cave and fall back into the rhythm we so easily sway to. But I don't look at him. I don't dare to, because I know what lies there: a perfect face, with two beautiful green eyes asking me to forgive him. To believe him.

The problem is, I don't want to look at that face and see what else waits for me: a fraud.

I sniffle and get out of the car, not hearing him when he says my name or, more accurately, not caring. I ignore him as he follows me into the house and punch a few buttons on my phone. He softly takes my arm in an attempt to turn me toward him. I hear some words leave his lips, but I find no point in listening to them when I have to question their integrity. These meaningless sounds follow me around the room while I gather my things.

He raises his voice then—just an octave, but the vibrations instill some kind of assurance in me. Some desperation makes its way to my ears, yes—a valid response to someone you love leaving you—but so does the aggravation he tries so eagerly to conceal.

"Where are you going? Delilah, stop it—talk to me! What do you think you're doing?" I open the front door, and Bodhi catches sight of headlights in the driveway. "Who is that?" he demands, immediately defensive.

I turn to him, finally meeting the gaze of the perfect man

who ran into me at a coffee shop. As I face him, I'm scared for reasons I both can and will never be able to fully understand. I look into his eyes and see every memory flash through my mind, the feelings I had during each one squeezing my heart enough to hurt, but also enough to remind me it's time to go.

There is so much happiness to be found in the parts of us we've carelessly shared and scattered around, but those are pieces I can't get back. They are missing now, and by staying, I'm only losing more of myself. I can't hold on to this hurt any longer, hoping that it turns into something less painful, something more familiar.

"You won't be at the wedding tomorrow," I start.

"What? No—" he begins to say, but I don't stop, knowing that this is how it has to be. Knowing that if I take a breath, I might break.

"I'll tell them that you're feeling sick. We'll go home—"

"Delilah, stop it—"

"We'll go home, and I'll drop off your stuff and pick up mine—"

"Delilah! This is crazy!" His eyes bulge as he throws his arms in the air.

I don't tell him that he's right. This *is* crazy. How could I be planning the end of us?

"I'll pick up my stuff, and that will be it," I say definitively. "I'm done, Bodhi. I can't do this anymore. I won't."

The crazed look in Bodhi's eyes tells me he's finally hearing me. He finally realizes I'm not as permanent as he once thought; he can feel that he's lost me. He can see in my tear-filled eyes that I know he's withheld another truth. That he messed this up too much to duct-tape it back together again.

"Please." He lowers his voice and gently holds my arms. "Delilah, listen to me, I've told you everything. Don't do this—"

The car in the driveway honks, and he whips his head toward the noise.

"Who the hell—?"

I move his arms off of me and step away, his attention drawn back to the girl no longer within his reach.

"I'd like to believe you," I say. "Really, I wish I could." And I mean it. My heart aches with desire for some kind of miracle that could fix this, that could make this all go away.

I wish that he would let me love him. I wish he wasn't causing this. I wish this wasn't so hard. I wish he would just tell me the truth. Because then it would be him.

It would be him, if only he'd let it.

"But you're still lying," I sob.

He shakes his head painfully slow, and silver lines his eyes. "You promised," he whispers. "You promised you wouldn't leave me."

My eyes burn with tears, but before he can take any other part of me, I turn away and face the road. "I'll bring your stuff by when I get back home."

And just like that, I walk away.

Each footstep collides with the pavement quicker than the one before, scared that if I'm too slow, I won't make it to the car in time before this tsunami hits me. His voice dies beneath the sound of a roaring engine, and I manage to hold it all in when I open the truck door. I hold it all in when I climb into the passenger seat. I hold it all in when I throw my stuff in the back and while I put my seat belt on. Through it all, I hold it in.

"Delilah?"

"Just drive," I croak. "Please."

He pulls out of the driveway, and when Bodhi disappears in the rearview mirror, too far to see, Luca touches my arm.

With that gentle touch, it's as though he pulled the trigger.

The pain and hurt gather and surge, erupting all at once. The sobs escape uncontrollably, and I can't see anything through the grief that threatens to overwhelm me. That's what this is, I realize: the beginnings of grieving. Everything is blurry and blue, and I'm grateful not to see the world yet. I'm grateful not to know what it looks like to live in a world where I was right.

I always knew. I *always* knew that this was how it was going to end—with me hurt. I knew it, and I let myself love him anyway.

I cry and cry until the salt stings my skin, until there are no tears left to cry.

I cry knowing there is nothing more I can do.

I can't fix this.

CHAPTER THIRTY-FOUR

Boston couldn't see the red blotches still lightly staining my face. The lights in her bedroom were low enough to conceal what the makeup couldn't, and the smile on my face hid the rest. She paced around the room in a frenzy of excited energy, unable to wipe the smile off of her face long enough to consider resting.

Once the night began to turn into the very, very early morning hours of the day, I convinced her we needed to get some sleep before the wedding. She resisted only for a minute before relenting, and sleep found her quickly; her chest rose and fell in symphonic breaths almost as soon as her head hit the pillow. She has always had this gift of shutting her brain off whenever she needs to. Her mind is like a machine with a built-in on-and-off switch. I look at her face now, void of any disturbances and empty of thoughts, and envy her.

Sleep never finds me. I lie beside her in the same bed, staring at the blinds of the window as the light quickly, it would seem, changes from dark hues of black and deep blue to the soft glow of morning daylight.

I slip out of bed, grab my bag, and make my way to the bathroom down the hall so as not to wake Boss with my rummaging around. After I wash my face off in the sink with some soap and pat it dry, I look up to find a terrifying girl in the mirror staring straight back at me. Her eyes are swollen, tinged with red streaks. Her nose is raw from blowing into rough napkins from a glove compartment. Her hair, although always disheveled in the morning hours, is rattier than usual from a restless night full of tossing and turning. There's a ghost of something hiding her gaze.

With the makeup gone, a stranger emerges, and the sight of myself makes me want to cry all over again.

Instead, I reapply the mask of a happy girl—one untouched by the knowing—and when I finish, I stare back at someone who looks a bit more like myself.

Today will be the last day I have to hide. The last day I have to pretend.

I can get through one more day, I tell myself. *Just one more day.*

I place a pin in the smile I practice in the mirror, memorize the feeling of the excuses in my mouth, and collect whatever strength is left in me. Once I've achieved something close enough to normalcy, I push my bones to pack up my things and go throw together some breakfast.

Bridesmaids bump and brush up against me in the crowded room. Although it's a sizable area with three vanities and extra counter space, with all of the makeup, curling irons, and discarded clothing strewn about, the space continues to seemingly shrink in on itself. Many of the girls lean into the mirror to artistically apply a sharp streak of eyeliner or dab on much too much blush. All of them speak over one another, and I find it difficult to believe any of the conversations coincide with each other. All of the words collide and crash in mass pileups around us, and I do my best not to get caught up in any of the wreckage.

Boss gets ready in the center of the chaos, somehow shielded from the carnage that surrounds her. A hair and makeup artist runs her brushes across Boss's skin and tames her hair as they cheerfully chatter. She keeps cooing sweet words about Boss's beauty, though it's not difficult to hear the jealousy or to spot her ringless finger.

I got ready quite quickly, myself. I don't care to place bait out for bites of attention when the attention is better spent on the girl waltzing around this mansion in her beautiful fitted white gown. While all the other women are applying and reapplying layers upon layers of hairspray and foundation, I take a moment to just take it all in.

I watch what feels like one of those moments with a definitive end unfold before me in slow motion, each gasp and bit of mischievous laughter drugged to prolong its profound effect. Perfect white teeth flash around the room carelessly, and the scent of hairspray leaves a permanent trace in the air. Eyes all around me crinkle with the giddy drunkenness that comes with an abundance of serotonin, and I search for any bottle left unattended, desperate for some kind of high of my own. Of course, there is nothing left for me to grasp, and none that would be accessible anyway. Each girl manufactures it on her own and gifts none of it.

Perhaps it's cruel, but it is also the very design of life; in almost everything, we must be self-sufficient. People can only elevate what you already feel, can only expand the feelings that already exist. This happiness possessed by the rest of the room cannot be charitably donated. No—to feed off of their joy, I would have to already have its taste staining my mouth.

I leave the room without making an excuse, seeing no need to add to the indecent amount of chatter overflowing from the space. When the door shuts behind me, it's like I've placed heaven-sent earmuffs over my ears. Though deadened noise is at a nearly bearable level now, I can't help but feel that this pounding headache isn't due to the onslaught of words, but rather the ferocity of the tears and sobs that racked my body last night.

I dig through my clutch, fish out the pills I'm looking for, and swallow them dry. I don't care enough to find a drink to make them go down easier. I do realize, however, that I haven't had anything to eat since breakfast, and although they are mild painkillers, having them on an empty stomach may do more harm than good.

I float in and out of the venue's many rooms like a phantom, taking this moment between acts to drop the facade. No one really pays attention to the hollowed-out girl peeking in and out of each one, which only serves me better. The fleeting memory of me will pass quickly, and I'll be forgotten before I leave.

The wedding venue is a large mansion nestled in the woods of Park City. It skillfully hides itself from the rest of the world in the winding roads and curves of the mountain, yet leaves room for a stunning backyard view of a forest untouched by man's hand. Looking out at the ocean of green, you wouldn't expect to be so near civilization.

I don't find any food in the plethora of rooms I peruse, and although I imagine that the boys would have some sort of sustenance, I leave their door untouched. Instead, I find myself leaning on an iron rail and staring off into this endless sea of fir trees undisturbed by city lights, mulling over what has already been thought to death.

The questions left in Bodhi's wake eat at me more than I thought they would. I thought that once I cut ties, I could ignore the holes in the story. Out of sight, out of mind. But as I stand here, with the only noise being the breeze whistling past my ear, I can't quiet the questions down.

The one that plagues my mind most, of course, is the phone. Even with its supposed tie to his past, I can't deny that something is unbecoming about its existence. About the call. And his explanation only seems to deepen the lies.

And what was the investigation he was involved in? It feels awfully coincidental that the detective would have his "old" phone number and not his current one.

Unless it had something to do with his parents. That is something they could potentially be investigating, and it would easily explain Bodhi's involvement. What it doesn't explain, though, is why he didn't mention the investigation to me at all. Especially when I gave him multiple chances to do so. Even as I sat silent, he could have confessed. He could have spoken up right then and there, and when I walked out the door, he could have blurted it out. When I got into the truck, he could have called to me. Even when I was gone, he could have texted, called, or hell, sent an e-mail. Instead, he did exactly what he did before: let the space between us grow so vast that when the silence is one day broken, it cannot be bridged.

I wish, for a moment, that the phone call had gone a different way. I wish I had picked up and heard the detective say something to make me believe that the call was a novel one —but he said they were following up with Bodhi. If that had been their first time contacting him, then this wouldn't be a lie. It wouldn't be another lie.

"I meant what I said before."

I jump at the sound of Luca's voice. He's leaning against the railing maybe a foot away, but I don't remember him walking up to me or finding a place to settle in. I was so lost, staring out at the blanket of deep green, that I didn't notice him. *I wonder how he always manages to find me.*

"What?" I ask, confused.

He examines the view now, too. I watch him look out at the various shades of green and brown with a stern gaze, like some of them don't quite fit, like something is missing that he can't quite pinpoint. "That you didn't deserve what he did. You still don't."

I look away and stare out at the same emerald sea, trying to ignore the weight in my chest. I let the wind speak its truth and sweet nothings against my skin. The cool breeze is a welcome reset to all that has gone wrong. I let it kiss my lashes and lips, willing it to take away what I've seen and said.

Luca shifts to face me, no longer hiding behind the pretense of admiring a view. I don't have to look at him to imagine what shape pity takes on his face. I don't have to see the worry etched in his brow to know he's concerned for me.

You can see a lot without seeing anything at all, the same way you can see a whole lot of nothing even while looking at everything. It's this single truth that angers me, that fuels this self-loathing. I saw a whole lot without seeing anything at all. At least not what mattered.

"You going to be okay?" he asks.

"Of course," I automatically reply. When it becomes apparent that this answer won't suffice, I add more solemnly, "I *will* be fine. What other choice is there?"

This seems to be enough to, at the very least, get him to look away. Whether he accepts my adapted answer, though, is uncertain. I don't know that I believe it much myself.

"I'm here, though," he says to the mountain. "If you need me, I'm here."

And the funny thing is, I believe him. Despite all of the hesitation I've trudged through, and despite the slow start to this friendship with him, I believe that if I asked, he would be someone to lean on. I believe he has a good enough heart that he would drop everything on a dime to show up for some girl he hardly knows just to lighten her load. Last night was more than enough proof of that.

The problem is, I don't know how to accept something as kind as this.

So I answer with a soft sad smile, agreeing to nothing, making no promises.

He doesn't press me to speak about it, and he didn't last night either. All Luca knows is that Bodhi and I broke up, and it was messy. Once I could catch my breath and get something out that wasn't a sob, he asked me just one thing: What could he do?

All I could think to ask was that he tell no one about it. And he agreed.

In the darkness of his truck, I quietly put an incredible amount of makeup on top of my preexisting layer. Then, once I collected myself, I asked him to take me to Boston's. She barely noticed the time when I finally walked in. Never noticed the sad tinge to my every expression.

"Have you ever been in love?" I ask him as I stare at the trees. "I mean, before Ali. Were you ever in love?"

"Yes," he says without hesitation, and I know it to be the truth.

"H-how did you survive it?" I whisper, admitting that I have never before felt so much for a single person, requesting some kind of reassurance. Something to get me through this.

"A part of me didn't," he confesses simply. "A part of me didn't survive it. But it wouldn't be love if you weren't giving up a part of yourself, would it?" Luca pauses before speaking again. "The good news is, I grew where the missing pieces were and became the person I needed to be for when I met someone who could show me what real love was. Because the secret was that, though it felt like it at the time, that wasn't real love."

I swallow the emotions rising in my chest, holding back the tears threatening to form.

"It might not feel like it right now," he says, "and it probably won't make you feel any better hearing this, but that wasn't love. If he loved you, he wouldn't have treated you the way he did. If he loved you, you wouldn't be feeling like this. No one who loves anyone would willingly let them feel this way.

"You'll grow where those missing parts of you are, and you'll love again—only the next time, it'll be real. It'll be what you need." He places a gentle hand on my arm, and it's this bit of mercy that allows a single tear to slide down my cheek.

Somehow, it feels more sad than if I had cried until there was nothing left in me.

I place a hand over his, still not having it in me to look at him right now.

"You probably should get back in there." Luca tilts his head toward the mansion. "But I can stall for you if you need more time."

Shaking my head, I take a deep, shaky breath. I fan my face for a second, hoping that my makeup isn't terribly affected.

As we straighten to walk back inside, Luca takes one last look behind us. "That was a beautiful sunset."

I pause and take a look for myself. But the colors have almost completely drained from the canvas, leaving only bleached clouds and a darkening sky.

"I didn't notice," I murmur before going through the doors.

No one notices when I come back into the room a few minutes before it's time to leave. The bridesmaids pair off with their groomsmen, and mine doesn't look at me once. He's too busy staring at the ass of the bridesmaid walking in front of us.

What I remember of the ceremony is that it was beautiful, but someone sat on the remote to my life and fast-forwarded through the whole thing. It's all one gilded blur that somehow got me to where I sit now—in a stolen chair, hidden behind a shrub, sipping on some fizzy drink alone. I chose this spot because not only is it out of the way, but it also happens to be where the waitstaff walks by with trays of appetizers and drinks. I could stay here all night and leave full.

Out of all my life's moments, I think strategically moving a chair to hide behind a plant and get drunk at my best friend's wedding is by far the lowest.

Luckily, today has been so hectic that no one has taken notice of Bodhi's absence. Still, I've rehearsed my lines well. I know that to a total stranger, my words would be taken at face value, and any sadness would be attributed to a girlfriend missing her boyfriend. But I don't know that I'm in the best position to lie to someone who knows me as well as Boss. She'd see right through me and likely press until I relented.

So, behind the shrub I stay, sipping these wonderful drinks. Forgetting.

I watch, sip, and sulk further into the leaves for a long while. No one tells you how boring weddings can be when you're part of the wedding party. Of course, there's no place I'd rather be than supporting Boss and Max, but I can't help but feel like a puppet used to fill some photos that they'll look back and point to with their children, reciting the names of their old friends.

Other than the photos, there isn't much required of me. The happy couple is too busy making the rounds to take notice of a runaway bridesmaid—

Runaway bridesmaid. I giggle aloud at the thought.

I swap my empty glass with a full one on a passing tray and sip at it. The bubbles tickle me with their warmth the whole way down. With a sigh, I peek at the party through the branches. Gemma has begun moving around the tables collecting single women for the bouquet toss, and although I should make an effort and get up, I doubt Boss will be able to spot me missing in the growing crowd of women on the dance floor.

And this chair is so comfy.

I sink in further, letting my eyes close for just a second, only because I'm so relaxed and warm and my eyes are too heavy.

Hiccup!

I clasp a hand over my mouth only to let every giggle slip through my fingers. Soon, I'm in a fit of laughter at myself because I'm just *so* funny, and I'm starting to think that this wedding isn't as bad as it was earlier.

I hear a yell come from around the corner, and when I turn

to look, the world goes topsy-turvy—or I do. My head gets dizzy, and the world spins around a bit. I close my eyes and try to hold still, but another loud noise comes from the corner.

I try to get up and struggle to find my footing with these heels in the grass, so I decide it'd be easier to get around if I wasn't wearing them. I sit on the ground and begin to tug and pull at the straps, but the clasp won't undo. Frustrated, I use all my strength until the one strap snaps off. I slip my now-free foot from the shoe and tug at the other one until it does the same. I leave them where they are and stumble toward the corner, laughing at how funny walking is. I've never realized it was so hard to walk before, putting one foot in front of the other over and over and over again. I hold onto the wall to help me, the rough brick scraping against my palms.

The shuffling gets louder and louder the closer I get to the corner, and I want to tell whoever it is to quiet down, because I can't hear the music anymore, but I can't see them yet, and then I laugh again because *Duh, I can't hear the music! I'm walking too far away.*

I stumble around the corner, tilt my head in confusion, and squint to try to get a better look.

There are no lights on this side of the building, but I can make out a person lying on the floor while a man swings his leg into their side. Soft grunts escape the beaten person with each blow, but they're quieter than before despite me being so much closer. I stumble my way toward them, trying to yell at them to stop, but my mouth is having a hard time forming words; the muscles, like taffy, won't contract or extend to say anything right.

I get within six steps of them and trip over something in the grass. With a yelp, I fall face-first onto the ground, barely sticking out my jellylike arms to take some of the fall. The grass tickles my face, and suddenly all I can think about is how funny that is, and how funny it feels. Laughter comes much easier than the words and I roll over to my side, clutching my stomach from the pain the deep humor provides.

Why am I on the ground? I wonder, then clutch my mouth to smother another barking laugh. Everything is so warm and good here—I think to myself that I don't ever want to get up from the grass, so I spread out and stare up at the dark sky with its twinkling lights.

"Delilah," someone says. "Delilah, get up. We're leaving."

I try to protest and point to the stars, begging whoever it is to leave us alone. *It's so beautiful! Why would I want to leave?*

Something shifts underneath me, and I start to laugh again as I feel myself float up into the sky.

Oh, we're going to the stars. Okay.

I giggle again, and through the buzzing in my electrified skin, I feel something squeeze my face and force it to turn, which hurts so much I want to scream at them to be gentle.

"The drugs have already kicked in," the voice mutters. I laugh at the voice with the blurry face and try to tell them that's ridiculous, I would *never* do drugs! I reach an arm out, but it falls back down to the Earth, and I follow it as it falls until I see something on the ground.

Wait, wasn't I looking at that earlier? What is that?

I squint and widen my eyes a few times and try to clear the picture, and after a second I see someone lying there in a suit with a baby-blue tie, but they aren't moving, and there's a lot of red paint everywhere.

I start to get upset, and I hate this feeling more than the fuzzy one—it feels harder to breathe, like that one time I had an anxiety attack in junior high in the middle of a hallway after school. *I have to clean up that paint, it's going to stain, and those ties—I bought those for something. What was it?*

My head hurts from all the feelings and things swirling inside it, and then my body starts floating away from the mess, and with every step I feel myself forgetting . . . something. *What was just happening?* I look up to find that I'm not flying, but an angel is carrying me, further away from the noise, the mess, and the worry. I try to smile at them and tell them I've always known angels were real. I want to ask the angel if they saw me in the clouds when I was little and flying around with them.

Do you remember me? I try to ask.

The angel looks at me like they heard, and I laugh because I didn't hear the words come out of my mouth.

"Be quiet, Delilah," my angel says, still looking at me. "We're almost to the car."

I obey and squint to try to make out the angel's face, confused as to why they would need a car when they can fly, but the only thing I can make out is a pair of beautiful green eyes, and even though there's something about them I feel like I should remember, they're familiar enough that I feel nothing but safe, so I close my eyes and fall asleep to the sweet scent of cinnamon and sandalwood.

CHAPTER THIRTY-FIVE
AFTER

The smell of the cinnamon rolls placed on the plastic blue plate between us brings me back to the wedding. I remember it more clearly now, having let time do what it does and the drugs having passed through my system long ago. The memories cling to certain things now—things that have absolutely nothing to do with the night that I will always look back on as the first day my life was stolen from me.

Of course, a million little variables had to conspire to create that night, and every night before and after it. A million little moments led to that one night, but it will always be the night where the taking began.

And the memory of that night has found solace in clinging to the scent of cinnamon and the color of those stupid ties.

"How did you do it?"

My question is no more than static penetrating the air, easily ignored and just as easily fixated on depending on the listener's mood. I try not to lean into this psychosis, to feed his ego and alter this fantasy he has created. But looking at that plate and remembering the shape of Luca's beaten bloodied body on the grass, and how sick I was for weeks after remembering I did nothing to help him, I can't help but ask.

As usual, he does not seek any clarity. He sees the questions coming as though he has given me the prompts himself, and perhaps he has. The dessert and the color of the plate may be staged to remind me of that night.

After all, he know me better than anyone else. Myself included.

"You know what I find fascinating?" he asks. He adjusts the tiny projector's lens in an attempt to clear the picture before he begins the movie. "People love to say that 'anything is possible,' but rarely do they believe it." He pauses. "For some reason, people place mental limitations on what they're capable of and what is possible when in reality, you can do anything you want to. You simply have to be willing to do what is necessary and think of every single variable, even the seemingly insignificant ones."

"But how did you do it—at the wedding?"

My captor leans back, the movie ready to start. "I promised a handsome sum of money to a server to spike one of your drinks. His car was unfortunately found wrapped around a tree that night. His brake lines had eroded and, well, you know how those canyon roads can get, especially at night."

My stomach rolls over itself.

"I knew exactly where you sat, and knew where you would hear a scuffle, and knew you would investigate. I knew how to get you out of there. The rest, well—I chalk the rest up to jealousy, I suppose." He turns to me with that dark look in his eyes, and I hold back the urge to vomit. "You can manipulate all kinds of emotions to get the results you want, Delilah. Jealousy is a self-reliant machine, but trust"—he looks to me—"is the easiest to fabricate. And affection can be bought—for the right price, of course.

"If you know someone, and you understand how they tick, anything is possible. I just had the patience most others do not."

CHAPTER THIRTY-SIX

The hum of the engine hits me first. It vibrates softly through my body, nearly lulling me back into the comforting dark space I've been wandering in. There, it is calm. In the dark, there is no pain. It is a kind friend extending an offer to forget, at least for a little while.

It's the smell of stale dirt that hits me next. The particles in the air tickle the hairs of my nose as I breathe deeply, its dry taste already coating my mouth in a vaguely familiar way.

The heat comes next, and though there's a breath of cool breeze steadily blowing onto me, it is slight in comparison to the compressed air that surrounds and suffocates me. The air is old and stubborn and will not change, no matter the efforts made to do so.

It isn't until I see the image of Luca, lying lifeless on the floor, covered in blood, that my eyes snap open as the rest of the memories claw their way back to me, desperate to be remembered. The moment they open, I'm blinded by an unbearable light, and instantly the sensation of searing hot needles being shoved into my eyes takes hold of me. The pain, so intense, coaxes a soft groan from my gut, and I turn my face into the soft fabric below me.

The hum of the engine, the taste of the dirt, and the heat all fade away behind the pain. The thought that they could ever be felt above this mind-bending agony is preposterous. For hours, it seems, there is nothing but this pain. I lie here, tightly squeezing my eyelids shut against the cloth, until the splitting headache and needles subside to a dull buzz, but it still hurts. Not wanting to risk a relapse, I keep my eyes closed and try to rely on my other senses.

I know that I'm lying down; the soft bounce of what reminds me of uneven pavement meeting tires jostles my body around. Up and down, left and right, I softly bump around, a slave to its movements. I hear a symphony drenched in the sound of static—like an old radio, maybe. It's familiar, the tempo at which the cello strings meet the bow. It's something I listened to with—

With Bodhi.

The longer I lie here, hiding from the pain, the clearer the memories become.

There were green eyes, the scent of sandalwood accompanying me as I was carried away—away from the wedding. *How —wh—what happened at the wedding?*

No memories precede the image of what could only be Bodhi's eyes. After they meet mine, it all goes dark. Nothing. The next thing I remember is the hum of the engine.

A car. I'm in a car. A car with cloth seats, hot air, and a cloud of recognizable dust.

Spurred by some unknown source of courage, the need to know something, *anything* more builds up inside of me until my skin tingles with adrenaline. Just one peek at what's happening around me would tell me so much more. One peek, and I might know what's going on.

Tentatively, I crack my eyes open, face still smooshed against the seat. It hurts, yes, but the pain has dulled into something bearable. I attempt to move my skull toward the left.

Everything doubles—no, triples as it spins around and

confuses me. I see the backs of six car seats where I logically assume there are only two, but their phantoms move about in chaotic patterns before me, causing a whole new pain to build up inside my brain.

And everything is so bright, it's almost blinding again. I can't make sense of how *everything* is this bright, like when light reflects off of a ripple in the lake just right and it hits you in the eye. But this is *constant.*

I force myself to blink until the frame comes into focus, and the driver, plus two identical versions of him, becomes visible. They all have identical perfect hair and identical white button-up shirts with the sleeves rolled up.

Even though everything I've tested out so far hurts, I try my voice. I find my throat is parched, the sound difficult to place, but a groan of sorts escapes me and three pairs of emerald eyes glance back.

"You need to rest," Bodhi says, his voice echoey.

"What?" I croak. "What are you doing?"

The three Bodhis reach for something in the passenger seat.

"Go back to sleep. We're almost there."

There? The dusty air is no longer comprised of enough oxygen. My lungs expand and contract rapidly, grasping for more of it, and the panic partially shields me from the pain of the hot needles that shoot into my brain when my eyes snap fully open.

My muscles don't possess the strength to lift me off the seats in the back of the car, but I try to force them to anyway, exerting every ounce of energy in my body to shakily lift myself so I can see where we are. Thousands of Joshua trees and cacti litter the desert outside the windshield. For miles and miles, there's only one singular road, and beyond that, nothing. As far as the eye can see, there is nothing; there is no one. Just us.

And that is the most terrifying part.

"Delilah," Bodhi says, looking back at me, "lie down. You're going to—" He looks up just in time to see he's veering out of the lane. "Shit!"

Before I can brace myself, the car hits a massive pothole in the road and jerks to the left. My body slams into the side of the car, and before the world goes dark again, I hear the *crack* of my skull hitting the window.

CHAPTER THIRTY-SEVEN

The dolls are littered around me like wedding rice. Each one's hair is brushed and twisted to create some fancy updo of my choosing, and each one is dressed in the tattered remains of beautiful ball gowns. I'm not yet old enough to understand that we are poor. I don't yet realize that these dolls, with smeared faces and missing shoes, were all that my mother could find at a nearby garage sale. But, like most young children, I am shielded from the devil that is comparison. It won't be until my eighth birthday, when Katelyn sees the hand-me-downs from my cousins and asks where the tags are, that I realize that some kids grow up differently than others. For now, though, I am six. I'm playing with my dolls and know nothing other than what is.

The squeaky hinge of the front door snaps me out of my dream world, and I race to greet the person walking in.

"Daddy!" I squeal.

His worn face quickly turns into a beam of sunshine as he bends down to scoop me up. Dad hugs me tightly, swinging side to side, and kneels in front of me when he sets me down.

"I missed you, peanut," he says, smiling. The dirt on his face itches to be washed off, but that is simply proof to a child that her father has been away, hard at work. His clothes are rumpled and tinged with the smell of sweat. His eyes are a little more tired than when he left in the morning, but his smile is always in the same place as before. This is what it looks like when Dad comes home.

"You'll always be my little girl," he says, softly pinching my chubby cheek. For years, this sentence will fail to be understood in the way it is meant. I'll be fully grown before I realize how bittersweet those six words truly are. His little girl won't be so little anymore when she sees her father's mantra for what it is: a wish spoken aloud.

"Duh," laughs the little girl who cannot yet understand. She pulls her father's hand, and he follows—the gravity that pulls a father to his child's happiness greater than any physicist's theory. "Come look at my dolls!"

Desperate shallow breaths rip me out of the dream. Already, its memory leaves me, withering before I have something to grasp onto. I grapple with my mind for a moment, torn between the dream and the now. But when images from before I fell asleep flash before my mind, I wish I had stayed focused on the dream.

My eyes snap open and a dull throb inhabits my skull, but adrenaline keeps me from feeling the extent of it.

No. No, no, no, no.

I choke on a sob and throw my hands over my mouth to stifle the noise. *What happened? What happened?* It's all I can think, stuck on repeat over and over and over again. I remember the car, and the dry air that consumed me. I remember the feel of the cloth and looking up and seeing him in the front seat—

Another sob racks my body at the memory of his bottle-green eyes looking down at me in the back seat. His robotic voice telling me to sleep. Telling me to be quiet while he carried me in his arms. *While he carried me away . . . from what?*

And then I see it—the unmoving lump on the grass.

Oh. My. God. My limbs shake uncontrollably as I curl in on myself. *We left* someone *on the ground—a person. Bodhi did.* I remember stumbling toward the two of them, wanting to help, but I wasn't myself. I couldn't think, let alone walk. I saw the blood and the same baby-blue tie that the groomsmen all wore. But that face . . . it was so bruised, caked in crimson, that it takes me a moment to realize who it was sprawled lifeless on the grass: Luca.

There isn't much in me, my stomach empty of all but the alcohol I consumed, but the need to purge this sick revelation overcomes me as dry heaves constrict my throat. *Bodhi attacked Luca, and we left him, and he dragged me away and stuffed me in a car and took me . . . where?*

My eyes dart around in vain attempts to make sense of my surroundings, but every inch of the room is cast in an eerie blanket of shadow. A small rectangular patch of moonlight paints itself onto the floor, but it isn't enough to see anything around it. In the corner, I swear I can feel someone standing there, leering at me, even though I know better than to believe monsters live in the shadows. I blink a few times until I'm convinced my head is playing tricks on me. The shadows smooth into a void. *Nothing is there. Nothing.*

Being almost completely blind to my surroundings sends my body into high alert. My chest rises and falls quickly, and I force my shaky arms to push me up into a sitting position. The rough feel of a naked mattress beneath my palms turns my stomach, but as I move my weight, the springs give way to weathered groans. The sound makes me jump, amplified by the dead air, but then I freeze.

I wait for the sound of approaching footsteps. For the floorboards to creak. But I'm met with nothing—just my heartbeat, my breaths. The utter silence. *He isn't here.*

I let the mattress release a final groan as I remove the full weight of my body. My head spins wildly, but I steady myself with deep breaths and blindly reach in front of me, looking for a way out of this dark silent nightmare. It takes a few steps forward until my fingers meet a wall, and I press my hand flush against it. I follow the gritty barrier until I reach a corner, then turn to keep going.

My fingers graze what feels like uneven paint, or maybe a crack, and then they snag on something sticking out of the wall. I reach up and down, side to side, until I find what I'm looking for. My hand grasps the cool metal of the doorknob, and cautiously, I turn it.

Against all hope, the door opens.

A hallway only a bit brighter than the room greets me with its lifeless air. There are a few more windows along the right side of the hall, and particles float around like ghosts in the dull shafts of light. When I step into the hall, I look up through a window, and my breath catches.

Tens of thousands of tiny pinpricks of light litter the sky. There are so many, it's nearly impossible to believe that they are indeed stars. And even more impossible to believe that something so beautiful can exist in a dark place like this.

I take another step into the hall. To my right, I see what looks to be a wall. *Dead end.* To my left is a hollow kind of darkness—the kind that holds something inside. I walk in the more promising direction and swallow hard. Six steps forward, and I'm surprised to find that I can actually see more in here.

The far right side of the room is lit by windows bigger than the ones in the hallway. The new moon hanging in the sky does nothing to illuminate the ancient carcass of what was evidently once a living room. Only the stars peeking through the clouds show me what little there is to see.

A dusty couch sits behind a smashed coffee table, its top broken in the middle as though something—or someone— slammed into it. Next to them is a small stand with an old record player. Time hasn't touched it the same way it rests heavily around the rest of the room. Dust has rested everywhere else, but not on the record player. It maintains a sense of purity in this haunted room, like someone has maintained it. Hasn't let it be forgotten.

I need to leave, to find a way out. But for some reason I walk toward it, drawn to this item so clearly out of place, and find a crate of vinyl records on the floor next to it. The first few are worn and illegible, but flipping to an empty sleeve, a familiar name stands out: Led Zeppelin.

"You shouldn't be out here."

I jump, startled by the sound a hushed voice can carry in the quiet of these walls.

Bodhi sits in a chair in the corner to my left, shielded from the minimal starlight illuminating the room. I shiver at the thought of his eyes prying at my shaky body from the shadows, raking up and down it while I forced my weak limbs and dizzy mind to move blindly forward. If he hadn't spoken, I might have walked out without ever knowing he was there.

Yet somehow, I doubt he would have let that happen.

In the quiet of the night—or perhaps it's always this silent here—I hear the fabric of his clothing brush against itself as he shifts in his seat, perhaps getting a better look at me or deciding what other truths he will deny me. The light, though dingy, illuminates my every blink under its magnifying touch. He can see everything, while I'm left staring at the ghost of a man, trying to picture what expression he uses to gawk at me. Beneath the weight of his hidden gaze, my pulse quickens. *I need to get out of here. Now.*

"Bodhi," I shakily whisper, my own voice too loud even hushed. "Where are we?"

The sound of shifting fabric rips through the night air once again. I swallow, anticipating the worst.

"This is my father's cabin. You'll be safe here."

"Safe?" *His father?*

"Yes. I will keep you safe here," he vows, and though I know he thinks this to be true, my stomach turns. All I hear is that he will *keep* me.

"From what?" I ask.

"From *who*," he corrects, as though he knows where my thoughts lead. "I won't let anything happen to you, Delilah."

I choke down the fear working its way up my throat and hold back the tears threatening to spill. I do my best to be brave, trying to remember what it was like to talk to him before. Trying to be the girl who knew him as a loving boyfriend, and not some psychopath. "Who?" I whisper. When he doesn't answer, I repeat myself a little louder.

"From Luca."

I laugh at this—at the absurdity of what he's just said—but when he stays quiet, I realize he isn't kidding.

"That's ridiculous."

"He isn't a good person, Delilah."

"What would you know about being good?" I spit. My head spins, and I steady myself.

He ignores me. "I know you won't believe me, but it's the truth. From the minute I met him at the dinner—no, from the minute he pulled up and dropped you off, I knew there was something off about him."

It hits me then, just how deep this jealousy of his runs. How dangerous it is, how dangerously deep its roots have grown. I'm too stunned to speak.

There is no way that something as simple as Luca giving me a ride has brought me here to this moment. No sane person gets jealous and then does all of this. No sane person just *steals* another person.

Images of every moment leading up to this flash before my eyes: Luca dropping me off. The three of us talking at the dinner. Bodhi saying he didn't like Luca. The fights and the lying. Bodhi watching as Luca drove me away. And, the worst of them all, Bodhi kicking into a limp and lifeless Luca.

There will be no coming back from any of this. There is no forgiveness to be given. This is something that cannot be undone by a simple apology.

The only person I need protection from is the man whose delusions have led him to believe he's *protecting* me.

I can barely manage a whisper. "What did you do?"

"What I had to." His tone is deliberate. Cold.

"Take me back," I whimper.

He exhales. "I can't do that."

"Please," I beg, the panic rising in me once more. "Bodhi, please?"

It's quiet for a long time. Long enough to convince myself he might be considering it. Long enough to think I'll find some sympathy in the dark corner.

"No," he says, the frightening finality in his rejection undeniable.

A single tear runs down my cheek. "Bodhi, please!" I cry. "Please? I know you love me. I know you're—you're just trying to protect me, but please. Please, Bodhi, can we just leave now?"

The tears run faster down my cheeks while I plead with him to just listen. I beg and cry some more, trying to reason with him. I tell him I won't tell a soul. I tell him I love him, too, but he can see it for what it is: a lie. I whimper and plead and sob, but he remains silent in the chair, uncaring. Letting me get it all out, it would seem.

And at last I realize I've lost him, if I ever had him to begin with.

Whoever I thought I knew is gone. I'm staring at a shadow of that man and realizing that I was wrong to ever love him. I was wrong to ever love.

"I knew you'd hurt me, you know," I whisper. "I knew you would, I just—I didn't—" I gasp at the thinning air, the room closing in on me as I gasp again and again, trying to get enough air in my lungs.

"You need to go lie down," he says in a strained voice, dismissing any last shred of hope of getting through to him. "You're not well. You hit your head pretty hard in the car."

And even though half of me is stunned that he hasn't strode

across the room to wrap me in his arms and hold me together, the other half snaps out of the panic. I nod at nothing in particular but stay standing where I am, wondering what I did to deserve this. How did I go my whole life being so careful, only to end up with a rarity—a statistic? How does someone so cautious end up being caught so completely off guard?

My thoughts drift to the only person who could have prevented this. Who could have warned me and kept me from ending up here.

I should have asked the detective for something more. He might have told me to run, had I given him the chance. Given him the truth. Would I be safe in the arms of my mother if I confessed right then that I knew Bodhi? That the phone belonged to him?

"I answered your phone," I confess. Maybe I say it because I want some kind of confirmation that there was never any outrunning this. Maybe I say it in hopes that there will be one final excuse to wipe this all away. Maybe I say it to piss him off. Maybe I say it because nothing makes sense right now, so why would any train of thought of mine follow a logical path? I don't know why I say it, but I do.

"What?" he says, his voice as dark as the shadows that conceal him.

"I answered the phone that you had hidden in the drawer. I found it, and it rang, so I answered it." I don't have to see him to know that his every muscle has stilled, frozen in an attempt to hear what I'm saying more clearly. Frozen like that moment when we were lying on my bed for the last time, but neither of us knew it. "I spoke with a detective. That's how I knew you were lying to me, again."

He's quiet for long enough that the rest of my thoughts start spilling out.

"I keep thinking about that day we walked around looking at the statues," I think aloud, staring at the charcoal floor, "and the girl across the street who saw us. She saw us, and she was terrified, and she ran, and I brushed it off, like you did that day. But I've been thinking about it, and I've realized she wasn't looking at us." I pause to look at the shadow in the corner. "She was looking at *you*. She was terrified of *you*. Wasn't she?

"I've tried to remember her face, but all I can see is her fear. It's so strange to have that one moment stuck in my mind. It plays on a loop over and over and over again, because a small part of me knew something was missing, something was wrong. But I overlooked it, because I didn't want to imagine there was a real reason for her to look at you that way. But there is, isn't there?"

A breeze billows outside, filling the silence. What little light there is dims as a cloud covers the stars above us.

"Yes," he quietly confirms.

"Who was she?" I ask, even though I expect nothing more than lies to come out of his mouth.

But for some reason—perhaps the layer of darkness protecting him, or the fact that he already has me and doesn't plan to let me go—he says something that I know is not untrue. Something that even he wouldn't lie about. There's no good way to spin the name or reassemble the four words that leave his lips; it is simply the truth.

"Her name was Marcy."

"Marcy?" I choke.

It couldn't be the same girl. *No. How could it be her?*

"Marcy Mae Thomas?"

His silence is confirmation enough. The blood drains from my body and I can't move, not even to blink. I'm frozen in fear, staring wide-eyed at the man not hiding, but lurking in the corner. He doesn't confess it, but I know without a doubt that he murdered Marcy Mae Thomas. I feel it in my bones.

This isn't a simple outburst stemming from jealousy—this is years and years of faulty crossed wiring in his brain. This is something dark and empty that lives inside of this man. Something that I don't think can be reasoned with or shocked.

The man who murdered Marcy is sitting across from me, and he has no intention of letting me go. He will never let me leave here alive.

"Go back to bed, Delilah," says the person in the shadows, a person I do not know—and never did.

Out of fear, my feet shuffle back the way I came, and in a daze I make it to the bedroom I woke up in. As the darkness envelops me, I accept that it has now become a prison. This will be the last bed I sleep in. The last floor my feet pad across. The last doorknob I touch. The last window I gaze out of.

If I don't get out of here, this will be my final everything.

Things begin to piece together like fabric sewn to make a quilt, and my heavy eyelids close. It's almost the same shade of black behind them as the room, but they close anyway.

Bodhi's mysterious loneliness once was endearing, but having no ties to any other human should have been the first sign. I think about him lying about having the phone and not caring about me going over a week without hearing from him after our fight. About how he was in Utah for a *week* before showing up to apologize, leaving me to feel—

I clutch my hands to my mouth, holding back the quick rise of bile, and sink to the floor. Bodhi was in Utah when the girl who looked *exactly* like Marcy went missing. *He was here. He was here, and I had no idea. I don't need someone to tell me that she's dead—I know she is.*

How long was he watching me? How many times did he follow me and Luca running errands for the wedding? How long has he known that I'd end up in this room?

Something wet slips down my cheeks. I swipe a hand across one to find that traitorous tears have been falling steadily from my eyes. I remove my dampened palm, but don't stop the tears from falling.

And I'm next.

EPILOGUE

The brown box filled with the remainder of my possessions meets the metal of the small moving truck with a satisfying *thump*. The sky shines brilliantly above, and the reflection from the sliding door momentarily blinds me when Collin pulls it shut. As the metal door slams into the truck's floor, it sounds like leaving. It sounds like leaving this all behind me.

"That's the last of it."

"You're sure you'll be fine? I really don't mind coming with," Collin offers once more, even though I've told him time and time again that I don't need someone to babysit me. I can make the drive on my own.

I place a gentle hand on his arm, squeezing it to reassure him. "I'll be fine."

His face flinches ever so slightly, and I can feel the tears he's holding back. I know that it isn't fair for me to leave like this, but staying isn't an option. I just can't.

Mom shuffles around in the cabin of the truck, likely arranging Tupperware containers filled with baked goods and adjusting the seat even though I'll move it as soon as I get behind the wheel. Dad stands nearby with his hands in his pockets. The scared look on his face now feels permanent. Leaving won't help him get rid of it, but staying hasn't, either. And I can't stay for him.

Kayden leans against the truck with his arms folded, staring at me. He's hardly said a word to me since I've told them I'm going. He's angry, and I can't blame him. I would be angry with myself, too, if I could. I know his anger is rooted in fear, but that's not enough to keep me here, either.

Memories of *him* stain this place so deeply that I see him in places we never went. He is in every stranger, every café, every glance. I can't escape him here, and I can't live with him all around me.

"Well," Mom says softly, her voice wavering. She's busied herself as much as she possibly can to distract her mind from this moment, but it's here. Her eyes, a perfect mirror of mine, glisten with emotion, and without another word, she pulls me into the tightest embrace I have ever been given. She holds on so fiercely that in her arms, I almost feel safe again. I almost beg them to take everything back out of the truck. To let me stay wrapped in this hug forever.

"I love you, little Lilah," she whispers into my hair. I know it breaks her heart to let her little girl leave like this, after everything, but hurting her right now hurts me a little less. Mom inhales sharply, pulls me in tighter, and then lets go before more of her tears can seep into my curls.

I walk up to my father and take in his face, still so filled with fear. Sharp stubble covers his face beneath the dark circles. He hardly even sleeps, let alone shaves. Every night, he sits outside my bedroom door waiting to wake me when the nightmares come. Every night, he holds me while I scream that he's still here, that I can feel him watching me.

I won't do that to him anymore.

"I'll be okay, Dad."

He nods, knowing this whisper of a wish is all I can give him. The worry will fade in time. I throw my arms around his neck and hug him tight. I try to memorize the feel of his cotton shirt against my cheek, try to replace every other memory from the past few weeks with this one—the warmth of my father's arms wrapped tightly around me.

I'm not in the desert anymore. I made it out.

Collin quickly pulls me into an embrace, letting his chin rest atop my head. "See you in two weeks?"

I nod against him and pull him a little tighter. He got so old so fast. What happened to the kid I built forts and swung on the swings with?

"Two weeks," I promise.

His arms fall away, and I turn to Kayden.

He still stares at me, not saying a word. Somehow this feels far more difficult than any of the other goodbyes, because this is my baby brother. I'm supposed to protect him from pain, and instead, I'm inflicting it on him by running away from my own. How could I ever make him understand the desperate need for this selfish act? I can't. He would never be able to understand, and I pray he never does.

"I'm so sorry . . ." I nearly choke when I've stepped close enough to him, the rest of our family out of earshot.

His lips pull to the side, and I see the wave of emotions he's holding back. "How could my big sister do this to me?" he probably wonders. I don't know how to explain that his big sister died months ago, and I'm doing what I can to hold on to whatever is left.

"I don't think you should go," he says quietly.

"I know," I whisper.

He looks at me then, really looks at me, and lets go of whatever walls he had up. And for the first time since I came back, he cries.

"Kay," I break, pulling him in even tighter than Mom did me. His grip is solid, like he can fasten me into place. Like he can keep me here. His tall figure shrinks in on his little sister, leaning on her for whatever support he can find, and he falls apart.

"Don't leave, Gray," he sobs. "Don't leave."

And the rest of whatever is left of me shatters inside my chest. I crumple as his anger dissipates into this fierce pain, and I don't feel strong enough to hold the two of us upright. But I don't have to: a strong hand finds its place on my back, giving me enough support to stay where I am until I can find the words.

"I . . . I can't," I croak. My eyes slide shut when he lets me go, because he doesn't deserve anything he'll find in them. I'm too hollow to offer anything but the one tear that glides down my cheek—the last bit of life in me. He deserves so much better. He's still just a kid, still my little brother.

The air grows hollow with his echoing footsteps as he retreats into the house. The slam of the front door will haunt me for months to come, I know it. *That* is the sound of something irreversible. The sound of the final nail in the coffin I've created.

"He just needs some time," Mom says. "He's just scared about you not being around—"

"I know," I interrupt. I don't want her to say anything else. The leaving may be more important now, but I know that once I get some pieces of me back, I won't be able to handle any more regret than I'll already feel looking back on this moment. I have to leave before they add anything else to this pile of grief.

"I love you guys," I finally say from the driver's seat. The window rolls up once I've pulled away, and the crestfallen faces of my torn-up family tattoo themselves inside my skull. The last of the Arizona air zips through the opening before the glass cuts it off, and I take in a deep, ragged breath.

This is the last of this place that I'll ever have to inhale.

I don't stop until I've crossed the border into Nevada, and even then, I only stop to fill up the tank. Mom's snacks and treats get me by until I make it to my destination.

I don't feel sore when I step out of the truck and look at the face of my new home. I just feel one step closer to freedom.

Renovations on the bookshop go quicker than they realistically should. The previous owner let the list of issues pile up, using duct tape as a fix-all. With nothing to occupy my mind other than work, I keep my hands constantly busy. From the moment I wake until right before my head hits my pillow in the upstairs apartment, I pour myself into fixing this place.

Sleep should be easier to find when I fill my days with endless manual labor, but I find that I just stare at the ceiling most nights, not trusting what I'll see when my eyelids shut. The ceiling is smooth and boring, predictable and plain. I don't have to worry about what I'll see up there; it is the same blank canvas night after night.

When my family comes to visit and help me with the last of the renovations, there isn't much left to do. It isn't until they're there that I finally sleep. But I don't tell them this.

Kayden stays in Arizona, still angry with me for leaving, and I don't blame him for it. If it had been him who did this, I would be angry, too.

Their visit is a blur, and I hardly register the time passing. Before I realize it, I'm staring up at the ceiling, alone again, while the breeze stirs through my open window. I know it should frighten me, having the window wide open like this, but it's the only way I feel safe. The air is too fresh, too full of moisture, compared to how it was back there. It's the only tangible reminder that I'm out.

Shipments start rolling in a week after my family's visit. Beautiful copies of books I've read and dreamt of owning pile up in boxes while I finish the last coats on the shelves and touch up the baseboards. The books take up every bit of available space in the back room while I ready the storefront. I leave them untouched, unable to stomach the smell of fresh parchment just yet.

Night greets me the same way it has every night before, like the host of a wake. I feel every minute of her tick by and watch the shadows in my room shift. The only noise that drifts through my window is the sound of the occasional slow-moving car. No blaring horns or rowdy teens make me jump through the night. Not out here, on the outskirts of the city.

The next morning, I busy myself by sweeping for what must be the tenth time this weekend. Nothing collects underneath the bristles, but I swipe at the floor anyway. I do this again and again and again until the sound of the door clanging against the lock of the deadbolt makes me whip my head around.

Through the glass, I see a familiar face I didn't expect to ever see again, really. I swallow hard and make my way to the entrance. The lock turns easily, and the visitor's smile tries to bring me a bit of warmth, but I'm too numb inside for it to reach me.

"Hello, Delilah," he says.

"Hi, Luca," I reply quietly.

He comes in and tells me how great the place looks. Says that Boston told him about the move and that I had been working on reopening an old bookshop. He tells me she misses me and wishes I would return her calls. I nod as I know I should, not yet feeling guilty for the space I've put between me and everyone I love. The person they know is gone. I don't want them to have to grieve her, or for me to feel guilty for not feeling bad about it.

"You must be working day and night," Luca says, taking in the dark circles beneath my tired eyes. I shrug.

He finds the boxes in the back and lifts the lip of one of them to reveal the untouched literature inside. "Whoa, are all of these books?"

I nod, but stare at the ground near his feet.

"There are so many! Why are they not out on the shelves?" he asks.

Words have trouble finding my lips. After a minute of silence, Luca says my name, trying to pull me out of whatever trance I'm in.

"I . . . I can't seem to bring myself to open them," I whisper, trying to explain but not knowing what keeps me from completing the easiest task on my to-do list.

He takes in the image of the ghost before him before pulling out his phone and holding it up to his ear. "I'm ordering pizza."

Luca spends the rest of the afternoon and part of the evening making me eat a few slices while he puts the books out on the shelves. He doesn't make me touch a single one of them, seeming to understand before I do that these are still reminders of before.

I point to certain shelves and areas of the room, and he doesn't complain when I change my mind and have him rearrange multiple sections. Once the last box is unpacked, he takes the broken-down cardboard to the recycling and returns to find me sweeping again.

"Have you been sleeping?" He doesn't sugarcoat the question with a kind tone; he just asks in a way that demands the truth.

"A little . . . more when my family was here," I confess.

He nods and takes the broom from my hands. "Come on," he says, setting the broom against the wall. "You need to sleep."

I don't argue as I follow him up the stairs to the apartment. He sits outside my door while I dress in shorts and an oversized T-shirt, then waits while I brush my teeth and climb into bed.

"I'll stay outside your door, if that's alright. You can come get me if you need anything."

I nod, but when he turns away, my chest clenches in fear. "Wait!" I shout. Luca turns, his eyes wide with worry. "Can you . . . can you stay in here?"

He relaxes and walks back in, agreeing without a word. I

show him the trundle underneath the bed, and he settles in for the night.

"Get some sleep, Delilah. I'll be right here when you wake," he promises in a hushed tone, seeing my worried eyes stare at him like they're the only thing keeping him there. I nod and let my face turn back to the ceiling.

Within minutes, my eyes close, and sleep finds me quicker than it has in a long time. When morning comes, I find Luca sitting on the floor against my bed, the trundle pushed back and him in its place. His arms are wrapped around his bent legs, and he stares with a sober face at the wall in front of him. When he realizes I've woken up, he tells me to shower while he gets us some breakfast.

He stayed by my side the whole night.

Three mornings later, I wake in the same way I have every morning in between: with Luca seated next to the bed, keeping me safe. I sleep sixteen hours on the fourth night, finally letting myself release the fear gripping my every molecule that I'll wake up back in there, alone again, and trusting that he won't leave. And when I wake, I find him sitting in the same spot.

On the sixth day, I'm finally enough of a person to question how he's been able to stay with me for so long.

"Don't worry about it," he says with a small smile. Hours later, when I question him again, he tells me that they don't need him at work right now.

"And Ali doesn't mind you staying here with me?" I ask.

Luca flinches and says grimly, "No. Ali doesn't mind."

Part of me already knows what he implies, but none of me can attempt to be there for someone else right now, so I leave it unsaid and simply squeeze his hand. He gives me a bitter smile and accepts this as the most that I can give right now. This is the best that I can do.

Ten days later, Boss and Max come to see the store. Boss cries a lot and tells me how much she missed me. She apologizes again and again, like this is all somehow her fault, and I stand there like a statue, patting her back while her tears wet my shoulder. Max has to pull her off me, and they only stay for a little while longer before he urges her to leave. I know I make it more awkward by not being the person they knew before. The person in this room can barely muster a polite smile, let alone react like they expect.

Luca stays and waits for me to get ready for bed again before climbing into his spot on the trundle. I stare at the ceiling for a long time before I hear him say my name. Somehow seven letters, spoken so softly, can hold so much. The question is deep and complex, but at the root of it is the same concern: Am I okay?

"I'll be fine," I whisper. It's the same promise I made to Dad when I left my family months ago. The same promise I made to Luca while looking out at the trees.

I don't believe it any more than I did then.

The springs underneath Luca creak as he shifts, and I feel his hand wrap around mine.

"Of course you will."

My eyes slide shut, and for the first time in a long time, I feel a whisper of something. It's not much, but its small spark is enough to lift the fog from my body and let a single tear slip out.

For the first time in a long time, I feel something other than this never-ending emptiness.

Luca leaves after sixteen days. I don't cry, but I do feel his absence. He promises that he'll come back in a few days, and I believe him.

During those days between, I sit in the store cataloguing the books and updating the stock. I find it in me to pick up some of them, and it feels a little less like dying than I thought it would. I force myself to go to the grocery store, but I do so at five in the morning, wanting to see the least amount of people that I can. I find that I'm able to leave the person behind the checkout stand with a small smile. It's nothing like the smiles I used to give so easily, but it still is something.

I clean up the clothes and things around my room and realize Luca must have been doing that before I woke up, because they hadn't started collecting until he left. I clean my apartment upstairs and call my family. Kayden talks to me for a minute, and I almost cry hearing his voice. I still feel the hole I've left in his world in his voice, but what I feel most of all is how much he misses me. He agrees to come up for opening day with the rest of the family in two weeks.

I begin texting Boss back, but not nearly as much as I used to. I mostly let her know I'm doing alright, and she tells me the same. She visits once before Luca comes back, and this time, there are fewer tears and more talking to me like I'm an actual human being. She only gets overly emotional when she tells me how sorry she is that she couldn't see I was going through something during the wedding. She tells me she should have seen it; she should have known.

It's not her fault that I hid it from her. It's taken me a long time, but I don't blame her anymore. I don't tell her that I ever did.

Luca returns four days after he left. When he looks me over, he gives me the first real smile I've seen since he showed up here. Like he's seeing a piece of the real me shining through the corpse that's been rotting inside these walls.

I find that he's the only person I'm able to trust. He is the only one who doesn't know the person I was before, the single person whose motives I don't constantly question. If we had met any other way, I would have cut him off like everyone else in my life. He would be one of the casualties, along with Molly, Dennis, Rachel, my brother's friends, and anyone else I met before. What if they had planned to meet me the same way Bodhi did?

If Luca hadn't been forced to meet me at the wedding, I would have been too scared to let him help me like he has. Without him, I know I wouldn't be making my way back to myself. Without him, I would still be staring at the ceiling every night, praying not to close my eyes so I wouldn't see his face.

The nightmares don't come when Luca is with me.

"I'm sorry," Luca says one day. "I'm sorry I didn't come to see you in the hospital."

"It's alright," I tell him, but he only shakes his head.

"I wanted to be there, to make sure you were alright."

"I am alright," I remind him.

He looks at me like he's maybe seeing this for the first time, but it doesn't take the sorrow from his eyes. "I was out there looking," he whispers. "I looked for you every day that I could. As soon as I could."

My vision grows blurry, and I don't swipe at the tears that fall. "You did?" I murmur.

He nods. "Every day."

I swallow the lump in my throat, and Luca does the same, both of us choking on the emotions these memories dredge up.

"I'm sorry, too," I whisper.

Luca's face snaps up, two lines of confusion burrowing between his brows.

"I'm sorry I couldn't help you," I cry, and the tears flow freely. "I'm sorry, Luca, I'm so sorry for what happened to you. I swear I didn't know—I didn't know he would do that to you." Luca's limp body on the ground, beaten and bloody, flashes through my mind, and all I can think is how I didn't do anything to help him. I know now I was drugged, but for some reason, it's this guilt that has slowly buried itself into my bones and haunted me every day since I first woke up in that cabin. "I should have helped you," I sob.

Luca rushes over to me and grabs me by the face, his eyes desperate for me to hear him. "It's not your fault, Delilah. I don't blame you for—"

"I should have known—"

"It's not your fault," he says sternly.

"I didn't know he was capable of that, Luca, I swear—"

"Delilah!" he shouts, and I go silent. "It's not. Your. Fault." His eyes plead with me to believe this. My tears stream onto his hands, and when I can't say anything else, he pulls me in and repeats it again and again. "It's not your fault," he hushes me.

I continue to sob into his shirt while the memory replays in my mind on an endless loop. Luca is the only other person that Bodhi hurt directly. Had Luca never met me, he would have been safe. He wouldn't have been beaten nearly to death and hospitalized, only barely pulling through. He wouldn't have apologized for something as ridiculous as not being able to search for me while he was recovering, because he wouldn't have had to know me. He would have been better off never having met me.

This time, when we finally make it to bed, Luca reaches for my hand without a word. Without question, I put my hand in his, and we fall asleep.

———————

The shop opening comes and goes quickly. When my family comes into town, Luca stays with Max and Boss, and I find that it's harder to sleep without him here. Even with the comforting sound of my brothers' snoring and my mom's sleep-talking, it is difficult. They leave easier this time when they see that I'm looking better, more alive, and Kayden apologizes for the way he left things in Arizona. I tell him that there's nothing to forgive.

Luca comes back when they leave, and we fall back into our little routine. He makes a lot of phone calls and does a lot of remote meetings for his charity while I work in the store downstairs. Slowly, his clothes start piling up in the guest room, but he always sleeps next to me on the trundle. I don't mind it, though. I'm scared that once he sleeps somewhere else, I'll be too scared to ask him to come back if I can't sleep on my own.

For months, we live like this. Luca leaves on the occasional trip when he can't get the job done virtually, but the trips are always short. I don't tell him that I can't sleep when he's gone, but I don't have to. He can spot the dark circles that find a home under my eyes each time.

He doesn't tell me outright, but I eventually figure out that Ali had been cheating on him the whole time they were together. He doesn't talk about it, and I don't make him. I offer him the same kindness he's offered me. Because even just the thought of *his* name makes me shiver.

I gradually start to forget about the desert, for the most part, only thinking about it when a customer with striking green eyes or a similar cologne walks through the door. Then it all comes rushing back, no matter how hard I try to push it back down, to box it back up. I'm better at holding it together until they leave now, but the memories of him haunt me all the same.

They found the ketamine used to drug me and a trace of Andy's hair in the back of Bodhi's rental car. The same place he had me lie while he drove my inebriated body to his father's cabin. Andy had been discarded in a canal, just like Marcy, her head bashed in just the same. He was convicted of both murders and an attempt on me.

It later came out that Bodhi briefly dated Marcy right before he met me, and yet he spent every minute in that cabin telling me he didn't kill her. He was innocent—it was all Luca. Everything was always Luca, though it only made sense in his twisted mind. My stomach churns with the memory of the look on Bodhi's face every time he said his name—the unmistakable hatred and resentment.

I honestly think that Bodhi thought he had killed Luca; otherwise, he wouldn't have taken me away from the wedding when he did. The thought of Luca's body lying lifeless on the grass is the only nightmare that plagues me now, and the only thing that reminds me I was dreaming is when I wake and see him sleeping soundly next to me.

No one knows why Bodhi killed Andy. He won't confess to any of it, let alone give a motive. But the evidence was enough to convict him. Now, he sits on death row.

Because of me.

Because I escaped before he had the chance to kill me.

Truthfully, I still don't remember most of the escape. I was dehydrated and delirious beyond what any human should have to endure. I just know I got out of the cabin and ran. I ran and ran and ran until my legs could no longer hold me up, and then I clawed my way through the Arizona dirt and dragged my body as far as I could. I know the sun rose and fell twice while I huddled beneath a desert bush. I know I felt the tickle of bugs crawling over my sunburnt skin, and I know I felt the rasp of dry breaths slowly dying in my lungs, growing more shallow with each second. But eventually, I drifted off into a dark, dark place. The next thing I remember was the blinding hospital lights, the beeping of a machine telling me I was alive.

I tried to tell the people crying all around me that the machine was faulty—that it couldn't be true, because I felt anything *but* alive—but my dried lips stuck together, and I was too weak to part them.

They sedated me for the first few days until I could wake without screaming and thrashing out at anyone who came near me. Never once did he lay a finger on me the way he did the other girls, but he hurt me all the same.

Eventually, I realized I was out of the desert. I had made it out. But that was when the numbness set in.

Until Luca showed up at the shop, I hadn't felt a single thing. I was too scared to, knowing how agonizing it was to feel.

My family did what they could to comfort me, to make me feel safe. They walked on eggshells and tiptoed down the hall. They listened at my door to see if I was awake. After the first night home, I knew I had to leave. I was always going to have to leave.

Somehow, the manager of an old bookstore had gotten hold of an old resume of mine and asked to interview me to operate and manage his shop. He explained the on-site living situation and how I would have free range to do whatever I wanted with it, so long as I got approval for any major changes to the establishment.

I agreed immediately when I saw the shop was located in Utah. Away from there.

I didn't tell my family for weeks until they heard the unmistakable sound of packing tape ripping its way across cardboard in my room. They protested and cried and begged me to stay, but my face stayed in the same emotionless mask it had remained in since I returned from the hospital. Eventually, they realized there was no changing my mind. I was gone the week after that.

And now, a year later, I'm glad I did it. Because I'm slowly becoming me again.

Luca still stays here with me. He's patient when I go numb like before, but he's always there, sleeping next to me when I need him, though his mattress is much nicer than the trundle he was sleeping on before.

"Can you help move those books over to the corner?" I ask him.

"Of course," he says as he grins up at me.

I smile back at him, and though it's something I've done a million times, it still feels a little strange. Sometimes I feel like I'm not allowed to smile anymore. But whenever I'm around Luca, I find it doesn't feel as sinful. It's easier to be okay around him.

He leans down to scoop up the box, and I watch him straighten and walk toward me. He leaves a gentle kiss on my cheek, and I smile softly at him again. This time, the strings pulling them up are a little tighter, pulling up the corners just a bit higher.

I may not ever be the same person I was before everything Bodhi did to me, but I do know that I'll never have to fear the pressure of Luca wanting me to be her. He's the one constant in this after that hasn't tried to push me back into a mold that no longer fits. He's happy with me just the way I am. He doesn't ask me to change. He thinks I'm perfect, even while broken.

Luca begins unpacking the box, and I quietly watch him handle the books with care from behind the counter. He's something I never saw coming, and yet he's become someone I so desperately need in every part of my life. I don't want to go back to being that scared girl ever again.

He looks up like he knows I've been watching him, and it's right then that I make a small wish that I'll never have to know what life is like without him.

LUCA

I n the shop she has been successfully running for a year now, I help her organize the books. Over a year ago she was taken to that old desert cabin. More than 365 days ago, Bodhi took a drugged-up Delilah to the middle of nowhere thinking that when she woke up, she would understand. Thinking she would listen to what he had to say. How foolish of him to think she ever would.

He never knew her in the perfect way I do. He never knew just how deep her distrust in him ran. That she would never believe him because he made the alternative so much easier. He started too many lies he could not finish. It was doomed from the start—from the very first moment he ran into her and tangled her in his past.

"Can you move those books over to the corner?" Delilah's question holds much of the tenderness it once did. Not when we first met, over a year ago; back then, she was much more guarded, still very much hurting. But the same tenderness from when she finally began to trust me with the most vulnerable parts of herself.

"Of course," I say, picking up the box of books. I leave her with a quick kiss on the cheek, to which she smiles in return. A smile that has only recently found a near-permanent residence in her arsenal of expressions.

For a while, I know she felt disingenuous smiling. She did not know how to go from the scared girl fighting her way out of a wooden hell to anything somewhat normal.

She does not remember much, but I know she has tucked away the memories somewhere deep in her mind. She still mumbles in her sleep, pleading for him to just kill her. She feels guilt for living instead of dying—this much, I know. I cannot understand why, but putting the pieces of herself back together was almost too much for her. It almost made dying in the desert look like the peace she believes she will never feel again. She does not remember it when she wakes, but even in her sleep she still thinks of him. Still wishes for it to be her, not him, that will be dead soon.

Because Bodhi now sits on death row for the murders of both Marcy and Andy and for the attempted murder of Delilah.

Sitting through the trial was a whole new hell in and of itself. Delilah would not sleep. She could not stomach eating. At times, she would shake uncontrollably for no reason at all. It was only twelve days that she spent in the desert, but time does strange things depending on the company you keep, and when you think you are trapped with a murderer in the middle of nowhere, it seems that each day can feasibly fit eons inside them. In her mind, she spent enough time shackled to the man to break completely. I could not begin to understand that concept, or what she has felt, but I am beginning to understand the consequences the feelings bear.

They found Andy's hair in the backseat of the rental car, along with photographs taken of both her and Marcy before their respective disposals. From the looks of it, they were still alive when the photos were taken, as neither bore the signs of the blunt force trauma that spelled their end. It was concluded that they were drugged the same way he did Delilah at the wedding, with the ketamine found hidden in his glove box. This is true, though there was nothing in the toxicology report to indicate as such.

Marcy was simple for the police to connect Bodhi to: an ex-girlfriend, one he dated briefly before Delilah, who had a nasty habit of sticking her hands in other people's wallets. Not that she needed to—no, she had a job that paid well and parents with deep pockets, but she was enamored with the thrill of taking. She took too much cash from Bodhi, though, and up and left him before he found out. He did not report the missing funds to the police. Perhaps he just didn't care, or perhaps he didn't want to chance finding out something about his parents. I do not know and I do not care, but it certainly complicated things for him when Marcy wound up dead and the police came looking for answers.

Connecting Bodhi to Andy, however, was more challenging. Other than appearances, the two women had nothing in common. Age separated them, as did geography, and they had no common company. But when evidence turns up? Looks are motive enough for any jury. To them, she had the misfortune of appearing eerily similar to an ex-girlfriend, which, I suppose, is true. Had she been brunette or stick-thin, her life would not have served the purpose it did. She would have been spared.

Taking Delilah, though. *That* was the trickiest part. Not to prove—Delilah was the only testimony needed to sentence Bodhi—but to make happen. This was the most delicate piece to the puzzle, and yet the most crucial. One wrong word would alter the course of this story. One wrong word might pivot the narrative in the wrong direction.

Bodhi had to take Delilah, and she had to believe he was capable of such a thing. But how do you convince an innocent man to abduct the girl he loves?

You tell him what you're doing. Then you embellish just a bit.

Bodhi had seen ugly people before—was raised by them. It was not difficult for him to see the monster concealed beneath my skin. To believe me when I said I was going to take Delilah. It was not impossible to imagine that my claws were so deep in the justice system that no one would stop me. That I could make it so they never started looking for her.

When he showed up at the wedding, just as I knew he would, and I told him the things I knew about him—down to the last sullied detail of his miserable childhood, things that no one but him should know—he believed everything else. Believed that there was a group of us willing to drug and abduct and kill Delilah. Believed that no one would take the word of someone who has spent his adult life lying about his identity.

He knew what might happen if he took her—I know he did —and he took her anyway. Tried to save her despite it, hoping that hiding in the Arizona desert for twelve days would be enough to keep her from this fate.

And he ended up in prison, just like he knew he might.

What a waste of time and energy.

It should have been more challenging, but with Bodhi being who he is, I got lucky—if notions such as luck exist. Had he not been so adamant about forgetting his past, had he been a bit more forthcoming with things as trivial as last names and details about his history, it might have been impossible to drive a wedge between the two of them. It would have been improbable to make her believe. Unlikely for me to split them apart.

I never thought I would have to drive her away from someone, as she had never *wanted* someone. She was too afraid. I made sure of it.

Four years ago when I found her reading on that swing in the crisp spring air, living so perfectly, being so *human*, I knew I would do what it took to make her mine. It is not love, not infatuation nor an obsession, but a subject to be studied. A result that needs analyzing. I have never known what it means to be human, but she appeared so unapologetically *it*. Who better, then, to show me?

For years, I have watched her and molded her into a person

ready to accept the lie that I am. For *years,* I have crafted her likes and dislikes, manipulated the media she consumed, and laced her life with traces of me. Made wanting me feel like breathing. Made being with me feel like fate.

She still does not know Ali was never real. Never once did she ask to see a photograph, but if she had, I had some photos taken with a stranger tucked away and ready to use. A fake girlfriend was necessary to get her comfortable, to get her close. I knew that she feared attachment, because I had molded her mind to fear what she might lose until I was ready to keep her. To tuck her away.

We were not supposed to have been together yet . . . but meeting Bodhi complicated things.

The minute I watched him slam into her and give her that charming smile with that obnoxious dimple, saw the way her face flushed with color, things had to change. We were always going to meet at the wedding, but once *he* got involved in her life, I had to make him go away. Had to move up the timeline. And what better way to force her to be dependent on me than to become her anchor, the singular thing holding her in place after all I would make him put her through?

Indeed, I was fortunate with Bodhi being who he was. My only real task was to falsify enough to get him into prison; he put enough strain on their relationship without a nudge from me. Besides the phone call from me pretending to be a detective investigating Bodhi for some mysterious case, that is she had to start really spiraling somehow. But the rest? That was all him. I suppose that is what happens when two scared people find each other, though. They make it difficult to stay.

She thinks that she will never trust another man again because of what Bodhi did. But what she does not know is that this hesitation grew roots in her long before that. I made sure of it.

If he had left in any other way, it would have broken her into pieces too small, too complicated to put back into place. A simple breakup would have been too easy to heal from. I could not stand to follow her around that hot, godforsaken place any longer, and thus she needed to leave it. Needed to never come back.

It had to be horrific, whatever drove her away. That place needed to be poisoned so she could come back home—come back here, where I stood waiting for her.

And as "luck" would have it, the perfect opportunity soon fell into her lap, just waiting for her in Salt Lake City: her dream job that came with a place to live.

From the first time I saw her, I knew I needed to understand what made her tick before introducing myself into her life—into the experiment. I needed to analyze every modicum of her essence. What each tear indicated. What her tells were when she lied. What she kept hidden under the surface. I tasked myself with becoming fluent in her very existence so I could lure her into choosing me.

I needed to enter her life in the most innocent of ways. So, I orchestrated Max and Boss's meeting and falsified the friendship between Max and myself.

I became a contortionist of sorts, bending and folding to fit perfectly into all of their lives. Creating a person they not only loved, but trusted, all so they would one day lead me to meet her. I examined their behaviors and habits, the inflections of their voices and the tilts of her loved one's heads, for years—*years* before I even greeted Delilah with a smile I replicated from the hundreds of photos of her grinning friends and family members I had collected and hoarded.

How incredible the internet and zoom lenses can truly be.

It might have been easier to simply take her from the beginning. To cover my tracks, to get away with it the way I know I could. But I have learned much more about being human this way. I have learned how they break, and how they piece themselves back together. How fickle emotions can be, and how intertwined they all are. How one cannot exist without another.

Like how she hates him for what she thinks he did, but also hates herself for letting him. How she loathes being alive despite thinking he first tried to take her life.

It is all so confusing. And all so educational.

My "work trips" have become less frequent. She still thinks I have clients to visit and a charity to run, but really, I am making sure that the room is ready. Making sure it is perfect. Once the mock window's light is properly timed, it will be complete. It is too unpredictable to place a real window in her cage—too many variables to account for. The LED skylight will have to be a suitable substitute for sunlight.

The crack in the wall from Andy's skull smashing into it is the only remaining blemish, but I do not think I will cover it up. I imagine the mental adjustment will be difficult for her, seeing as it has been rather tough altering her perspective of Bodhi, so perhaps a daily reminder of whom she lives for will do her some good. There is no reason for it to be difficult once I put her in there.

I have been tugging at the strings in my face to convincingly play the part of human for much longer than I originally planned, but I am flexible. I am patient. I can keep up the ruse until it is time for the final bow.

There is not much time left in the "before," and when the time is right—when the appeals run out and they no longer need Delilah for the trial, and when it's finally convenient for her to disappear—I will take her away. Keep her all to myself. Watch my little specimen act and think and breathe and read. Witness her be human. Not so that I can, but so that perhaps it will make more sense why people do what they do.

Delilah smiles at me from behind the counter where she types in book prices. It is calming, listening to the rhythmic beep of each book being entered into the computer. The clicking keys reminds me of the low battery signal my surveillance system began emitting last night, and I make a mental note to grab batteries on the way back to my actual home—not the one I have been pretending to live in with her, but the one in which Delilah will soon be joining me.

I smile back at her, a smile I mastered years ago. One so seemingly normal that even someone who has suffered as Delilah has could not detect the emptiness in the act. When she turns away, my face slackens to something more comfortable. Something that conveys the nothing I feel inside.

She was hollowed out for so long, I began to wonder if I had turned her into something like me. Into something that cannot feel. Though I was wrong, I can't help but wonder if such a thing is possible. Perhaps one day I will find out. Perhaps this was not just about a monster understanding a human, but discovering if something human can be rendered void of all that makes it so.

The book in my hand pauses in midair, frozen in the midst of a thought.

This is when someone might feel something like guilt, perhaps even pity. But the sourness never comes.

It was always going to end this way.

Why would I feel badly about that?

ACKNOWLEDGMENTS

I never expected to be sitting down to write the acknowledgments for *my* book. This project has been a long time coming, and the end has felt so out of sight for so long that it was difficult to imagine it ever truly happening. But here we are! I have been so overwhelmed with support, so this may be a bit long.

First, I'd like to thank my parents, who have always been incredibly supportive of every venture of mine, whether that be my Etsy shop, my stint in retail arbitrage, becoming a certified childcare director, or my writing. A significant part of the reason I was able to finish this was your unwavering belief in my dreams. I love you! Thank you, Mom. Thank you, Dad.

Thank you to my brothers. Their brutally honest opinions and hilarious feedback were imperative during this process. Without them, this book would have been, well, let's just say this book wouldn't be what it is now without them! Thank you for all of our chats and for thinking I could do it. I love you guys!

I'd also like to thank every single one of my friends who have asked me for updates and encouraged me to keep going with this dream of mine. You know who you are, and your excitement and enthusiasm are a big reason I pushed myself to complete this project!

I want to thank my editor, Cleo. Your hard work and dedication helped me reach a point I could never have achieved on my own. You've helped smooth out the sharp edges of this book and made me feel confident in the final product. Thank you for your patience and for taking care of my baby.

Thank you to every single seasoned author who responded to my messages and questions, and who gave me such great advice. The writing community is such a supportive group, and being part of it is nothing short of wholesome.

And finally, thank YOU, dear reader! Thank you for taking the time to read this book. You are incredible for even reading a single one of the words I wrote, and for giving Delilah's story a chance. You all have filled my soul with such gratitude. Writing a book is an incredibly vulnerable experience from start to finish, but I'm glad to finally be sharing this with you all.

ABOUT THE AUTHOR

Ashlynn Poulsen is twenty-three years old and lives in Utah with her family. She has four younger brothers, two dogs, and more books than she can possibly read. When she is not writing or daydreaming about her fictitious worlds, she enjoys cooking, gardening, knitting, reading, golfing, and sewing.